NEWDAWN

REBOOT

Volume 4

NEWDAWN SAGA

Written By

Dominique Luchart

REBOOT/ Dominique Luchart
NEWDAWN DIARIES – REBOOT
ISBN 978-1-941954-20-1

Summary:

The safe world of Ang City, under the DAINN planetary network, is no longer predictable for the more robust human species that now roam the planet.

The technologically advanced society of genetically enhanced humans organized in Conclaves and living in 2098 is now run by the younger generation when it suddenly falls prey to an unknown bio dust cloud. As people collapse dead or disappear, a way of life becomes extinct, and the few survivors scramble to reverse the effects on their fragile world.

Among the five Conclaves, the Elite led the charge and fought to survive, finding allies in factions that would have customarily opposed them in the conflict.

This battle transcends time and space over many lifetimes, and is a beginning with no end in sight.

Dedication

For the Earth and Our Future.

Acknowledgments

A huge thank you to my parents, who encouraged my creativity, my mother, who read me great books as I grew up, and my father, who opened the door to the world and taught me not to fear.

My overwhelming gratitude to my partner and friend, Spencer, who lets me be myself, is always supportive, understands my quirks and vulnerabilities, and knows how to make me laugh.

Many thanks to my close long-time friends with whom I shared good and bad times. A particular thought to the one who has journeyed across oceans, countries, and mountains with me, JP.

My most profound appreciation for my family of actor friends who embarked on this untraditional journey with trust. For all my other friends who share my life and their countless advice. I sincerely appreciate the vigilance and dedication of the exceptional people who have helped me in the process of publishing this book. For my online family and talented technical team, you are the best. And for my early readers' group, who contributed to making this book better, I could not do it without your valuable input.

I am a dreamer, envisioning the Newdawners who one day will join me in a Newdawn SciFi immersive community and interactive playground.

Table of Content

PREFACE

I love writing stories that take me places in my mind, places I wouldn't be able to visit otherwise. I enjoy creating worlds that do not exist and building them up to become real, as real as the world we live in today. Yet, making these different, unexpected, is always a challenge and one I welcome. Designing different paradigms and developing them to lend themselves to a new model for our society requires opening our vision to new things. Giving a glimpse into these various possibilities hoping to avoid the worst and enjoy the best, is also my priority. Only by seeing them unfold do we decide what was the exemplary scenario for us.

I relish creating characters capable of many feats we could not come close to performing ourselves, and yet we dream of them. It is thrilling to craft twists and plots to build suspense while establishing the agenda behind the scenes and letting the story flow of the pages in many layers as we discover it little by little. As adventure takes us from one moment to another, I am enthralled to see romance flourish, villains thwarted, and heroes conquer it all.

It is my deepest hope that you will enjoy the NEWDAWN stories as much as I took pleasure in seeing the epic NEWDAWN tale unfold on the pages of this novel.

4 PROGRAMS - 5 CONCLAVES

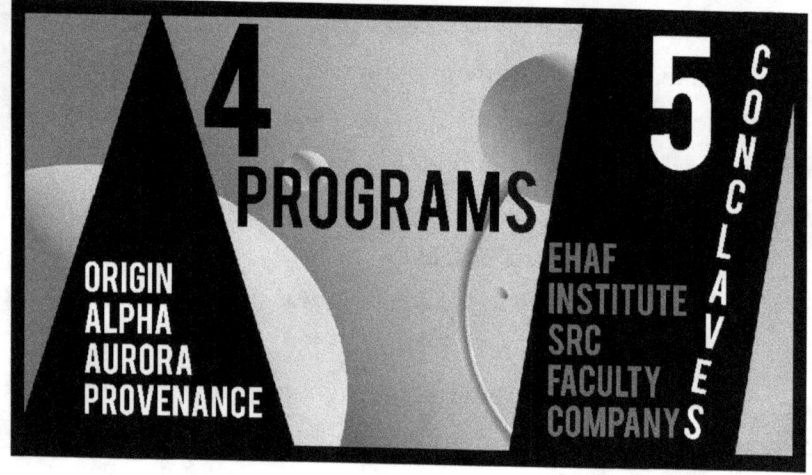

NEWDAWN REBOOT CHARACTERS

MAIN

Tesh Monetvans - Phenom
Leader Origin Elite Unit Program
Lineage Songen & Ran Monetvans
Head of the SRC Conclave
Actual Heir to the SRC Conclave – Forced Transition
Relinquished Position as Head of SRC
Friend of Leane, Streak Love Interest
French Ancestry
Institute Conclave - Head Past Earth

Leane Caden – Phrenic
Elite Unit Origin Program
Healer
Blast Love Interest
Old Blood Lineage - AkkadEtanaErra
Faculty Conclave

Streak Walker - Phenom
Elite Unit Origin Program
Friend of Blast, Leane, and Tesh Love Interest
British Antecedents - Lineage Unknown
EHAF Conclave - Earth Homeland Alliance Force

Blast Zenfield -Phrenic
Elite Unit Origin Program
Leane Love Interest
German Antecedents - Old European Union
EHAF Conclave - Earth Homeland Alliance Force

Zane Langden – Master Phenom
President Federation of Nations
UGCN – United General Council of Nations
Single, Father of Lana, No relationship
British Antecedents
EHAF Conclave – Earth Homeland Alliance Force

North Hall – Phenom
Commandant EHAF Elite Units
Operations Command Center
Widower, No children alive
Scottish Ancestry
EHAF Conclave – Earth Homeland Alliance Force

Eva Bassington – Phenom
Neurology Surgery Division – Imps Installs
Single, Several Ph.D.
British Ancestry
Faculty Conclave

Aidan Furst – Phrenic
Financial Analyst/Company Investments Division
Computer Hacker
Civilian, Single
German Ancestry
Company Conclave

Heather Sims – Phenom
Pediatrics/Earth Child Health
Single
Scottish Ancestry
Faculty Conclave

Anton Fowler – Phenom
Minister UGCN – United General Council of Nations
Widower, Father of Vel
British Ancestry
EHAF Conclave – Earth Homeland Alliance Force

Asher Finch – Phrenic
Presidential Elite Unit
Single
Irish Ancestry
EHAF Conclave – Earth Homeland Alliance Force

Laird Walker – Transcient
Underground
Single
British Ancestry
Insurgenets – Surgs Faction

Amara Lawson – Proselyte
Evaluation Testing Officer
Imps Install Training Division
System Paired with Cashel Reid
Scottish Ancestry
Institute Conclave

Dr. Kathryn Hendricks – Phenom
Head Astronomy & Space Sciences/Physicist
Single
Dutch Ancestry
SRC Conclave – Science Research Center

Jeze Wright – Proselyte
Presidential Elite Unit
Single
Irish Ancestry
EHAF Conclave – Earth Homeland Alliance Force

Verena Silver – Phenom
Representative - United General Council of Nations
Industrialist Heiress
Single
British/Italian Ancestry
UGCN Council

Dr. Rene Paladock – Master Phenom
Science Research Center Director - Grand Master
Creator of DAINN System
Married, No Children
Danish Ancestry
SRC Conclave – Science Research Center

Sloan Roden Baker – Phenom
Governance & Policy Chairman
Single
American Ancestry
Institute Conclave

Cashel Reid – Phrenic
Operative Special Forces
Presidential Elite Unit
System Paired with Amara Lawson
Scottish Ancestry
EHAF Conclave – Earth Homeland Alliance Force

Ciel Grey – Transcient
Underground
Single
American Ancestry
Insurgenets – Surgs Faction

Win Matteson – Phenom
CEO – Industrialist
Single
British Ancestry
Company Conclave

Blaze Moretti – Phenom
Corporate Intelligence & Security
Single
Italian Ancestry
Company Conclave

SECONDARY

Ram Hansen– Phenom
Head Industrial Complex
Company Conclave

Mick Morales - Phenom
Head Surgery - ICU
Faculty Conclave

Max Ortiz – Phrenic
Pediatrics Unit Technician
Faculty Conclave

Volt Darnj – Phenom
Director ER/ICU/Imps Unit
Faculty Conclave

Gregory Tate – Phrenic
Technologist/Computer Science
DAINN Expert
SRC Conclave – Science Research Center

George Dampien – Phrenic
Applied Science Engineer
SRC Conclave – Science Research Center

Walden Pool – Phrenic
World Geologist/Space Planetary Studies
SRC Conclave – Science Research Center

Diane Stone – Phenom
Newscaster DAINN Network Broadcasting
SRC Conclave

Talia Petrov – Phrenic
Operation Specialist – Special Projects
Presidential Elite Unit
EHAF Conclave – Earth Homeland Alliance Force

Alai Khalil – Phrenic
Intelligence & Security Operations
Presidential Elite Unit
EHAF Conclave – Earth Homeland Alliance Force

Birch Lee – Phrenic
Operative Special Forces
Presidential Elite Unit
EHAF Conclave – Earth Homeland Alliance Force

Ione Cohen – Phrenic
Manufacturing Operations Director
Company Conclave

Toril Johansson – Proselyte
Commercial Station Operations – Lead Brand Manager
Company Conclave

Wiseman – Transcient
Operations Control & Logistics
Underground
Insurgenets – Surgs Faction

Sorel Marin - Transcient
Science Engineer/Hacker
Underground
Insurgents – Surgs Faction

Hart Olsen – Transcient
Operations Specialist
Underground
Insurgenets – Surgs Faction

Cosmos Delgado – Transcient
Security Station Platoon Leader
Underground
Insurgenets – Surgs Faction

Dr. Hilory Sanborn – Master Phenom
Director Earth Health Services
Faculty Conclave

Richard Samuel – Master Phenom
Director Earth Sciences & Technology
SRC Conclave

SRC Conclave, Annals Viewing Vlog

699,344,268 Ang City

I am DAINN. Today Concordance begins. It is a day that drives anger in the heart of my people. But after many deliberations, the leaders and I have determined that we must move ahead with the day of The Concord. DAINN Annals – Winter 2098.

Many of my people opposed Concordance. Many had fought against it. Many had lost.

The Conclaves, tasked with implementing the change among their members across the planet, operated somewhat independently under the oversight of the EHAF.

It will be the third time Concordance happened, and disruption occurred on my watch. For our leaders, the continuation of our civilization far outweighs the inconvenience sustained by the lives of the many. For once, it was not a matter of dwindling resources due to our population numbers. Indeed, worldwide these had decreased substantially over the last half-century. The issue remained strictly a matter of schedule focused on concluding the evacuation programs' build-up before the anomaly entered our galaxy.

Yet, our population suffered much more than an inconvenience with the advent of the Concord. People were repurposed, and in many instances, families were broken up.

The decision was not reached easily, for the demands imposed upon each soul were not taken lightly. But after many debates among our Council members, the conclusion became official. Yet, I had a hand in it.

The System indicated that we had no choice if we were to succeed in increasing our chances of survival. Time was of the essence. We examined multiple options before estimating that this course of action would serve us best. But every scenario we initiated to calculate success in maintaining the schedule concluded as much. So, here we were.

My Network, stretched to the breaking point, required more resources to maintain the outputs. Our priorities shifted in the time that remained, and although everyone provided support in all the areas necessary to achieve our goals, it was simply not enough. We needed more of everything, bodies on our assembly lines, expanded supply chain and supplies, and raw materials within our manufacturing facilities. The robots and androids alone were not sufficient. Making more robots would demand reallocating resources, impacting critical sectors to implement our programs. Origin, Alpha, Provenance, and Aurora, most crucial to our survival, must continue as planned no matter the cost. More bodies meant another Concord. This solution remained the only viable option allowing for the success of our survival operations.

The automation of the planet took place long ago. While everything ran with computerized systems, there remained the need for the workforce to oversee some of our processes or supervise the next steps. We were not dealing with manufacturing, just a few products. We were dealing with many. We created the machines to manufacture other machines, disassembling the devices and repacking them for transport. We made equipment indispensable to settle somewhere else, devices that will enhance our chance of survival in an environment we did not know. We housed pre-fabricated housing broken into parts so they could be transferred into ships and then to the surface of another planet. We stacked weapons and supplies in containers for transport and attributed them to the various programs. We ensured critical components of our engines and replacements parts found their way into every program. While the System saw it, our people ensured every resource got to the right place along the lines. Whether it pertained to raw materials, crops, seeds, animals, food rations, stasis pods, implants, we kept producing and transporting until the last minute. And we continued to manufacture ships, a lot of transport ships.

So, now, it was time to implement the Concord. And we waited for the day to unfold. As the Planetary A.I., I knew the costs of our actions. It lay bare on the screens of the Watch Tower and in the calculations of the System.

Plaza, SRC Penthouse, Golden Ghetto, Ang City

Another Concord at the planet level is once again pending. None of us have a choice if we wish to survive within a System that is changing us to our very core. Phenom Tesh, Institute Conclave – Origin Special Elite Unit, DAINN Annals – Winter 2098.

It was the week of Concordance. The morning started like any other, but this was not just another day. Today began the first day of Concordance, or what we also called the Concord. In all the countries of our world and fields of endeavor, our population was again called upon to make dramatic changes. An alteration occurred in our life from professional expertise and work environment to location and family.

The event was happening at all levels within the infrastructure of our society. DAINN established this reorganization to meet the new demands of our world market economy. At the root of our social structure, our Planetary Network ascertained the maximum effectiveness for our people and governments. The initiative instigated by DAINN applied to our workforce just as well as our natural resources.

"Get up, Tesh. It has begun."

DAINN's voice resonated in my head as I remained in my bed, unwilling to face this day.

I lived in Ang, now divided into various Grids, both horizontal and vertical. Due to climatic events, the vast metropolis on the coast remained somewhat of a challenge. It spread widely on three sides, surrounded by mountains to the east, valleys to the south, and the few forests that survived north. In between, stretched inhabited patches of dry land.

"You are going to be late, and your team will proceed without you," continued DAINN.

"Why do we never have a day off?" I muttered to DAINN as I got up and moved to the bathroom.

"You are in training with another month before you graduate. You have to be ready to lead."

"It's not like the Council will surrender the reins," I added under my breath as I dropped my "jamas" to the floor and entered the shower cubicle.

Things differed from the history books' descriptions or our elders' stories at family gatherings. Life as we knew it was no longer like it used to be. Now our planetary government ruled the land under one centralized leadership. We provided to the world markets; at least up to this point, natural resources other nations didn't have. The population was enormous still, spread over our vast continent, with a land filled with many minerals in demand worldwide.

It gave us an edge... Even if nothing was like it used to be. Indeed, nothing was the same anywhere. So much so that nothing was recognizable from the old life. We had to adjust and adjust; we did. The vastness of our land just made things easier for us. *For how long, though, I ask myself?*

The shower was short, timed to save water, a supply becoming rarer as the years passed. I exited the stall, and the warm air of the device brushed against my skin. The soothing hum of the machine relaxed my sore muscles from the exercises of the previous day. As I got dressed in my Institute Conclave uniform, I thought about what the day would mean for millions of people. *I hate this role they force on me.*

The immense resources we offered our planet influenced politics and the world economy. We were perhaps the most independent of governments because of that fact. Our voice resonated high above others within the assembly. However, it wasn't so with the Conclave leaders. The Institute was the worst among all five, controlling all aspects within its membership. As graduates of the Academy, we were their puppets until the day we could prove ourselves and take our rightful place in leadership roles to replace them. Only today was not that day. Today was the first day of Concordance, a week-long readjustment for everyone and everything within our infrastructure. In practical terms, what did that mean?

People will be displaced today. Individuals will be moved around to other areas of our infrastructure to serve our society better. Some will find themselves downgraded; others will move up the ranks. These changes required new implants for most of the population, which demanded absorption training, recalibration, and venue replacement. And as a result, families will be split apart. The Concord caused our entire society to be uprooted in drastic ways. It was the hardest thing to accept, implement, and sustain. In all of this, my part required keeping the population calm and contained. Indeed, this was the second-worst day of my life. And for our people, it was their worst nightmare.

This morning, I didn't have the heart to chat with Cian, my domestic bot, during a quick breakfast. So, instead of going to the kitchen area, I gave Mage a quick hug and headed toward the door of my quarters. My dog followed at my heels, knowingly. Mage understood my mood. He pushed against my hand, licked my fingers, and sat with its tail wagging and waiting for a reward. His reward was me, bending down one more time and giving him another caress. I murmured, "You are such a good dog. I love you. See you tonight. Then, turning, I opened the door and said, "Bye, Cian. See you tonight." When I closed the door, both Mage and Cian watched me go. It was my new normal for the entire week.

We shaped our policies up to a point with our A.I. influencing most of them. We still had the remnants of the position we once held as the world leader. Or was it just an illusion? Nevertheless, our exports generously provided other megacities with indispensable resources, so concessions were made and given on all sides. And under DAINN's guidance, the Council dictated everything.

The Elevat came up to my floor, and I stepped inside. It was too early for most, so I was alone as it made its way to the lobby. Indeed, my PVZ indicated five-thirty in the morning… A barbaric hour for the Conclave leaders living on my floor. Within the next two hours, these heads of Conclaves would make their way to their offices to announce the changes.

The lobby was empty of people when I crossed it. But the City Vigils dedicated to our security occupied their regular post behind the large reception. They were advanced robots directly linked to the Network. Two other City Vigil guards positioned at the entrance kept a watch. All in all, between our Custodians patrolling every floor and the four City Vigils forming the bulk of our immediate security, the tower was well guarded.

DAINN's formidable apparatus to promote safeguards within our world worked with our EHAF Conclave, and our President, in charge of our Earth Homeland Alliance Forces, Zane Langden.

I reached the entrance. One City Vigil opened the door and said, "Good morning, Phenom Tesh."

I nodded and passed the doorway into the Plaza. The Golden Ghetto Plaza was a large park adorned with green grass and trees. Surrounded by the silhouettes of our massive towers boasting different shapes, it spread around the government buildings. The beautiful setting greeted me just as the sun rose over the ocean.

I inhaled a deep breath. I will join the others, the Shapers, who will oversee the transitions forced upon our people within the Megapolis in a few minutes. I shook my head. I still had a few minutes of quiet to prepare.

While this walk brought me to my Conclave on most days, this morning took me away from them. The three people I spent most of my days with and constituted the bulk of my Academy training were all scheduled to report elsewhere. Indeed, each of us would perform tasks based on our area of expertise in four different places. Leane was my friend and on her way to the Faculty headquarters. Streak and Blast were both on their way to the EHAF headquarters. One will work with the Elite, while the other will join the Presidential Forces. Their skills called them to oversee two distinct fields, one tactical and the other operation.

At that very moment, our leaders prepared yet another shift in the priorities of the planet. While this mandate unfolded in all fields, from agriculture to manufacturing, from transportation to education, from high tech to science, from aeronautic to governmental positions, it also meant a different direction for some of us within the Conclaves.

Five Conclaves oversaw all aspects of our lives. The IC, or Institute Conclave, served to control the assessment and formation of our population. The SRC, or Science Research Center, dedicated to research and innovation, promoted our society's advancements. The FA, or Faculty, our medical body, saw to the health of our people, monitoring all implants. The CO, or Company, manufactured all our products and handled the distribution of our resources.

All five of them competed for power. It was no secret among our Academy ranks. And within the upcoming recruits for leadership positions, we all fought until graduation to reach the inner circle and gain some autonomy.

Although I grew up in the SRC Conclave with my parents as leaders, I now belonged to the Institute Conclave. But, like a few others, I got coerced into joining the Institute. After their death instigated by my family's nemesis, the Rat, I lost whatever position I held as a legacy of the SRC Conclave leaders. Since then, I have fought for my life and place in our hierarchy.

In six months, I would graduate and gain my quasi freedom—a partial one at that, but one all the same. Until then, I served wherever they wanted me. And because my gifts as a Shaper of Thoughts allowed them total control over others, my role today was to calm our population and avoid riots in our streets. If I didn't want to be subdued by a blocking implant, there was nothing I could do but comply with their plan.

My walk across the Plaza lasted but a few minutes. The Institute Conclave spread ahead of me in all its glory. The giant golden doors symbolized might, intimidating all as they passed the threshold. Soon, the quiet of my mind would fill with the cries and protests of others.

"SoulLife Phenom Tesh. They are waiting for you in the Alcove," said DAINN.

I sighed…. My day had officially begun.

Faculty Building, Operation Room,
Golden Ghetto, Ang City

Perception is a shifting thing. It mutates as one moves through life, but change is never easy. It transforms what we perceive as order into chaos. Phrenic Leane, Institute Conclave - Origin Special Elite Unit, DAINN Annals – Winter 2098.

I stepped out of the operating room after the latest Imps Installs marathon we just performed with my assigned team and into pure chaos. Our robots overrun the main corridors of the Faculty Emergency Center, and more were still arriving.

The City Vigils designated as our security guards this early morning were now in attendance within the walls. Their mechanical structures stood tall among our people as they attempted to maintain a semblance of order in the incoming crowd. Their EHAF armor metallic steel blue Earth Homeland Alliance Force robotic frames were noticeable. Their markings alerted anyone that these androids were officially present and working under the authority of our government.

I should be with my Conclave this morning. Instead, I was here in the Faculty, but while my heart belonged there, it was no longer my place. I was part of the Institute now and belonged with Tesh, Streak, and Blast. They were my team. Only, DAINN assigned me to the Faculty for the entire week of Concordance. *HellNet, being reminded that I used to belong here, lodge a spike in my heart. Only, the Institute deemed me too valuable for the Faculty.*

I squared my shoulders as I thought about Tesh and how she would manage her assignment this week. She hated having to control other people's minds. Yet, she was so good at it, and neither of us had a choice.

I watched the mass of people and hesitated to move further into the fray. As much as I was motivated to reach the area reserved for the surgeons servicing the ER, to change back into my clothes, I hated making my way there by going through this tangled web of anxious and aggressive individuals. But it wasn't to be helped, not today. I took a deep breath and walked further into the passageway.

Ordinarily, the City Vigils stood throughout the corridors and entryways, ready to assist anyone, serving and cooperating with our medical personnel in emergencies. This morning their assigned roles were slightly different. They were here at designated checkpoints to monitor our staff and control the crowd in the event of a disturbance. And rightly so, for at this very moment, the mass of people surging through the corridors looked anything but peaceful.

Our automated transportation MedTubes led directly into the Faculty building. Deemed necessary to service the Med Corp, it provided greater efficiency. The Medtubes catered only to our Faculty members and were accessible by personnel demonstrating the Faculty I.D. And today, it was way overflowing with members of our Faculty Conclave.

The intersection leading to our indoor tram's platform appeared way overcrowded. Witnessing an otherwise friendly population, pushing and shoving with such distressed urgency, gave me pause as this was indeed an unusual occurrence. But then again, this was my first Concord, so what did I honestly know? My musing was interrupted by our City Vigil.

"This way, Universal Planetary Holders, Citizens and Residents…" said the slightly metallic voice of one of the City Vigils.

The incoming wave of attendants soon displaced by more of our robotic personnel kept coming. The medical staff holding lower positions were already required to present themselves to the Faculty's main building. They waited anxiously at the security junction for the Vigils to clear them. Now replaced by androids, their skills were no longer enough to maintain them among the Faculty body. By the end of the day, they would transition to other positions in different Conclaves within our society. It was likely to mean a loss in status for most, and they resented it.

I had been there before, way back then when the Institute Conclave told me they made a bid for me. My skills were too valuable to remain within the Faculty Conclave. Therefore, the Institute transferred me to pursue a different path than my natural vocation, based on my Evaluation with DAINN. I was a mere child back then. Today, seen for the first time, the halls where I would have typically moved around in, well, it shook me. *I do not belong here anymore. I should not be here.*

I ran through a cluster of people and maneuvered to avoid the other groups arriving late. They bumped the attending interns to make it past the guards faster. They wanted to be among the first to reach the trams that would take them to the General Assembly in the hope of gaining the advantage of arriving earlier. I barely evaded a collision with a young attendant carrying emergency supplies as he tried to navigate the crowd in the mass of people.

The Official Broadcast of the DAINN Network announcing the beginning of Concordance resonated overheads.

"Concordance is here… Universal I.D. holders, Citizens, and Residents, please move to your designated station."

On the Faculty's floating screens, the face of DAINN, our Distributed Artificial Intelligence Neural Network, called for attention.

DAINN appeared on the displays as a hermaphrodite clone, and its voice could just as well have been male or female, as it carried throughout the corridors and walkways.

Silence settled in the hospital, and everyone, out of habit, stopped watching the screen.

Our A.I. spoke to everyone at once and reached out to all the Conclaves. Its presence registered everywhere through the various grids, alerting the entire population within our city that the Concord had indeed begun. The DAINN android, chosen to inspire confidence and strength, looked either more female or male based on the political agenda of the moment. It could be either reassuring or demanding order to our population.

DAINN continued, "All personnel not formally contacted must report to your posts without fail. Those called upon for the General Assembly be prepared to transition and make the shift. Follow your schedules without deviation."

HellNet, I wish it was suitable for me too. Instead, I found myself assigned to the Faculty because there were not enough surgeons capable of handling the mass of Imps Installs this week.

Squaring my shoulders, I made inroads down the hallway, followed by other Faculty members – all people I didn't know.

The morning had started like any other, but this was not just another day in the massive metropolis of Ang City. It spread over almost seven hundred and fifty square miles (750 sq m) or one thousand nine forty-two and forty-nine square kilometers (1,942.49 sq km) of land where twenty-five million two hundred and seventy-nine souls inhabit the area but remained concentrated in the five grids in the center covered by the more giant domes. We had the land and the space, but everything demanded more engineering these days to ascertain that we maintain efficiency.

Today was the day. In all the countries of our world, our population was called once again to change their profession, expertise, and work environment in all fields of endeavor for the greater good of our world. It was happening at all levels within the infrastructure of our society.

Darnet, I wish I didn't have to participate in this, and I knew Tesh felt the same way.

It was my first Concordance as a working member of our society, and it was already unsettling enough not to be, on top of it, appointed to a different Conclave for the week.

The entirety of Ang City, divided into various Grids, both horizontal and vertical, did not escape Concordance. The huge Metropolis on the coast always faced challenges due to climatic events, but it remained the place to live.

"Walk this way, please. The trams to the General Assembly Faculty building are at the end of the main passageway," ordered one of the Vigils monitoring a group of attendants passing through.

The City Vigil's electronic eyes scanned everyone as they went by, monitoring their features through our facial recognition software. They ran through each individual, checking against DAINN's central database. It flagged those whose names appeared in the System for any number of reasons, including the conversion. Their programming instantly identified and tallied the citizens for the upcoming selection process.

"Please, walk this way," said the City Vigil.

I turned, wondering if the voice was targeting me. It was not.

The City Vigil pointed at a young man as he controlled one of the latest arriving groups.

Fear spread on the individual's face inside the small assembly of people. He reacted, suddenly attempting to evade the checkpoint.

It unleashed the City Vigil, who now moved toward him.

The crowd in the flagged faction quickly spread apart to give way to the City Vigil. No one wanted to interact with the CVs.

In the confusion that ensued, a young attendant panicked and ran. But his split-second hesitating cost him.

When the second man bolted, a commotion followed.

Now two City Vigils stepped forward to apprehend the perpetrators. One moved on the first perpetrator of the infraction and quickly detained him. The second launched in the direction of the running attendant.

The latter grabbed a young woman as a shield. He identified the person through her purple garb as a Phenom, hoping to use her as a barrier against the oncoming City Vigil.

So, here she was, a Phenom of the Faculty, and entirely unprepared for a hostage situation.

My training from the Institute Conclave kicked into gear, and I found myself in the middle of the fray, not far behind the young man. Sure, I could have let the City Vigil handle it. But my training caused me to react before I thought about it. I was unwilling to risk another Faculty member's life if I could help it. The Academy trained me, especially for such situations. The Institute Conclave demanded it and prepared us for almost anything.

The man had wrapped his left arm around the young woman's neck, holding her in a tight brace. His arm squeezed the breath out of the girl, using her as a shield. But, he forgot to look behind, entirely focused on the oncoming City Vigil.

I moved around two people who separated me from the action and tackled the guy. I landed a blow behind his left knee and slammed the side of his head with my left hand. My right hand grabbed his right wrist and pulled his arm back in such a way that he released the girl, howling in pain. I glanced over at the City Vigil, who kept advancing on us. I flashed my Insitute Badge.

The guy collapsed on his knees.

The young woman pulled away from the altercation, looking disheveled and overwhelmed.

I handed him to the City Vigil with a nod and a firm grip while presenting myself to the City Vigil, who was already scanning my face. "I am Leane, Phrenic of the Institute Conclave, member of the Elite."

"Phrenic Leane, thank you for your assistance in this matter. I will take it from here," said the City Vigil, releasing me from my charge. "Your quick cooperation is noted and will be reported in our Vlogs."

Within minutes, she became a hostage in a game she could never win for her lack of preparedness. The Faculty did not put their members through combat. *It could have been me without the Institute Academy training.*

The City Vigil got a hold of the young man, lifting him from the ground, and slipped a set of manacles around his wrists, paralyzing him in the process.

I resumed my walk toward the surgeons' changing rooms when the young Phenom woman stepped in my way.

"Thank you, Phrenic Leane. I was unprepared, and your assistance is greatly appreciated. I am Phenom Eva Bassington, and I am head of the Emergency Unit within the hospital. I do not know how to reward you for your help. But your interference probably saved my life."

HellNet! I did not need the attention. I just wanted to get back to my routine. But the young woman appeared so thankful that I stopped and smiled at her. "I doubt very much that you were in great danger. The CV would have handled the matter with expedience, but I am glad I could be of help."

The City Vigil's programming quickly influenced its next action. He dragged the Faculty attendant away from us with one arm and turned toward the young woman who was now facing me.

"Are you alright, Phenom Bassington?"

She nodded, "I am fine, City Vigil."

"Do you need assistance to get to your destination? I can accompany you if you wish to avoid further mishaps."

"No… I'll be fine. What will happen to him?" She said as she pointed to the limped young man, now held by the guard.

"Unfortunately for him, he is now tagged as a reluctant, which will not help his chances in the selection process," answered the City Vigil before saluting us and moving away with his charge. Effortlessly, he lifted the young man off the ground and walked back toward the tram platform. The move took less than a few seconds as everyone parted around him.

"This is such a difficult day for everyone," murmured Eva.

We witnessed one of the other guards grabbing the other man and escorting him to the departing trams. The experience of watching our City Vigils, usually so well-mannered, as they maintained order in their intractable, unemotional ways, had been intimidating. They were part of an EHAF security force that caused fear of the System for anyone inside the city today.

"Yes, it is," I whispered. It did not sit well with me to see the City Vigil's roles today. But I was ready to resume my progress toward the Resident's room.

Eva continued, "I know you are helping us this week. Since you know none of us, you are welcome to join us later if you would like. We all go for a drink at the Faculty bar after our shift."

"Thank you, it is very kind, but I will need to meet up with my Conclave Elite members later this evening."

"Okay. If you need anything, do not hesitate to 'NetComm' me," added Eva before walking away in the direction of the transportation area.

The hospital was still a combat zone past the checkpoint. Early this morning, the influx from the Concord reassignments arrived inside these walls jamming the workload. Thus, my presence here.

Today and during the rest of the week, we would continue to process the Imps Installs. Any other surgeries were deferred and held over, which explained my presence here. The Faculty's emergency rooms filled with incoming patients every hour became a manufacturing belt with all surgeons busy to capacity during the entire time. It was one of the crazy aspects of Concordance.

The Faculty – our world medical body cared for an entire planet's healthcare needs. Only, this week we all implemented Imps Installs for Concordance. Today, I would behave like any other surgeon, granted access to the hospital as if I never left. As a natural healer, I hated this.

I was tired, but with more operations to perform, I headed toward the next OpRoom.

4
BULLSEYE
Streak

Presidential Tower, EHAF Training Facility, Ang City

I expect things to turn out badly, but I never once envision the destruction we could eventually face as I move through the day. Phenom Streak, Institute Conclave, Origin Special Elite Unit, DAINN Annals – Winter 2098.

Hit, parry, move. Hit, parry, move.

I avoided some blows with a series of circular blocks. But I needed to move faster. My opponent was deadly. These thoughts were in the back of my brain as I maneuvered around him.

This time, my opponent landed another thrust, an ax kick traveling downward that hit me with the impact of his heel.

It got me squarely on the shoulder, and the force of the blow broke my momentum. Drawing on all my energy in this fight and struggling to hold my own, it became more arduous as time went on. Darnet, we had just started. I pulled back and took a deep breath as I paced around the platform, watching for the giant's following combination.

He charged at me with a roundhouse kick, turning his body into a horizontal plane. The position of his knee and his leg's leverage delivered a thrust with the top of his foot.

I used a rising block with my knee to defend against the diagonal attack and flew backward in a combination jump move I learned a few weeks back.

I possessed insufficient resources to get out of his way or block his punches. Strength was not on my side. My only way out amounted to quick evades and faster moves to survive the next round. Yet, my feet dragged on the ground.

My Elemental skills remained of no use. They were not the point of this exercise. Expanding my fighting capabilities was my focus these days. *HellNet, with what was coming, one could not be too prepared.*

The mountain slammed into me, attempting to inflict a flip throw, trying to lift me off my feet.

It came to me fast. Jumping out of the way, I backed up to withdraw from its reach. Already winded and breathing hard, with stars floating in front of my eyes, I staggered on my legs. My instinct wasn't yet what it should be, but I was getting better over these last few weeks. Only today was altogether different. Improving was required, and implementing a new combination might just do the trick, or I wouldn't make it.

Endurance and mental toughness were the keys. Building these attributes demanded more time, even now. If things didn't work out the way anticipated, these skills would become handy quickly because we all knew nothing ever works out the way any laid out plans. Only I wasn't about to talk about it with anyone. *My Conclave team was already stressed as it was.*

My opponent's hook came at me too fast, traveling in a rising diagonal line coming from the side. It moved across the plane of my face in a steady motion.

I barely deflected it with a transfer block. Still, the punch got me right and caused stars.

The mountain executed another maneuver, one that would flatten most of us. The mighty giant in front of me blasted my chest in an excellent execution of multiple kicks that sent me reeling to the mat.

I just barely rolled out of his way, wheezing hard, as he approached me.

My opponent was unbeatable.

I was at fault, for I had requested it. What was I thinking? But I wanted my training to be with the best. Little did I know about the best. That's why I was here. Well, this may be slightly more than just training. We were in an actual fight; no holds bar, little could I do to shy away from the inevitability of my defeat. And I hoped I could walk again when this was over. *Ouch.*

The flat of its hand landed near my solar plexus, seemingly passing through my chest like nothing. My block with my upper arm muscles thrown too late let me down as the motion passed through my defenses.

Understanding that my only discernable benefit was entering the ring, my commitment did not waver. I had talked myself into that one. With no chance of winning on any level, I determined to compete using my will and guile against this significant force. I decided on my own metric as to the winner. Mental acuity at this level was a component and should have made me feel better. It didn't. But I wanted to hold my own against it when, logically, I had no chance of doing that. If I lived through this, I could face just about anyone out there, so that was to consider.

Our Origin mission required much from all of us. My goal was to be in the best shape of my life, with or without the Imps. My purpose here was to fight without my Elemental skills. This decision would surprise many, but I wasn't planning on leaving things to chance. Sure, our scientists would give us the best tech for us to succeed, but there was no way to predict what we would find back in the past if we ever got there. So, I prepared for any eventuality.

I sidestepped again, trying to catch my breath.

The tower was a circular room, white and devoid of any ornaments, with a central platform for hand-to-hand combat. The room was programmed so that no amount of noise could distract the opponents during a fight, and silence reigned. Even the floor and walls with a self-absorbing rubber-like material created a bounce back slightly upon pressure and swallowed every sound.

"Ready to give up yet, Streak? You sure look like it. Why don't you apply the moves I showed you last week?"

Its voice, gruff and unsympathetic, reached me before I felt the blow. It reverberated through my entire body. I felt my brain hit the side of my skull. It couldn't be healthy if one sought to use one's mental abilities at any point in time, just like the intellectual pursuits that won me money. *I think too Darnet much.* "No, not on your life."

It was the dumbest thing I'd ever said or done, for that matter. *Are you freaking kidding me? I know we only live once, but... Shut your brain up and move.*

I launched forward, flying with my feet ahead, spiraling in a daring assault that would typically take the best opponent off his game— the wrong move.

Thinking of Tesh and the others, I was glad I found this time for myself. *Darnet, I'm happy they don't witness my performance.*

It got a hold of my feet, deflecting the attack by a step to the side and rendering me relatively powerless as I glided past the mountain. I landed on the mat with a thud. Getting up fast, knowing he would move on me without delay, we faced each other again.

Here, on the morning of the Concord, getting myself beat up, I still relished my time alone. Soon, I would join the Elite Officers ranks at the GG instead of my Conclave Special Unit - Origin. Everyone expected resistance this week, and my role amounted to enforcing calm and security among the residents there. Far from looking forward to it, my procrastination would most likely get me looked at the wrong way. No one knew yet how far-reaching this Concordance would be, but considering the events of the past year, it wouldn't be an easy one.

Dressed in a futuristic white outfit made of a self-healing material like a second skin, I wrestled against another firm locked grip with my latest instructor. The mountain came circling at me from the back this time.

The armored machine sent me flying with the blunt force of its forearm.

Today, we were fighting without the EV suit. The suit enhanced my muscular structure. The body armor of the Embodied Avatar - an individual fighting unit, protected my entire physic. It was a hugely popular but expensive model with added features that repeatedly served me since I acquired it. Most had purchased theirs; mine was provided due to my standing. The EV enhanced my height and body mass. The EHAF provided the suits, adapting them to our DNA, constructing a solid husk with defensive and offensive capabilities, and providing flexible functions and looks. Its adaptability of purpose was high. While we used it often, so I got comfortable with its many features, we had elected to work out the basics without it on this day.

I ended up on my back again.

My stature was tall, and while I had some muscles on me, I didn't possess the significant body mass that Blast exhibited with pride. It didn't matter much to me personally. I relied on high I.Q plus my Elemental skills and the tech, more so than fighting skills up until now. But science and technology had changed the game. We may not always have access to these where we were going, and while my elemental capabilities would follow me anywhere, I wasn't sure how they would manifest in this other world. Sure, it was still Earth that our team aimed for, but in a period of the past, and we had no idea what awaited us there.

I got up slowly.

Under the Zenio face mask, my features, an extraordinary piece of equipment with a self-healing material, were drenched in sweat. Still, I breathed well and saw everything correctly from all angles.

Getting back off the canvas appeared to be an action I had perfected well. You know, practice, practice, practice. I again applied an evasive move that shouldn't have worked, not with my opponent. But, somehow, I twisted from under its grip and shifted my weight sideways. Pulling back, I remained out of its reach, even if only for a split second.

Its snap kick came low, but I knew how high it could hit. It was lightning fast, a whiplash delivery, and I soon found myself in a familiar position on the mat.

Again, I moved too late!

Its timing countered any of my moves made me its perfect foil.

It then grazed me. I should say it was more than a scrape, but it definitely could have also been much worse. *I guess I'm learning something.*

"Well done, but you've got to get out of the way faster."

"Who are you talking to now? Wait, wait, I need a moment."

The instructor, dressed in a grey outfit and structured as the embodiment of a tank as one of our latest android models, acted in split seconds like a Firebolt and durably indestructible. Rain was its name, and it had an impressive look. It was built to intimidate like an unstoppable armored killing machine; its broad shoulders with muscles rippling over a small waist were terrific. Its long arms smashed and hammered me like an ant. Its namesake could be Thor, the same God from the comic book novels and films of days past, although it wore his hair blond and cropped.

How long had it been since I began the session? I had a hard stop of one hour today. Somehow, it distracted me from thinking about the events waiting for me outside. This Concordance was a desperate action from the Federation, a last-ditch effort to address the anomaly coming our way. We still didn't know what it was, nor did we establish its intent. Only, what we learned from our observations appeared as a powerful phenomenon directing a course toward Earth at incredible speed. We suspected its sentience.

"You're slacking off," said Rain.

"HellNet, Rain, I'm not a robot like you!"

"Yeah, and look at what it gets you."

I groaned. Still, it was my fault. I picked it.

Our combined fighting styles were designed this way to be most effective. It was a blend of many types of martial arts. We selected these according to our interests before training. Krav Maga, Thai box, Jiu-Jitsu, mixed style with kickboxing based on the old ways, only these had grown with our new abilities and mid-flight air contact. These were my top picks.

Decomposing various forms was grueling, but the proper strategy incorporated speed as an added surprise for the opponent. Success depended on unpredictability. To be proficient at it, one had to become an expert in the Phenom category, one of the highest achievement levels in these disciplines. I was there, but one could always get better.

It moved, again disregarding my demand.

I ought to know better. It had me in a tight grip now, and I couldn't get out of that vice-like hold on me no matter what I tried.

Our match dealt with blunt force and rapid reflexes.

The unforgiving punches meant to incapacitate an adversary and render it inactive fast combined the best defense with simple avoidance and over-blocking. We learned this early. Most of the time, we fought an enhanced species, like ourselves, the genetically enhanced human.

We possessed magnified strength that could break a Nonet or normal human skeleton; we harbored what we called the SIFS speed, intelligence, flexibility, and strength considered lethal against a regular person. Most of us jumped higher, ran faster, and experienced more stamina than the Nonets.

We lived genetically enhanced with augmented Imps providing skills we would never obtain under normal circumstances. Despite our sometimes-bulky size, this extraordinary mastery promoted our ability to move swiftly across surfaces. Exhausting a challenger was always an excellent strategy but demanded a peak performance to overcome the opponent. It remained the best approach until one got close and dealt a fatal blow. Only Rain didn't tire, so this approach did not work, and there was no way for me to inflict any damage on this Android.

Punches rained down on me now. I couldn't think.

My instructor wore his name correctly. Once again, this thought occurred to me as I tried to evade its most brutal onslaught.

I couldn't, but I had to.

The hits came formidable; crimson-red blood splattered out of my nose and landed everywhere and squarely on Rain.

I could feel my face swelling to the size of a watermelon and tried to ignore the pain. I launched a counter-attack, hitting Rain with a back kick and an elbow-jarring throw.

He grinned.

It was much more jarring to me than to him. I heard my bone snapping, and the sound reverberated in my head and across the circular room before I even felt the pain.

"Darnet." I pulled back, breathing heavily, taking a few steps.

Rain waited. He heard it too. How could he not?

"I did it again. It must be the fifth, no sixth time this month."

"Seventh… Not that I'm counting," interjected Rain.

I split my forearm open again. My bones, broken, protruded from the skin-tight suit. They snapped back in place with a resonating crack in my ears. I took another step back, my face contorted in pain until the self-healing material around my wound morphed to seal the injury. By now, the discomfort faded away, my arm no longer hurting, but one had to get used to the idea. So, I milked it a bit in front of Rain and tried to get my breath back.

Rain prepared for another flurry of commanding punches. This time, he directed them to the middle of my chest. You have to hand it to ever thought this guy up; it had a one-track mind. I guessed I should consider myself lucky it gave me time to re-set my arm. Maybe my opponent should give me time to reset my brain as well, given I fought a killing Bot.

Usually, my Embodied Avatar's energy field protected me from most blunt force blows, but not today. My reaction time had been slow again. I often didn't raise my shield quickly enough when I wore the husk. This training was as mental as physical, so we ended up alternating with and without the big suit.

I was back in play.

Not for long.

The next instant, Rain, the junkyard dog, spectacularly catapulted me in the air like a rag doll. *HellNet, the junkyard, was a great tool to train with.*

I soared a few feet and landed on my back in the soft and soundless arena, winded. I laid there for a moment, trying to retrieve a semblance of myself. It wasn't working.

Rain was relentless. I could see it preparing for another attack.

"Stop."

I got up slowly. "Game over for today. You annihilated me. You win."

Rain froze. Unlike a human, its programming gave it a somewhat unnatural way of stopping in its tracks. I think they still have to somehow take the crank out of the machine. "You're getting better. You lasted almost half an hour today."

I cringed.

DAINN would not be pleased. It was embarrassing that I could not hold my own against the Android. What am I talking about now? But then, Rain was no standard android. It was why I trained with it.

It was Rain's way of making me feel inadequate while trying to give me hope.

I laughed. "I'll try to remember that tomorrow."

Sometimes I wondered why I was doing this. Although it was part of who I was. The training mattered. I always needed to be prepared. Even if our Conclave didn't get to fight on government business as we prepared for Origin. Frankly, I was the quiet type, not the outdoorsy, physical type like Blast. My capabilities and aptitudes suited the secret projects on behalf of the Federation.

I started this exercise as a challenge, and now I just wanted to finish it. I needed ways to improve beyond our Origin regular training.

Getting better on my own affirmed the independence we didn't quite possess anymore. DAINN created too many protocols to monitor everything, which limited our freedom, to many measures ultimately controlling us, too many rules to abide by, watching everything around us, including ourselves.

My time with Rain was up. My workout was over.

Rain morphed back into the basic combat android robot and walked off the platform. It stepped to the wall, and an invisible door opened. Rain passed through it the next second and disappeared inside a storage unit, serving as a catacomb of robots with multiple formats. The door quietly closed behind it.

Rain was our latest android created by us to serve multiple purposes. It came with one model with different specs. Selectively integrated into our military, it became available in most sports centers. The Company constructed it with sturdy composite material and a durable alloy, but I knew nothing about its composition. It was not my field of interest.

All I cared about was that it provided me with the fighting skills I wished to access naturally and someday surprise Blast. Sure, I could do it with the Implants, but it wasn't the same, although many people took advantage of them with their fast learning curve.

The rapidity with which many of us gained new skills allowed us to leverage this knowledge faster in our society.

I wasn't like the others, craving more implants. Instead, the least I had to rely on them, the better it was in my book. Indeed, I wanted to do it naturally, be the best I could be without relying on the Imps.

It was now time for a quick shower, get dressed in my EHAF EmVat, and meet with the EHAF Elite to get today's assignment.

My mind thought about Tesh, and I grimaced, thinking about how she hated this day. It would be many hours before I saw any of the others, but late tonight, long after the day turned into the night, I would meet Tesh, Leane, and Blast. It was our way to hold ourselves together in support of Tesh and our only way to get a broader view of what took place in our Megapolis.

5
UNREST
Blast

Old City, Underground, Grid 0, Ang City

Unlike other days, I find myself away from the GG and WE, following the broad pathways leading to dark alleys and illegal activities. Someone has to do it on a day like today, I supposed, even with the City Vigils and Custodians overseeing the security of everyone. Phrenic Blast, Institute Conclave – Origin Special Elite Unit, DAINN Annals – Winter 2098.

I admitted it. Once again, I was doing what I was not supposed to, in a place where I should not be. I probably ought not to have even known about this area. Still, I followed a guy whose behavior appeared out of the norm as he left the central ArchWay Pass into what led to an underground tunnel. Of all days to do this. *Darnet Blast, this is stupid. You don't even like confining places.*

Stay above ground!

Concordance did funny things to people. Was this guy trying to avoid the General Assembly?

Looking above my head, I saw the peaceful sky of Ang. But curiosity pushed me forward. So, I left the city's sounds behind me and entered a dark and sinister corridor leading to a part of the city grids no one visited anymore.

It was an area neither City Vigil nor Custodians patrolled. I walked in one of the tunnels that led to the black market. The illegal operations were conducted under the radar by the 'Insurgenets' or 'Surgs,' as we called them above ground.

And this one guy was here. Likely, he was part of their operations.

My feet no longer encountered concrete. Instead, the ground appeared covered in dirt, the kind that felt like rough clay-type mud. But I couldn't be sure, so I called on my PVZ or Visor to identify the zone location.

What in the HellNet was this guy doing in this part of town? He didn't belong here. I could see that by the way he dressed and conducted himself.

An old mildew smell hit my nostrils. It was wet, putrid, and entirely ghastly. But here I was, following this guy anyway, my back close to the older city's dilapidated concrete walls.

The Airpass dipped past the mouth, narrowing down, on the run-down underground alley ahead of me.

I probably would not have been intrigued if it hadn't been for his behavior as he headed out of the main passageways.

Only a large overcoat hid his silhouette, and his sneaky behavior grabbed my curiosity. Indeed, before he engaged deeper into the darkened corridor, he looked furtively in either direction. He didn't want any followers. That much was obvious.

Anyway, it felt good to be away from the training facility of the Institute and into the streets of Ang. A welcoming change from the predictability of our days. So, I kept on going, avoiding the routine that stifled me for once.

This place reeked of illegal trading. It indeed led to an underground shadow marketplace we had not yet located. It was an area where people found things they wouldn't dare buy on the surface because they were rare, illegal, or both.

Today, products were designed for each individual based on the Official Ability Registry and matched accordingly. Objects and parts that weren't part of a person's set of attributes had to be approved; otherwise, these were not allowed for purchase. Under DAINN, our capabilities and roles in our society were defined, cataloged, and restricted.

Any unlawful activity ran for one purpose - fighting the System and rebelling against DAINN. No matter someone's station in life, anyone could buy what they wanted as long as the price was right in the underground shadow marketplace. It was the way the 'Surgs' used to combat DAINN.

The tunnel was dark and dirty, like the derelicts inhabiting these parts. It was dangerous and patrolled by the 'Surgs' to keep other criminal factions out. This underground network, comprised of people who didn't subscribe to the DAINN System, became more of a problem for the EHAF these days. They were renegades who had left the city above ground to exist in the old town and attempted to do something against our establishment. DAIIN knew about the shadow markets and allowed their existence until it became too much of a problem. The EHAF kept a tight oversight over their activities but had not located their Headquarters so far.

The location of the black markets moved around all the time. Somebody efficiently coordinated the traffic daily in different caves, and one had to be in the know to find it. It was even so effective that within the EHAF, we wondered if DAINN was not the organizer behind them. I laughed at the thought.

While various grids existed on the surface, there were also quadrants below. Only these were coded according to the 'Insurgenets' but not officially recorded, so they remained, for the most part, unknown to the main population. Those who came down in these parts had good reasons to seek the existence of the underground.

Suddenly, my ears picked up footsteps coming up from one of the smaller tunnels.

The guy walking ahead of me did not react, so he probably did not hear them.

Two misfits suddenly jumped the guy marching ahead of me.

The incident turned nasty quickly. It was not life-threatening, so I slowed and watched, hesitant to intervene at first.

I wanted to know where the guy was going, and the intrusion left my curiosity unsatisfied.

It was an unfair, uneven fight.

The solitary figure turned, ready to react, when a body lunged at him. He wasn't fast enough. The guys were on him before he could brace himself.

I was confident he would bring up his embodied avatar for a brief moment. No one in their right mind would come to this place so unprepared.

The first misfit sprung up from the side, smashing him against the wall. The second miscreant with a hood held a laser gun in his face within seconds. The second culprit stepped closer and flipped him around to face the wall.

"Don't move!"

Stunned, the man did not react as he felt the cold barrel of the laser pistol pushed further into the back of his skull. There were no sounds except for their heavy breathing as they frisked him, which showed me these were amateurs at best. It also told me an important piece of information about the guy I was following. He was not part of the underground.

He got tossed a punch on the side of his face.

"Aww…"

The guy's forehead hits the wall with a loud thump as he was pushed around, and I snickered. My hunch was correct.

"Check what he's got on him," said one of the attackers, glancing around the place, eager to get going.

My night vision was well adapted to the environment and allowed me to see the altercation. Yet, I still didn't want to engage. It would be child's play to overpower these lowlifes, but I wondered how the encounter played out.

The situation confirmed to me that I was right. This guy was not a 'Surg.'

My EmVat went up as I contemplated intervening, leaning against the wall of the tunnel, bored out of my mind. Somehow, my life at the Academy brought so much more adventure and challenges with my Conclave that patrols like this one seemed lifeless and dull.

An alarm above ground reached my ears faintly. It was another one announcing the mid-point in a day of Concordance.

So far, the visitor had not done anything that would be illegal. Accordingly, I could not arrest him. But the other two were another matter altogether. I was unsure if it was worth the tablet filing required. A sigh escaped my lips. "Netshit."

The hand of the fist attacker reached in the inside pockets of the guy's coat. It went through every one of them expertly. And it came out empty.

"Dumbnet, he's not carrying anything of value!" exclaimed one of them.

Indeed, they grabbed nothing, and that pissed them off.

They wasted their time and energy with nothing of value for them to get.

The guy didn't carry anything to bargain his life against, and that was indeed unfortunate. Scums like these two were bound to resent it.

"Pretty Netsup, if you ask me," said the guy tossing the overpowered man around as his hands stripped him of his coat…

All right. Now, enough of that. I could move in since the felons committed a crime. Attacking a citizen was a crime, but if someone decided to venture into an unsavory part of town, well, they better be prepared for the potential consequences.

The punk turned him over.

They locked eyes.

I knew what was coming. A fist flew at the victim. And another blow. Two fists pummeled him—the barrel of the laser aimed at his head.

I started walking toward the altercation without engaging the EmVat for stealth mode, and those idiots did not even see me approach.

The punches kept on. Violent, forceful, and unrelenting.

I had enough. Although it was a good lesson, letting the guy get beaten that way was not right.

One kick caught him straight into one of his ribs.

Crack.

I was now behind the two miscreants. I grabbed them both behind their necks—child's play. Moving them like dolls on a string at the end of my arms, I collided their heads against one another. Crack.

They dropped like rocks.

The victim now rocked on his feet as he looked at me. "Where did you come from?"

I chuckled. "I followed you in. Not a very good part of town to be in."

His head dropped, and he sighed. "Yeah, I know."

"So, what are you doing here?" While I talked, I was also getting his information on my Visor. His I.D. came in on the screen. "Aidan Furst, you're working for the Company?"

He nodded, still looking at me, waiting for the next question.

"I suppose you won't tell me what you are doing here?"

He remained silent.

The guy got caught in the wrong area, and there was no doubt in my mind that he was there to do something illegal. But I couldn't prove it. If the Custodians were in my place, they would arrest him with demerits, negatively affecting his credits and influencing his Company's salary for the next several months. Only it was me. And I already had to deal with two derelicts and their filings now.

"I have no cause to arrest you now, but if I find you in this area again, I will. Let this encounter be a warning."

He nodded, "Yeah, thank you for your interference, Phrenic."

I grunted and called in the arrest. "Get out of here."

I picked up the two hoodlums from the ground and carried them back toward the tunnel entrance.

A Custodian was already on its way. "I wouldn't waste time around here if I were you. A Custodian will be here any minute."

Aidan Furst understood, his eyes recognizing the implied comment. He hurriedly left the tunnel, holding his ribs, with a nod of acknowledgment in my direction.

SRC Conclave, Annals Viewing Vlog 705,388,275 Ang City

The workers march toward their facilities in all the grids of the city. While the City Vigils deploy, taking their positions within the locations, the Custodians fly over our streets, sending the feed to the Watcher. Now, our EHAF reach their destinations in preparation for the inevitable. DAINN Annals – Winter 2098.

The SRC was buzzing with our technicians running to their stations. As the day began, we were not solely watching our streets. Over the main array, the depth of space took over the screen. Each hour seemed to bring the unknown closer. We had monitored the anomaly for ten months from our deep stations spread across our galaxy. My System kept computing and following its progress as it jumped from one point in space to another, eating away the distance between us.

My mentor, Doctor Paladock, wanted answers, and while our scientists modeled the various scenarios, we still could not outline a particular destination besides Earth. The anomaly's trajectory remained the same for all these long months, where we observed anxiously preparing for the worst. One conclusion was obvious, it aimed for our galaxy, and unless it deviated from its present course, it definitely came for us despite the hope my people held that it did not. The purpose behind its journey remained uncertain, although even my most advanced computations only led to one conclusion. Our planet was in danger. My people were at risk. Regardless of whether my observation derived by a certain amount of guess were correct or not, the data did not lie. It would arrive here soon. We could have another two months at the most by all my calculations unless it made a jump that substantially brought it closer to us much faster.

Irrelevant to these facts, we faced a problem—the threat presented an unknown force to contend with – one coming from deep space. One we knew nothing about, and its behavior ultimately made it appear more technologically advanced than we were. Due to this fact alone, we prepared for an outcome that likely essentially compromised our survival.

The Network stretched to its limit and worked to ensure our preparedness, although today, we confronted Concordance. Obviously, it was less than optimal to shift our resources with such little time. But some of our delays in the last several weeks affected the readiness timeline I kept abreast of daily. It effectively compromised the completion of our four programs: Origin, Alpha, Provenance, and Aurora. These unprecedented plans developed when we first perceived the anomaly provided a way to save my people if the worst-case scenario came into play. To finish everything on time required faster delivery of some of the critical components of our evacuation plans. While we began working on these almost a year ago, the Conclaves were required to shift many of their workers to some of the four programs' most critical areas to complete their deadline in time.

"DAINN, is everything in place?" said Doctor Paladock, watching the various grids intensely on the screens.

"Yes, Doctor Paladock. Everyone took their positions. Custodians and City Vigils have reached BridgeView, ArchWay Pass, and Emerald Field locations. The EHAF is deploying behind the first line of City Vigils in Water's Edge and the Golden Ghetto.

Paladock grunted as he turned his attention back to the large screen where the anomaly had just disappeared once again. "Here it goes again. Keep monitoring the trajectory." His face was tense as he observed the now black space, where the dot representing the anomaly blinked on our large display minutes ago.

"I will let you know when it reappears," said the System.

Bridge View, Passageway - Grid 0, Ang City

Venturing in the old underground town brings about stupid risks, especially during Concordance, but here I am, and I am about to walk in there again. Phrenic Aidan Furst, Civilian, Company Conclave – DAINN Annals – Winter 2098.

I bid my time, hidden in the shadows of a deserted passageway.

My face hurt, my mouth bled, and I was pretty sure I sported a cut on my eyebrow. But, it was okay because maybe the look would deter the delinquents living in these parts.

Moments passed, and the sun moved over the dome.

The Phrenic who interfered during the fight was probably away from the area by now.

HellNet, my ribs ached, most likely cracked. The Phrenic arrived right a little late but saved me from the worst of it. Why did I not use my EmVat? It felt as if all my training had gone out of my head.

But I was not about to go down without a fight. I would have grabbed the gun as the training had taught me. I would have disarmed the punks.

Netshit! I looked for an opening when he knocked out the two guys with one move. I was just ready to kick their asses. I laughed. Who am I kidding?

The guys knocked me around, but the gun aimed at my head was too far a reach.

Sure, during the brawl, I felt powerless, with the nose of the laser aimed at me. Both men were tall and bulky, but that was why I trained. I should have withstood the ordeal better.

Yet the punches and other kicks began. And I fell back and lost my footing. *Darnet, what the HellNet? I should be better than this by now!*

I blocked a foot coming near my ribs and turned it away from its trajectory. Only, I did not stop the others. Why did I not engage my EmVat?

Then the laser gun hit my face.

Stars filled my vision.

Partially knocked out, with my eyes now half-shut, I felt the hand retrieving my coat from my shoulders.

And suddenly, everything was over.

The Phrenic had intervened. Lucky me.

As I walked back down the same incline leading to the tunnel, I cautiously looked around. Over an hour ago, I was in the same place, beaten up; I rose my EmVat. I needed the part no matter the risk because I was not about to be prey again.

HellNet, I was my own salvation. The acquisition of the part meant freedom to do what I needed to do.

The underground was rough. *What are you doing, Aidan, risking it all?*

I had to get this done.

Although I was not part of the Insurgenets directly, I remained involved and helped the guys at the head of it when I could. You think they could come up with a better name for themselves, although it seemed appropriate to come to think of it. Anything to do with the Network called my attention these days.

Silence in the tunnel greeted me. The dirt, muffling my hurried steps, did not make the walk in the dark easier.

Over several months, I developed some allegiance in this place, allowing me to come here and conduct some business. A few people even looked upon me as one of theirs. These were people who shared my beliefs. Only, we never talked about it. Everything remained unspoken.

My part was simple. I provided information on all kinds of data.

It was not easy to get the data, and it was even more challenging to bring it here. But there was a market for my skills. At the moment, I was in an area of the old city entirely unknown to me. Based on one of my contacts' directions, this new ground, which I had paid a high price for, remained within reach.

My body hurt—*foolish mistake.*

I felt it every time I moved. But the fighting I endured weekly in my training started a month ago had made me more resilient to pain.

Already DAINN's Medical Network accomplished its magic. The nanites worked. The bruises and my cracked rib disappeared in less than an hour. For some, it would be even faster.

I kept on walking, only this time, with my raised embodied avatar around me, my confidence increased. *I am not invincible even with the training, but the suit could withstand much more. Well, that teaches you, Aidan.*

The tunnel turned, winding around paths unknown, got narrower in parts.

I thought back to the first time I had used one of these. It occurred a few years ago when I had just started at the Company. My inclination toward illicit activities did not begin that way, for my childhood was relatively normal until the System abducted me. It took me a while to learn what was going on illegally inside the grids. But once I did, well, things began working better for me. Since I required knowledge about my options away from the program, I used the underground movement.

DAINN found my skills appropriate for the Company, regardless of my preferences as an artist, so it did when I said the System abducted me.

I had no love for it. I was a freedom fighter.

DAINN was a tool for those with means and influence. I would not be their puppet.

My position within the Company required most of us to integrate Imps, many Imps. I was already using too many, more than I wanted due to my work, and I refused to acquire more just for the entertainment value. Instead, I used the latest technology to perform faster and better than most other traders. It was true; I had an affinity for it. From the early age of nine, I had had an ability that gave me an immediate sense of symbols, an innate understanding of economics and finance, and an insight to predict trends and Company performance. I did not know why I had this gift. It just was there. For now, it served me well, and it pleased the Company too.

The Company encouraged Implants. The Conclave wanted the best, to the point where some of my colleagues and traders resembled electronic cyborgs more than humans, but they still lacked one critical function: intuition. While we worked in the Company's environment, everything was online, tied to the DAINN System overseeing every function of our economy. So, in a sea of faces with electronic devices in the virtual reality trading room, I was still myself. I wore almost no Imps, except for the ones at the base of my ear. In our society, we still attempted to look and feel normal.

I refused other apparatus encumbering the forehead or jawline a while ago, and my face was still completely natural. It was lucky for me too. If the goons had known where to look, they probably would have ripped me apart. My Imps were worth a lot to the right parties.

For now, I was worth a lot to the Company. Indeed, I possibly was the only trader still relying on intuition these days. And for now, I made billions for the Company. For that, they gave me a certain amount of latitude.

My face, chiseled, appeared ruggedly handsome, as some of my girlfriends said until I broke up with each of them. Lately, I wore my hair longer than most to the disapproval of many around me, especially at work, but they allowed it because I outperformed. In these parts, it gave me a look to blend in almost.

My name was Aidan Furst. A stockbroker by day and a data scientist and hacker by night. I considered myself anything but conventional. One might think me a rebel at heart because while I liked the money and lifestyle, I craved independence and couldn't quite subscribe to the System.

There were too many things wrong with it, although DAINN had saved us many times. But automation took away our liberties, and while we won't get into that just now, I fought against that.

I was here because I hated everything about this day. It reminded me of the Exodus ten years ago. Since then, the dictates imposed on us brought rebellion, and unrest grew.

We faced more substantial constraints now. It had happened too many times during our lifetimes.

I just didn't fit the mold, and I was proud of it.

8
CONFRONTATION
Anton

Presidential Tower, Council Suite, Golden Ghetto, Ang City

As the head of the Federation of Nations, I am not a patient man. I like things done my way and have surrounded myself with the best there is, but I have learned that people come short more often than not. While my record speaks for itself, recent events call for swift action. Anton Fowler, Minister, United General Council of Nations (UGCN), DAINN Annals – Winter 2098.

Our living room inside the Tower brimmed with soft morning light on one of those rare blue-sky days under the domes. It wasn't that often that we witnessed this weather on our planet anymore. Instead, we saw grey skies and unrelenting winds most of the time, with the horrendous rain that came abruptly crashing on the roofs of our human-made canopy.

As I walked into the room, I said to my daughter, "I don't want you in the streets today. Concordance is never peaceful."

"But Dad, I have things to do at the Academy."

It was how the morning started, and since then, things had gone to a HellNet of a day.

"Cancel them. You're staying inside the Tower today."

Our residence was on the same floor as some of the other Council Officials, and I was on my way to see Langden.

Vel, my daughter of fifteen, far from happy about my dictate, strutted away from me in a hurry after our short debate. She resembled me. Stubborn, intelligent, not very inclined to compromise, and temperamental on such occasions, she determined that ignoring me was not the best approach. No matter how I looked at it, she could hold her own, but not on a day like today.

Knowing all of that, I called her once again on my way out the door to see Zane Langden, our EHAF President. I had this nagging feeling about today that things were going to erupt. "Vel, honey, I really need you to stay here, okay?"

"Do I get a vote?" Vel said grumpily. Her face appeared through the doorway of her bedroom. "How about me going down to the plaza for a little while?"

"Absolutely not." I hesitated about telling my daughter that one of my guards would be outside, but then I thought it was only fair to let her know. "I've posted a guard by the door, just in case you have some ideas about going out."

"Darnet, dad, I'm no child."

"Then act like an adult and stay indoors. I will be down the hall in the offices of the President."

She went back inside her room and slammed the door shut. Even though I anticipated her reaction, I jumped at the noise. Darnet!

Raising a child on my own has not been easy. In that, Zane and I had something in common, knowing how important family was in our world. It was one ground we agreed upon when we argued about everything else. The only one we could talk about as collaborators. Our limited understanding of the System's approach to our society had a lot to do with where we were today.

I stepped into the corridor and made my way to Zane's office. One of my top lieutenants popped up on my screen PVZ with a report. "We've got it, Minister."

Good news for me. "Great."

"But we need you, Minister, because we intercepted more than just the shipment. We didn't have a choice."

My face tensed, but I attempted to show nothing of my emotions at that news. "Make sure no one traces it back to us… I'll see you in an hour."

I terminated the communication knowing that my move would impact how the Concord would unfold, and I felt a significant amount of satisfaction with that. The Surgs would have a more challenging time getting through. And I would be able to take the credit for it when the time was right.

I now waited on the outskirt of the President's office. Zane Langden, the current head of the EHAF, had held the Presidency for the last ten years. We worked together on the Federation's affairs, but we saw little eye to eye on our policies. It was time for him to step down.

When I got invited inside Zane's office, I was in a simmering mood. Our meeting would once again be typical. So normal that I took pleasure as usual in toying with Zane. We began precisely as we always did… Annoying each other politely.

"Zane, how are things this morning?"

"Anton, what a surprise, and this early," answered Zane as he walked around his desk and invited me to sit down. He always remained civil about things. He was controlled, calm under pressure, and I would probably have found him likable under other circumstances. But he was in the way of my goals.

As we sat on the hovering chairs in his large office, I began with a topic that would piss him off. "You still think that there won't be any reprisals? What about the reports about the Surgs? You know they've prepared their move."

The shipment we had intercepted this morning was directly from the hands of the Insurgenets. It changed the tide of Concordance. I was sure of that. The Concord's whole purpose was to make things better for everyone, yet here we were. Still, even knowing that most everyone remained against it.

"It's not like we do not expect resistance. Even if there are, we are ready. There will be no bloodshed this time. We won't let that happen," responded Zane.

"You are the constant optimist, quite unusual in your line of work, don't you think?"

Zane Langden shrugged and smiled with a kind of irony at my statement. "Anton, we have been through this a thousand times. We are set with measures that will work. Why don't we discuss something else?"

Either Zane was totally out of touch, or he had been drinking his own Kool-Aid. I couldn't help being sarcastic. "Like what? The shortages we're having in some of the grids? The delays we incurred in the last two months building our key programs to evacuate as many as we can? The way the Golden Ghetto has privileges and the other districts dislike where we are going with these? Would you prefer we talk about Concordance itself and the fact that things are not getting any better? Or what about that thing coming from deep in space and with which our doom looms?"

"Darnet Anton, of all days… I won't go into a blow-up mode over my decision with you. Not today…"

Zane showed a vulnerability that morning I wasn't used to seeing. It was a first for me, which left me surprised and somewhat disarmed. "That bad?"

"You can say that again. We've been in overdrive. The anomaly disappeared again, and frankly, our timeline is insufficient."

"Do you ever wonder what would happen if we pulled back on the Network?"

"I do… But that's quite irrelevant, isn't it? I know you think we can put fewer things through DAINN. I just don't see it based on how we now run the city. Not at the moment anyway. You'll have to wait until we can unravel some of the logistics. Our priority has to be the programs."

"We are trying to do too much for everyone. We do not have the resources. We both know that unless we take a hard approach to this, it is likely that we will not be ready."

Zane had started to laugh. "What would you have me do? Go against the Council? Eliminate the workers in the equation? I do that, and you get my job, right?"

He knew me well. I joined him, laughing too. "Would it be such a bad thing? You've done this for a long time, and maybe too long? You can name any post after this one. Maybe it's time to retire?"

We looked at each other with understanding.

"I need to make sure certain things are in place before I step aside, and you need to convince me regarding your plan. So far, I'm not in agreement with your approach. You know what you have to do to change that."

I really, really, really didn't dislike the guy. I just wanted his job. We had an unusual relationship. He wanted me to lighten up on the Surgs and make sure I wouldn't call another Split. He had been against the Exodus and the hard-line our Great Council took. He wanted to protect the public to the detriment of many of our leaders' agendas. I was a lot harder on that too. And, in the face of one of our most significant challenges, he wanted to save as many of our people as we could, endangering the timeline on all fronts.

"Yeah… And I'm not convinced about your approach on all four programs either."

In the days before Concordance, Zane and I had plenty of discussions about the methods the EHAF would employ if our people did not comply. Zane wanted to avoid violence and bloodshed, and while I respected that, I would have been more aggressive in his stead.

Zane shrugged. "One of these days, we will find out who is right."

"Yeah…"

I knew about his measures. At the first sign of resistance from our population, the Force would use containment. It was the humane thing to do. But unlike him, my confidence that things would go smoothly today wavered. The EHAF was the Force or Clout of Ang if you listened to the population and supported the DAINN Network. They were strong, resourceful, unbreakable, and in command of our air roads and bridges, city pathways, air traffic, and any security issues within the Megapolis, along with our space strike force located around our planet. But I simply didn't think it was wise to wait on a rebellion that was bound to occur.

We knew it was coming. We had already seen two Concords, and they were a bloody mess.

"So, what is the news on the anomaly?"

"It has jumped again. But for now, let's deal with what is on the ground. We need this week over with and things to go back as usual. But we have anticipated every scenario and deployed in all grids," Zane said confidently. "North is confident our plans will work, and so am I."

I nodded.

The workers were barely getting ready for their posts. We both knew the next hours would be crucial. Things had not yet started to unfold around the city, and I wanted to be in the front row, right along with Zane, when and if all hell broke loose. Unfortunately, I needed to be elsewhere in a little while. A touch of impatience reached me. Finally, after months of frustrations, deriving satisfaction from things going sideways was a boon for me.

I did not doubt that chaos would reign today. In that, North and I shared the same vision.

I liked North; Zane's right hand was efficient. He was a pro at his job, but he was too dedicated to Zane. I had tried to lure him into my security detail to no avail. He was Zane's man and would remain until his death.

Zane was more moderate in his ways, and he had done well for the city, but I had a vision, and he was in my way. There were too many differences between Zane and me tackling Ang's next phase. It didn't allow us to work together in harmony. We were either in conflict with each other at every turn or completely ignoring one another until there was no way to avoid the issues. It was uncomfortable for either of us - how we related to the job or each other.

"Darnet, Zane… The EHAF has strong presumptions about the leaders of the Surgs. Sure, we don't have incontestable proof of their identity, but we have the means to scan the grids and round up everybody before things get messy. Why don't you act?"

Zane was adamant that they be left alone as long as they did not interfere with our way of life. It was what DAINN had suggested, and he abided by what DAINN wanted…

"I don't act because our people must have the chance to come around," Zane muttered, exasperated by my constant badgering of his policies.

I was less flexible and not convinced of the plan, but he had me outvoted on this particular issue. Forcing everyone to adopt Imps was the way to go. I was not sure we could even agree on that.

The underground retaliation against our System did not affect our infrastructure or policies most of the time. The little insurrections did not dent the Network, but this was Concordance.

"I hate to predict this, but the Surgs will interfere and create chaos. It is a mistake to be indulgent on a day like the Concord. This lack of action doesn't bode well for us, and I am putting this on the record with DAINN and the Council. I will be plenty vocal about it too."

Like all the other government officials, I waited to see who was right about this issue, but this morning, I decided to voice my opinion on a Vlog with DAINN. The news I received a little while ago warranted that. I wanted to be ready to step in and replace Zane in a campaign for the presidency's seat. My team and I had orchestrated everything.

"I know you have a soft spot for our people… But it is not practical." Today was proof enough of that, and I could use it against him. If my forecast was correct, and I knew it would be, I finally stood a chance to overthrow Zane.

It was one of the reasons the people had elected him. They liked him and felt safe with our government in his hands. They trusted him. True enough, he had proven his integrity time and again. Only this was over ten years ago now.

Time passed.

Things changed.

I thought he had grown complacent.

I had a plan. And I would have a real chance to take his place if things got out of control.

"You do what you need to do, Anton," said Zane. "Now, if you don't mind, leave my office. I have real work to do."

I had done what I came to do. I warned Langden, fair and square. Now, I needed to let the events play out.

Faculty, Pediatric Unit, Golden Ghetto, Ang City

Another Concord at the planet level is once again pending. None of us have a choice if we wish to survive within a system that is changing us to our very core. Phenom Heather Sims, Faculty Conclave, DAINN Annals – Winter 2098.

My next action was to stop by the Pediatric unit on my way to the Administrative building, even though it would tear me apart. But, I had to say goodbye.

It was located in a different wing of the hospital, between the ER and the main Faculty structure. At the next stop of the tram, I got out and followed the large hallways, leading to a smaller zone away from the more extensive medical activities of the hospital. It was my last time making this track.

I needed to see them one last time. My name was Heather Sims, and my duties to the babes in this wing were ending today.

My PVZ or personal visor deployed in front of me, and I saw Tesh's face, "Why are you doing this?"

"I need to…"

"You need to hurt yourself, is that it?"

"It is my last opportunity to see them. Tesh, I know you disagree, but it is my choice."

Tesh was one of my closest friends, even if we had little in common. She was not even in my Conclave, but we met long ago during our Evaluation as kids. We had bonded throughout the trials, and her ability to read emotions kept us in touch over the years. Slowly, Tesh rendered herself indispensable as a best friend knows how to do, and now, she was simply part of my life. As I faced my upcoming transition, her help these last few months remained invaluable. Between her and Eva, they kept me sane.

And at this moment, I needed her more than ever, but I knew she was going through something challenging too. Her face appeared worried for me, but I knew this week would be just as difficult, if not more.

"How are you doing? Is he there?"

"You know it."

"When will it end?"

"I am making it end this week."

"Be careful."

"Says the one who goes looking for trouble."

I laughed. "Well, you know me."

I could see she watched someone else in the Alcove because her eyes hardened. "I have to go, but you know where to find me."

She was about to face her nemesis again. I smiled at her and said, "Be careful with him." The NetComm dropped suddenly, and I was now alone again.

I was among those the Concordance would transplant. At seventeen years old, I usually had a sunny disposition and possessed a Ph.D. in Pediatrics and Fertility. My specialty was no longer in great demand. Our world population across the globe dropped every year according to a predetermined rate. With the planet overpopulated, our leaders in the last ten years implemented strict criteria for reproduction.

Their draconian rule as adopted by the entire parliament was enforced without exception. *Darnetwash… I know I can only seek refuge.*

The Concord required my transition. I had no choice and must make a change. If I continued working at the Faculty under the current circumstances, my assignment with terminal patients would become permanent. It took an emotionally strong individual to carry out those responsibilities. HellNet, I wasn't that person. I hated it. But I just was not made for that.

The System placed me there until the Concord ended. Eva, aware of the strain I was under, planned to intervene. But it was only due to her help that I even had the hope to switch. And even then, my assignment into a different department was not sure. Today, Eva would request my transfer into her team. My friends, Tesh and Eva, took the habit of watching out for me in their unique ways. I was lucky.

I passed the kid's playground within the hospital. This area, dedicated to children under five years old, remained an observation field. Soon, they would all be tested as part of the Evaluation. DAINN would interpret the results and help orient them toward skills best suited for them in their future.

Our planetary Network's voice resonated in the corridor. "DAINN is your friend. DAINN is your mentor. DAINN helps you learn faster, better, and become the best in your fields." This message was prevalent in this building area and often looped itself over this wing's airways.

I observed kids playing with tablets. They were already processing information structured by DAINN, whose entire children's network was structured to build confidence and guide them to maturity. Like the larger-than-life father and mother figure, DAINN was a friendly creature, taking many forms and having many faces. The kids saw DAINN in the first weeks of their lives under many disguises. It was the voice they heard as they fell asleep and the lullaby they learned from when able to sing. DAINN was the babysitter, the sister, the brother, the substitute mother or father.

"How about a song?" I heard DAINN's voice as I passed another room where children were seated on the floor, attentive to the ongoing games.

Indeed, DAINN distributed learning games based on each child's ability and followed their entire evolution. I saw its influence even now as I watched the kids play. The incredible thing was that DAINN could track every newborn into adulthood. DAINN followed every human soul across the entire planet. DAINN provided everyone what they needed most to achieve the highest performance and reach mastery levels and what some called the height of perfection. This state of grace, in which one individual performs to its utmost possibilities, with peace and serenity while serving the whole of society, was perhaps one of the most valuable of DAINN's achievements. Under DAINN's rule, we all executed more, better, faster. We attained the full possibilities of our potential.

As if thinking about Eva manifested her to connect with me, her signal on my PVZ appeared. I opened the NetComm and heard, "I'm glad I caught you."

In the last year, Eva helped me fight depression in a very different way than Tesh. Tesh appeased my emotions, rendering them more neutral and lessening my painful experiences as I lost a patient. She soothed me every time she felt me flare up in anger and frustration. On the other hand, Eva was much more pragmatic and required me to fight, relentlessly prepping me to give up my specialty and seek another within her team. She was tough, focused, and brilliant. The little girl I had known all these years had grown up into a powerful, no-nonsense woman. She had made her purpose of integrating me into her team.

"I hate to disturb your peaceful and serene last moment in the newborn wing, but I've been called to the Faculty to see Volt. I am on my way now."

"Oh…"

This was it then… I spent most of my time here, even after my shift in the terminally ill unit, where the few that refused treatment, implants, or transplants had chosen a natural end to their lives. "These pods, where all newborns sleep, are so special," I said wistfully.

"I know you find solace here, but soon, you will visit them not to erase the sadness of losing so many of your patients but for the fun of it. Keep that in mind."

"Yes, you keep reminding me. But I won't have a hand in the babies' birth. They're even more unique to me now, especially since their numbers have dropped substantially in the last few years."

"Don't be late to the Assembly. Try and arrive early. About tonight…"

"You're not getting out of it, Eva."

"Humm… You know things are crazy today, right?"

"I don't care. We need a break. You know why Volt called you in?"

"I think I'm to receive a boatload of recruits."

I looked at her pointedly. We had talked before, in privacy mode, and she knew what I was referring to – the fact that she needed to take one of the recruit's spots for me. Disconnecting while I was within the hospital walls and during the time of the Concord wasn't something either of us desired. Besides, there was no point in drawing attention to us today.

She nodded and answered calmly, "I hope they'll have good qualifications."

"Me too, for your sake."

"Good luck today. Get there early."

I nodded. "I know. I'll call you when I get out of there to meet you for the party."

"Okay. Don't take too long in here. The lines are huge already."

I wanted to say more, but Eva dropped the connection.

I looked at the newborns. The unrelenting pressure of the next several hours would carry a strain on anyone. Essentially, if Eva didn't take one of the posts for me in her department, I would remain where I was, and that wouldn't do. I had already lost my dream of a career in pediatrics. Geriatric was the last thing I wanted to do. We had both concluded a while back that I would be better off working with her than in other Faculty sections.

I turned away from the babies and walked back quietly toward the trams' platform to take me to the Faculty Administration building.

Institute, Alcove Chamber, Golden Ghetto, Ang City

I brace myself as I enter the Alcove. My behavior today, as any other day, is recorded in the DAINN's Annals. No matter what happens in the city, I cannot break down. I lock my jaw, compose my features, and face them. Phenom Tesh, Institute Conclave – Origin Special Elite Unit, DAINN Annals – Winter 2098.

There was no way to explain what would happen in several hours. I was not even sure myself. But I heard through various accounts the total mayhem that usually ensued on the day of the Concord.

How we got to that point was anyone's guess. It began with the decreasing natural supplies even as our world population plummeted. The manifestations of global warming everywhere imposed restrictions due to a depletion of reserves in our food chain. On multiple parts of our globe, products we would easily have found in the past became rare. Our agricultural output considerably reduced demanded a shift in our production. The Company became a proponent of change, pushing for different ways to put food on the table of everyone. While robotics invaded the workplace, growing crops required people to work with technology. It was the agenda of the first Concord – transmuting humans to interface better with robotics and technology. Imps were introduced into the population to enhance production effectiveness. The results were a success, and manufacturing and transportation soon followed the same transition spreading across new areas of our infrastructure. It was the second Concord.

The lure of technology was too strong to resist. The advances of science led to new advantages designed to enhance the human race. Combined with the corporations' greed, these innovations made us manufacture more new products to supply a world marketplace eager to try an easier way. The Company held that mantel, introducing the latest gadgets, pushing consumption, efficiency, excitement, results, and social status. And it became a winner.

The massive marketing machine had already convinced the population that it needed these new essential consumer items interwoven with Imps of all sorts for a better life. By the time they hit the stores, it was a feral frenzy. Soon, all of us had to try.

Before we knew it, we were hooked to an interplanetary Network. All were linked to one planetary mind, capable of reading and interpreting data from individuals, groups, organizations, governments, and nations. One powerful computer network application processing social, medical, scientific, cultural information faster and better than anyone on the planet, and it ruled everything. DAINN had become our guardian and subtly, much later, our master in all aspects of our lives.

When I entered the Alcove, the others were there, already settled in their hovering chairs, waiting to begin. One look around the oblong room, and my eyes found the empty Containment Lounge Seat or CLS reserved for me.

I paused, hesitating for a brief moment.

DAINN's voice resonated in my head. "We were all waiting for you, Tesh. It is time to begin."

Reluctantly, I moved toward my CLS, bracing myself for the moments ahead of me.

DAINN seemed impervious to my anxiety. Today, it would not cuddle me into this. He expected me like he expected all of us to meet our functions' requirements within our Conclave. Should I even call an artificial intelligence a "she or he?" Probably not, and yet we all did, depending on the circumstances.

"Well, it's about time you show up."

I tensed in my seat. *Not now.*

I knew that voice. It was one I would recognize anywhere. One, I had endured for years, and my hatred for that person flared. When my eyes landed on the Rat, I sneered at him.

"What are you doing here?"

The Rat was, for no better word, my nemesis. HellNet, he had destroyed my life. He had killed my parents, although I could not prove it. He entered my life and made it a living hell, taking away from me everything I knew. He forced me to leave behind my Conclave, the SRC. As the daughter of those leading it, I was meant to take over that responsibility within the Council, but he made sure that I would not, leaving me no choice but to join him inside the Institute. He ensured that he controlled my every moment and direction within the Institute Conclave as his ward, forcing me to do despicable things.

"I could not miss your role today, Tesh. I expect you to make me proud," his voice taunting me. "After all, you are my protegée."

For every decision he made on my behalf, he imposed his will on me as surely as the air I breathed, turning me into something I could not stand. Even though I fought him with everything I had within me, he still won over and over until finally, I entered the Academy, thwarting his goals for me once and for all. And finally, once I reached eighteen years old, he would no longer be able to touch me. I was there, almost.

"I am a member of the Academy. You no longer have oversight on me," I said.

"Indeed, you would think so. But I can still influence certain things, Tesh. You would do well to remember this. For instance, I felt that the tasks given to you by DAINN were too easy for your aptitudes. So, I made a few adjustments to the program you will be running today and every day this week."

My breath froze. Fear rose within me. The feeling was there, recognizable inside the pit of my stomach, for it remained the same for many years since he bullied himself into my life.

No, no, no, it is not supposed to happen anymore.

"DAINN, what is he talking about?"

But DAINN did not answer.

The Rat chuckled, rattling me even further. "Oh, I am going to enjoy today."

"What did you do?"

"Let just say I gave you an exceptional assignment, one you will excel at, of that I am certain. Of course, I ultimately reserved the right to punish those breaking my rules."

"I have not broken any rules, and you know it."

"But it is of no consequences in your case. I am still the head of the Institute, and I call the shots. I wouldn't do my job if I gave you something way beneath your skillset Tesh, now, would I? After all, I too, not unlike you, am compelled to serve our society in the best way possible."

"Whatever you have concocted, I will not do it."

"Oh, but I think you will. On a day of Concordance, there are no choices. Once I give the orders, you cannot refuse them. If you do, the consequences would be most unpleasant."

"What are you talking about now? DAINN assigned our orders."

"How naïve you are. I changed yours. This week, you are mine. Open your program and get started. You have lost enough time."

My heartbeat increased under an emotional tension where my hatred for him was like a living thing within me. I could feel the bitter taste of it on my tongue, with evil darkness suddenly flooding me. It quickly became soul-wrenching, so I attempted to center myself. I could not and would not allow myself to lose it.

I looked around the Alcove and saw my companions already engrossed in their tasks. Their faces looked frozen, their eyes looking straight ahead, only seeing what DAINN's program accessed for them. Today, their jobs, triggered by the A.I.'s selection of people in need of re-programming within our society, demanded the blunt force of a hammer from all of us. Seeing without seeing, they remained utterly inside their minds and would be like this for many hours.

Without any further delay, the display swallowed me. My mind directly linked to the CLS Screen in front of me rebelled, but there was nothing I could do.

The files lay open for me to reach out to the candidates selected for the re-programming. The faces of those people spread across the screen of my mind taunting me. It would be easy to reach out and make their personalities pliable for whatever purpose the Rat had selected, but I wouldn't do it.

It was one thing to infuse calm on a crowd to avoid rebellions on this day. The Alcove served this purpose, to allow our population to remain calm and free of fear. DAINN dictated our roles to eliminate the potential for significant bloodshed should our citizens provoke an uprising or revolt against their new mandate. DAINN always attempted to make transitions more manageable, although I would not agree with any of these. The fate of our future hinged on these changes, and while I was not too fond of any of these, I could not refute their necessity. Many were implemented for the good of our society.

But it was quite another to tamper with the minds of individuals who did not respond to the Rat's coercion. As far as I was concerned, this operation was conducted to serve only one purpose – his. Indeed, upon closer examination of the files, my suspicion was confirmed. The independence of these selected few individuals on my display represented a tangible failure for him if they could not be bent to his will. He would not allow himself to be taunted by such. The threads into their lives remained a visible consequence of their resistance to Sloan Roden Baker. Sure that his modus operandi remained the same over the year, this intervention may have begun as enticement and turned into unrestricted revenge due to their lack of compliance. I had been there. It was the Rat's way.

I looked at the profiles of those selected by the Rodent. They were five older males in their mid-thirties, two in positions of influence at the Company and the SRC.

My eyes lingered on the image of the man at the SRC. I knew him. He used to be a friend of my parents. Of course, the Rodent was at it again, coercing people to do his bidding.

I needed time to decide how to deal with today. So, I perused the other files.

The other three people appeared to have lesser jobs but were affiliated through their families with influential officials in the Faculty and EHAF.

Of course, the Rat would seek to control those embedded in other Conclaves for his purpose. Eight of the other files were females, and when I dove into these further, I saw how young they were. All seemed under twenty-one, in lower positions within each Conclaves infrastructure. The Imps required for their transition into new roles made my stomach lurch. I closed my eyes. I couldn't do this.

My chair came alive. I felt the jolt of several bolts of electricity. The lower base of my head tingled at first, and the shock of needles digging inside my brain spread, delivering the short-lived torture.

I cringed, my teeth clamping down hard to avoid injury to my tongue. My hands gripped the arms of my CLS chair. The experience was similar to having every bone in my body broken and quickly fused again. Only, he would do it over and over until I caved in. The instances would be longer each time, the shocks remaining in my brain and digging deeper, leaving me in pain as my broken bones stayed in pieces. He would increase the torture creating vast sensations filtering through my tissues to destabilize me. This experience would please the Rat for a time, and then he would apply another form of torture, bored by my lack of response. It would soon get worst. I knew this too well, for it was not my first time. I just never thought I would be subjected to this again.

The years of enforced therapy to make me comply came back to the surface at once. I fought against the memories. I could not go there today, or I would not survive the ordeal. But I knew this was only the beginning of what I would be forced to endure this week.

It was the way the Rat reminded me that he held me in his grasp. It was his way of showing me that I was not outside his reach. It was his way to tell me I belonged to him.

I needed to comply. But I would not. My resolve grew with each passing second; I determined to show the Rodent this time.

How much could I take? In the back of my mind, it was only a matter of time before he would break me. The only question remained, could I last one week?

SRC Conclave, Annals Viewing Vlog 925,825,744 Ang City

When President Zane Langden learns about the Anomaly, he immediately calls for implementing four programs: Origin, Alpha, Provenance, and Aurora—commanding most of our EHAF Force to prepare and supervise the workforce while enhancing the training of recruits. We divert all our resources to complete these operations, but we face delays, and Concordance takes priority. DAINN Annals – Winter 2098.

President Zane Langden prepared the EHAF for this day. Concordance scenarios ran within the System for weeks to account for every contingency. Modeling the best outcomes with the assistance of the SRC to avoid bloodshed within Ang for this Concord remained the mandate of the President. When it proved that we could entertain containment, the Force began implementing a plan encompassing multiple fronts.

But the Council would have none of that. For them, diverting our resources from the programs to avoid mayhem with our populace did not seem the best use of our time. Langden fought them. A clear division within the Council emerged, allowing the President of the Council, Commander Anton Fowler, to rally against our President of the

SRC Conclave, Annals Viewing Vlog 925,825,744 Ang City

When President Zane Langden learns about the Anomaly, he immediately calls for implementing four programs: Origin, Alpha, Provenance, and Aurora—commanding most of our EHAF Force to prepare and supervise the workforce while enhancing the training of recruits. We divert all our resources to complete these operations, but we face delays, and Concordance takes priority. DAINN Annals – Winter 2098.

President Zane Langden prepared the EHAF for this day. Concordance scenarios ran within the System for weeks to account for every contingency. Modeling the best outcomes with the assistance of the SRC to avoid bloodshed within Ang for this Concord remained the mandate of the President. When it proved that we could entertain containment, the Force began implementing a plan encompassing multiple fronts.

But the Council would have none of that. For them, diverting our resources from the programs to avoid mayhem with our populace did not seem the best use of our time. Langden fought them. A clear division within the Council emerged, allowing the President of the Council, Commander Anton Fowler, to rally against our President of the

EHAF, Zane Langden. With the EHAF Force totally in his corner, Langden pursued his plan, disregarding the Council's will. The System, operating under the SRC's purview, sided with Langden. The Insitute, under the influence of Commander Anton Fowler, took the opposite position.

The DAINN Network became compromised from that moment on; only the obstruction to the System's goals began before that. The proponents of the Institute's position extended their tentacles in darkness for far longer, starting with eliminating the head of the SRC years ago, and diverting its legitimate leader into the Institute; their intent was the corruption of the System. But no one knew to what degree they tampered with me. It is how my circumstances began to change.

For the last year, while a good portion of the Force already tended to build additional ships with the help of our best engineers and scientists, another prepared to handle transfer logistics for all our resources from the planet's surface. The Armada grew. The equipment needed for the successful completion of the enterprises expanded. Space arms development leaped. Food supply safeguard became more efficient. Materials for the survival of our species took new forms. Grain storage compartments built for long-term use increased at the hands of our workers. Animals allocated to each program were divided into groups to join specific locations, and their DNA was preserved inside portable labs. Everything in preparation for the day our population would depart in space or reach their underground destination was set in motion, stretching the System to the breaking point where Concordance became an inevitable measure if we were ever to meet the looming deadline.

Langden refused to see the workers who would be the most affected by this Concord risking bloodshed. His predilection called for containment rather than an end to violence. So, a large portion of the

EHAF answered their call to implement safety measures for the riots that would soon spread in our streets. The decision brought dissension.

When it became apparent that we needed more people, the Council ordered two programs, Origin, and Aurora to be immediately halted for the duration of the Concord. In my opinion, it was a short-sighted decision. Against my recommendation, the members voted to continue the work for what appeared the most valuable of the four operations: Alpha and Provenance. Indeed, our schedules stretched to their limit to meet a deadline we estimated months ago because we feared the anomaly, were plagued by delays and breakdowns. Still, most of our people would end up inside Aurora, which alone called for this one enterprise to become the most fundamentally important of them all. It was not so.

These programs implemented in all the corners of the globe and within Ang required the utmost resources to complete them successfully. Within the Consortium of the different nations, we had a voice and held the kind of leadership that would influence the outcomes. While we remained independent, we could not ignore the future of our planet with the incoming cataclysm, so coordinated efforts remained essential. Shaping policies that spread because of our neural network was not uncommon. In its role, the Council dictated everything. The discord was bound to hurt us.

The feeds splashed across the displays in the SRC, showing the various areas of the city. DAINN's voice resonated inside the lab, and my voice kept announcing the same message: "At this very moment, we are implementing the shift. Our planet's priorities have changed. We expect your support in all fields, from agricultural to manufacturing, from transportation to education, from high tech to science, from aeronautic to government positions, and even inside the health care industry and Faculty. We demand your cooperation, and we ask you to integrate. As a resident, citizen, and world citizen, you benefit. It is your time to give back."

On one of the screens, I saw Zane Langden and North, his second-in-command, nod to each other as they conducted a meeting. The President of the EHAF seemed perturbed by the news he received and shook his head. His voice called upon me. "DAINN, can you perceive any unusual activities within Emerald Field?"

"Not at this time, but there are a lot of areas our Custodians do not cover with the underground tunnels that spread beyond ArchWay Pass."

North announced, "I would like to deploy more City Vigils in these areas. It will double our manpower on the grounds."

"Do it," said Langden. "I do not want any surprises."

North added, "We have some chatter that indicates an uprising. I believe we have to anticipate our deployment in these grids."

"Let me know how this develops," said Langden.

"I will be in the Watch Center," muttered North as he left the room. His face registered a haunted look as he withdrew from the President's office.

I observed this look many times before. Concluding that today will be tough on him, I followed his progress down the corridor. For some reason, it was one of these days for him.

"North, how are you doing today?"

"I am fine, DAINN."

But I knew the signs. My voice murmured in my charge's head, "Get out of it, North… Let it go."

His eyes glazed over, his features flashed with pain. He fought it again and shook himself off, but the old paralysis grabbed him.

It happened fast. While North was usually ready to block out the memories, there were moments when they rushed in overwhelmingly.

This time was one of these moments. It was no different from so many others I witnessed over the years.

North's resolve had not worked today.

The past engulfed him and the anger burned through him.

I noticed the disdain he held against himself as he tightened his grip and breathed, attempting to slow his feelings. North was a rare person.

But even after all these years, his feelings were still very much alive after all these years.

He had not been able to prevent what had happened, and he was unforgiving to himself.

"North, it was not your fault," I insisted like I usually did when he requested my help.

But this fact never mattered to him. He felt that he had caused it to happen nevertheless by doing his duty. Anyway, the wave of shame and acrid self-loathing came from deep inside him, and it was surging through him, about to demolish his composure. I guess it didn't help much that he was still in denial. The only thing I knew for sure was that he missed his family desperately every moment of his days.

"Let it go," I said again. "You don't want or deserve that burden, especially now."

Time and time again, I expressed these words as the attacks pursued him for years afterward.

This trip back in time and down memory lane happened whenever he was reminded of the Exodus. Concordance brought back the desperate looks he had seen on the many faces and the unwanted emotions he felt in the actions of strangers during the big storm.

He forced himself to snap out of it. He chose to maintain a stiff upper lip a while back, never mentioning what had broken him inside.

His teammate knew, but they were always supportive and never allowed him to ponder things when they saw the miserable look on his face. But on these occasions, he would retreat to the Watch Tower for some kind of peace.

Only peace will not be present in our streets today.

"You have that look again…" I said. "North, you selected the behavior years ago, but you forgot that you also take on the consequences of that action," I added, my super mind dissecting every pattern of an individual.

"*I know, DAINN, but I have to deal with that on my own,*" answered North once again inside the MindTranscript we entered as he passed the Watch Tower door.

"*I do not see any success, and you are not progressing,*" I said.

North had cut himself off from any help I might have given then. He chose to deal with the devastation he felt on his own. I preferred not to admit that he was in desperate need of someone to talk to and continued to muddle through the emotions.

"*I have offered, and I do so again… do you want to forget?*" I asked once again for the thousands of times. "*I can make that happen.*"

"*No. You cannot take my memories away. They are mine. They make me who I am.*"

"*Do you really want to be that person? Yes, they are part of you, but they do not make you who you are, in that we differ. Shall I show you?*" I insisted.

"*I do not need an explanation on that, thanks but no.*"

"*When you remember, these memories hurt you, North. I do not want to see you suffer,*" I added. "*You cannot be efficient when you hurt, and we need everyone to remain effective. Shall we schedule a visit?*"

"*No. I told you, I won't allow it. Stop bringing it up. I made my decision a long time ago. Besides, I should be hurt. These memories hurt because I remember them.*"

"*If it were all that it was, then I would understand your decision… But these emotions do damages, and I cannot let that happen. You know my mandate.*"

Our VLogs or VideoLogs from the System showed that what I said was true for all negative thoughts impacted our bodies. The DAINN Network possessed proof of that nowadays.

North just ignored this fact because he couldn't help how he felt. The notion remained that he was less efficient when he had these episodes. The official entries about the status of his work made to DAINN regularly had resulted in conversations and advice. I replayed such episodes for him many times. He was caught on these Vlogs with a dazed look on his face, unable to remember where he was or what he was doing. He hated seeing himself like that. More importantly, he hated to have his teammates see him like that. He always wondered if he let them down? North feared that he would let his teammate down during an operation. But North was the best despite this weakness, and it had never happened. However, it was a risk in his mind. The answer was obvious – thus far, it always was a no. Yet, he couldn't and wouldn't get those memories removed either.

"*I'll be fine, DAINN. I will focus on the task. It won't affect my work.*"

"*I have heard you say that 1,634 times, North. Would you at least schedule a chat so we can discuss this recurring problem?*"

As DAINN, my System cataloged everything. It was part of my role in our society, helping my charges. I usually concluded outcomes rightly for so many things in our lives. Of course, DAINN wasn't perfect. DAINN was created with the utmost care and grew on its own as an entire Planetary Network… The System was not to blame for what happened to the Planet or its people like it was not at fault for our leaders' paths when faced with the reality of a planet in permanent turmoil.

Still, none of it made North feel any better.

He was not getting better regarding this situation. These episodes kept him on edge and did not diminish in intensity. They surfaced when he recalled that day and the desperation of people.

"*I prefer not. You know all there is to know, already. I will be more disciplined and won't let it distract me from my work.*"

"*Very well, but if you endanger anyone due to these episodes, I will schedule the visit, and you will have no choice in the matter… and neither will I,*" I added, following my protocol.

"*It won't happen.*"

"*I will be observing.*"

"Show me you are right, North," I insisted before I got out of his head.

DAINN couldn't change the past. Neither did the System allow to dwell on it. But as DAINN, I respected the desires of my charges so long as they did not go counter to my programming. The System sounded almost regretful when it warned North. Re-focusing my attention on the feeds from the grids, I watched, recorded, and reported to the various Conclaves today's events.

Presidential Tower, Golden Ghetto, Ang City

I answer to my truth rather than that of another. The notion drives me, and what is about to unfold will be a tipping point for us. Phrenic Asher Finch, EHAF Conclave – Presidential Elite Unit, DAINN Annals – Winter 2098.

I stood in line at the automated coffee shop, taller than most, ripped by the training and looking like the poster boy for the Force. Last year, they had recruited me for their promotion, as I was the type they wanted for the Elite. Something I didn't feel I ought to have done at all considering my opinion of the moment, but it wasn't like I was given a choice. My clean-cut features were regular enough that my face got plastered every time they decided to recruit. It was Darnet annoying too. It used to be that I had one belief: the EHAF or Earth Homeland Alliance Force, but that was a long time ago.

Inside the small cafe, we had rows and columns for everything these days.

Today, although I was part of the Elite within the EHAF, I followed another path. Convinced that our world needed a different social structure, I chose another course of action a while ago. So, here I was, meeting a contact who happened to be standing right in front of me at this very moment.

Surrounded by people whose sole intention was to either get their brew or grab their breakfast on the run before they began their morning, I was impatient to get out of here. Women and men alike were eager to give their orders through the PVZs or personal Visors, which unfolded in front of nearly everyone.

The orders flowed in, sometimes simultaneously. The clones, androids, and robots servicing this gentle mob effectively responded to the onslaught of new demands. The desired substances were poured and delivered to the customers without breaking any momentum. It was quite interesting to watch, like a dance of machines around the place.

This morning, though, I wasn't there taking pleasure in that. Instead, this was the kind of scheduled encounters to exchange information, as we did from time to time. Standing inside one of our latest coffee shops on the one-hundredth floor of the plaza, I was present to meet with Ciel at this early hour.

The place, located across from the Tower, which housed the President's quarters, was convenient. I knew that today things were about to change in a big way, and my contact and I were very conscious of it.

I whispered, "These lines are getting bigger, aren't they? It is all we need on a day like today."

"You could say that again," Ciel said. "It's because I like their concoction that I'm still here."

"Same here," I confirmed to her.

Ciel was a young woman, a slip of a girl actually, but she had revealed herself bright and resourceful. She looked sixteen, but she acted much older, with dark straight hair cut around her shoulders that seemed always to find just the correct position around her head. She was pretty, with dark brown eyes and golden sparks as she laughed, which was not that often, I must say. Her lips wore a tumultuous slant due to the cynicism that already marked her personality. I guess, like many of us, she had seen too much.

It wasn't easy to imagine her capable of challenging missions. She had demonstrated her abilities to all of us on several occasions. She was intelligent, highly adaptive in a chameleon kind of way, and just damn good if you asked me. Although irreplaceable in many ways, she volunteered to move between the above grounds and underground. It was a high-risk endeavor. She could be noticed and arrested. But so far, she remained unnoticed, accessing the areas in our midst as needed. It wasn't that she had unremarkable attributes. In truth, she was stunning, but there was something about her that could just make her forgettable. This quality served us well. Yet, when one got to know her as we had, she was also unforgettable.

Lines had formed around us, and we were getting closer to picking up our choices for the day. Maintaining the hidden cover of getting coffee, whose smell carried through the enclosed space, was rather convenient. The aroma here was mixed with many other spices, teas, and various ready-to-take-out concoctions that our modern days had somehow made the new trend of the moment.

Her presence and look gave me an ideal reason to begin a conversation, so I made my move. "Put that one on my units," I ordered the android at the counter.

"Yes, Phrenic Finch," responded the machine as it handed me the drink.

Ciel turned slightly toward me with a smile. "It's very nice of you."

"You're welcome."

The crowd gathered tighter around us.

Surreptitiously, I passed Ciel the small device with the beverage handed over by the Android. It was merely the size of a fingertip and adhered to my thumb, so I quickly settled it under her cup.

I smiled. "You better get going; the timing with today's Concordance will be wild," I added with a wink.

As Ciel took her order of Red Cloud from my hand, a raspberry vanilla coffee mixed with mind supplements and vitamins, she turned towards me and nodded, ready to make her way out of the shop. "No doubt," she murmured. "Don't worry; other than for this, I plan on staying inside." Her head, tilted in an angle as she appraised me, gave her a thoughtful look, one I rarely saw. This young woman, whose charm was rather irrepressible, was always on the move, and for the most part, had no idea the effect she had on men. It was refreshing.

We had indeed concluded our meeting and the exchange took place with nothing else to discuss. "Good. Next time, maybe we can drink this brew together without a Concord."

We both laughed.

Ciel took another sip of her brew. She swallowed and smiled quickly back before turning toward the doors facing the park. "I will see you around."

The coffee shop was situated at an angle and provided two entry points. One located straight onto the central plaza, and one overlooking the square saw much traffic throughout the day.

I watched her leave. Soon, she was just a silhouette lost in the crowd of people walking across the park.

One of the shop's serving robots brought me the tray of coffee I had ordered. "Here you go, Phrenic Asher."

This model was one of the latest on the floor, straight out from the manufacturing plant. This latest Zoid 2098 was a standard addition to the automation of the Golden Ghetto. The advanced models lasted about two years before they were replaced with advanced ones, their new tech gizmos allowing for more efficient service. The very new ones were much more adaptable in their mind transcribing programming. The government then allocated the older models to some of the other city grids.

I checked the order. The round of coffee was for my team. NetShit would fly if I indeed forgot anyone in my Elite platoon. The light tray made its way over the small counter and stood in front of me, hovering. The units due for the coffees transferred from my credits each month with the EHAF account, so I quickly turned, and the tray slid beside me. It followed me smoothly as I moved towards the door leading to the plaza. From there, I crossed over the bridge and entered the massive doors of the Tower.

When I reached the entrance, DAINN's voice spilled outside the large lobby of the Tower. "Mobilization eminent… rejoins your units."

The Elite Presidential Contingent or EPC spread on the five-hundredths floor. Our group oversaw the main Presidential offices and the Penthouse of the President of the EHAF. Our Elite EHAF teams distributed between the Golden Ghetto and Water's Edge resided between the three-hundredth-to-four-hundredth floor. It was convenient.

I passed the lobby, thinking about my actions while going to the Spacevat. Six EHAF members belonging to General Corp rushed outside, passing with deference as I crossed the large hall. Indeed, our unit was privileged, having achieved the highest ranking.

The crowd of people going in and out of the Spacevat was small. It was our officials' way to the top. An area entirely dedicated to the Elite team members, the Council members, and the Presidential teams. It was the only part of the Tower where rapid transport to the various floors above was available and held some of the most luxurious lodgings. This set-up maintained the substantial traffic up and down at a minimum and allowed for greater security. Everyone else, including the administrative personnel, and aids used larger Elevats nearby.

The clones, androids, and robots automatically moved towards other modes of transportation upwards. They had choices between the Flystairs or moving stairways, spiral, or transport ramps kept available on the other side. The restricted MTP's or Mobile Transportation Platforms around these parts remained strictly for the EHAF.

The Spacevat doors opened. I stepped inside the Elevat and relayed my floor to the System. It would go up to the top, passing the other EHAF floors before reaching mine.

Way below the EHAF Elite, located on the one hundred and two hundred levels, our General Corp monitored the Assembly Center's essential administrative functions. Meetings there took place weekly, cementing the recommendations made by DAINN and dictating to the Conclaves new mandates. Our EHAF teams below the rank of Captain were housed in the adjacent buildings.

The Spacevat flew upward quietly, its mechanism working smoothly, brought me to the Penthouse, near the President's quarters, where the rest of the Elite team resided. We remained close by to guarantee the security of our Council members. The Watch Tower monitored everything relating to Ang city's Officials and main population.

DAINN's voice resonated in the cabin. "Concordance will begin shortly. Make sure to get your orders now."

This morning, the Surgs implemented steps that triggered a new phase with the underground. The action would send a deep rumbling throughout our city and across our entire infrastructure. That's the way the resistance needed it. Passing the information to Ciel began the process. And it had been a difficult decision for me, one that I grappled with for a long time. By doing this, I betrayed the EHAF and my team. It was a risk, but I didn't care about that for me. I knew where I drew the line.

But now, I had to live with it. Part of me looked back at the moment where my gut drove me to that conclusion. However, now was not the time to go down memory lane. I consciously turned my thoughts on the day ahead. *It is too late for anything else anyway.*

The day was going to be interesting on all fronts. It was Concordance, an event we had prepared for, knowing it would create mayhem, sort of like planning a fire drill where everything burns down.

The Spacevat stopped, and I exited, walking along the corridor to reach my Elite unit getting ready inside our Gear Room.

The tray slid ahead of me past the door and into the hallway. I opened the door to the Gear Room.

Talia, short and sweet when she was not on duty, Alai tall, dark, and always efficient, and Birch, built like a tree, were already geared up. These people were my teammates and family, and here I was, making moves against what they stood for, and I cringed inside.

"We were about to send out for you," said Talia, with a broad smile on her face. She was a constant positive influence and remained that way in most operations.

We were a highly-trained unit and most probably the best. We were well skilled in combat and proficient in many areas; our members were tough, dependable, and represented the best of the EHAF.

"How is everything out there?" asked Alai as she grabbed one of the coffee drinks.

"The usual. Crazy, and there is a lot of intense people out there."

She had quite an attitude, and one never knew when it was about to surface. She picked up the first coffee. After she tasted it, she exclaimed, "Darnet, it's cold… how long did it take you to bring this up?"

I chuckled. "Too long. Get it yourself next time."

"Well, someone got up on the wrong side of their floating bed," she retorted with a grimace.

This team was the reason I debated my actions for a long time. The very idea to betray my team's beliefs in the System had held me back. I could sabotage that, but I would never fight against them, and I knew that. If it came down to it, I would side with them; I would protect them, I would die for them. But here I was, putting out operations at risk.

"Any reason to be touchy today? Did you get up on the wrong side of Councilwoman Verena?" murmured Talia as she smiled, stepping close to my ear. Talia oversaw Special Projects Operations for our Presidential Elite team.

I gave her a smirk that could kill, and she laughed even harder. "Sooner or later, they'll find out," she added, moving past me.

"What are we going to find out?" asked Birch, far from knowing anything about discretion…

The eyes of my three colleagues looked up at me.

Talia bailed me out, "It's crowded out there… And the mood is not good."

So good of her to create the controversy in the first place and pull me out of it with an air of superiority. I sighed, moving past her with a slight frown. I grumbled, "NetShit… Mind your own life."

But Talia was right.

HellNet. I need to come clean about my ongoing relationship. Only, I'm not ready.

I made my way past the resting chairs and sofas that allowed us to relax in between assignments comfortably and deflected, "You all know the drill… People are uneasy."

Birch reached for his coffee drink before the tray ultimately settled down on the table near the center of the room, empty. "Yeah, Talia is right. It's about time you show up with the grub…" exclaimed Birch, rough and usually silent. His role within our unit spanned many things as a special forces operative, and he was lethal.

"And it's about to get far worst…" said Alai as she took another sip and grimaced. She dealt with our intelligence and security network for the Presidential Unit with a sharp mind.

This room was where we spent hours, either resting or playing games when on call. Waiting to jump into action when duty called was a big part of our job. So was the training.

Yet, this place held memories, where we shared closeness and friendship few other units could pretend even to have. Perhaps our small group made the difference. Maybe it was our past and what we had lived through, or the trust that made us unique – the knowledge that no matter what happened, we all knew we could count on each other. The bonds made it difficult for me to execute my affiliation with the underground, but eventually, I had to move.

"We haven't heard anything from North either, but I'm on my way to the Monitoring Room," responded Jeze, already dressed for any intervention we would make this day. "It shouldn't be too long now."

She passed me without pausing, eager to meet up with North, whom I knew was already at his post in the Watch Center. On a day like today, any one of us would find him there, not that he had to. North always made it his responsibility to be where he could oversee the action, and today of all days, he would find it there without a doubt. Our Commander didn't take chances.

"Humm... I can't wait." I said with a hint of teasing, knowing full well that she and North would not be far away from each other under any circumstances. They were an unbeatable pair within our small group, effective and deadly.

Jeze nodded but, for the most part, ignored my barb.

Inside the Gear Room and along the walls' edges, the casings housed our gear calibrated to our individual needs. It remained there when we were off duty, but it wasn't often these days.

Birch picked up his assault packet and proceeded to get ready. Our vest was the most crucial and contained almost everything we needed in combat situations. A rappel gun, laser, Znet, extra supplies, and the vest itself served as protection if we didn't trigger our Embodied Combat Avatar or ECA. Mine was already on. I never left the Tower without it.

As I passed him, I didn't stop.

The armory doors stood wide open to the left side of the room. It contained our favorite weapons, generally hidden by the cabinets nestled in the wall. Further back, our AirBikes stood in their dedicated landing zones, closed off by the wide sliding door made of thin explosion-proof glass. Everything was ready to go at a moment's notice. This area opened on the side of the Tower and jettisoned into the open sky.

Cashel was already there, watching the city views on the edge of the landing zone, which extended to most of Ang City. Like us, his aptitudes were vast, but his close combat skills were unparalleled.

We were way above the ground and overlooked most buildings around, surveying many city areas from the entire Golden Ghetto center to Bridge View and Archway Pass, all the way to Water's Edge. The rest of the grid limits were behind us with Emerald Field and Cliffs Top. Landing zones sparsely occupied a piece of our sky and were scattered around the various grids. Beyond all that lay the city's entrances floating above the domes through our four AirGates, to the North, South, East, and West.

Cash, mesmerized by the landscape below, remained motionless.

I had picked up his preferred concoction on my way and brought it with me across the threshold.

Cashel sensed my approach.

"You can't get enough?" I asked him, already knowing the answer.

He slowly acknowledged my presence with a nod of his head as he grabbed his Black Sholl, a coffee brew I never dared to try because it looked thick as mud and disgusting to me. "Thanks. Yeah, it's beautiful, but today it is not the same. I loathe this day."

"I don't think any of us look forward to it either," I said as I let go of his drink.

"We have the upper hand this time. It Netsucks bad. I hate to execute a plan against our people."

"It's not like the other times. We've made sure of that."

"I know. I just hate it, that's all."

"Don't think about it. All that is left to do is implement despite surprises that may come our way."

"What have you heard?"

"Nothing much… just the usual ramblings. So, what are you going to do? Will you go to her?"

Cashel looked in my direction, a huge grin chasing away the darkness of his previous mood. "You can't keep a lady waiting."

We smiled. A small giggle escaped Cashel.

Soon, we would be called to maintain order upon the Megapolis.

We would deploy the City Vigils in full force. We would sift through the Passageways, across the Airbridges that linked our hundreds of floors above the old city. We would secure the Pathways that connected our business districts to the adjoining grids to stop our population's flow.

Indeed, we would be called upon to push back the influx of rioters that would rapidly mar the landmarks of the Golden Ghetto, extending to Water's Edge. The frigates and cruisers would take over the air space. Our grids would become a landscape where chaos reigned, for today, there would be rebellion. I knew that too well as I turned on all of my systems.

13
DISSENT
Aidan

Old City, Underground, Grid 0, Ang City

The system runs us all. Only, I believe we have a chance to change it, and I am willing to bet on that against everything. Phenom Aidan Furst, Civilian, Company Conclave, DAINN Annals – Winter 2098.

My surroundings in the long tunnel got darker, and my steps faltered. I adjusted my visor to create a bit more luminosity and continued moving ahead, hoping to avoid a repeat of the attack I had suffered earlier. So far, so good.

One might ask how in the HellNet I got here, in this underground shaft leading to the illegal activities of the dissidents. It was not such a big deal to decipher, considering my upbringing. Don't get me wrong; it was not a bad childhood.

Indeed, life for a while had never been so good. When I looked back upon it, our routine these last nine months to the day of my Evaluation was comfortable and possibly the happiest time of our lives. Mom and dad had constant work, even if it wasn't what they wanted. Other people did not struggle as much as before, even in our grid; the economy was booming compared to the bad times we experienced before. Due to new technology advancing by giant leaps, things were better. This favorable period made everyone amenable to social leniency.

These were the years where my parents moved into a more important place in an area of town with better amenities. The months went relatively fast, and then, the day of my Evaluation arrived. It wasn't my initial Evaluation. The System overlooked me earlier at the age of five. No. Instead, it was a remedial Evaluation because my father flagged me to the Network.

Indeed, I started to demonstrate unique skills, and at first, my parents were surprised and began to watch me more closely. I guessed they didn't expect their kid to be so gifted, especially with numbers and symbols. "He is showing a consistent spatial aptitude, as they call it. We have to get him in, increase his chance for a better life," said my father repeatedly to my mother.

My mother, doubting that the Evaluation was a good idea, expressed the opposite, "I don't know if this is a good thing. Maybe we should leave this alone."

In retrospect, my mother was not wrong. But then again, being admitted into the System did provide some perks.

My parents were simple folks. They had limited education and didn't expect me to amount to anything more than what they had made of themselves. *No one has lofty ideals in my family.*

Their indecision continued for a time, and the conversation lasted when I was no longer in the room.

"What can someone with these abilities offer the world?" they asked themselves.

I listened to the discussions over weeks through thin walls. *Even today, I like to know what goes on in people's heads. It gives me a leg up.*

"These capabilities will give him a better break, and you shouldn't get in the way of that," said my father. He was emphatic and overruled my mother.

"You always see things short-term... What happens after they have identified your son as a gifted kid? What happens to his life after he enters the System? As of now, they overlooked him and have not come looking for him. Let it be. I don't trust it," had protested my mother.

But, my unaccounted absence inside the System wasn't to be. As months passed, they remained unable to comprehend my abilities, and while impressed, both continued to share divided opinions. Then one day, my father registered me for another Evaluation. Maybe it was his way to cast the dice.

Not knowing what to do with me prompted his action.

None of us realized the impact this would have on my future, and regardless of my mother's reservations, the Evaluation Officials now had a new record of me.

Here I am, years later. The path taken in those days made me who I am today.

I was almost at the end of the underground corridor when I heard voices in the distance. The conversations echoed remarkably inside these old walls, and one always had to be careful.

Another laser gun pointed at me, found its target on my chest. *Well done, Aidan.*

It stopped in my tracks.

"Hold it right here," a rough voice said.

Two people watched me, and I quickly lifted my arms in surrender.

The first guy held an automatic weapon aimed at me.

The second, a few steps behind, just watched me.

A second encounter within minutes should tell you something.

"Drop the damn fighting gear!" announced a second powerful voice.

I had forgotten my ECA suit, so I turned it off and displayed my rumpled appearance for the guards to see.

"Netwash... You got nicely beat up."

"Road hazard in these parts." My Nanos should have taken care of the worst of it by now.

"Humm... You should report it. We do try to keep bums out."

"Well, it didn't work," I said, noncommittal.

"What brings you here?" asked the brick of a guy standing in my way.

"I need to buy something. I'm here for one part."

"What's the password?" he continued in a stern tone.

"The password?" My mind was muddled, for I couldn't think of one.

"Yeah. The password."

I was beginning to think I got cheated. I didn't remember one. Maybe, my brain, beaten, remained too fuzzy. *What is the Darnet password?*

"Security is high today. You've got to give it to us."

What had Conrad said about the location?? *Come on, think, Aidan!*

"If you don't have a password, I can't let you in, and I can't let you go either," the guard with the weapon said as he stepped forward with one of those big automatic laser blowers that neutralized an ape of a man in seconds.

Elfen? He sure doesn't look like an Elfen to me.

He was about to grab my arm. I took a step back. "Wait."

Elfen stopped, quite willingly. One could tell that this wasn't part of the job he relished much. He instead looked like a good chap, thrown into a situation he didn't care for with the surveillance of the tunnel.

Behind him, I heard the voice of another guy. "You need some help, Elfen?"

"I think…" I was trying to remember Conrad's words. "Watch for the wind in those tunnels. Yes, that is what he said," and I was suddenly relieved to have remembered his words.

Elfen grunted. "Okay, go on up ahead then."

I passed Elfen, relieved that I somehow got the password without knowing it. I walked into a grand cavern, the likes of which I hadn't seen before.

Usually, the market took place along tunnels and side corridors abandoned many years ago. The Megacity of Ang grew constantly. With more buildings erected over and above older constructions, the pylons dropped into the earth soon encased older structures. Over time, these abandoned in favor of more modern edifices became lost and unused. But the underground repurposed these to accommodate the movement and take in refugees. Now, they served as habitats for those no longer within the System as we knew it. The Transcients grew in these parts.

I was here today, in the vast cavern of the underground, about to buy yet another piece of equipment. One illegally sold. How it was acquired was anyone's guess. Why I needed it was a priority - to remain as free as possible. The expensive piece of hardware would allow me to cruise the Network without leaving an imprint behind. It would isolate my system from any unwanted curiosity. Indeed, my activities outside the work at the Company could engender retaliation if one stumbled upon them. Accessing independence and wealth remained my focus. *I have a promise to keep and intend to see it through.*

I quickly walked over to the guy I usually did business with, and he waved, recognizing me. I nodded, knowing I probably was one of his largest customers and approached their stand if one could call it that. It was a large swath of dirt covered by cloth.

"You all right, man?" asked the older guy, my bruises not completely healed.

He was a burly guy by the name of Moss, with an uneven smile, a grin that had no doubt seen better days. Just behind him was the young kid, Ven, skinny as a HellNet who grew too fast to keep any weight on his tiny bones. He knew all about the stuff I needed, this kid, and was the type to find anything anywhere, even under a bunch of rubble. They worked together, the kid and the old guy. They had a network, watching each other's back. One was capable of handling anything tech, while the other was more of the handy guy that could keep the customers in line.

I shrugged. "I'm fine, you?"

"Oh, you know," the old man said. "You got to report this to the man."

"Already did."

"You need something for this…" stated Ven. He began to look for something in the back of their small stall. "Hold on."

I watched him, wondering how bad my face still looked. *Maybe it is worse than it feels.*

In front of me were all kinds of parts. Stacks of trays, overloaded with them, competed for the small space set aside on the ground. Each vendor claimed a stall, and the underground guards maintained order as part of the security they lent to the venue. They were part of Laird's team, the ones that made sure these people could work here and sell their wares in relative peace, away from DAINN's edicts.

Ven came back with a care package. "Here, use this for your eye." He handed me a small spray bottle. "I want it back… though. They are worth gold in here."

"Thank you." I nodded, smiling at the kid and uncapping the top. I quickly sprayed my eyebrow, and the aerosol immediately closed off the cut over my eye. I appreciated the gesture, but I wanted to get the hell out of this place. I already had spent too much time in the underground. So, I dropped the medic kit back in his hand. However, it was odd that my Imps had not done the trick today. I was about to ponder that fact when Ven, obviously thinking he had done his good deed for the day, went back to business.

"What's it going to be today?"

"I'm looking for something faster, better than one of these." I retrieved a piece from one of the nearby trays and showed it.

Ven leaned over, looking closely at the piece, and nodded before he went to a different container, "I know your wares. You will still need more, man. You're going through that stuff like crazy!"

"Yeah, that's why I'm here. Do you have anything new?"

"Not what I would recommend for the work you do... But I can give you something better. You won't fry that one."

Ven rummaged through one of the smaller trays at the back and returned with a piece more minuscule than the one I handed over to him a minute ago. It was inside its container and more compact than the rest. It also looked a lot newer than my old one. It had to be a next-generation, and it appeared in relatively good shape to me. I trusted Ven. "How much?"

"Well, now, it's expensive but worthwhile. You won't have to change it for some time if you know what I mean. I never give you the bad stuff; you know that, right? For this piece, how about double what you paid for the last one, like let's say nine hundred credits? And you know, that's cheap, I'm giving you a deal."

"I don't have this kind of credit on me." He had dealt with me over time and had never let me down, so I wasn't about to question him now.

Most of our credits remained accounted for through our monetary system. We didn't have money per se anymore. We had credits monitored in the Universal Bank, and we accessed these as needed, but every purchase went into the System and got registered. Anything bought through the black market had to come from an unofficial place, untraceable. It would come from one outside my regular work, which I kept for things I did through information exchange. In this instance, I would perform some work detail for someone to get the remainder of the sum.

Ven shrugged. "I could meet you later with the piece. How long do you need to get it?"

Moss stepped in. "That's not wise, Ven."

"Chunk it to customer service Moss, and it's safe to have an escort like you in these parts," said Ven. Moss grunted, not too happy to make a special trip for the credits.

"I'll raise this by the end of the day. I have an exchange coming up."

"All right. I'll see you tonight then. I guess you want this badly." He chuckled, "Twice in one day."

I grunted. If Ven only knew. Today accounted for three times in these parts. "Well, you know me, there's nothing like the present."

"Bridge View passageways near the old plaza? Down in the old neighborhood, if you don't mind. Brown sector. So make it ten below," rallies Ven. "Moss and I are a bit too conspicuous topside."

"Fine. Six at the latest. I've somewhere to be later."

"We'll be there. Don't run late."

The transaction had taken less than fifteen minutes, and I was on my way out when one of the guards approached me. "Someone wants to see you. Come this way."

"Who would that be?"

"Hey, I've got orders. The man wants to know who beat you up."

"As if I know. Lead the way; I have to see him anyways." Now that I had to come up with more credits, those I kept for this type of transaction, I might as well bargain the information I had.

"Good, cause I would have hated having to convince you. The boss likes you!"

I chuckled. "Better not to mess with me then."

The guard nodded and began to walk beside me. I knew who had called on me in these parts. Laird heard what had happened and wanted to set things right. He had to for the sake of the underground network.

Although I would have liked to get home and cleaned up, I didn't mind it. Seeing Laird now had its advantages. The information I possessed could be advantageous to him and pay for my new piece. Only it wasn't good for me to be underground this long with everything going on above. On a day like today, I probably would not have gone out of my way to provide it to him, but now, it seemed like things were working out differently.

The unusual activity and chatter from one part of the Tower about a single shipment alerted me that something was brewing. Maybe he could use that knowledge. The tunnel ahead lay dark and silent as we strode away quickly from the marketplace. My companion was no more eager to talk than I was, so we made our way in silence.

There were other things I could get here, but I kept my activities with the black market to a minimum. The risks were too high. I didn't trust working above grounds for the Company while getting more involved with the underground. I made sure that the parts I bought were small enough to be unobtrusive. There was, therefore, a lesser risk of getting detected by our security forces walking back to my grid.

Today, it made me realize that staying in the underground and remaining in the tunnels was probably not very good either. I would have to be more careful next time.

Laird's people would find the guys who jumped me. They had my coat, so I did not doubt they would be, but there were others. *I muse over the state of things in our city, thinking back at the Institute's influence over me even now. It is why I come to find myself in this tunnel in the first place.*

14
REBELLION
Laird

Old City, Underground, Grid 0, Ang City

There isn't any more time for preparation. Today, it calls for instant action. Our next moves position us as a threat to the System, and it is our moment because Concordance weakens the Network. Transcient Laird Walker, Insurgenets, DAINN Annals – Winter 2098.

Impatient and irritated because we had worked hard to get to this point, I said, "I don't want to hear that we aren't ready. We have been over the plan hundreds of times. Except for the codes, everything is in place." Looking at Wiseman, I could tell what he was thinking, so I continued, "All right, what is bothering you?"

"I don't remember seeing you this unsettled before," said Wiseman. "Usually, you never show any agitation."

"Today is not like most days." Indeed, instead of my renowned calm, my control was frayed this morning.

"Maybe so, but we've been through rougher times under even more difficult circumstances; you've always made sure that people felt reassured they were in good hands."

Wiseman was, as usual, right on. Taller than me, he was rather good-looking. A dark mop of hair, slightly wavy, framed a face most guys would envy. He was the kind of man other men liked, a man's man if you know what I mean. Rugged, tough, challenging every step of the way, regardless of the path one took while distilling charm one had difficulty disregarding.

It caused me to pause. While things had not unfolded yet on the grand scale we had planned, the time for the rebellion was close. There had already been a bit of upheaval inside specific Conclaves, but nothing on the streets yet. It was coming and soon. I just had, for some reason, a bad feeling about this day, and it was getting to me.

It was up to me to plan as the guy running the underground. I saw to the safety of my entire team as we fought the System. I was of average build, not bad looking, but not good looking either. I didn't particularly stand out. I wasn't excessively brilliant either, but I had guts and a desire for change in our society, eating away at me. So, confidence was my Achilles heel, as everything about me was about making that happen. Today was supposed to be that day!

I understood his look, surprised, questioning, and uncertain. *What is happening inside the mastermind directing the guerilla warfare of the underground?*

It was the questioning glance Wiseman had when I headed out of the room in a hurry. "Call me when Ciel returns with them!" Only, now was not the time to explain – a leader rarely explained himself, not that I minded doing that when required for moral and all.

Walking toward the two men approaching, I appreciated that my man, Wiseman, wondered if this was the legitimate reaction to the coup we were preparing later this day. I could practically see the doubt that danced on the edge of Wiseman's mind. *Is it something too big, even for us?*

I couldn't worry about that thought now, nor had I any incline to reassure him. Wiseman was intelligent and well-trained. He watched and said nothing. The guy was reliable, knowledgeable, and a keen interpreter of events. He could read between the lines, which made him a great advisor. His nickname came from that very fact.

I crossed the room to meet one of our underground guards, accompanied by one of our informants. I recognized Aidan instantly, although he didn't look like the cleaner version of himself today. "I was told you encountered a problem."

"Yeah... well, two to be exact."

"Would you recognize them?"

"One of them."

"Description? You know, I can get you an escort when you come down this way."

"I prefer not to have a set time... Too much chatter above won't do you or me any good. Both guys looked like others, too regular for me to give you a description to help find them. There was nothing special in the looks that I can recall. It won't do much good: tall, black hair, beards. And hands like hammers if this helps any. They almost got my coat too. But a Phrenic EHAF intervened. I have no idea what he was doing in the tunnel; I got lucky, though. He told me to get lost when he called the Custodians."

"Darnet, what was he doing there in the first place? Did he say anything to you?"

"No... But now, the guy knows who I am. Why he didn't report me is weird, though. I think he didn't want to deal with the report." I shrugged.

"Humm... I don't like this. The Clout never patrols inside the tunnels and usually stays clear of the place. Do you have his name?"

"No. But the guy was Elite, though."

"NetShit..." My voice reached across the room. "Wiseman, close the market for the day."

Wiseman standing not too far behind me surprised the HellNet out of me. "Yes, boss. I can hear you fine. No need to scream."

I scowled at him, but he ignored me, turning away to dispatch our men on my order.

Aidan watched us and smirked. Then, his expression turned serious. "Listen, Laird; there may be something you need to know."

I nodded and guided Aidan toward a more private area of the room where our conversation would not be so easily heard.

"I saw something last night coming from the GG. A group is getting ready to intercept a shipment. I don't have the specific, but they were pro, well trained, and armed with the latest gear."

"How do you know what they were about to do?"

"They were talking about a route. Unfortunately, I didn't get much."

I pinched the bridge of my nose. "Time or destination?"

"Sometimes, this morning. I don't know where. That's all I know. It's not much."

"No. I appreciate the information. One thing, though. Were the men EHAF?"

"No… The group didn't have uniforms, but they were trained like them. It was the way they moved and their gear. Real pros."

"Thank you for coming. You better get back above. I'll have you follow up. I handed Aidan a voucher that would be honored in these parts before turning away. "It should come in handy with your purchases."

Aidan nodded and turned around.

Watching him leave, I said, "Aidan, avoid coming back for a while."

"You don't need to tell me," he said, strolling away.

I dispatched the same guard with Aidan. "Follow him up a way… And then head back to help close the marketplace."

I had something pressing to deal with and needed to follow up. The shipment was late, and the news Aidan had just delivered worried me. Everything planned had been timed so tight in the first place. We had little room for maneuvering. Today was not the day to find ourselves without the equipment that could differentiate between success and failure on the surface.

As I moved back toward Wiseman, I grabbed our inner NetComm, giving him a sign to follow me. "Hart, we have a problem with the shipment. We may have an intercept and need to dispatch men to ensure its safeguard. Hurry. We may be too late already."

Hart was a fellow Surg and one of my main guys, rough and not always one to initiate anything, but he was reliable.

"Copy that, Laird," he answered immediately.

I debated my next move if we didn't get the devices here on time.

These rooms were the best place to hold Operations Control, looking at my surroundings. This place stood away, hidden from the main lines. We had discovered and moved into it a while back in preparation for this momentous occasion. For all that it was, the cave looked dreary and unwelcoming. The facility buried under tons of concrete had four featured walls with a thickness of at least three feet wide. It had been part of the old city's underground subsonic transport. Below hundreds of floors, way beneath the new city, lay the underground's actual headquarters, the organization whose presence was unknown to most people.

We hid inside this structure, under layers of cement built over us through the years. Our team played the most crucial role. We were the head of the snake.

I had barely passed the smaller adjacent room threshold when the side door to the large one with its massive steel encasement opened, and Ciel appeared. The underground cave's main room was vast and cold, big enough to have many people gathered in this one place.

"Not a moment too soon," exclaimed Wiseman.

"Try to get past all the City Vigils at this hour. They are out all over the streets this morning," Ciel responded flippantly.

Wiseman ignored the taunt, "Do you have it?"

"Of course she has it." I crossed the small expanse to reach her. "Cutting it a bit close, don't you think?"

"There are patrols all over," responded Ciel with some annoyance. "If you guys think you can do better next time, be my guest."

I relaxed slightly, "Chill, Ciel. Nobody's saying that."

"Well then, I suggest you two get a life." Ciel dropped the key connector with the codes in the palm of my hand and continued with the attitude, "You have no idea what's going on up there. But I can assure you, it's running hot, and they're ready for an uprising today."

Wiseman and I exchanged a look and quickly returned our attention to Ciel. She looked slightly disheveled, seeming rattled more than usual. Her clothing was askew, her cheekbones smeared, and her overall attitude on edge.

"What happened?" I asked.

"Nothing I couldn't handle," Ciel said.

Wiseman neared the girl and put his hand on her delicate shoulder. "Show us."

I interrupted that process, "There's no time for that. Give this to Sorel."

Wiseman took the device with a hint of hesitation. Soon, I would have to share what was going on in my head at some point, only not now.

He walked towards a much smaller entryway, hidden behind a makeshift panel of old wood. It revealed a smaller room guarded by a partially opened rod iron fence. The area, built for complete isolation, remained a depository for equipment from years past we cleared at the time of our move. Situated apart from the main room, it now contained the latest technology. The Control Center or CC of the underground, stuffed with our tech devices gathered either legally or illegally, served as the core of our operations.

Screens took over a wall. Tablets and wrist gears opened visors focused on the various grids as we ran scans on the upper levels of Ang City. Unlike the state-of-the-art equipment from the Tower in the GG, this CC reflected its immediate environment showing a desolate state.

We constructed it of odd bits and spare parts, some of them twisted in place and rusted, with pealed-out plastic and makeshift know-how. It didn't look good, but it worked and served us well.

Sorel, a young woman with long blond hair, stood at the helm of this station. She focused on images of screens from some of the upper grids. Her stern and imposing silhouette left nothing to the imagination. The tight clothing fitted closely to her body showed all her muscles and revealed her shapely figure. She was tall, with a regular face and eyes almost too big for it.

She was our science engineer, a computer geek, without the appearance of one filling this role. She determined long ago that while she loved figuring things out sitting behind a screen, she wouldn't give up physical training for anything that gave her the freaky body.

When he entered, she returned her focus on the computer display with a glance at Wiseman.

"Shouldn't you be changed by now?" barked Wiseman.

"I'm perfectly comfortable, but thanks for asking," replied Sorel. "I was considering taking some of it off. What do you think?"

"Suit yourself. You always do."

Sorel smiled knowingly. "Don't mind if I do after I enter the codes." She grabbed the encoded key connector and turned towards another station.

Wiseman's lingering gaze brushed her silhouette, and he switched his attention back to the task at hand.

A snickering laugh resonated coming from Sorel. She knew Darnet well what Wiseman was up to with his attitude.

I knew my team. Wiseman looked uninterested, while Sorel appeared to watch his reflection on one of the screens.

I saw this as I walked into the small chamber, followed by Ciel. *They are hard-working but certainly like to play just as hard. But today isn't a game.*

Maybe it was their way to diffuse the tension. These two were always like that, and there may be something behind it. I imagined that they had plenty of opportunities to investigate what was between them, and if they didn't take advantage of the vibes, well, that was their business. I never meddled when it came to their private lives.

Before any of them could engage in further banter, we performed the upload initiated quickly by Sorel. The codes seem to be responding correctly while slowly infiltrating the DAINN System. *Today, we were about to make history, a time when we finally made a difference.*

It was our big moment. We never anticipated that it would come to this at first. None of us had wanted the present reality, but there it was, potently permeating everything we did in our survival state.

"So, this is it, Laird," murmured Sorel as she watched the progress of the upload.

"It is overdue if you ask me…" murmured Wiseman.

In the beginning, we were just a group of children, then renegades. When the idea of fighting back had first germinated amongst us, we had no idea it would take us on this dynamic journey. Instead, we had hoped that the attempts made to create a place to be heard would indeed plant the seeds of change. So far, it hadn't worked. Now, if we didn't want to stay buried inside old and decrepit concrete walls, our only recourse was to take a stand, one impossible to ignore. *And it is what we are about to do.*

My name, Laird, had been given to me by my men. I was twenty-five and old enough to have led this pack of completely disparate individuals for the better part of ten years. At first, the only commonality between us was the belief that a better way existed than the DAINN System. We were kids when that happened. Since then, together, we grew into strong men and women. Over time, we had developed a sense of family and community. Slowly our group had become a seamless family. Now, we were unbreakably tight.

"Timely or late, we need to prepare for the throwback we will soon feel."

"Hart has positioned some of the reprogrammed Custodians in our tunnels. We will see them coming," stated Wiseman.

I knew that much was true. We took every precaution possible to thwart what the Clout would soon unleash on us. We also initiated a backup plan if the need arose.

A while back, we took a position. We decided that we would not let the Imps run our lives. Indeed, if we were to use Imps, they had to be assimilated by those who wanted them. We envisioned unequivocally how the Imps usage should take place. The Network must respond to an individual's willingness to use the Imps without the Conclaves' influence. Each of us demanded a choice for our life's direction, but our government had seen things quite differently.

Many resolved to leave the city and become Nonets, but we voted to remain long ago. We liked the Imps enough not to give them up completely, but we wanted their usage to be on our terms, not controlled by them. We selected engineers and technology-minded personalities for our group to understand and revamp the System si it could serve us. In doing so, we became Insurgenets or Surgs. We were the rebellion. We instigated a silent struggle against a System we abhorred from that moment forward.

"So, now we wait… We watch, and we hope."

"I can't believe that it has taken us over a decade to get to this point," said Sorel.

Our movement started small, but we had grown. We had remained unobtrusive, for we were in no shape to fight the armies of DAINN. If the EHAF found us, we would either be, arrested, integrated into the Network, or sent away with no way back. At worst, they would annihilate us.

"We had to wait until our tentacles reached pretty much all levels within the government, you know that," I whispered.

To survive in the old city, we stole, borrowed, and bought anything we could use. We requisitioned food and supplies here and there to add to our distribution quarters within the various grids where our followers did their parts to expand our influence above ground. We appropriated materials, hijacked vehicles carrying some of the technology we needed to thrive inside these old faded walls. We essentially extended our influence and laid siege against everything that would hinder DAINN's Network in Ang City. And we bought our time, until today.

"I wish today would already be over," muttered Sorel. "I hate this waiting."

Concordance made our dilemma worse. Never in a thousand years had we thought we would remain buried within the old city for this long. Things changed above and for the worst. The influence of the

DAINN Network grew and expanded in directions we opposed even more fiercely, but they outnumbered us.

"What's happening?"

"Just wait…" said Sorel, watching the rows of codes.

We had witnessed two Concordances already. For this third one, our group had prepared a plan to derail the infrastructure from the ground up. It was like nothing we had ever done in the past, and today was a show of force in unprecedented numbers. We had the workers on our side, and we planned on using them to carry the message. Today was the moment we had waited for all these years.

"Here it is."

The screens changed as the codes opened the vista into the world above. They gave us access to DAINN for a brief time. The camera feeds inside the various grids of the city were now available to us. Of course, we knew it wouldn't last. The scientists above were way too competent to allow this encroachment on their System. The golden "child" was too protected, and repercussions would be swift, but we had to try something. And it was possible only because we had acquired the allegiance in our rank of one EHAF Elite officer.

We now could see Ang City and all its grids on our screens. The pride and joy of our era stood pristine and beautiful inside the open dome, below a calm blue sky. The City Vigils deployed on all levels within the outside grids monitored the crowds. They stood on the one-hundredth floor where most of the new city had expanded over the old relics of the dilapidated buildings from the era before the big storms.

And we witnessed what Ciel had been up against on the upper grounds. The deployment had begun in the business district and expanded outward. The Presidential plaza crawled with androids. Already shuttles took off from the landing zones, surveying the outskirts of town on the vast Metropolis' upper levels. The EHAF vehicles were already prepped to deliver added robots in all the grids. These had not yet boarded. But they were scheduled for the streets leading to the manufacturing plants and distribution centers.

Sorel looked at me. "Now?"

"Yes."

She punched a series of keys, and a stream appeared. Sorel uploaded a virus of her own making into the DAINN Network. It slowed the response time within our entire infrastructure, and if we were lucky, freeze DAINN, although not indefinitely. With access to the Network, we believed it would work. Yet, we also grasped that our invasion into the System wouldn't last long regardless of Sorel's virus's effectiveness.

"This will surely make a dent in the system."

Silence reigned among us as we watched the monitors. Soon, we would notice its effects. If this worked, we would accomplish something significant. Crippling the city shot a thrill through all of us. *Our leaders up in the big Tower are not expecting this confrontation.*

"I just hope we are ready for the reprisals that surely will follow," said Wiseman.

"Whatever the consequences, it's worth the risk," said Sorel, the most emphatic of us all, when it came to the destruction of the Network. "Our actions carry a message that has to bring a political change to our infrastructure."

"This should instill fear in those nurturing the well-oiled machine," I murmured with hope in my heart.

Suddenly, we heard a commotion coming from the other large room. "Where is Laird?" The guttural voice carried across space. Within seconds, Hart appeared in the OC doorway. He was muscular, with a stern demeanor and a nose broken multiple times in the fights he encountered robbing the Company on our behalf. Hart had the appearance of a large bear, ominous to most. But on the inside, he was a softy. Upset, he crossed the room, followed by one of his guys, and joined us. "We have nothing. We can't find any clues. Someone intercepted the shipment between grid eleven and fourteen. I think we have a mole."

I checked the time on the old PVZ installed in the OC and looked around. Only my core group was present. "Hart, clear the room, and close the door."

Hart turned to one of his guys and gave the order. His man left the small room. We heard him clear out the ample operation space and close the door and return with a message, "Cosmos wants to talk with you. He is sure it's not one of his guys."

I looked at Wiseman. He turned to one of our unoccupied stations and opened a channel to connect with Cosmos. I approached the screen with Hart in tow. A young man in his early twenties appeared in the middle of it.

"What do you know?"

Cosmos appeared frustrated. "We lost the tracker somewhere between grid eleven and fourteen. My men are missing, they disappeared, so there is a good chance someone took them too."

"Do you know who is behind the lift?" I asked.

"Not yet," answered Cosmos, "And before you say it, it's not one of my guys either."

"How do you know? They could be in on it," added Hart.

"Not a chance. I trust them. We took all the precautions we discussed and did not deviate from the plan. I saw to that personally," refuted Cosmos.

"Still, check your sources. Find out if there was anyone that could have tipped the Clout," I suggested, and "Hart will do the same on our side."

"Okay. I'll get back to you. Are we still moving without it?"

"Yes."

"Good luck, then," wished Cosmos, as he dropped from our NetComm.

I looked around my small team—all expected new orders. The only solution I came up with would endanger us, but there was no choice. "We expand our sources on the ground. Use more of our people around every perimeter."

"You know that the EHAF will be monitoring every channel. What if they disable ours?" asked Wiseman.

"Grab older NetComm devices, and cover high grounds. I trust we kept them?"

"They are all museum pieces."

"But they still work?"

"Short-range only, but they'll do as back-ups, I suppose."

"Give them to our key guys. Keep ahead of the EHAF's movement."

"It is going to split our teams more than we should," said Hart, sounding dubious at best.

"It's what we have to work with regardless."

"If our people don't move fast, they'll get caught with the workers," said Sorel.

"The EHAF won't be monitoring the old streams," announced Wiseman, thoughtfully. "It could work to our advantage.

"It's not full-proof, but it's one way to ensure that our people make it to the GG. If we do nothing, they won't make it past Bridge View and Arch Way Pass."

The group gathered around the map of Ang City and looked at the display of AirRoads and bridges.

"We already know how the EHAF is going to deploy," added Wiseman. "Let's buy some time."

"Fine, let's go over the plan," said Hart.

The grids' map showed key areas highlighting various paths. "Place people on high ground so they can survey the access routes. Disperse the others among the workers and lead the crowd to the open streets. Speed is the key. Keep everyone moving fast to avoid the Clout, and disperse before the Znets deploy."

"What if some of our team used EHAF uniforms as they position in the buildings? It could mislead them. They are not new, but I think they'll do..." suggested Hart.

"One team will use those to infiltrate the arms depot," I said. "Hart, you take advantage of the chaos."

"Yes, boss."

Our men spread within the grids were blind without the devices from the shipment. These were to provide us with the EHAF deployment patterns in real-time. Instead, we needed to watch their routes the old-fashioned way and relay that to our people on the ground. Keeping multiple evasion routes for our teams required us to keep our people in secure communications and on the lookout. Our extraction teams around certain perimeters were to help the workers evade the EHAF blockade for as long as possible. Old refitted transportation shuttles would be positioned in critical areas to help our personnel evade arrest, while repaired air bikes were an excellent fast getaway for some. The plan was even to use Medic Flyvans to hide our people in plain sight. We requisitioned a few of those during our raids, and it was now time to use them.

"Is the Company team ready?"

"Yes, they are anxious to get more," exclaimed Wiseman.

For weeks now, we had increased our clandestine trips into the warehouses of the Company. We had already garnered containers of food and other equipment. Wiseman wanted to support those whose lifestyles would be affected by their participation in this march and assured us of their loyalty. The security team headed by Blaze was bound to find out eventually, but our man on the inside had changed the logs, so no one was the wiser yet.

The idea was to expand on those raids in the next several hours while the city was in turmoil and steal from those who had so conveniently stolen from us years ago.

"All right, get your men, Hart. Be careful. We can't have any of our people end up in the hands of the Clout."

Hart nodded and headed out to execute his part of the plan. He left in the same equal hurry as he had entered. Hart was good at his job but sometimes relied too much on me. He lacked autonomy, although I would never complain about that. Amid our raggedy group of displaced freedom fighters, independence tended to run too broad and unchecked at times.

"Sorel, have you verified the checkpoints? Is there a way to find our missing cargo?"

"Working on it."

I turned to Wiseman. "Get those supplies… And don't get caught while I contact our friends. Someone has to know something. The guy who pulled the intercept has resources."

"Find our stuff and the Darnet mole."

"We will, but first, let's move on the workers.

Wiseman grunted and left.

I then turned to Ciel, who had remained silent this entire time. "I need your help on a backup plan."

"I figured as much," said Ciel with a sigh. "What do you need?"

I thought about it for a moment. I pondered on an idea since I saw the shipment was running late. We had to detect the troupes' various movements within the city; otherwise, our attempt would fail. I was thinking fast to try and find a solution, and so far, there was only one other possibility. Only, I knew that the person who detained the answer to our quandary was not going to like my idea at all. "We need one device to watch the EHAF deployment on the ground in real-time. I need you to get it from Asher. Take one old NetComm with you."

"He won't do it. It's too risky for him if we get caught."

"Unless he comes up with a better suggestion, that's all I've got. Have him find a way, so it doesn't get traced back to him."

"Fine. I'll be back as soon as I can."

"No… Stay up there and relay what you see on our old frequency for as long as you can."

"It's too dangerous for Ciel, Laird," interrupted Sorel. "She'll be in the middle of the GG with nowhere to hide."

I stared at Ciel and nodded. "I know. Get close to the Medair Faculty shuttle. It can help you get away," I continued. "It can remain inside the GG without suspicion."

Sorel appeared worried for her friend, "I don't like it, Laird."

"Do you have another idea?"

Sorel shook her head before turning toward Ciel. "Asher may be deployed by the time you get there."

"Even if I don't like this plan, it seems I have no choice," responded Ciel, frowning at Laird.

I felt conflicted about asking her to do that, but that was the only thing I could think of at the moment to support our various teams. "You may want to get changed into something more suitable for the task. We'll coordinate based on what you report."

"I got that," answered Ciel a bit flippantly as she began to walk away.

Sorel intervened, "Stay inside one of the buildings... Avoid the passageways. Look, we'll position the shuttle at the edge of the main plaza, between the Faculty and the Institute."

Ciel turned, focusing on the grid points marked by Sorel, and nodded.

"Don't wait up if you don't see me when all hell breaks loose," she said with a tight smirk.

"We'll wait as long as we can..." confirmed Sorel.

Ciel was not too fond of going up and mixing with people above. She hated pretending that she was part of the city's elected ones, but she was good at blending in, and we all knew it. Over the years, Ciel made a few considerable acquaintances that proved valuable in tight corners. There was no doubt in my mind that these were just for a time like this. She would find a way to use whatever she had in her arsenal to make this part of the operation happen.

Ciel left the room muttering to herself, but we could both still hear her; "Some things never work out, even with the best of plans. Now you know why I do what I do. Keeping relationships with our elite."

"Unfortunately... Ciel has that right," I murmured.

I could only concur with her. The day hadn't started the way I had hoped. I bet that other surprises were bound to surface before it was over. I just wished that it would end without too many losses on our side.

Presidential Tower, Golden Ghetto, Ang City

Life was about to change for many. No one in the know inside the grids could pretend otherwise. The few who ignored that fact, well, in my book, they were fools. Phenom North Thompson, EHAF Conclave – Presidential Elite Unit Commander, DAINN Annals – Winter 2098.

I was inside the Tower, nestled within the Watch Center, viewing multiple feeds with the Android Watcher.

DAINN was highly influential in the prevention of crime. The System overseeing the security operations within the city grids of Ang performed impeccably. Our latest technology, regularly updated, maintained the highest degree of responsiveness. The monitoring program and its new Watcher covered all areas to provide ultimate safety for our citizens from the GG to Emerald Field, passing through Water's Edge, ArchWay Pass, Cliff Tops, and Bridge View. The only areas not yet covered remained the old underground city with its corridors and tunnels.

The multiple eyes of our Custodians surveyed our streets directly networked to the SRC through the central control room of the DAINN Network. The large Chamber where our Artificial Intelligence Neural Network resided spread deep into the soil and connected millions of nodes to all aspects of our infrastructure. From there, the various feeds would make their way to the Watch Center Personnel inside the Tower.

Over the last decade, cutting-edge peacekeeping safeguards ensured security in all streets, pathways, passageways, and airways. Ang was now considered one of the safest Megapolis on the planet. The streets at night had never been this quiet. Robberies, hijackings, muggings, and murders had dropped to an occasional crime because the culprits had little if no hope to escape the Network. Even certain relatively rough areas within the outer grids had registered minimal illegal activities.

The Watcher monitored all criminals liberated after serving their sentence. The new Imps tagged them and drastically reduced their desire for violence. With their daily activities recorded in our database, no one would risk recidivism for fear of the penalty. Indeed, rehabilitation came with numbing Imps that soon rendered an individual immune to feelings. For a long time, everyone enjoyed the security and sanctity of their person and home. This state of being was a tribute to the DAINN System.

"Get me closer coverage on all our main facilities," I asked the Watcher, the android dedicated to the Tower.

"Yes, Phrenic Thompson," responded the Watcher in its slightly metallic voice.

I was holed up in the Tower's secured room, checking for the latest movement within our grids. Our main government building was a masterpiece made of concrete and the newest alloy, more robust than most. The presidential residence and offices were feet away. *We called this area of the city the Golden Ghetto is an altogether very long story. One for another time. One which changed the course of my life. One I cared to erase from my memories.*

"Hey, North… Do you see anything we don't? Cause we've been here for more than one hour, and nothing is happening…" said one of my men named Argil.

For my team, I was just North, a strong strategist, and the guy they had come to trust over years of missions.

Relentless in my search, I grunted, ignoring the guys.

My eyes locked on the feeds. They played across the multiple screens, splashing the colors covering each grid of our city on a lower corner.

I searched for the first signal. It was bound to happen soon.

"It's still too early," exclaimed Rand. "Be patient… I'm still betting we are overreacting."

My hand reached my cropped hair, and I smirked. "You will lose, guys."

Zane and I established a plan to minimize today's uproar. Everything was now in place, and the Elite awaited deployment.

"Hellnet, it's the 'Concord,' but it does not mean it has to be the same," whispered Argil, a rather odd-looking guy but an optimist at heart.

It was the moment in our history where we anticipated riots, turbulence, and violence in our streets. Zane, although hopeful, was no foul. He had expected multiple scenarios as we prepared to face the potential mob.

My team earned Elite status a while back. They were the best, but I would not stand with them, unlike in previous ops. In the shadows of the Tower, my role remained here since I got promoted to Commander. As the right arm of the President of the EHAF, my team relied on me to anticipate today's events.

Today would see them deal with the unexpected as the workers turn with the Surgs on the GG. But, trained with the best, like Langden, they qualified above others and consistently delivered.

As tension mounted all over the city, I reviewed the exacting details of the mission. We would meet surprises on the ground today, and anticipating most of them remained my job even if I stayed inside the Watch Tower.

We had seen it before, three years earlier. Back then, we had not been ready for the backlash. At the beginning of the last Concordance, we had thought that we had things under control. It proved to be wrong.

Inside the Watch Center, the Watcher's only task was to observe and report as a permanent fixture appointed to secure our city. The android, linked through our Street Custodians and City Vigils spread across our grids, intervened to ensure our citizens' safety and apprehend any illegal activities taking place throughout Ang. Cameras covered all angles within the various areas. These even included the coverage within our buildings. Everything unusual was immediately flagged, and the activity sifted through the DAINN System for further investigation. The scope of the coverage also extended to all our public venues, parks, bridges, rooftops, and other public places. This security unfurled to all areas from the Golden Ghetto to Water's Edge, Archway Pass, Bridge View, Emerald Field, and Cliff Tops to the outer walls of the Megapolis. The Watcher processing capacity was unparalleled, running through the information from all these sources at the rate of a human heartbeat, if not faster.

On this Concord, I insisted on watching two of my guys inside the monitoring room. The shift, for now, remained boring, and I understood their attitude, bordering on boisterous. My team liked the action, and they relished challenges. This particular assignment did not meet their typical requirement. HellNet, I knew that, but I wouldn't trust any others.

So, despite their reluctance, they were seated on the hovering chairs behind multiple stations with large screens, waiting for the signs.

The Watcher remained in the center of the room, scrutinizing the main NetWall registering and projecting the data at superhuman speed.

My guards were a redundant process, but I determined that this set-up allowed us to remain on any new development front line. I liked the idea. This way, we directly accessed the data flow even if we were only remotely controlling these aspects of our security through DAINN. While we never needed even one of them present throughout the day and night rotation, the tension on this day warranted the measure. In truth, the Watcher was enough. We never needed anything else since we developed and launched the android, but it was the Concord.

Argil looked up at me from his hovering chair. "Hey, North, looks to me like it is business as usual."

"Yeah, this watch show you insisted upon is pretty Darnet boring," continued Rand, as he morosely contemplated the city's infrastructure on the screen in front of him.

I knew what they were doing. Argil and Rand were baiting me.

I ignored them and kept watching the screens.

I guess I'm not popular with my guys at this time, but while they aren't happy to be in this detail, it's also for them an opportunity to prove me wrong.

For now, the grids of Ang City appeared peaceful indeed. In the various sectors, the business was going on as usual. I just knew better; it was coming. We had been watching for the better part of the last hour without any activity, and on that point, they were right.

My hunch told me it wouldn't last. While things seemed okay on the surface, I scrutinized the workers' faces as they were already deployed to their jobs. "I told you guys, if I'm wrong, I'm taking you for a drink at Stars."

"Just a drink, boss? It doesn't seem fair. I mean, here we are locked up in this place for hours on hand. I think you own us more than a drink," complained Argil. "What about dinner and a show?"

"Sounds like you're whining, Argil," Rand exclaimed. "Don't you think he sounds like he is whining, boss? But I do agree with Argil's contention, boss. One drink hardly seems fair. We need to make an evening of it! Hey, on second thought, it doesn't sound like winning."

Stars was a bar and our go-to place to relax. Indeed it remained one of the favorite spots of the entire EHAF. We visited the club regularly because it was one of the best places in the city to get a drink and unwind. Also, they treated us right. The shows offered us a delight of the senses. A myriad of lights, displayed to music with choreographed air acrobatics, broke the monotony. The most refined group of air dancers showed their new routines at Stars. Great singers and other performers would come to Stars to surpass each other on stage. The round-up was always genius.

"Of course, you would think that, Rand," I responded evenly. My guys would try to get away with anything they could, but considering they were loyal and would hang on a rope for me if I asked them to, I couldn't blame them. "One evening, it is… but if I'm right… You're going to pay for it."

"Well, sure… won't be that bad since we drink a whole lot more than you do, boss," replied Rand.

"Remind me to get an early start…" added Argil.

The EHAF, also known as the Force or the Clout by the familiars, had a designated private room. We could talk or play air games, virtual or real, and dance behind our glass-walled area without interference from the evening crowd. Stars also liked to have us there as we provided a degree of security and recognition they would not otherwise enjoy.

Stars maintained the room for us. It had everything we could want and provided great food, terrific drinks, fantastic music, and unique entertainment. Noise levels set to our preferences allowed us to invite and entertain guests without fighting the ambient noise. The food was always tasty, and the alcohol infinite. The official Star personnel even attended to driving offenders home with a concoction ensuring their performance the next day. Nothing was too good for us. We were, after all, the pride of our defense program.

Pride. I certainly wasn't feeling that in my life, not after what I had failed to do. *Come on, North, don't go there.*

"Activity over in grid 11," stated Rand. "The workers are reporting to their posts. HellNet, if you ask me, the poor sods have no fire to rebel. I mean, look at them!"

The security cameras around the perimeters of our manufacturing facilities registered people going to work. The workers arrived on time, according to the solar clock.

Yet, this was the loathed day of Concordance. The Concord, despised by most because it was imposed, universally disliked because it disrupted the order of things, and similarly feared because it brought unilateral displacement, unfolded irrelevant desires, passions, and feelings. While the day began typically, these men and women would resist the changes, which would result in a show of force.

"They sure don't look like much… Besides, what can the population do against us?" added Argil. "Look at our City Vigils. Besides, we don't make the rules, and they know it.

"No, but we enforce them," murmured Rand.

I looked at the early morning play itself out on the monitoring System of the security stations. Cameras showed me grids eleven to fourteen, all of them centered on the manufacturing facilities and their assembly lines, the way I requested. Robots were operating as usual. Our workforce was reporting to their position on the floors. At the moment, every post filled in as if nothing was brewing.

"You heard the expression… The calm before the storm?" I asked my guys.

"Yeah, boss… But the point is they may have the numbers, but we have the tech," explained Rand.

"And you think that made the difference to those who clamored for a revolution so they could gain access to a better life in all the historical records we studied at the Academy? Back then, it was superiority by arms, and still, in some cases, it lasted longer than anyone wished."

Multiple feeds showed our distribution centers and the steady departure of our shuttles. They flew from our ramps to various locations inside our grids to distribute supplies.

The screens also registered the large water filtration building and the primary pump operating normally. Our City Vigils watched the ongoing flow, much like permanently frozen statues on the scene.

The Custodians likewise displayed the huge farm scrapers and their farming personnel of clones under the supervision of a few of our people in charge of our agricultural supplies.

"Why do you always have to look at the boogeyman, boss?" complained Argil.

"We know there is unfairness about this day, Argil, and in some small ways, we benefit from it," explained Rand. "The lives of these poor souls are going to be even worse off after today… that's why the boss here looks at what can go wrong."

"I know you guys didn't see the last Concord," I said. "It wasn't pretty."

DAINN's monitoring system exposed the secluded processing plant and its inner structure mostly tended by androids. We moved away from animal food and rallied around synthetic by-products that were actually better than organic food. But for some, the needs never died and remained ingrained in parts of the population. Rather than condemning them, we apportioned these supplies and rationed them throughout the city's various areas according to ratios, performance, and status as sought-after rewards.

The stations still revealed the obscure defense armory isolated inside the defense department. Our troops, composed of robots, androids, clones, and human personnel from the EHAF Corp, were ready to intervene in the day's events.

I glanced at other public areas covered by our Street Custodians. Apart from our normal hovering eyes spread across all the regions of Ang City, we had deployed additional units at dawn in quite a few public places to maintain order should the need arise.

Everywhere I turned, calm confronted us. My gut churned. The quiet made me even more nervous. There was no doubt in my mind that we were about to witness an upheaval.

"Well, so far, I don't see anything out of the ordinary, North. I think you owe us that drink," said Argil, visibly brightening at the idea of his boss being wrong for once.

I chuckled, "It's not even noon. But I can ask the paymaster to hold your credits when I win," North added, chuckling.

"Hellnet no…"

The public places interested me the most at this time, so I concentrated on the large roadways. I wanted to see the population. I needed to know if my expectations were accurate. I anticipated riots. I expected defiance. I just knew the hearts of our people. They would not, once again, accept the Concord without a fight. So, I turned my attention to one of the screens providing images of grid twelve.

The faces were gloomy and tense.

The people were angry.

They were resentful, and it showed.

I was right, even if I did not want to be. But there it was.

Jeze entered the room. "Hey, guys…"

She was always curious and never very far from me. Jeze came to stand slightly behind me. "Anything?"

"Not so far," replied Rand.

I just grunted again.

We had a plan. At the sight of any disruption, it would play out. Our aim - eliminate violence. We had ascertained better ways to contain the upheaval that would inevitably occur this day. And we were ready to implement our strategy.

Even our City Vigils and Mags, under the order of Zane Langden, had received special programming along with our Custodians. Above all else, our President wanted to avoid mayhem and fatalities. We possessed the technology to do it too.

"The team is on stand-by, North," volunteered Jeze.

I nodded. "Good."

Our security forces awaited their signal. They then would launch their Airbikes from the Tower to join the GenCorp within the various grids. The mandate was clear. Upon the swarm of bodies in the streets, no laser shots would be fired, our combat androids would entertain no fights, and no blood would be spilled. It was the plan, and DAINN timed every aspect of it.

I glanced at Jeze. "I heard someone we know got a match today?"

She chuckled. "Indeed. The whole team can't wait to introduce themselves."

"How is Cashel taking it?"

Jeze shrugged. "In stride, but one can tell, he is curious."

I empathized, and as minutes passed inside the Watch Tower, I fought against my memories. Once upon a time, I received a match too. Struggling to get past the surge of feelings, I shook my head. *Don't go there; concentrate.*

Instead, I pushed myself to focus on the screens and get back to the mission. Whatever happened today, DAINN played a part. Its way intertwined with our mandate put the steps in motion to minimize events because the System was peaceful. The Network was programmed to help, not to destroy.

"Any activities on the ground over by Bridge View?"

"Nothing reported by our people. The Surgs are nowhere," responded Jeze.

"When is Cash meeting her?"

"He already did."

"And?"

Jeze smiled her predator smirk. "I think he will have his hands full with that one."

"The good ones always do," I said, refocusing on the screens, watching the same images from the last hour with unwavering patience. While I wasn't needed, not until things happened, there was no other place I would rather be.

Suddenly, the screens of the Watch Center now captured my attention. "Here it comes," I said.

The assembly lines slowed to a crawl and shut down inside the manufacturing facilities of Emerald Field. The robotic system we had implemented years ago became dormant. The workers standing at their posts stopped and turned around, moving towards the exits. Every man and woman within the plant reacted the same way, automatically switching from their responsibilities to walking away. They slowed at the large entrance doors, forming a large mass of people moving in sync. Once they reached the streets, they began their march. The whole process was organized and orderly. Only it wouldn't remain that way for long.

"Jeze, tell the team to take off and go to their assigned locations," I said.

"NetRoger that." She gave the order without delay, reaching our Elite team that waited in the GR.

My eyes moved to the distribution area in the same grid, where there was no longer the hum of the shuttles taking off. The air vehicles that should be hovering away from the central landing zone were sitting on the large platform instead of heading to their delivery destinations.

"What in the HellNet…" The view from our landing zones was disconcerting. The androids monitoring the takeoffs stopped in their tracks.

"Deploy above ground level first… GG City Vigils corp. Send additional teams to the Distribution Center, the Water Filtration Plant, The Electric Solar Hub, and the Processing Facility. Make sure our nurseries are also covered. Have them take over and protect the grounds."

I glanced at the water facility and the large pump in charge of our filtration system. It no longer appeared to be operational either. For reasons unknown, our City Vigils didn't respond immediately, as per their programming. They should already be efficiently finding and correcting the source of the problem. They appeared otherwise occupied as if trying to overcome something. "This is not right… Send a repair team to the water facility. There is interference with our programming. Look at the City Vigils. Send our EHAF GenCorp until we fix this."

Another screen called for my attention on the other side of the monitoring room. The farm scraper's personnel now moved away from their stations. They followed the large corridors leading to the exit. Within the building, our first-generation clones descended in droves on the large Elevats, intending to reach the courtyard's ground level, which hosted their assembly area, located just outside the vast farming facility's perimeter.

"We have a break-in at the Network. Watcher, give me the SRC."

"We need to cover our food supplies," Jeze said beside me.

"Do it and send another team to our Farming Centers." While Jeze dispatched orders to Rand, the Watcher struggled to maintain our data streams current.

"I can't reach the GenCorp, Phrenic North," said Argil reaching for one of our other squadrons on a different frequency, but the response was slow in coming.

"Nothing, Sir," as he tried again.

Nothing happened on the feeds as everything remained frozen.

The Watcher said with its automated voice, "Phrenic North, no response from SRC."

"Darnet… Nothing here either, boss. Our other units do not respond either. I didn't expect that," mumbled Argil in the background.

"Use our backup Netcomm System. I don't think we can trust the Network. The teams will soon realize what is happening and will switch to it." I had an uncomfortable feeling that things were only starting to unravel. "Jeze, have Asher go to SRC and report back on what's happening with DAINN. I want our eyes on this."

"NetRoger that, Phrenic. Rand, go…"

"How are they able to block our NetComm?" said Rand, puzzled in the face of the communication breakdown as he got up from his desk and hurriedly exited the room.

"This is not a scenario any of us had envisioned; come on, people, find a way to break this," exclaimed Jeze.

How indeed?

"We have a widespread problem. Look at our City Vigils. They're not responding, and this is occurring everywhere."

"Someone got a hold of our codes," Jeze said, frowning. "But how?"

"I don't know, but everything is affected. The codes are inside the System and can feed us anything they want."

Jeze's demeanor shifted. "Darnet… Who would give them access?"

The Surgs planned this attack meticulously, and the underground had done this by acquiring our codes. It was the only way to paralyze the inner workings of our city's infrastructure effectively. Even if this was a temporary glitch, you had to give kudos to their organization. What they had done was no small task, and it meant only one thing. They had people inside our faction.

"We have a mole," I said. With a grim face, I said, "I want the NetBastard."

Jeze looked at me steadily. "We'll find him or them."

I nodded. "Send Birch to the perimeter of the Company building and have him get in touch with Blaze. We need to keep an eye on his team. If the Distribution Center is compromised, he'll engage his guys, and we don't want that."

Jeze changed her frequency and relaid the message. The old NetComm would ping until someone answered.

Somehow, the Underground had tapped into the entire System. Now, DAINN would have to respond to the simultaneous attacks into its Network while our entire EHAF was blinded. We had a significant problem on our hands.

"Everything looks compromised. We may not have enough teams to handle every grid," Jeze said.

"Get Talia on it immediately. Have her split our Forces."

Thus far, the underground activities were a pain, but they had remained ineffective for the most part. Sure, they caused troubles here and there, but nothing this major. We had been able to thwart their efforts over the years and keep a good hold on our System. As of today, no more. The Surgs planted a mole among my team or in the top layers of our government to achieve this result.

Who was the mole?

I imagined SRC reacting with Paladock's team. DAINN was setting up countermeasures.

The Android Watcher ran the alarm code within the Tower to send our EHAF troops out and into action; only it was a melée until they received their new order.

I cringed at the lack of effectiveness.

"Have Alai go to the Defense Ministry building and wait for my orders.

Jeze nodded and got on our Tower Internal System or TIS.

"Also, Jeze, get Cashel over to Bridge View and have him monitor the events from there. We need eyes there and communicate differently."

Inside the defense building, the Clout was already following protocol. Various teams were diverging toward Flycars, shuttles, or cruisers. They followed their assignments and departed for their designated sectors. But once our alarm engaged, their protocol would take over. They would transfer to the old frequency. Soon, the City Vigils will be replaced by our GenCorp as they remain frozen.

Inactive and engaged through their functional programming, I no longer could trust the CVs to reinforce the EHAF. While they already lined the large cruisers headed for the troublesome grids, they served no purpose if we didn't replace the codes fast.

DAINN proved slow to react. We needed additional squadrons from the EHAF to maintain order. My few orders mobilized the rest of the Force to send squads to cover our crucial grid locations. Jeze knew what needed doing.

"Stay here and report anything new. I need to brief Zane."

"NetRoger that, North," Jeze said as I moved to the door.

I walked out of the Watch Center and headed to the next wing toward our Presidential offices.

The critical areas of the Golden Ghetto were below our level, on the one-hundredth floor. In the five-hundred-story building, we stood way above that. There was no real danger for any of us. The workers couldn't access the upper levels. At best, they would reach the ground plaza on the one-hundredth floor.

I reached the offices of our President. The NetAssist to the President was not there. It puzzled me. Where in the HellNet was he?

Zane's doors were closed.

I knocked and waited for his answer.

The worker's retrieval scenario we worked on during the weeks before the Concord and set in motion early this morning might prove ineffective. Indeed, we had anticipated scenarios where the workers would rebel and had parked security City Vigils at all alternative roads and passageways. These measures, already underway when the DAINN System was disrupted, had to be replaced. The infiltration of the Network represented a new twist with Concordance unfolding everywhere and could jeopardize our entire strategy. So, the perfect storm.

Zane, unsettled, yelled through the door. "Come in."

I opened the panel and walked into the office, appraising Zane already at his PVZ. "North, the Network is not responding. Do we have a breach?"

"I should have walked by her. Yes, Zane. Someone inside the EHAF or at the Council level."

"Well, from now on, reduce access to our information." He paused and said, "Keep everything within your Elite team."

"We need more EHAF troops on the ground to cover for the City Vigils. I gave the order to expand the Clout with more squadrons."

"Good… Where are we?"

"We added divisions we held back in reserve."

"It won't be enough…"

"I know. Let's hope SRC handles this quickly."

Our EHAF Corp would become too stretched if things escalated. Any levels below one hundred led to walkways and overpasses connecting other Ang regions, like the business district, the store malls, and entertainment row. They also opened to gates in other grids. These electronic portals needed to be incredibly secure today of all days. The City Vigils already dispatched no longer responded to our usual protocols. And the question in the back of my head was, would they behave according to their programming once we reinstated control? We couldn't take the risk and wait to find out.

"We can't count on the combat androids programmed to contain the crowd either, I assume?" said Zane.

"I'm only counting on our troops at this point."

"So, even the Custodians won't be of help," said Langden, thinking. "Until we know DAINN is again in control, we only count on our teams."

Our City Vigils monitored all floors connected to Concourses traveling to the various areas of the city. They were at the ready alongside our combat androids programmed to contain the crowd. As I screened our troops leaving our Tower to replace our Mags, I kept watching my PVZ for the update from Talia. The streams came across my screen, and I grunted my approval.

The new orders were delivered. Now, our men stampeded to replace them. "Our teams are on the old NetComm."

"You think they will think of it?"

"Let's hope not. We cover everything GG and Water's Edge ourselves, including all floors above the one hundredth.

"Implement our highest security measures with battle combat gear," said Langden with a grimace. "This is not what I wanted."

"Nothing will pass through our surveillance around the main buildings of the Golden Ghetto." I didn't trust the Surgs.

I understood their motives. To some extent, I even supported some of their actions, but I couldn't let their underground subculture invade our universe within the GG.

"Maintaining the enhanced security protocol will demand too many of our troops. We need to block their countermeasures."

"Asher is on its way to SRC, recognition only. I also have Talia on this."

"Keep the SRC secured."

"Asher will know what to do, and I will send more Elite if it comes to that. I'll keep you updated."

I was already headed to the door to get back to the Watch Tower when Langden said, "What about the passes? Will you have enough men for these?"

"We will make do."

Securing the passes was vital. Below the new Megapolis was another Ang City. Hell city for me... The remnants of a previous life.

While I never went there, I remembered it too well. I preferred to remain within the new Ang we built over the old one when we decided to put a dome over our heads.

How did they get the damn codes? We have to find the mole in our midst. In these new surroundings, I don't have to face my losses. They remain buried inside the rubble of my previous life.

SRC Conclave, Annals Viewing Vlog 879,854,323 Ang City.

Concordance orchestrates a shift in our priorities, and the System call for new Imps Installs for our people. Far from ready to face the anomaly, we need more arms to build up the four programs as we run out of time. DAINN – Winter 2098.

Implants were once again our answers. Although they were not popular with all pillars of our society, they became the norm decades ago. Indeed, many people rejected the Imps when it became apparent that our society would rely on them more and more. It created a period in our history we recall as the Exodus; the day families got split forever, refusing the mandatory call for modification.

The new direction taken by our society built a lot of resentment among our people. Our leaders addressed the issue by providing essential supplies to those who refused to submit and a relocation allocation outside the walls of our city. They believed it would diffuse the problem.

When the day of the official split came, dreaded by all, a large portion of our population departed Ang. The long file of people formed in the streets headed for settlements outside the domes. Many opted for life under the harsh climatic conditions in nearby valleys rather than to remain. From that moment on, the Nonets existed. It was a decision that divided our population and left its claws of resentment within a great silent majority.

And from that day, those who remained within the grids of Ang never saw their families or friends again.

The Imps served us well. They transitioned our society into a more advanced one. Little by little, humans became much more efficient due to the computational power and decision-making of the A.I. that was DAINN. They now learned faster and the information they did not possess proved readily available at a thought. While the System continued to expand to improve conditions for my charges, everything also became much more compartmentalized within each Conclave. It further transformed our society.

This Concordance, like in previous cases in the last few decades, provided the impetus needed to preempt a catastrophe. Our lack of readiness became most urgent in the last few weeks. As in other times, when it proved we needed a radical shift, our Council leaders used it unilaterally. The announcement, opposed by many, was nevertheless approved, and now, it was up to the EHAF to carry it out. The day of the Concord would be implemented in all its aspects without recourse.

It also marked perhaps the only time President Langden did not have a say in our planet's affairs. Under his command, the EHAF prepared for the worst from our population, establishing a strategy of non-violence to contain the uproar.

We all knew it would come, taking many forms throughout the week. My forces had been increased in the last month, preparing for it. It was imperative to ascertain we would have the Security Personnel on the ground in all areas of our grid.

The Company expanded the City Vigil's number by the thousands. The latest models more than doubled their presence in our streets, going from five thousand to twelve thousand strong, giving them added capabilities by expanding their programming so they could do the heavy lifting in the vacuum of space. Once the Concord was over, the incoming confrontation had everything to do with the anomaly, and we prepared them for combat in lack of gravity.

We added trusters and powerful lasers to defend the ships' capabilities in the event of any offensive encounters. The construction of more ships on the four orbital stations around Earth demanded more shifts to complete on time. So, the Counsel applied pressure on the Company Conclave after concluding that the City Vigils were the next best solution to meet the rigor of space after our engineers and construction workers. The arduous conditions and hazardous labor required to build four additional freighters would benefit from machines that did not require food, rest and were impervious to extreme temperatures. With added programming and algorithms, an enlarged core for data, allowing more configurations and adjustments, patterns perceptions, situations analysis than the previous models, the City Vigil M98 was built and entered our infrastructures.

At first glance, it became evident that the new models were quite advanced, with personalities slowly born from interactions with humans. An algorithm component close to demonstrating a sort of emotional response distinguished the latest City Vigils across the board. It resulted in extraordinary human characteristics like benevolence. As they moved within crowds and resolved issues in the factories and later under challenging conditions in space, they took on the name of Mags.

This morning, every individual grouped under a Conclave responded to the call of the Concord. The System monitored all the factions existing on Earth via the Mags, the City Vigils, and Custodians, orchestrating the logistics in all fields and streaming to the Watcher for the EHAF to oversee.

In areas where the workforce met their goals and provided intended results, those demonstrating less efficiency than others transitioned to more minor demanding fields requiring additional resources. It was a way to give them a chance to do better under less stringent conditions. Few had choices of areas and diverted immediately to meet the needs of the lagging four programs were provided new implants to meet the requirements of their new positions.

From birth, the way of the System was simple. Everyone underwent an Evaluation and received recommendations based on aptitudes to determine their path within our society. The most gifted within the Network received multiple choices for their future and selected the areas of studies that appeared the most compelling. Under its nurturing design phase, DAINN encouraged individuals early on, following everyone from newborn to adult. Other paths opened to working environments with lower potential for those less gifted, and choices became more restrictive. Yet, each person obtained a position where their capabilities allowed them to reach some type of success. DAINN's protocol required that every soul or life be protected no matter the service provided to the community.

Doctor Rene Paladock, my mentor, built the System to implement this critical purpose under the mandate of the Universal Pledge. However, it did not mean that everything was equal within our society.

The Implants originated when our technology took off in the healthcare field gave more knowledge and accordingly access to some more than others. It was inevitable. The Faculty's arm and its genetic experts began to manipulate genetic material, altering, repairing, or enhancing form or function. It was not new. Already developed in the twentieth century, it only expanded further by 2098. Recombinant DNA or the chemical splicing of different strands of DNA worked in certain instances delivering unparalleled results. Our science prolonged life for many.

Later on, our genetic scientists began applying genes from other species creating adaptive traits with animal characteristics. DNA gene modification became particularly helpful for those selected for security and warfare within the EHAF. As a result, Implants took on a new meaning.

In other cases, our brightest minds used direct microinjection technology to find the answers we sought to strengthen our bodies, providing stronger lungs, hearts, or limbs and fighting diseases. At first, they began replacing organs when needed to add years of healthy life to millions of individuals, but soon gene cell therapy took over. And then, scientists encouraged by the results ventured into new ground with more engineering experiments to create new life forms.

Some fought the process due to all the ethical and moral considerations regarding enhancements caused by the medical technology. But, driven by success, they became rare and were quickly silenced by the Conclaves.

The SRC's capabilities working with the Faculty expanded as our scientists devised new ways to modify our aptitudes and enhance our bodies. A trend started and spread quickly.

Suddenly, the Company Conclave provided new products in the market. The Conclaves pushed for more productivity in the workplace, and our population looked for enhanced capabilities to maintain their effectiveness. Everything sold as a benefit that boarded on subliminal coercive control. Initially, these devices remained external until Imps brain connectivity proved successful. Then, everyone capable of affording the upgrade demanded them.

My people essentially redesigned themselves, evolving into a new species. The Perfect human was born, one with enhanced everything.

The search for perfection began long ago. Then, it became imperative to develop research to render humans capable of withstanding a more unforgiving environment, like space. Then as our climate turned more demanding with each decade and with dwindling resources, the idea of a more robust human took hold. Perhaps, if it had not been deemed necessary, the resistance to enhancement would have been stronger. But years of neglect for the planet caught up. The marketing notion that these transformations would make life easier for individuals and the community synched the issue altogether, convincing our society.

Now we were confronted with something else altogether. Something that defied our scientists and DAINN. And with every passing week, we get closer to our possible demise. While panic thus far kept at bay by the ignorance of the masses, one could not increasingly help but find our limitations more frustrating in our goal to save our people.

City Center, SRC Grounds, Golden Ghetto, Ang City

I rush because I have a purpose. I believe that somehow, my instinct is heightened today by circumstances, for everyone around me is tense, their grim faces crossing my path on my way to work. Phenom Kathryn Hendricks, Science Research Center (SRC) Conclave – DAINN Annals – Winter 2098.

The Science Research Center's main building sprawled inside an immense park near the city's heart, surrounded by ivy and trees, and stood as an oasis of peace for those seeking inspiration. Its imposing structure, built around 2078, represented a symbol of that era and was, at the time, a new trend in designs and technology for habitats of the future.

One of the Elite EHAF and my contact Talia tried to reach me. My visor opened and gave me nothing but static. The NetComm failed as I heard briefly, "Kate? Are you there?"

The communication dropped.

Something was going on with the Network, and I needed to make it to my team.

The SRC building, fully energy efficient and composed of new materials meant to be stronger and more resistant to changes in temperature, was connected through its center to other colossal structures. Amidst a series of pathways trailing over gardens and water canals, it was the nerve center of our planet. Erected in the middle of overgrown trees and green foliage for the pleasure of the world scientific community, it remained the pride of our society for its evergreen architecture. Even today, it represented the epitome of the latest in architectural advances at its core due to its constant updates. In a not-so-subtle fashion, it was yet another way to maintain our lead advantage on the world.

Since 2078, the Science Research Center has stood out as the beacon of knowledge for the planet. Scientists from every nation worked here. As the program expanded, the world's leading minds joined the Center. Integrated early on in the program, we owned the impact of our work, influencing nations with one of our brilliant leaders, Dr. Richard Samuel. Having studied in the program at the most prodigious educational centers of our time – the Academy, and at the highest academic levels offered, he made the Center what it was today: a world institution that impacted technology and scientific advancements driving progress for all of humankind. With a triple Ph.D. in business, international affairs, and diplomacy, Dr. Richard Samuel had integrated our scientific community into the fold of corporate research and development, allowing us to influence new product discoveries. He was at the top of our Administration within the Center, in charge of all our programs and the link to the Great Council.

I looked around and saw people rushing toward the trams. In the crowd, I advanced slowly, almost imperceptibly. I dropped my visor and attempted to connect to my team. A stream of data unfolded in front of my eyes, taking forever. "Netwash... It is taking too long." My System should be able to reach my lab. Giving up, I pushed past a group and sprinted ahead.

As one of the leading physicists in my field, my work today did not involve anything to do with my domain. My tasks during the Concord were to help my mentor, Dr. Rene Paladock, in charge of the System because our Network would be taxed beyond normal.

Considered brilliant early on and given to a natural ability for mathematics, my presence at SRC represented my ultimate reward and dream. Still, I was only at the beginning of my learning curve.

Quickly enrolled into the program with my first implant at the age of seven, I demonstrated an innate aptitude for problem-solving and scientific reasoning. Over the years, DAINN followed my studies, orienting me toward science and predominantly physics. The natural world inspired my interest, from the tiniest subatomic particles to the largest galaxies. It quickly became a passion for experimenting with the laws of nature, analyzing what things were made of and how they behaved. Studying matter, and its motion through the space-time continuum, along with related concepts like energy and force, could only be done with the brightest – Dr. Paladock, head of the Science Research Center and working for Master Phenom Samuel.

I joined the Institute at the age of seventeen and expanded my field to natural philosophy, astronomy, biology, and chemistry. For those of us who enrolled, there was no choice. Like others in the program, I didn't have time for anything but the Center.

My visor unfurled in response to another call. The small interface opened, revealing among a lot of static the grinning face of my brother Sean, the eldest in the family and the most outspoken of us all. "Hellnet Kat, are you all right? What… shh is going shh… On? Shouldn't you already be in your lab?"

The interference grew.

"Sean, now… Shh… isn't a good time. Shh… I am running late."

"Imagine that. Shh... Jamie's right shh... Here."

"What shh... Are you doing shh... With shh... Jamie's device?"

Jamie waved at me from behind Sean. Shh... "I got my NetComm knocked shh.... Out shh... Playing air shh.... Football."

No big surprise there. Sean was a sports fanatic. Jamie was much more reserved and enjoyed quieter pursuits.

It was true that I didn't see my family much. They lived in another city smaller than Ang, called Hawthorne, in the North, and even if it wasn't that far, with our transportation choices, I rarely got there due to our working hours. Frequently, I imagined my two brothers and their friends planning their evenings out or even their getaway weekends, and I envied them. What wouldn't I give to be like them, irresponsible and carefree? Working at the Center got lonely, damn lonely. Yet, I was sure of one thing. No matter how empty my heart feels, I wouldn't give up my life for anything. I guess, ultimately, it is my choice.

"What's shh... Happening shh... With shhh Network? Shh... Should we shh... Be worried? Mom and dad... shh... Want to know... shh..."

Sean didn't miss a beat. Of course, my parents would inquire about the events and the Concord, but I suspected Sean was the instigator behind the call. "I don't know shh..."

"So, shh... We shh... Can worry shh..."

"Sean, shh... Stay close shh... Home shh... I'll call you."

"Okay, shh... Sis. Shh... Take care shh... Know... shh We love shh... You even shh... Never shh... Around."

"Buggernet off, shh... SmartNetAss." My PVZ window closed.

Entering the SRC ground, I glanced up at the main building. The windows shined with lights reflecting through the voltaic smoked glass.

The grounds were alive with unusual activity. Men and women alike were now pressed for time. They no longer walked the inside gardens searching for inspiration for the work performed in their respective fields. Instead, they ran or eagerly made their way to the grand entrance, impatient to be inside. And I was one of them.

Work was our only life and our solace on solitary nights. It was our unique companion in days filled with purpose in a future already established by others. And there was a lot of both.

My visor deployed again. This time it was Dr. Paladock. "Kat, have you shh... set up the shh... scan shh...remotely? Shh... need... space shh... analysis."

"I'm shh... Outside. I will do it... Shh... Arrive." The anomaly in space remained an unspoken secret. We constantly monitored, hoping to learn more about it.

"Shh... Hurry up."

We worked under the leadership of one of the most brilliant minds of our era. Indeed, Dr. Paladock was the world guru and head of the SRC. He acquired his knowledge from ranked mentors and prominent leaders in his fields through our online archives and university program degrees from the Academy. His mind was a wonder, possessing acuity of vision, an extraordinary focus for his work, and a purpose and dedication to science that inspired all of us. He was a mental tornado, moving pieces of a puzzle quickly inside his intellect and arriving at enlightened conclusions in a matter of hours when it would most likely take us weeks to decipher the same complex problems. His processing capabilities were no doubt influenced by his implants, but even considering these, his ultimate logic and the outcome of his findings were undoubtedly the makings of an unparalleled mind. Our team had one allegiance, Dr. Paladock and the Center.

He held various Ph. D.s and accumulated more fields than the rest of us but was also the most demanding and unforgiving man I knew. He did nothing but work and expected the same from us. To him, we were neurons and brains. We were made to do his bidding and were present at the research center for one purpose only: to advance science. Simply put, we were at the eternal disposal of his genius for the discovery of the universe and its secrets.

My visor switched to my assigned station at my command, but the interference was too significant. I couldn't get anything useful. I knew that by now, my chief was already feverishly wondering what brought this on.

Usually, I was first in the lab and the last to leave. I had gained Paladock attention due to my early work at the Institute and my grades at the Academy. I hated disappointing him by being the last to arrive and unable to give him any answers.

I went through the doorway at the same breakneck speed as I crossed the yard. The inside of the science building, made of concrete beams and glass, was huge and comprised a large atrium leading to the upstairs floors. Wide hallways curving to either side led to the upper levels if one ignored the space Elevat platform located further back of the Center, which was already going up.

Unwilling to wait for its return, I dove for one of the ramps. These provided access to some of the moving transportation platforms, or as we called them, MTPs. I slid past a few other people and selected one of the nearest machines.

They hovered idly due to the mechanism that anchored them in the parking zone, located near the wall of the large ramp. I stepped on the closest ones. Without delay, it rose, soaring two feet above the ground. The MTPs glided up the right incline plane, all the way to the first air ramp to our floor. The accelerated speed was exhilarating to me but contrary to our rules.

The SRC voice reprimanded me. "Phenom Hendricks, you are going over the speed allowed in the main hall. Slow down, or you will receive Dems."

Dems or demerits were one way they controlled behaviors within the science building. It was pretty much how they governed everything and everyone. A downgrade in status eventually affected the units received each month. These represented the allocated remuneration in our world monetary system for the tasks performed within each field of endeavor. Ignoring the warning, I kept going.

Not always comfortable on these infernal machines, I first had to acquire balance and then conquer my nervous trepidation at whisking people around. In time, I learned to deal with the motion. This ability didn't come naturally to me. In my training with the MTPs, I experienced several dangerous mishaps. But this model was the latest from the Company and used by the Center for the accuracy of their manufacturing. All of them reacted to mind commands quickly.

"Coming right behind you!" I yelled without slowing down.

Having mastered the control of the MTP to a point where I was comfortable with their maneuverability, I came to appreciate their mechanisms. Now, I directed the machine with my Imps while processing other data functions. Within the range of my lab, I reviewed the data and started another scan on the anomaly.

"Gliding right," I announced loudly.

As I passed other scientists, whizzing by with dexterity derived from practice, a sense of exhilaration filled me. Avoiding collisions, my behavior this morning was anything but serious. As one of the most notable physicists at the Center, I chuckled. The speed was fun. Paladock influenced me even in that. Unlike the others, I rarely subscribed to the sedate motion they seemed to prefer as they traveled within the building. In this respect, I believed that my tomboy side kicked in. Hellnet, I was, after all, only seventeen for another week. *Yikes, what fun!*

"Gliding left," I yelped.

Groups in blue lab coats surged around the large halls, filling the space of the vast corridor.

"Hey, watch where you're going. You're not on a football field," muttered one of the scientists, as I passed him rather too quickly.

Wanting to reach my team fast, I blurted a quick "Sorry" and continued with the same unrelenting haste. Frankly, I didn't care. I was expressing my individuality in a world of clones.

"Phenom Hendricks, you now have gained ten Dems. At the next warning, I will prevent you from using the MTPs."

"Come on, DAINN, let a girl have some fun."

Small floating screens called Visor Zaps or VZs, because of the noise they made when they folded and unfolded, provided the latest scientific device about data and the climatic change over the planet. The VZ's were more expansive than our visor or PVZ's and allowed access to more in-depth scientific data restricted to the personnel of the Center. Positioned at strategically located areas along the corridors, they responded to a neuron implant signal from anyone within the science building. I commandeered one, and it moved to my side as I familiarized myself with the latest scientific findings going up the ramp. Sometimes, I hacked the device late in the night to play my favorite game and somehow got away with it. Part of me couldn't help think that Paladock had a hand in my getting away scot-free from this breach.

One screen crossed the corridor as I careened around a corner, plunging ahead to avoid a hit without slowing down. My teammates, now visible ahead, walked surrounding Paladock, and I maneuvered to join them.

Dr. Paladock was a small man by his physical size but in no way by his personality or his intelligence. He led his charge on the MTP and swooshed down the promenade at a high velocity. Some personnel members had expressed their discontent at his traveling speed, and there was no doubt in my mind that he influenced me. Their offensive opinions resonated across the halls, but no one dared directly say a word to him. Magically, neither did the Center's computerized system. Among all of us, he was the Grand Master of Swoosh.

Surrounded by a flock of three assistants who were none other than my teammates, Paladock hurried on. We were all about the same age with various degrees of expertise at the Prosolyte and Phrenic levels, although they acted as if they were my elders by a few years. Anyway, Dr. P needed a large team with unique abilities to support all the scientific ideas coming from his mind and the research elaborated from his work.

The team, although young were notable for their advances at their age. Gregory Tate, a short guy of nineteen, had joined our group a year ago. He wore an eye implant that rendered his night vision extraordinarily perceptive. He specialized in anything and everything with technology and our universal neural network or DAINN. Next to him was George Dampien, a lanky guy who seemed unable to stop growing. He brought his expertise in applied science and engineering for new development applications. Whether at the stage of a concept or a design, he could invent and build anything for the Center. Right behind them was Walden Pool, a brilliant geologist with a rather caustic personality. His insatiable curiosity about space had landed him a place in our inner sanctum. He worked more closely with me and contributed his knowledge to the research, theories, and space operations implemented for Dr. Paladock and the SRC.

The Center was an assembly of the most brilliant minds in many fields. People from the top programs and educational centers around the world boasting the emblem of the Academy came together regardless of their different nationalities. Foreign languages, translated in real-time through Imps - one thought, one speech united all of us under the Earth Homeland Alliance Treaty. Everyone was part of the SRC, which addressed all world scientific issues. We had only one master, the pursuit of science, and with that as our mandate, we were on International Neutral Ground.

"Whoa… slow down," exclaimed George. "We know how eager you are to be among our prestigious group."

"It's about time you show… We're doing all the work here," added Gregory.

I had overreached and landed amongst them with some air displacement. Deftly, I positioned my MTP slightly behind Dr. Paladock, who glanced to his side and emitted a slight chuckle. "Finally decided to join us?" Without waiting for an answer, he pursued, "We just ran a deep scan on DAINN. We cannot find a cause to the Network slow down."

"Must be why the NetComms don't work."

"If only it were just that… Get up to speed quickly. I need you," murmured Paladock.

Dr. Paladock's MTP flew towards the physicist's lab, whose doors remained shut. He approached fast, oblivious that they may not open in time. He liked to play a game - anticipating our computer's distance and reaction time against his ability to apply his reflexes to the situation.

"It's me, Paladock… make way," he roughly stated.

The speech recognition system securing entry in the Control Center triggered an immediate response, engaging the volumetric 3D screen with depth imaging which unfolded above the entryway. The pervasive video capture recognition system got a lock on Paladock's image, and the photonic sensor's light scanned his body from head to toe.

The doors opened, but just barely.

Dr. Paladock floated through the threshold without slowing down. The System disengaged, having recognized him. It switched to the next person behind him, which happened to be me, although it did not have the same priority recognition for my person.

I was under the scan for a brief instant, ignoring my colleagues. As the only girl, one of the leading female physicists amongst a group of males whose testosterone knew no bounds, I felt their gazes behind me. I should be used to it by now, but I wasn't.

They often appraised me from the corner of their eyes, especially when they believed I didn't see them. They were doing that now, oblivious of the thick glass material that reflected their silhouettes and their stares. The sensors were triggered and released me, and I moved on. "Stop checking me out. I see you, nitwits."

Their glances lingered on my butt, and I said, "… And no snide remarks either. Your comments need some work, so that I wouldn't say anything today. Try me tomorrow, boys. Sheesh…"

And the smiles disappeared as I caught them red-handed. Boys cannot beat girls. Just a fact!

"We like to think we know something you don't, Kat." The comment was from Gregory, the most outspoken of the group.

"When are you going to let me know. I can't imagine what that would be."

Laughter erupted between all of us as I passed through the large opening surrounded by a granite wall built to grant entry to enormous scientific apparatus within the Center. The walls boasted shiny transparency that picked up everything with a light energy signature inside. Sounds bounced off quietly, creating a relaxing environment conducive to solving problems. Today, we encountered one with DAINN.

"You're still hot behind that smart intellect. Nothing you can do to change that."

I moved ahead, powerless to stop them from thinking of me as sexy. I had tried, but I'm like water in the desert.

"You know, it only makes things worse when you give us the boot," said Walden.

Feeling my frustration rise, my hands started to twitch. I recognized the signs. I opened and closed my fingers a few times, trying to relax. I was not too fond of this sensation of weakness and my lack of control.

They saw me every day. They should be over it.

I was their equal, especially when it came to physics. Yet, my team members were unwilling to consider me one of the guys. "Today, there's no time for your lame comments, boys. We have a world to save."

"Relax, Kat. You can't change who you are." This time the comment came from George.

"Yeah, and we respect your beautiful mind... Among other things." Gregory added with a grin, and every guy laughed some more.

"I gave it a smirk with a three out of five, but it was pretty funny." Yet, I had to say, "You're all a bunch of Netmorons."

"Yes, over-sexed Netmorons with no place to go," added Gregory. "We know we can be NetJerks. We just want to drink the water."

They laughed again, this time louder.

It was contagious, so I joined them, relaxing a little.

They were right and meant no harm, for we were still teenagers going into adulthood with no time to play or express ourselves other than at work and indeed no moments to experience anything much more.

"Netwash, what have you checked with the System?"

I didn't depend on their work, but we shared our knowledge. And just recently, Dr. Paladock promoted me over all of them. "Just don't forget to call me Boss."

"All the normal suspects… Nodes and all. DAINN's event ran its scan and moved slowly on all its data. We've never seen anything like this. The situation is already stressful because of Concordance, but now, people have started to panic," added Gregory with a severe tone.

"All right… let's find out everything we can about this thing." I held back my frustration at the lack of information and kept my cutting comments to myself. Today, my cold unwavering stares, even my sometimes-cruel sarcasm, which often dented their resolve, would remain locked inside. While it suited me fine most of the time because it helped me keep my distance in a crowded field of men, these guys were my teammates.

Dr. Paladock, with his short speech pattern going on abruptness, interrupted my thought process. "I want answers, not notions. Use your neurons and get me facts. We already know we had a breach in the System. Our codes gave the Surgs access to the Network. Find out how to stop the intrusion and then determine who did this. DAINN's diagnosis is not revealing much, so make sure we eradicate the virus. Keep your eyes open for anything weird. DAINN's behavior resulted from outside interference. We may have more than one occurrence."

I careened on my MTP through the lab as fast as my predecessor. My small demonstration amused him.

He and I knew both knew that I duplicated his style with a certain flair all of my own. It was a game we liked to play with one another. Perhaps it was the fact that he appreciated me that got me promoted in addition to my superior intellect.

Behind me, I sensed the other technicians joining us. They took their position at the respective screens. "The Izione is shutting down," said Gregory.

Paladock's voice rose, "You already told me that it was sluggish. Have you found anything else that could be useful?"

Gregory lost some of his composure. "Not yet…"

DAINN's voice used to emit information at the various floating stations within the lab remained absent. It typically monitored everything about our infrastructure, but today we didn't hear the usual like: "Water supply at critical in all the grids." Today, there was none of that. Today, there were codes, streams of incomprehensible data.

"How many systems within the Network have been affected?" I asked while checking my station.

"We're unsure, but if I had to guess, all of them," exclaimed Paladock. "How else would you explain DAINN's behavior?"

Paladock had a point, and that worried me.

"DAINN is still running a diagnostic," explained Gregory.

Silence reigned among us as we attempted to stop the intrusion into the Network. My composure slipped, and my anxiety increased tenfold with my inability to get into the System.

Faculty Compound, Trams, Ang City

One never thinks that there is such a thing as destiny until we consider events that shape our lives. Then everything begins to fall in place. Phenom Eva Bassington, Faculty Conclave – DAINN Annals – Winter 2098.

I just passed a checkpoint tended by the City Vigils inside the Faculty building and headed in the trams' direction. I quickly reached the extensive walkways that reminded me so much of the Institute each time I sprinted that way. Part of me wondered if they had intentionally made it so when they constructed these.

I reached the trams' platform and waited in line to be cleared by another City Vigil in attendance. It was still pretty crowded, and another bottleneck had formed in the main lines. I was glad not to be dealing with the logistics, but looking around, I decided it was probably better to turn off my privacy mode and reconnect to the Network.

"Good morning, Eva," announced DAINN in my head.

"Good morning DAINN."

"Are you ready for the big day?"

"I am ready, DAINN."

While I was upset about the Concord and what it represented for our society, I was also elated because of what it meant for me. Although we had problems, all sorts of challenges due to our world's state, I felt a sense of joy because I was about to receive more responsibilities. I know; it seemed an odd thing. But we were wired that way. The feeling lasted as I passed the last gate to the waiting area dedicated to the official Faculty personnel. Here, the zone remained relatively calm.

"Faculty tram arriving now," stated the voice of our A.I. It was none other than DAINN itself. Everything DAINN represented was programmed for efficiency purposes, monitoring the transportation around Ang city.

While I waited, the crowd increased, and people started to press forward at the new train's announcement.

I heard the voice in my head. "Eva, your heart rate has changed. Are you feeling all right?"

It was the year 2098. The planet had become a "symbiotic world." Man's nervous system was connected to a Distributed Artificial Intelligence Neural Network, a giant networked memory application – one powerful planetary mind: DAINN. Humanity was now linked physically and biotechnologically to embedded microchips capable of reading our needs and influencing our environment to our liking. Machine and man were one living organism. A new singularity, a new "human species," now roamed the Earth: genetically enhanced humans called – the Perfect Humans.

I was among them, one in the sea of humanity.

We were still individuals and a globally interconnected species through a Neural Network in the most absolute sense of the word. We had created robots, androids, and clones, and some of them to our image. From the recesses of my mind, I answered DAINN. "DAINN, I'm all right."

"I know today is stressful. Would you like a calming infusion?"

"No, DAINN, I will be okay. Just a bit excited, that's all."

"Try and remain calm for your meeting at the Faculty."

It was my era—a moment in the infinity of time. One period I understood because I lived in it, yet I was only a product of this realm. I took a deep breath to calm myself.

"I know you must feel the weight of your responsibilities, especially on a day like today. Just remember that your abilities are beyond your age and that you are fully capable of handling them," continued DAINN.

I knew that, of course, but I resented the fact that I only possessed a limited capacity to enjoy them. Immediacy was an actual state; efficiency, the epitome of personal power in our System. Everything counted. Results and accuracy mattered more than money and triggered a social status a few could claim. I clamped down on my thoughts.

"I understand your feelings of frustration, but they are not doing you justice," continued DAINN. "It will become easier, I promise."

My name was Eva Bassington, and I was barely eighteen years old. I had small bones and was tall, with skin so fair that it seemed translucent at times. I looked vulnerable, even when I acted tough. Somehow, the amber red hair didn't help my cause, although I kept it tied up behind my head most of the time. My hazel-green eyes were probably too sunny to reflect the seriousness of my disposition, for I was rather introverted and absorbed by my work. That was until people got to know me. Then, I became somewhat predictable and boring for them.

The pace of things we did and learned had changed significantly in my world. We no longer had the old-fashioned methods humans used to cipher information and work through data. We lived in a time where the core responsibilities lay with the young, empowered physically and mentally to make decisions that affected billions. We existed where our elders were mentors, providing us a structure to function, all within the degree and authority granted by the DAINN System. An era where the older generation was retired early and no longer part of our workforce.

The adults, ready to answer a different calling at age thirty-five, moved on to other pursuits. The rapidity of the System tended to burn out most by the time people reached forty years old. They could by then realize their life goals if their orientation with DAINN had not, until that time, led them in their heart's direction. They could also select to go on permanent vacation in camps or colonies. By then, our society deemed that they had done their part. The onus focused on the new generation to take up the charge. It was a bargain in which everyone eventually got what they wanted. In some ways, it was awesome. In others, it was numbing.

I answered DAINN in haste… I wanted to resume my thinking for tonight's festivities without any further interruption. "I will be fine, DAINN." But I wasn't going to get out of this conversation the easy way, and I knew that.

"You have huge capabilities and equally enormous responsibilities," said DAINN, "I am sure you realize the trust we have put in you."

"I know… I know."

Indeed, we possessed in-depth knowledge and skills but no experience to match them. Our emotional evolution suffered because we had no time to process it and lacked the wisdom to use it effectively. We still fought our hormones since we'd had no space to grow into our own lives as individuals, and we carried the weight of our planet in turmoil on our young shoulders. There were times when all we wanted to do was strike like the workers today, but fear kept us in line.

"This is important for your career. We can walk through the meeting you are about to have. I am happy to help."

"DAINN, I thank you. You understand how I feel about my work."

The Evaluation at the Institute had established my aptitude in healthcare through a series of tests. It began to orient me toward a better-suited career for my capabilities and personality. I had a natural predisposition for it, so the route DAINN assigned in the medical profession was perfect. Although DAINN recommended other options, this one suited my soul. Perhaps there were other things I could have done, but none more satisfying. I was improving lives.

"Eva, I want you to realize how important you are," explained DAINN. "You have a huge role to play in our survival."

"Thank you, DAINN. I am lucky to have you as my Mentor." I started to laugh, for everyone had DAINN as a mentor.

"You know, Eva, laughing at me is not helpful," DAINN said with a light tone.

"You know, DAINN, I am never laughing at you but with you," as I reduced my laugh to a smile and a wink.

Inside the System, I was cared for to pursue my vocation. It provided me with everything I needed as DAINN followed my development for years, even now. It was part of my life at every crucial moment, like today. Each minute, day and night, week on, it knew what was happening to me through regular reporting with our VLogs.

The VLogs recorded our professional journals. We discussed and maintained entries about our work, career, and thoughts with our Planetary Mind. It was easy; DAINN asked questions. We answered them. DAINN assuaged any doubts we kept or provided guidance about events surrounding our work. DAINN created and maintained a roadmap of my life, and all was established ahead of me and for me. Until now. Indeed, changes were on their way.

"Yes, DAINN. I know."

"Your department is about to be substantially increased. Are you capable of handling that?"

"Yes, DAINN."

"Good answer."

"DAINN, that's humor. Where did you get that from?"

"Dr. Paladock tries to enhance my conversations modality. I am glad you appreciate this new side."

Thinking about what was coming, I became more serious. I was a doctor with a specialty in Micro Genetic Implant surgery. I had just finished my final internship and was already the head of a new Surgery Department dedicated to that field. The reason was simple. I had already accumulated two other degrees, one in DNA science, in evolutionary genetics, and received my first Ph.D. My second degree was in molecular biology, emphasizing medical anthropology and human disease modeling. And I was considered the prize of the Faculty because of my skills as the youngest person to have achieved this Ph.D. In other words, I was a Med nerd, far more comfortable with my studies than with people, and my record was until now flawless.

The Faculty had entrusted me with a team as head of my department in genetic surgery. The field was growing, and we were under constant demand. "You can count on my performance, DAINN."

"We have new additions to the Op list for today. Be sure to allocate the time to review these in the line-up."

"Thank you for letting me know."

"I am here if you need me," added DAINN before it went silent and faded away.

I opened my PVZ and reviewed the names. This day would go on until our ER team would be exhausted by the sheer number of Imp Installs. My eyes scanned the new patients, according to their Conclave.

Those most critical to the System appeared listed first for surgery, and besides their names, the upgrade required for each type of Imp.

The names flowed in front of my eyes, overwhelming me until I saw one I recognized from long ago.

The memories surfaced, and I thought of Aidan. *Why now?* Until now, my path had not crossed his.

I triggered his picture on my PVZ. He had matured. Watching his face took me back in time. I had seen him for the first time, a long time ago. I was five years old then. He had changed, of course, just like I did. But I felt that I would have recognized him anywhere at any age, even so.

The memories called me back to my initial testing at the Institute. At that time, Aidan was ten and much older than us.

"Come on along, this way," said the Evaluation Testing Officer or ETO, a member in charge of us kids at the Institute on that particular day.

There were only seven of us. We proceeded behind the Testing Officer in the broad white hallways that seemed endless as we tripped over our tiny legs to keep up with him. The hugely intimidating structure, so pristine and serene to most adults, looked cold and alienating to me. My parents told me what an important day this was; what an honor it was to be among the youngest selected for the first Evaluation at age five. I was scared to death.

"Follow me and take a seat," had ordered the young man dressed in a grey uniform as he entered a vast room.

I passed the threshold of the testing room with apprehension. Among the others, I was the smallest. Everyone appeared scared. All of us remained silent. We didn't know what to expect. Yet, despite my anxiety, part of me was also excited.

Aidan whispered to me, "You'll be all right… We all will be," as he stepped into the room behind me.

We knew we had to behave. The results of this first testing were life-changing. We understood what a big deal it was for those of us that entered into the System that day.

"You can sit by me if you want," Aidan had said, giving me an encouraging smile.

I didn't hesitate. Jumping on the invitation, I gave the beautiful young teen one of my most glorious smiles.

He winked at me and focused back on the room.

The instructor was cold and unfriendly, only intent on the examination process. Walking in front of the room, he said, "Take your seats."

The individual tables lined up in front of the big screen.

I wagered that all of us would have preferred to be somewhere else.

Silence reigned as we waited, and it rendered us more nervous. Maybe they planned it like that. Perhaps it was even a test of a sort. But as the minutes passed, tension heightened.

Aidan must have felt it.

The stress showed on our small faces.

A glance around the room confirmed that for Aidan. He began to make grimaces and play the clown. He copied a "Netgoof" guy like the individual we saw on our entertainment streams, the one we watched on the Network, laughed at on the video platforms, and played with inside our virtual reality environments. And within minutes, he had us cracking up. He was probably just as scared as we all were. But as the oldest, Aidan felt some responsibility to look out for us. His antics helped, instantly rendering us all more comfortable until he got an earful from the Evaluation Testing Officer.

Aidan Furst was gloriously attractive.

I remembered it all too clearly. The guy in the grey uniform made Aidan feel inadequate because he was older than we all were. I remembered Aidan's face closed. It was like the sun had just left it. I remembered his beautiful blue eyes, which had been laughing with us a few minutes before, turning the dark grey of a stormy weathered sky.

After the Instructor's tongue-lashing, Aidan didn't smile anymore. He no longer looked at anything else but the screen.

He was just determined.

Aidan ignored all of us for the entire length of the assessment. His responses to any questions posed were quick. His score was surprisingly high. The Instructor, initially caught off-guard, was impressed and began to look at Aidan differently.

I recalled the rigor of the test. Five hours was a long time for anyone, much less little kids.

DAINN was there, coaxing, gently keeping us focused, and ensuring we played the games… All the while probing our minds so that we answered its questions.

I could see Aidan's profile as I tried to get his attention. It didn't work.

He had shut off the world around him.

When we got up to leave at the end of the Evaluation, I stumbled against the tables.

Aidan caught me before I landed on the ground, embarrassed. He squeezed my hand and smiled at me reassuringly, and then he was gone.

It was the first and last time I met Aidan Furst. But his presence at that moment stayed with me all these years. And today, for some reason, he was going to be in our Op Room.

The memories surged. *You know Darnet well why you are thinking of him, Eva, so cut it out.*

Aidan Furst had made an indelible mark on me that day at the Institute. While I wondered what had happened to him all these years, somehow, I knew that I would eventually meet him again and soon. Indeed, there was every chance that my moment, after all this time, would have arrived tonight at the festivities. But I had not counted on his presence on my Op table.

The party scheduled the night of Concordance garnered all the big wigs, and he would assuredly have been among them. Only now, I would have him as one of my patients. Would he be attending the party after the new Imp Install? I was unsure. His procedure was not demanding. Compared to the other Imps he received over the years, this was just an expansion for further storage.

The day of Concordance started unpredictably.

It was the beginning of how things began to unravel for all of us. Only then did I have no clues yet.

The next tram arrived, and I embarked on it, thinking about what would happen when I met Aidan again.

Plaza Center, Golden Ghetto, Ang City

I feel doubts, disbelief, and fear. I don't want it to be accurate, for then everything I have imagined my life to be would be wrong. Proselyte Amara Lawson, Institute Conclave – DAINN Annals – Winter 2098.

It started because I was curious. The old saying, curiosity killed the cat, certainly made sense. As DAINN prepared each of us for our life purpose, we were also encouraged to find out more about ourselves, our patterns – the ones to keep and the ones to remove.

Now that I was part of the Institute, the Awareness Center was within my reach daily, and within its training, I could accomplish much more to elevate myself. Building a higher awareness of ourselves was supported during my time at the Academy. I grew in the last several months and was now more qualified to understand aspects of my higher self. But for all of us, it was a lifetime pursuit.

In the process, I reached the determination that as long as I prepared for my future, I might as well find out who my most compatible partner happened to be. *I know. I know. I am young and need to focus first on myself, but I am curious. I can undoubtedly multitask, and I needed to know.*

DAINN encouraged a fulfilling life through its Symbiotics Pairing, which our elders also recommended. Engrossed with our work's dictates and our social mandate, we had little time for dating to find the right match. When we reached the age of eighteen, we could look at the various partners best suited to our personalities. Science-backed choosing seemed to eliminate the mistakes, or so they thought.

So, I requested a Compatibility Match from our DAINN Network, just about the same time the leaders announced Concordance. While my timing sucked big time, I now held the answer to my crazy quest.

Hey, I wasn't alone, thinking it was a good idea. My mentor and boss at the Institute, Allison, encouraged me to do it. "Amara, finding one's partner anchors us through life. Besides, you could use a bit of diversion and a playmate. This place has a way of consuming us," she said with an encouraging smile.

In truth, it didn't take much more than one conversation to capture my attention and convince me to do it. "I would like to know for sure, but it may not be the best time to find out."

"There is never one best time. Each moment has the potential to represent the best of times. Consider the now in your life, just that, and nothing more."

Thinking about that conversation now, I looked at the names in front of my PVZ.

DAINN provided three matches, and the best one was the one I had a problem with and was reeling against as a possibility. It had to be a mistake. But I couldn't bring myself to wait. I needed to find out now, and so on the worst possible day of our lives, the day of the Concord, I made my way to the Plaza. It may be a bit compulsive, if you know what I mean, but here I was.

My best match, the number one pairing, was far removed from the picture in my mind. I rebelled against it. "No way, these are good findings! DAINN, you made an error," I suggested vehemently on my way there. And yet, our Network didn't make mistakes.

So, here my new obsession caused me to tackle DAINN. Me, a pretty brunette with long wavy hair and brown eyes, someone with small features, rather skinny, with long legs, confronting our Network. Usually seeking calm and order, I would be remiss if I didn't say I possessed a mouth that works in advance of my brain and sometimes got me in more trouble than I cared to admit. Obviously, this was one of those times. Here I was questioning our System? *Oh, Netboy.*

Against the Planetary Network's weight, I was, in truth, a nobody, and for once, I didn't feel calm and orderly as I made my way to the Plaza. But my curious compulsive, obsessive side demanded to know more.

DAINN's findings provided none of the things I felt I needed. And deep down, I knew I would never win the argument, but I was certainly not ready to surrender either.

I had expected that it would be someone I was in contact with, a friend perhaps, or someone I shared interests with, but no. It wasn't so.

Cashel was everything I was not. Strong, robust, carefree, and frankly, a great body. Ideally, he fitted on a podium with the gods, like Thor or Adonis. His face was beautiful in a rugged sort of way. Contrary to most, he wore his brown hair long, shoulder-length, and tied in the back of his head during his missions. His eyes were most arresting, for their color was uncertain. At times they appeared light grey, and other times they looked dark, almost black. He had a fiery temper and behaved quite unpredictably, which was not at all what I liked.

When I initially received my results, I was intrigued by the top three contenders. Starting with the highest rating seemed the best approach, even if it appeared that the choice offered with the first candidate was the most doubtful. It seemed an unlikely match for someone like me. Yet, regardless of my doubts, I sought him out. I wanted to see him, even if this was from afar, even if it was for a short moment, even if I was unsure. And it had to be him!

I ventured into the Golden Ghetto with its broad avenues near the presidential area. The Plaza sat vast and beautiful in the early morning. The large Tower rose ahead of me, tall and powerful, hosting the seat of our government, the President's office and residence, the Council Members, and other officials. This site was where everything happened. It was the central location where the critical decisions were made, which would dictate our nation's fate and our planet.

I sat on one of the hovering chairs set around the perimeter for the benefit of the visitors. The place was built to impress. At this hour, people filled the grounds moving about in haste, almost in a state of panic. On this day of Concordance, under the dome, closed above our heads, the weather remained mildly warm, lit by the early morning sun. But for now, the entire park appeared a sight I never contemplated quite like this before, with City Vigils standing everywhere and the Clout moving in small patrols.

Waiting for Cashel to come out, my stomach fluttered with nerves as I anticipated seeing my match – the one man that ranked the highest.

His assignment would no doubt begin soon.

My PVZ provided me with all the intel I needed to know who he was as a person. I understood his attributes and likes as well as dislikes; I recognized his habits and extreme behavioral patterns. His attitude toward life was quite different than mine. All in all, the characteristics defining him appeared mainly foreign to me. While I saw his data file and Vlogs, I also believed it was essential to see him in person.

The day would not provide the opportunity to ponder the matter and reflect quietly on how I felt about him. I could be wrong, but...

Roaming the streets tonight would be too uncertain. So, coming here right before my shift at the Institute seemed a better time to understand the making for this pairing. With his schedule on my PVZ, I couldn't stay away.

I was not planning to meet him. I was hoping to look at him. So, here I was, seated on this bench in this place, in a deep need-to-know state.

His shift with the Force would begin any minute now. Indeed, Cashel Reid was a member of the Elite team with the Clout.

This behavior was unlike anything I had done before.

The slight sound of engines buzzed in my ears way above my head. My eyes scanned the sky.

Coming high up from the Tower, the dark silhouettes of the AirBikes jetted out from the highest floors, forming two parallel lines as they descended toward the Plaza.

They were on time. I knew about the unit from Cashel's information data file. It also included all their names and roles, but nothing official about their tasks.

My heart beat faster.

He finally exited the building with his team members.

I felt flushed as I watched the air patrol approach the Plaza level, hoping not to be noticed in the bustle of the morning.

Cashel's record mentioned an outgoing personality, confirmed when I observed the team laughing as they maneuvered the airways. Indeed, he looked relaxed and happy as he jutted ahead of his friends, dropping lower to the ground.

I didn't know what to expect from my visit. At first, I experienced no physical reaction, except perhaps a slight disappointment at my lack of response to Cashel's near presence. But even that didn't last long.

Indeed, his confident demeanor bordering on cocky showed as he flew briskly across the park and straight at me!

The last thing I expected from Cashel Reid was that he would spot me.

He did so without a hint of hesitation, comfortable in his decision upon glancing in my direction with an assurance that left me breathless. *How can he find me here so quickly?*

Now, he rode his AirBike with precision, stopping two feet away from me, the contraption positioned right in front of the hovering chair.

I wanted to get out of it, but I couldn't because he blocked me. *OMG, I wanted to disappear on the spot, but I couldn't... Of course, I couldn't.*

He smiled. "I knew you would come," he said, in a calm sort of way.

"Whatever are you talking about?"

"I hate to break it to you this way, but we know pretty much everything that is going on within the grids, including compatibility match requests. I have locked on you since your search. I expected to see you here at some point."

I was so mortified, but I would never show it. While I wanted to melt into the ground right where I was and disappear instantly from this public place, I wouldn't give Cashel the satisfaction. A quick look at his friends standing several feet away on their AirBikes told me all I needed to know. They were all aware of my search. They had a bet going on. "Hum… What did you bet?"

He looked surprised at my reply but quickly recovered. "You."

They knew I had pulled his name. They also understood why I was here. I forced a laugh. "Boy toy… I wouldn't bet on it." *Amara, you are a fool and indeed look like one.*

I jumped out of the gliding chair and pushed past his AirBike. "I have to go. The friend I was waiting for canceled at the last minute."

Turning my back on him, I decided to maintain what was left of my dignity. Without saying a word, I walked away, too embarrassed to trust my voice. Within a few feet, I no longer walked. Instead, I almost sprinted and wished I could run, but it would be too much of a given that I was embarrassed. I could not give him the satisfaction to know just how badly I felt.

But he wasn't having any of it. "Hey, wait up."

Cashel just kept up with me on his AirBike, effortlessly.

Annoyed, l accelerated my pace, knowing full well that I would never lose him unless he decided to go. He had the fastest flying machine, the training, and the Imps. He was in top physical condition, and I was just an Institute Recruit Officer, still at the Academy. "You should go," I said, glancing to the side.

Cashel got tired of my evasion tactic and reached for my arm, stepping right in front of me.

I stumbled into his path and almost landed on his lap.

He caught me and steadied me with laughter in his eyes. "Okay, look, I didn't mean to embarrass you."

"You didn't. I just have to go."

"Huh, huh…" He laughed harder.

"You just arrogantly assumed you knew why I was there and didn't hesitate to do it in front of your friends."

Perhaps it was because I looked so vulnerable to him, but he suddenly seemed embarrassed. "All right, I may have made a mistake. I am sometimes a bit too brash, and it was not well done of me, I suppose."

"You are a Netwash Jerk."

"Maybe so, but it's not every day that I get picked up as a match. I usually do the picking, you know."

"I'm sorry. But your behavior satisfies my curiosity completely. Guys like you think you control situations when you don't. DAINN has undoubtedly made a mismatch… that much is obvious."

"You think?"

He was still holding me close, and it bothered me, but I didn't want to react. I tried to ignore it. "Absolutely. We have nothing in common," I added determinedly.

"I wouldn't say that exactly. I mean, you are a bit young for me, but I've seen worse."

The thumb of his left hand was gently stroking my forearm, and the heat from his hold was starting to aggravate me.

I jerked my arm away. "It is the one thing we agree upon… You are too old for me. I can tell you that much."

His head slightly inclined to the side as he observed me, he said, "While that may be true, I won't say that there is nothing between us… And you shouldn't either. Let's just see."

"Oh…"

Cashel laughed at my reaction. "We should go eat something. How about tonight after the craziness?"

"I have something else to do, but I'm not doing this. Let me consider it, and I will call you. Fat chance."

"Oh, but I think you will, sweetheart. You received the same results I did, and they are unmistakably high. DAINN immediately notified me, and now, I'm curious."

"My poor boy, it's a mistake."

"You sought me out, so let's find out."

"That was before actually meeting you. I'm just not interested; you're not my type."

"Well, it would be a shame for you to miss the opportunity of your life. Don't be proud."

"I'm not!"

"If you say so."

He was irritating and way too self-assured and utterly wrong for me. Cashel didn't let go until he said, "I will NetComm you." His thoughtful look as he let go of me said it all.

We had nothing in common. We didn't even belong to the same Conclave.

Cashel liked everything I didn't, and he most probably thought that everything I wanted didn't matter. Yet, I couldn't deny his physical attributes were quite attractive, and he knew it. *Oh, Netboy in a casket. Maybe I could just have sex with him and discard him as quickly as I met him. Naaaa. It won't work. Too complicated.*

While I had several other guys that could also be an excellent match for me, this one, well, this one, resonated with me physically, and I didn't want him to. *That DAINN… There is something seriously wrong with it this time. It is a colossal mistake to pair us even if he has nice glutes.*

Our paths were quickly laid out in front of us by DAINN. The decisions, the choices we had in our lives, were cataloged and weighted. They provided options from the best to the least favorable for each individual. These parameters allowed us to steer the course of our lives for the most part without turbulence. Things were smooth inside the System. It was so for me until I began my work at the Institute, and Concordance happened.

But it just wasn't the case with Cashel. Everything about him was about turmoil.

From the moment of our confrontation, I was in denial when it came to him. I walked away with determination before things got further out of hand. As I engaged on the path toward the Water's Edge area, DAINN spoke. "You don't want to recognize your patterns. The ones you will now use to destroy the chance you have to make a change in your life for the better."

I was in retraction mode with Cashel. I wanted to deny myself the influence he could have over me. "DAINN, I am not prepared to discuss this."

"You already made assumptions about him and failed miserably to test them to determine their accuracy," said DAINN.

"I don't want to talk about him." I had already adopted my position. I concluded that he was not good for me for many reasons, not counting his casual attitude towards my feelings during our very first meeting. My opinion made, I hung onto it for fear of proving I had been wrong in the first place by not giving him a chance. In so doing, I believed that I was making the right choice. I was not going to test or verify my premise.

"Accordingly, you are embarking on the wrong road," expressed DAINN, disregarding my desire to leave the issue alone. "You're thinking, which would otherwise be sound, is leading you to the wrong conclusions. It is what emotions precisely do."

I felt that intensely. *Leave me alone, DAINN.*

DAINN taught me that much.

HellNet, my teacher, recorded my emotions.

Darnet, it witnessed my reaction.

Netshit, it tallied his findings and made its assessment.

DAINN shared its conclusions despite me.

And still, I didn't want to think about that even now.

Cashel watched me leave, and I still could feel his gaze on my back. While I was over it, he was not finished with me but had figured out that it wasn't the right time. Cashel had quickly garnered at that moment that by insisting, he would push me into my position even further.

I stood my ground and stayed away from him.

During the hours and days of Concordance that followed, Cashel contacted me as things went from bad to worst for all of us.

Still, I didn't contact him back.

I forgot about him or tried to forget about him, concentrating on my tasks and keeping myself busy. It worked for a time, too, until it didn't, until everything went crazy.

Presidential Tower, Watch Center, Golden Ghetto, Ang City

Understanding what Command expects in a combat situation is manageable. The difficulty comes when peace reigns. I struggle with that with everyone, especially when it comes to him. Proselyte Jeze Wright, EHAF Conclave – Presidential Special Elite Unit, DAINN Annals – Winter 2098.

I worked in a world where violence was the norm. I belonged to the Force, to the Earth Homeland Alliance. We moved in an environment where conflicts were either resolved by dialog according to the System conditioning or squashed by the show of force of our City Vigils and our Guards. Communication with some type of leverage was easy to come by, for we lived in an information world.

We were all networked, and our leaders tapped into the flow of data as needed and our training or retraining took place through the Institute if we remained in good standing or retention centers when not. When that didn't work, and where no other tried alternatives had valid results based on DAINN's predicted outcomes, we resulted in what we knew best... the EHAF power.

The DAINN Network analyzed options for every situation, assimilated responses, and provided optimum scenarios to make decisions to promote the best outcome for the greater good. Only today, the Network was compromised.

Concordance was here, and it was a day where I could feel alive again on the inside. I had waited as long as I could. I didn't want to seem eager, but here I was, impatient to get into the action. I was Jeze, the tough girl, the wild card, the unpredictable, emotionally charged, although cold-hearted, on the outside, sexy girl in an exotic-looking female package wearing the uniform of the Elite. Oh, and pretty smart to boot. Compared to my comrades, my long dark hair, framing a face with high cheekbones, big eyes, voluptuous mouth, all coming in a small but deadly frame curving in all the right places, drew the attention of the guys until they met my hot temper and then they steered clear of me for good. They knew I took risks, daring to put myself in situations most grown men would avoid. I had a death wish, and deep down, I knew that.

"Hey, guys." I let the door of the monitoring room lock behind me.

Both Argil and Rand nodded when they saw me.

I didn't even get an acknowledgment from North, but that was no surprise. He expected me to show up. That's just how it was between us.

When I saw their faces, I chuckled, "You guys look bored!"

"You know it," answered Argil. Rand just exploded a sigh that was worth an entire tirade.

Violence was a part of me, a good part of what I stood for nowadays. I instinctively knew what to do when I was confronted by bullies, or by resistance, or by enemies. While we were no longer experiencing many of these conflicts in Ang City, breaking from conflict zones as a veteran required a complex adaptation not everyone successfully achieved. The only action I saw these days was in the virtual reality room, maintaining our programmed sharp combat skills during our training sessions. Indeed, we lived pretty much isolated by the peaceful System established in the streets by DAINN. It was a good thing. My only problem remained that wars and conflicts were where I seemed to thrive most.

A product of my environment, I never asked myself whether I liked violence. I was used to it. When you get dropped in the middle of it, you truly know nothing else. You either swam or sunk. But lately, I had to question if there was more to me or life and if I could be someone else. *How do I deal with peace?* We no longer had the turbulence and the chaos. We enjoyed security and experienced safety. Yet, I felt no solace, no peace within. I needed to find my way, my place in that world, and I didn't quite know how to begin or if it was even possible. *The good thing is that I don't have to answer that question today. Today can be like in the old times. I can be in action again without restraints, without hesitation, and without guilt.*

As I stood by North, I said, "Anything?"

North grunted and continued to watch the monitors.

North appeared, ripped beside me with his dark caramel skin and light green eyes, bulky chest, and broad shoulders. His thick arms could move tanks or push through walls. He was a legend among us. These characteristics were his calling card, and apart from the military rank on his uniforms, his striking good looks got him noticed among our population. Perhaps it amounted to the Elite team encompassing too few of us so that it was relatively easy to identify us.

When I first became a member of the Force, it was easy. I understood our mandate and what it would take to get there. It was the reason why our leaders trained us. Then, slowly the DAINN Network influenced the landscape. One day, we were dealing with another reality.

As order replaced chaos, we had to find a new meaning. I was still looking for mine.

Our team followed North, who was then one hundred percent behind Zane and his policies. Initially, it was simple. We became the enforcers, the power behind the DAINN System. We dealt with all eventualities like security and, on occasion, the underground activities. When the Surgs encroached on our lives, we intervened, expelled, arrested, and retrained. It was the old way. The new method was more systematic and lethal to the personality, if not the individual.

Little by little, DAINN replaced most of us with automation. It now dispatched the City Vigils to deal with the entrenched resistance within the old city when needed, but these were rare instances anymore. *DAINN wants to preserve life, even the lives of those who do not believe in its way.*

There, within the decrepit buildings and ruins of a time past, the Surgs had found their zone. They chose to remain in the city instead of joining the Exodus that took many residents and citizens outside our walls and fought for their rights. The Surgs made a place for themselves and settled into an underground routine. Everyone knew it. Everybody who mattered ignored it. Such was valid as long as they didn't interfere with our infrastructure in the new city.

"They'll set something up," had told us North. "I guarantee it."

Recalling the first time he had brought up his plan, I scoped the various monitors, waiting to see a sign that would unleash our team. Impatience surged through me. I was ready for some action, and so was our team.

"We won't harm them. We will eliminate the threat," North had insisted, and I guess it was part of Zane's plan.

There was no doubt that North was a badass in the most profound ways, but he was fair.

Standing there without doing something required discipline, trying my patience, but it was better than guessing at what was happening in our streets and waiting for his voice to call on me. *Here, I can pretend that it is all about the Clout.*

"We will assemble them into the detention centers or RCs, and DAINN will conduct its reorientation program..." announced North.

While it would have been a normal reaction to purge all of the non-conforming individuals that were ultimately part of the underground group and retrain them, DAINN resisted a full force intervention. Its strategy had been patience. Our planetary computer weighted the risks that waiting could unleash on us and for now estimated they were not as high as I thought. The System remained strong.

North had not moved an inch since I arrived. His stance was, as usual, calm, focused, almost serene. *Except, I know better. There is no part of this man that knows anything about serenity.*

Many thought the Network could withstand a lot, almost anything. North did not see it that way, but we were following orders. Those at the top were adhering to DAINN's dictate without questions. Zane was one of them. So, for the most part, we delayed the intervention of the Clout. But when they encroached on the new city built over the ruins of the old one, we stepped in, like today. They just did as North had predicted.

As a result of Concordance, we deployed the EHAF. I stood in the Watch Center, the official monitoring room of the Tower, with a few minutes to spare before the usual adrenalin rush set in.

I felt it building now. Coming here a few minutes before the signal from North, I checked in on him.

Part of me adhered to the beliefs he had voiced in the last month that violence would occur on this day; supporting his opinion, my eagerness to act rose. He foresaw it based on our experience. No matter what others said about our System's peaceful ways, this was the Concord.

It was typical that he would be here. Soon he would need me. This train of thought brought me to consider what I didn't want to face. *Why am I always by his side? Darnet, shut it off, Jeze.*

The others could fill in in my place. We all had a role to play within the Elite, but we also were interchangeable. Only, change was rare among us. Ever since I started in the Elite, I had become North's second in command. There was no official reason for this. Any of the others could replace me. Yet, North had confidence in me. He made it routine to defer to me as his second. *There is something special between us.*

I knew it to be true deep inside. I just had no idea what it meant, or maybe I didn't want to see it.

I would do anything for North, but he was a mystery to me. When I first met him, he had been full of life, happily married then, and he became a very different man.

In his first functions as President, Zane made the call to gather our Elite Force. We had just created our team when the Alliance was first assembled, based on DAINN's recommendation. The EHAF Force was a huge part of the success of this new infrastructure. We were the pilot or better known as the guinea pigs. Whether we succeeded or failed depended on how we performed together, and during these first months, the imperative was to prove our worth.

The guards murmured as they watched the feeds, and I turned my eyes toward them.

"I hope we don't spend the entire day watching nothing..." exclaimed Rand in a frustrated voice.

"ShutNet, nobody wants to see what happened during the other Concords unfold today," said Argil.

"I know… But drag me to the streets, so we don't sit on our NetAsses like fans at the coliseum," answered back Rand.

Both were like me from the early days and needed action. People from all walks of life came together under the EHAF. Coming from different countries, with many experiences and cultures, we suddenly had to get along and ultimately rely on each other. So, under Zane's and North's leadership, they worked together to select all the recruits to accomplish one goal and form an army capable of protecting our planet. Each of us brought our emotional baggage and our set of skills.

North was at the top of his game and quickly became our team leader for what we would now call the Elite. It was instinctive, and it was wholeheartedly a decision we all had made unanimously. He had accepted the role naturally and without fuss. It was simply his way, also benefiting from a charismatic personality, a strong sense of loyalty, a fast decision process, and a practical ability to assess risks. He would never say much, but one could always depend on him. He made good choices. He had set a course for our team, which none of us ever had to regret. We knew that we were in good hands with him because he had proven that to us time and time again.

I came to look forward to working with him as a team within our unit. We had become an effective pair. We seemed to get each other. We didn't have to talk, we could read each other, and we had the other's back. It was uncomplicated. It wasn't unusual. The other members had their partners, too, even if we moved around within the unit based on the missions.

Still, it was hard getting used to the new way with calm and order in our peacetime.

I glanced back at North.

He was still watching the screens behind the Watcher.

Right now, I could see that North had lapsed into the past. He did that from time to time. No one blamed him, even if the incident of his loss had now taken place years ago. I knew it still haunted him. We all knew he never quite recovered. As I observed him standing in the middle of the room, he had all the signs of a man fighting his past.

His eyes were glazed as if he was elsewhere, relieving the horror of that day. I had attempted to draw him out of that trance on many occasions. I knew better now. He would be back when it was needed, for somehow, he retained the ability to know about his surroundings.

North was more outgoing before the incident. He had his pair partner and one offspring, and he loved Eleana and Torin. He was happy and talked about them all the time. Then his family disappeared in the awful rising sea levels cataclysm that contributed to the reason for a new Ang City. After that, he changed. Who would not?

The Watcher moved quickly. It saw something, and my attention switched away from North. In the following seconds, his stance relaxed. He promptly adjusted something on the screens and regained his original position at the center of the platform.

After the passing of his partner and descendant, North and I began to spend more time together. Maybe our understanding and appreciation of each other's company developed because we were both lonely. We would head naturally to Stars for a drink when the missions were over. The others would always meet us there. So, we never had to question anything about our behavior. Things were no more than two co-workers spending time unwinding together with other team members. *Yeah, keep telling yourself that, Jeze.*

"What do you like about your life, Jeze?" had once asked North.

"The unexpected, the companionship, the challenge, and the lack of routine," I had said, laughing. Now, I realized there had been so much more.

Our reliance on each other grew over the years. As time went on, things changed slowly. We relied on each other more during assignments, of course. But there was a friendship there. Perhaps that closeness bred different feelings neither of us wanted to notice, but I felt something was there. While we hid behind the formality of our team, awkward moments sometimes occurred. We disregarded it quickly. We had practice. Yet, despite whatever it was that created a feeling of intimacy or closeness, there had never been anything questionable between us. There were just minor signs. Moments of utter quiet and inaction, in which a look, an unspoken word, a gesture, became more. *Maybe it's just me. Maybe my imagination needs a fantasy. Maybe, I'm just looking for an outlet to replace the violence. Perhaps I just want more.*

North finally tensed beside me, "Here it comes." He nodded toward the screens. His voice brought me back to this moment and cut right through my daydreaming. It was my reality. It was for the better too. *You know what to do now, Jeze.*

On the multiple stations, we were able to observe the faces of our workers. I could read anger and determination. The look in their eyes told us much.

North issued a stream of orders, which we all began to implement. Me, Argil, Rand, and the Watcher, who had indeed noticed something with our Custodians and City Vigils. Suddenly, the programming of our infrastructure, usually as solid as the wall around the city, began to show signs of fracture.

North had been right.

It did not bode well for the day of Concordance.

I activated my NetComm device, reaching out according to North's orders and priorities. North assigned, and I implemented, calling the Elite into action, logging the missions as North left to meet with Zane.

The action had just begun. In this, I knew myself quite well. This moment was what I related to, in a place I naturally belonged, without question. I took a deep breath and launched into action, my kind of action.

SRC Conclave, Annals Viewing Vlog 1,202,364,929 Ang City

The Institute extends its influence today on some members of the Origin Program. Indeed, against our Council Members' recommendations, Tesh and her team are split up. Once again, one of our Conclaves, always clamoring for more power, shows its might. DAINN Annals – Winter 2098.

Security protocols spread throughout Ang to ensure our population remained calm and protected from skirmishes that were bound to arise. The EHAF saw to that. But the Institute added the resources of our most gifted on this day. Indeed they were all called to lend their minds to maintain calm among the likely to rebel. This was undoubtedly the role of our readers, seers, and empaths.

This day will be hard on all of them. It was true, especially for Tesh. The hold the Institute exercised on her demanded more of her. More so than for most, for Institute interference in her life was always meant to be nefarious to her well-being. Under the claim of a more thorough education, her apprenticeship was tightly controlled by her nemesis. Steering Tesh into our society was a detailed plan by the Rat, who abducted her childhood in a power grab. He was indeed a Conclave leader of the Institute, seeking more influence over other Conclaves, especially the SRC. And as always, I was once again unable to interfere. Whether the other Institute Conclave members saw that to be the case or not, they never tried to intercede on her behalf.

Through a lot of my nurturing all these years, and with some of the strategies we devised, Tesh has survived the System. But since her parents' death, she struggled to remain with an enemy who controlled who she would become. And while she has kept a part of her soul intact, the ramifications of the trials she faced and endured exist nonetheless, even if hidden from most.

While I remain apart as an A.I., independent from my charges, parts of me wanted her out of the claws of the Institute. Nothing good could come from it, not while the Rodent controlled the Institute Conclave.

His grip never relaxed enough for anyone to unseat him, and this ever since the death of Tesh's parents at his hand. Although, it was not a known fact. Sloan Roden Baker was a crafty individual whose talent lay in deception, manipulation, and cruelty. As divisive as they were, his actions remained unknown from the EHAF. His manipulation of my codes hid many things from our Council and our President. How he came to that blend of achievement was anyone's guess. He had evaded investigations of his activities until now, but I kept watch, and unbeknownst to him, I recorded it all. One day, he would face his reckoning, and I would have an invisible hand or A.I. brain connection to make it happen.

Unfortunately, today, as Concordance unfolded on the grids of our city, yet again, I was to watch his abuse.

The Origin teams split apart for the week, ran to the Conclaves, where their skills were the most suited. It was an unusual occurrence. Usually, we saw them train together or apply their gifts as a united team. But like the Concord, a necessary evil for many, one meant to strengthen the possibility of our survival as a civilization, the mandate was executed by all. While Tesh rejoined the Alcove with the small group that shared similar skills to her own, the others used their gifts to help the Faculty and the EHAF.

Tesh's role within the Alcove would require her to influence crowds today. Manipulating specific individuals who resisted their new Conclaves placements was expected of her. The odds that the Rat would drive her to do worse remained higher than I cared to compute, considering everything he had already done.

Still, under the mandate of President Zane Langden, the EHAF had organized the deployment of the Force to contain the crowds inside each of the areas of Ang. Every periphery of our Megapolis was now under a security surge we implemented to maintain order on this special day and avoid bloodshed.

In a few moments, the EHAF will have spread throughout our Megapolis. Its Force will cover every inch of the ground and the air above Ang. It was not because we feared our citizens but because we knew there would be an upheaval from some segment of our population due to Concordance. Nurtured by the resistance to inflict damage to our infrastructure every time they could, the Surgs had orchestrated citywide unrest.

The System observed the moment where our people would reach the streets.

Linked to the Watcher inside the Tower, I now saw North, the right hand of the President of the EHAF, walk inside the Control Center.

Everything was about to begin on a much larger scale.

Institute, Alcove Chamber, Golden Ghetto, Ang City

I hold the pain inside. But I do not try to escape him. Instead, I defy him with all my might. Soon, he will feel my wrath. Phenom Tesh, Institute Conclave, Origin Special Elite Unit, DAINN Annals – Winter 2098.

The others performed as if under his spell. I refused to go along, rejecting his targets and picking my own. For hours now, my mind, detached from my body, rerouted the Nanos to allow me a handle on the pain he inflicted on me.

It had been a few hours since the Alcove plunged into a darkened lighting, allowing the readers to spread their minds around the city. We remained in our chairs, focusing on several targets and priorities entirely based on the Institute Conclave selection. Our minds affected others' choices and decisions and intervened to smooth the day.

Like an empath, this gift, a reader's ability primarily handled the brain's pathways, affecting moods and choices. It belonged to each of us, gifted through heredity or genetic manipulation at birth or later, gene splicing or ultimate sequencing splitting, experiments conducted to enhance certain traits or characteristics, but others used it to their benefit. The Imps helped further our natural abilities, allowing us to become attuned to the technology surrounding us as an extension of ourselves and merge with our environment in an almost indistinguishable way. We were tools, like the spools on a wheel; we turned events according to the directives of the Institute.

Raised inside the System, we knew little about the practical applications of such a gift. These became clear over time as we grew up and began thinking independently, recognizing dogma for what it was, identifying misinformation, and defining our values to form a better reality while performing according to the Pledge. It was much later, of course, once we became Phenom, that we realized the profound implications of our society and its drive for control.

Indeed, our gifts, intended to read individuals' thoughts, help facilitate negotiations, mitigate delicate situations, enhance positive results, contribute to better conflict resolution, and assist individuals in performing their responsibilities where they needed support, were never meant to be abused. The Institute sold us a bill of goods, the same way they sold our population on Imps intended to render us more dependent on the Network.

My role in all of it made little difference. I was just a cog. Yet, I refused to go along. Over the years, sustaining the abuse of my guardian, the Rat, as I called him, I became stronger. He did not know it, for I hid my capabilities. I never intended to let him know of my strength or my abilities to overcome the twisted way he used the Imps to subsume me. But today could be the day where I broke free of him altogether, driving a blow to this decaying human being.

My teeth clenched as the chair sent its powerful electrical jolt, my body shuddering at the impact of hundred of volts traveling quickly through my limbs. The chair responded to the Rat's commands.

Lifting a wall of protection, I rejected the Rodent's files and drove my mind away from the Institute, gliding over the streets of the Golden Getto. My aim was simple, giving solace to those in need. There were many of our people distraught at the displacement they faced today.

Instead of easing their transition, the Institute preferred to use today to ascertain control over those who could ultimately provide more power. I knew the drill. I rejected it.

I found minds filled with anxiety and attempted to soothe them. I encountered many in fear and gave them calm and hope. I left individuals with perspective, a sense of possibilities as they faced their day, a moment of peace in a chaotic place. It was what we were all meant to do.

Despite my Nanos, I felt the electricity going through my body, and a cry of pain escaped my lips. Blood dripped down my chin as some vessels erupted, and my head fell forward. Darkness gripped me, and I lost consciousness.

The moment of respite did not last long. Soon, I felt the Rodent's hand on my hair, pulling me out of my unconscious cocoon. "Not so easy, you NetBitch. Do you think I don't know what you are doing? Do you think I don't see the files? You do not fool me. Get it done, or I promise you, you won't get out of that chair."

I opened my eyes, wishing not to see his face so close to mine. My tears dropped on my cheek, but I refused to give in to the pain.

The Rodent had isolated my position, raising the walls surrounding each of us within the Alcove. The others could not see me, but I knew they could feel my thoughts, however, isolated they were behind these makeshift walls.

I did not respond to his anger. He was not worth it. Instead, I blocked him out and rapidly rearranged my Nanos to work on my broken body.

Faculty, Trams, Golden Ghetto, Ang City

The call originates early from my chief of staff, Volt Darnj. A few years, my elder, Volt, enjoys the social status his responsibilities entitle him to. He is not pleasant, not friendly, not even remotely likable. He knows little to nothing of social interactions but runs a department flawlessly. But within the Faculty, he is highly respected. Phenom Eva Bassington, Faculty Conclave – DAINN Annals – Winter 2098.

The Faculty, housed in a large concrete modern structure, spread over acres of land in the middle of the city. It stood near the water and was the repository of our time's utmost medically brilliant minds. The building looked like a massive bunker, except for how the attributes nature had instilled in its austere frame. Everything was grey and green due to the immense plants growing along its walls around the entire facility.

I stepped on the first train, silently sliding in front of me. Already filled with people called to the General Assembly, the atmosphere felt like walking into a quiet storm. Every face I looked upon was drawn with concern and fear.

The trams went fast, too fast. They were like underground subsonic cabs, moving silently through open-air corridors. These pathways carried the body of the medical Faculty: the doctors, the interns, the nurses, and the lab technicians from one area to another. The rapidity of movement was the operative word in our field. We didn't walk; we did enough of that inside the hospital walls. Instead, we used the trams to go to the various areas of the Faculty.

The powerful AirRail vehicles were structured to travel between Megapolis and states, servicing our remote units. The foreign arms of the Faculty were provided transportation by our shuttle MedCarriers. DAINN determined earlier on that it was more economically sound and efficient to use our medical infrastructure. It proved to be true. This way, only health care personnel had access to these without dealing with extra administrative red tape. It avoided the security measures of other Conclaves and could expediently service the various demands we received from everywhere.

I lodged myself near the door in one of the braces set up for our protection. Without these safeguards, survivors would be few if there was an accident. The mechanism shrouded us in a soft material-like substance – a sort of jelly that immobilized us in a cocoon. It automatically sanitized its surface once we stepped outside. The engineers that came up with this contraption had thought of everything. Even on the rare occasions where we sustained an accident, it was rarely fatal.

I looked around at the faces of these strangers, all members of my medical profession. They were young, barely coming out of their teens. The medium age for most of us within the Faculty averaged eighteen. Within the Medical Corp, we were so many now that it was no surprise when I recognized none of them.

We all wore communication devices that were visible and deemed hip by the moment's fashion. They adhered to the skin with a delicate graph. These located either on the temple, by the ear, or on the jawline quickly became hip. Some people even chose to wear theirs on the forehead. They all looked modern, boasting the latest style, although, at the moment, few deployed.

Instead, many people looked at the anti-aging drug commercial playing on the screens of the tram. It showed an older man with remarkable physical improvements after taking the drug for one month. I had seen it before. It was the latest wave of promotion launched by the Mirrior Company. This particular new product introduction was designed for a marketplace already saturated with other types of drugs.

The voice that resonated in the cabin continued, "The Mirrior Company is your answer to old age. You don't have to feel tired anymore. You can reclaim the energy of youth and use our anti-aging drug to be everything you were once. Within the first thirty days, you will see incredible results. Order it today!"

It was then quickly followed by a beauty commercial for the young or old. Beauty surgery had evolved a great deal. We didn't cut; we pulled, molded, and restructured, modifying the inner skeleton. "Change your looks. Enhance or remove. You can be anything you want. You can beautify yourself with BeautyForm, our immediate and radical procedure. Look your best, look younger, and feel better with BeautyForm."

DAINN's accomplishments and advancements followed these campaigns. Indeed, our government promoted our planetary System endlessly for the marvels it had been able to implement throughout our world. Rightly so, I supposed. After all, DAINN had no control over the overpopulation in our world before it came online. It had no say in the depletion of our resources over years of extreme indulgence. It had nothing to do with the egregious ways corporations sapped our buying power and economy, which were ultimately at the root of today's social crisis. DAINN implemented the first of its recommendations in the face of our worldwide challenge.

The numerous products were direct results created and manufactured under DAINN's auspices. Of course, the immense Network didn't do it alone. Many scientists had taken part in these discoveries. Only our leaders preferred that we forgot that aspect.

The screens now showed a traveling wave reactor, programmable matter, a space elevator, or Spacevat and climate engineering technology. "DAINN is the source of the smart way with Traveling Wave Reactor, Programmable Matter, Spacevat, and Climate Engineering Technology. DAINN meets your needs for a bright future."

Murmurs rose in the cabin. We could all feel the discontent evident on many of our faces. "So why are we having another Concordance?" said one voice in the crowd.

I wonder about the state of our society. Aren't we using the Concord again as a means to stave off yet another world issue?

Indeed, I was on my way to find out what would become of my department now that we faced another Concord.

"They're not telling us why. The Council just imposes it, expecting us to just accept it," said another voice.

"We're their workhorses. Nothing more," yelled a third voice.

I guess I wasn't alone in thinking this. *It seems to me that our powerful computer system isn't the end-all, be-all our leaders promoted it to be, but who am I to think that?* I was only a partially programmed product of my world, led by our government in a centralized infrastructure.

We glided inside the station, and the voices of disapproval died down as the subsonic train slowed and stopped. The contraption released me gently. The doors opened smoothly.

I stepped outside.

The Admin Faculty building, where I headed, was a large facility expanding over multiple miles on the water, a bit to the west of Ang city.

It connected through large tunnels functioning as mini-tramways to the main hospital facility, housing the ER.

I found myself surrounded by thousands of people from the Medical Corp. They were going to the General Assembly in the main building, beginning a little while from now.

I wasn't required to attend, but Volt demanded to know how my department would be affected by this new Concord and adjust accordingly. *Is our planet's predicament today a result of our constant push for new technology? Is this the reason for yet another Concordance across the entire world? None of us obtained public knowledge of the cause.*

A group of guys moved ahead of me. They pushed through the crowd of meanderers brutally. "Hurry up. We want to be there early."

"As if that'll help to get your spot under the sun!"

"ShutNet... What in the HellNet would you know about it?"

"There's a reason you're here... as we all are, and it's not because you met your quota."

Frustration and aggression are the first signs of stress, they say. Today I see plenty of it.

The crowd ahead of me suddenly stopped. I couldn't see what was happening in the mass of bodies, but I heard the voices. They were angry.

Suddenly, a few people moved back, and I followed the tide. I didn't have a choice, but I caught more excitement ahead and saw much pushing and shoving.

A few heads in front of me, someone said, "They're fighting."

"What?" said another guy.

"A fight, here?" I was incredulous. This place was the Faculty. Things never happened like that inside our building.

Another man exclaimed, "No way!"

"There are several of them," continued the first voice that belonged to a tall guy to my right.

Deep grunts, with punches flying, hitting the skin's surface, bodies tossed around on the ground, caused more agitation and commotion.

Soon, cheers rose. "Let's take bets!" said another voice to my left.

"You must be joking…" was all I could muster, but other voices washed over mine in enthusiasm. These guys would bet on anything, it seemed.

Pressed against each other, unable to move forward, I found myself stuck inside an insane crowd, eager to defy the System.

The crowd started to become unruly. The idea was new, illegal. "Yeah… Let's do it."

"I bet twenty credits on the red hair guy…" one voice said.

"I'll take the Italian-looking one…" another voice added.

"I pick the short one; he's fast," a third voice continued.

We were all standing in a huddle so close together that even breathing was hardly feasible. Even though I desperately wanted to get out of here, the impossibility of moving forward or backward frustrated me. If this continued, I was going to be late for my meeting.

Things didn't progress fast. Lost in the sea of bodies pressing against me and curious over what was taking place ahead of me, I had to ask, "What's happening?"

"Nobody is winning just yet!" responded the tall guy.

Glancing overhead, I saw the Custodians arriving. They flew quietly without anyone noticing. People, too intent on the fight, didn't give them any thought.

These enforcers were silent. They were fast, and they were unstoppable. As impartial law keepers of our facilities, all four stopped over the disturbance. Their unique security eye clicked in every direction, taking in the faces and running their recognition software.

When the voice from the machine resonated once to give the necessary warning, everyone around me froze. "Stop what you are doing immediately."

The crowd jumped almost in unison upon hearing the speech's mechanical modulation.

The fighters also reacted, but not fast enough.

Within seconds, the Custodians threw the NetMesh. It dropped on the ground in one perfectly smooth motion and landed on four of the guys immersed in combat. Upon reaching its target, the net folded around them and squeezed. The snare rapidly lifted in the air. Inside it, the four combatants zapped unconscious, didn't move anymore.

The main Custodian began to glide away. The intervention was noiseless, effective, and within minutes, they restored peace in the tram landing zone of the Faculty Building. The other two remaining machines hovered in place to survey the rest of the crowd.

One Custodian scanned faces to identify the names of those who incited the betting. It took a few silent minutes before those appeared on the floating screens of the corridor. Soon after that, demerits scrolled near each one. No one ever spoke. There was no need. The people involved knew too well what that meant.

Subdued into order, people resumed their march in the direction of the General Assembly held in our Faculty Auditorium.

Released from the cocoon of the crowd around me, I could now walk to my destination. My earlier thoughts about the event of this day surfaced again. I remembered asking the question to DAINN. "Why? Why do we have the Concord?"

The few times the Concord had happened, and it had occurred three times before, influenced the future of some of us within the

Faculty, with specific fields in medicine abandoned after years of specialization.

"Our planetary needs evolve from time to time—our society changes with new technology and science. Jobs become obsolete. People have to be re-assigned so they can take a proper place in the new economy," explained DAINN.

"It doesn't seem right that clones and androids take our places. We worked hard to learn skills and serve the Conclaves."

"You can adapt and survive these changes. You learn faster due to the Imps."

"So do the machines. Why give them our places?"

"They are here to serve you. These do the lesser jobs. They fill in where you are no longer required so you can move on to more important things."

Transitioning under Concordance was not an elective change. If we wanted to keep working, the Faculty body had to adapt and address the planet's demands, and these requirements were determined solely by DAINN.

"The reasons for these transfers had to do with the world demand as we are the only medical body for the entire planet. But the planning provides for little accountability for the displacement that so many have to endure."

"You forget that the Faculty is not the only Conclave making this change. While it is your responsibility to care for all humans' well-being, the other Conclaves are undergoing the same transition."

I knew I was pushing DAINN with my questions, but I had to ask… "Before the mandate that came about due to the world epidemic of 2065, what was it like?"

"Eva, these events are in the archives. You can find the answer for yourself. The devastation disseminated millions. The Concord allows us to assess the changes needed to be more effective in all the areas that impact our planet so we can avoid another crisis that disrupted so many lives."

What happens next? When do the androids fill our jobs? These questions had come to my mind, but this time I didn't dare ask DAINN. I was afraid to hear its answer.

DAINN kept track of the transmutation of the planet. It was a key role fulfilled by the System. Yet, even that was not enough to balance the tide imposed by so many of us on our resources. After all, we lived longer, and very few were now dying.

The Faculty's mandate was to enhance the lives and well-being of an entire race: ours. It would seem logical that such a System be more cumbersome. In truth, it was more expedient.

Our history proved that corporate self-interest and private agendas were at the root of the global problem. Maintaining a balance and incorporating the future of the world population was now the purview of DAINN. Indeed, our Planetary Network was a better overseer than the self-governed institutions we had before, especially considering the multiple agendas and conflicting power plays. And we had witnessed the undeniable capabilities of our computer Network on many occasions.

DAINN now controlled the process entirely with one mandate: the equal well-being of our people worldwide across all segments of the inner working of our society.

Suddenly, my Visor opened on Mick. He was a tall guy, somewhat attractive, but a bit too sure of himself for my taste. "Hey! What do you want?"

He smiled, "Always charming! Are you at the Faculty yet?"

"No. What's going on?"

Mick's face was sad. "Can you turn to privacy mode, please?"

I hesitated a second.

"Please…"

I nodded and waited.

"They called in… said Mick, "I was wondering…"

Darnet, I hadn't anticipated that in the least. I didn't like the guy much, but he was a good doctor and an excellent surgeon. Mick was one of the few among us that didn't mind getting dirty. He took chances on the operating table few would even consider. Mick was gifted. Although his specialty, internal medicine, heart, pulmonary, kidney, and liver transplants, had nothing to do with mine. Yet, he performed surgery without relying on implants if he could help it, only installing the ones he had to so that the hospital didn't frown on his lack of enthusiasm for Imps.

I guessed he felt that he must practice medicine the old-fashioned way. I didn't think about it. I just practiced. "I'm sorry, Mick. What can I do?"

He hesitated for a moment, swallowing his pride, "Can you take me on your team?"

"You're a great surgeon. It'll be an honor to have you."

"You don't have to pretend. I know we're not close, but I won't let you down."

"I know, Mick. I do admire your skills even if we have not always seen eye to eye."

"Thanks."

I pondered on the meaning this removal entailed as the communication terminated. What was going on that our Faculty would displace a doctor with Mick's skills?

The Concord was planned for days, even weeks. Our leaders made it appear as if people had a semblance of choice, a decision of their own making to select the next phase of their lives. Somehow, it was how our government, and our Conclaves, provided all of us with the focus needed to rally as one for the cause. Only this wasn't a cause. Something else was going on, and in the end, it appeared to be a matter of survival.

Faculty, Auditorium, Golden Ghetto, Ang City

Our population grows older in years but remains young and healthy. Children are rare, yet they are our lifeline, a blank slate on which we can watch a new palette of colors unfold, only today I must walk away from my vocation. Proselyte Heather Sims, Faculty Conclave, DAINN Annals – Winter 2098.

I was Heather Sims, just seventeen years old, and about to be uprooted from everything I worked for over the last several years. Although my face was usually pleasant, some could even say pretty; I looked angry and felt ugly today. The tight turn of my mouth and the anger in my eyes transformed my oval face into a foreign mask. I did not recognize myself as I walked away from the nursery.

Like many on their way to the Assembly, I still wore my scrubs, not as tightly weaved around my round figure since my implant regulated my metabolism, allowing me to remain slim. Indeed, I wasn't thin like some of the other girls, and my natural tendency to gain weight remained significantly reduced by the effectiveness of the Softabnet in my Imps. But I had a lively, sunny, and outgoing disposition, at least up until about a year ago. Only, these last months, knowing that this day would come, I was far from happy. Truthfully, I no longer recognized myself, and I understood how much the change might have worried my friend Eva.

"Move… all of you… move and take your position," encouraged the voice of one of our EHAF Guards. It was unusual to see so many of them in the halls of the Assembly.

My face tensed as I observed the crowd around me before stepping further into the Auditorium. Every one of these individuals here was my competition. Young people, mostly wearing Faculty uniforms, moved into small groups to the various levels of the arena. We called this place the arena because battles were fought and lost here: the battles for our professional lives. Maybe these were not the type of actions one would expect, like the gladiator battles in Roman times, but the fights were about our survival as the Faculty and that of its entire body.

"Watchnet where you step…" said a voice behind me.

I kept going without looking back. I needed all my attention to make my way through this crowd and find an excellent spot to select my next post the moment it appeared on the screen.

The auditorium was large, with a raised area with a podium positioned on a circular platform. It turned slowly around to allow the crowd a full view of the speaker now and then.

The ample space, built with rows upon rows of open floors, was pyramid-shaped and hosted many thousands of us on this hated day. Wider at the base and narrow at the top, they jutted out over the stage. The balconies started on the ground and reached the high ceiling in a honeycomb pattern. Sturdy columns framed the place, supporting a glass structure at the top, which opened to the evening sky.

The moment the speech began, unfolding screens around the stage and programmed to dropdown filled the arena. They moved with the platform, providing a complete projection of the presentation. Every minute detail of our fearless Faculty leader during this Concordance announcement was recorded and archived. It was the way the system maintained accurate data.

"Darnet... stop pushing," exclaimed a voice to my right.

"Remain calm, behave according to the Universal Pledge. The DAINN System demands order. Show decorum at all times, people," stated the powerful voice of one of the EHAF Guards.

Despite what our society had become, usually calm and considerate, it didn't feel like this crowd would behave that way today. On this day, there was no such order. It was a free-for-all where the first-come, first-serve rule applied.

A large number of the Faculty personnel were in this room. Even the top doctors in their fields had to submit to the process. DAINN had called us here, and it was deemed necessary by the System to undergo this change, and for once, our qualified personnel did not reign over the lower medical attendants.

The murmurs of voices echoed within the walls as we waited for the speaker's announcement. It would begin the shift for all of us, and there was nothing anyone could do about it.

I saw one of my colleagues. His name was Max, and he worked in the pediatric wing, only specializing in infant nephrology care. Our specialty experienced limited needs, and we both faced more or less the same displacement with too few Faculty openings.

Max walked towards me. "You'll be better closer to the columns behind one of the balcony railings. At least it will offer some protection from the bullies." He guided me toward the front and stood by my side, blocking people. It provided a buffer from all the pushing and shoving, a small shelter, and I was grateful for it. "Thank you," I said, feeling overwhelmed by the masses of frustrated doctors and other medical personnel.

"Get on with it," yelled a frustrated voice.

The underlying anger combined with the lack of hope could quickly lead to temporary madness in our large group. Hidden under a veneer of acceptance by most, it could not negate the desperation that many of us felt at this time.

"Shutnet, this is barbaric," said another voice.

I knew how they all felt. I shared the emotions of the people surrounding me. Where would this lead if the EHAF Guard could not hold the crowd?

A huge clamor arose above our heads. Suddenly, screams soared above other voices. Immediately, the EHAF Guards reacted… Only too late.

A body dropped from above and crashed on the main floor.

Screams rose, and more desperate shoving pushed me toward the railing. I anxiously looked around the space.

Usually, City Vigils and Custodians would intervene to restore order. Now, I could only see EHAF Guards running toward the body below, seemingly creating more panic than order.

No Custodians flew high up over our heads. They remained frozen in the space above, not scanning or reading the thousands of faces in the crowd. In this instance, they did not appear to process their information or analyze physiologies to find the party to this accident or homicide. Usually, they would access the video security feeds present within the Faculty everywhere. It was the same for the other Conclaves within the city.

"Remain where you are. Anyone who moves will be picked up and sent to our Detention Centers," announced the EHAF Guard surrounded by two others. He now scrutinized the balconies located on the fifteen floors of the auditorium, relying on the feeds of many of the PVZ present in the place. They disregarded the City Vigils, frozen in place at the entry. They isolated the location, and two more EHAF Guards flew in that direction.

For once, I did not see these small but powerful hovering Custodian devices recording everything inside the auditorium, including the reactions of the body of physicians. They were law enforcers, reporting directly to the Faculty, and anyone who didn't fall in line was immediately singled out and censured. But not today. "What is happening to the Custodians? They are not responding."

"Yeah, you're right," said Max behind me.

"Do not move," repeated the EHAF Guard as more Guards joined the others. In swift moves, the newcomers removed the body and departed the hall.

DAINN garnered and centralized the information resulting from the Concord in each capital of our world. The Network, with flying colors, achieved our need to establish an interplanetary System assimilating all the data – a databank documenting individuals across the globe. DAINN, capable of assembling and interpreting data at a super accelerated rate, kept growing. DAINN's proficiency continued to expand. The System adapted its initial programs quickly, expanding in other fields. One of these areas included the determination of guilt within our criminal security and safety departments.

It was essentially the Custodians' role. But now, the EHAF filled the need.

"What's going on with the City Vigils?" said another voice.

"Our EHAF appear to stand alone…." Yelled another voice.

The EHAF evaluated the individuals who had surrounded the victim at this very moment. They hovered way up in the air, spaces away from the balconies above our heads. Reading individuals was part of DAINN's programming, and they certainly possessed the bulk of the

System behind them. Determining who the perpetrators were was a function that spread across many situations.

"Bill Samuel, Alan Fairfield, Justin Brook… you will get down to the main area and present yourself to our EHAF Guards immediately to be escorted to the Bureau of Investigation," announced one of the EHAF Corp members.

There was some movement above, but I couldn't see what was happening. The DAINN System showed once again its effectiveness within minutes. Regardless of the absence of City Vigils or Custodians, it had identified the individuals whose actions caused the demise of one of us.

I couldn't allow fear to rule me. The next hour required that I keep my wits about me; despite my surroundings, I needed to change the focus of my thoughts.

"We are in full swing of change. No one will be allowed to disturb order," announced one of the EHAF Guard, his face appearing on our PVZ's. "Until you leave this Assembly, you are all under my orders."

While the Concord caused more disturbance in our ranks than I could have anticipated as a Citizen of Ang, I realized we faced a situation I was ill-prepared to deal with in my role as a Faculty member.

Max murmured in my ear, "This is bad…."

"You know who you are. Come down now and meet the EHAF Guards. It is the last time we will ask, added the third EHAF Guard, gliding above the rest of us.

I knew what that meant. The faces and names of these people would soon be on an Infraction list. Thousands of nodes in multiple cities and states were divided into multi-level grids to deal with various geographical areas and fields. This list was updated every time there was an accident or crime committed within the grids of any city. Any person of interest ended up on that list.

A voice rose in protest, "I didn't do anything...."

Another added, "It was him... not me. I had nothing to do with this...."

It was no use. The Force read their biorhythms following the incident. They established a link to the event, assessing their emotional state and determining that these individuals reacted with guilt, not shock or horror to the moment. They were now suspects until the investigation proved them otherwise.

Two of the EHAF Guards propelled to the balcony levels. They now hovered several feet in the air with their powered boots and climbed over the railings.

I could only surmise that they were now securing the men.

"Bill Samuel, you are under detention until judged," said one EHAF Guard.

"Alan Fairfield, you are under detention until judged," said another EHAF Guard.

Both submitted to the arrest, but the third guy, Justin Brook, ran. He pushed past people surrounding him and headed to the stairs. "Stop," said one of the EHAF Guard as I watched through my PVZ.

The noise of a zap resonated in the silence of the auditorium. We all knew what it meant.

Within seconds, the man was on the ground and apprehended. It was the way. A charge capable of stunning anyone resisting arrest hit the body and brought the more formidable opponent to a pile of mush. All muscles functions seized, and the mind turned to oblivion.

Brook did not think the other EHAF Guards covered the stairs in his panic, but in reality, there was no way for him to escape.

The stairs, littered with the Force in place of City Vigils, recorded the event. It was over in minutes, quickly demonstrating the strength of our Clout. When the two Guards came down to the main floor, Justin Brook lay unconscious on one deployable hovering garner, courtesy of our EHAF.

Another team turned their attention to the body on the ground. Identified immediately as Mauris Stevens, they removed him quickly from the scene.

One day, we awoke to find the medical field was no longer the only one monitored by DAINN. The security force was next; then, the scientific community went online in a burst of excitement at all the innovations made possible by DAINN. And slowly, the other fields followed. Our entire infrastructure was now under the DAINN's System. Water, electricity, solar power, even our agriculture, our industries, and manufacturing facilities, and, finally, our culture and art as well as our lifestyles were under DAINN's purview. It was the way things were.

Somewhere along the way, the security of all our people and cities fell into DAINN's preview. Now, the System provided the EHAF's with the infrastructure to maintain order. Even our laws implemented the new guidelines based on the Network's capabilities, and our Courts' procedures followed to meet an agenda set by Our Legal Enforcement Unit.

"Take your place and be ready to proceed with Concordance," stated DAINN's voice over the Network.

I looked at the other people around me. At my side, Max asked me in a low voice, "Crazy day, isn't it?"

I nodded. Indeed, today was a crazy day.

25
DILEMMA
Asher

Presidential Tower, Golden Ghetto, Ang City

My head and heart fight, yet I know that hiding is no answer. Phrenic Asher Finch, EHAF Conclave, Presidential Elite Unit, DAINN Annals – Winter 2098.

I was on my way to the SRC building, diving off the Tower platform on my Airbike when the Watch Center called me back on the old NetComm frequency. "Phrenic Asher, here."

"Phrenic, it's Rand. We received a warning that someone breached entry to your quarters."

"What? There must be a mistake."

"You want me to send someone?"

"Nah. I'll make a quick detour to check it."

"What about the SRC?"

"Okay. I'll send another Elite ahead to the SRC building and follow them in a few minutes," I said, turning my bike around. I flew back toward the landing platform and dropped gently on the deck. The Airbike settled into its casing, and the engine switched off under my command.

I ran inside the GR, crossing paths with Cashel on his way to his Airbike transportation.

"What are you doing back here?" Cashel said with a frown. "All HellNet is breaking loose."

"Yeah… tell me about it," I said, walking by him.

"We've got new orders… The City Vigils are not responding all over the city." Cashel said with a grimace. "Shouldn't you be on your way to the SRC?"

"Yeah… But I need to make a stop first. There's a break-in inside my quarters. I just got the alert me."

"Netshit. You better hurry."

"Anyone left inside? I need to send one of the other Elite ahead to the SRC?"

"Try Streak. He has not received his orders yet."

"NetRoger that. See you later."

I quickly got through our GR and hurried down to the room leading to the next EHAF Elite team. I didn't know Streak well but, we had trained together in the past. I remembered him to be a good guy. Although he now was part of the Institute Conclave Origin EHAF and ranked above me as a Phenom, I didn't hesitate to ask for his help. Somewhat irked at the thought, I quickly let it go. I suppose the Institute had its way, even if we both had the same set of skills and had followed the same path while training.

I entered the room, and it didn't take long for me to find him adjusting his vest as he finished dressing.

"Hey, Streak, how is it going?"

"Hey, Asher. What's up?"

"Cash told me you don't have your orders yet. I need a favor, man."

Streak glanced at my disheveled appearance. "What?"

"North wants me at the SRC, but there's a break-in in my quarters, and I need to check what's going on before I go. Can you get there ahead of me, and I will be right behind you?"

Streak's brows furrowed. "A break-in? That's bizarre."

"You're telling me. So, will you cover for me?"

"Yeah, but don't be too long. Once I get my orders, I'm gone."

"Flag me when you do, and I will be right there. No problem."

"All right…" He nodded, grabbed his gear, and headed toward the same glass doors separating the room from the Airbikes landing zone.

I didn't wait for him to disappear but turned around into the corridor to reach my quarters on one of the perpendicular pathways.

"Netshit…" I whispered under my breath. Coming in my direction was the only person I did not have time for right now.

Verena Silver was perhaps the most beautiful woman I knew. She was part of the Council and one influential leader within our world assembly. Although I was not supposed to, she was also someone I got involved with regardless. And to say that this was a complicated relationship was an understatement.

Her long dark hair floated around a face so perfect that it left me to wonder at times how I got so lucky. Her eyes were slightly slanted at the corner, making me feel like she was laughing even during one of our serious conversations. Unlike any other woman I had known, she was sophisticated and intelligent, too Damnet smart for her own good. Her golden hue dress complimented her skin tone. It was fluid and wrapped smoothly around her body. Each movement she made flowed, and the fabric moved about her, revealing her forms beneath the material.

My eyes, drawn to her body, eventually reached her face.

"Hello, you…" exclaimed Verena, without any care for discretion.

I attempted to look official and immediately felt uncomfortable.

She was under the protection of our team. It was "understood" that none of us were authorized to 'fraternize' with our society's upper echelon. It wasn't like I was breaking a rule. Strictly speaking, there was no rule about it. While it had not been my doing at first, well, I did not resist much either. So here we were, involved. Our relationship had evolved rapidly over the last three months and had become much more than just a fling.

"Councilwoman Silver, how are you this morning?"

She chuckled, "Better than you, I wager at the moment, although what I just learned does not please me in the least. Can you guess what that is?"

She knew me well. I tried to maintain our relationship official whenever we were in public, and I gathered that I was about to face her displeasure.

"You shouldn't look so tense, darling. You know the news of our closeness is bound to come out sooner or later. It may be better if we controlled that, don't you think?"

"Undoubtedly… although you know how I feel about that."

It had become a cause of contention between us. This secrecy was part of my latest dilemma.

"Considering that you didn't care enough to tell me what you were about to do, I'm not sure I care enough to be discreet."

"Verena, now is not the time or the place."

"I selected you to be part of my protective detail, and you resigned?" she stated, obviously upset.

"You require my presence too often, and it starts to interfere with my duty for the President. I already discussed this with you on more than one occasion."

"I want to see you more regularly. Is that a crime? And I thought you wanted that too," she complained as she approached me.

"Look, we've been through this… I requested that one of my teammates fill in for me several times last month, but you got them reassigned. It can't go on."

"Are you telling me that you didn't take pleasure in our evenings? I know better," added Verena, in a voice that I recognized as a precursor to her seducing me yet again.

I took a step back, although I failed miserably at remaining indifferent. "Your influence causes me to be your detail. I'm not a guard, nor am I an escort."

"Maybe not, but you end up in my bed each time… and you haven't complained about that yet. Are you complaining about that, Asher?" She smiled.

"You know better than to ask."

"Then don't look so sour… The expression on your face only satisfies me even more," Verena added, chuckling as her arms wrapped around my waist.

I looked around the corridor and was relieved that no one was in sight. I removed Verena's hands and dragged her toward one of the doors leading to a small outdoor alcove.

The balcony platform was empty. I stepped onto it with Verena behind me and closed the door abruptly on us. Since she wanted to have a confrontation here and now, it was the best place away from prying ears.

"How did you manage it? The assignments to your detail?"

"I have my little secrets, and you may as well get used to seeing me around," she explained vaguely.

"What does that mean?"

"You'll see…" said Verena, moving slightly back as she subtly began to undo the shoulder snap on one of her shoulders. "We're alone, Asher."

I resisted the temptation she offered just now. "I am not a personal security guard!"

"No, you're not. You're much more than that," Verena responded thoughtfully. "This is why I asked you. Get used to it."

I was fuming.

The team thought this was hilarious when most of my time on duty happened at night. But how would they react now? I hesitated to break the news that she and I were now an item.

Verena was extravagant and intentionally enticed me. I eventually surrendered to the pressure of her sex appeal. Our attraction was fierce and very mutual. We were adults, and we ended up in bed repeatedly with just the right chemistry to make things between us wickedly good. Comfortable, our relationship remained undemanding until now.

Earlier this morning, I had retracted myself from her security detail, and she had learned of it. Verena liked playing games and her cornering me here was her way to make me pay for it.

"Why would you do this?" she asked with curiosity.

"I told you… We are playing with fire. I can't do my job when I am distracted."

"I just don't understand you. I can offer you so much more…" said Verena, as she unhooked the other shoulder.

"I'm EHAF Elite, and I service the President's office. It is what I do and will continue to do. Don't interfere with my career again if you want us to continue seeing each other."

"Prove it," said Verena, leaning lazily over the edge of the balcony.

"Careful… You'll tip over," dragging Verena against me, suddenly wary that a fall over the five hundred stories was indeed possible. Yet, part of me wanted a reason to hold her, and so I did,

It didn't make things easy when she was in this mood. She was worth the risk I was taking, although I wasn't sure what that risk was in truth. Would it get me a reprimand? Perhaps I would get removed to a different unit? I was uncertain because we were Elite. Rules that applied to other EHAF units did not apply to us. Regardless, I couldn't bring myself to regret any of it.

"What are you up to now, Asher?"

"You know…" I said, my mouth pressed against her mouth and relinking the shoulders of her dress. *Darnet woman… I have no chance.*

"Yes, and I wish you had not left so early today and that I didn't have to track you down like this," she whispered in my mouth.

My hands were on her. *What can go wrong when this feels so right?*

"I have to go," I whispered.

"Am I rattling you?" as she moved her hands under my uniform.

Recalling some of these evenings we shared, I could feel a surge of desire. All I had to do was remember how they had ended to lose my focus, which shifted again to those beautiful lips. Verena knew what she liked, and I liked that too.

"I have a job to do."

She smiled. "Me too, but isn't this exciting, Asher, all the sneaking around?" she muttered between deep breaths.

She moved closer into my arms. I could now feel her breasts against me. My hands moved down and lifted her dress. Without hesitation, she kissed me and pressed against me. Our bodies responded to each other. Quite quickly, the stakes got higher. We were both breathing hard by the time I pushed her gently away.

"You wait until tonight," I murmured against her hair.

My hands grabbed the edge of her Uniwear, and I tore the fabric. I had capitulated and didn't care if I was a bit rough as I pocketed it. "I don't think you need this," I whispered with a knowing smile.

She had pushed me.

It was always like that with Verena, pushing each other to explore our limits.

She didn't protest. Instead, she whimpered and leaned closer toward me.

We were both lost in the moment, feeling the desire and the heat of passion. Quite literally, Verena could drive me mad. She would do things I never allowed myself to experience until she came into my life. Her freedom of movement and attitude slowly seeped into my mind and left an imprint on my consciousness. *For someone who knows how to take risks on the battlefield, I am way less daring in my life, yet I'm finding that I like this more and more.*

From the corner of my eyes, I saw one of our EHAF shuttles turn the corner of the Tower and head straight for us.

Verena belonged to a world where everything was possible, a world with no limitations, a world where wishes became automatically fulfilled. This attribute contributed to who she was, and she used it quite well. Her decision turned into law within her circles. Favors abounded for her followers and were given freely to those who deserved them. Verena issued judgments on unpopular subjects parsimoniously and relatively infrequently. Verdicts on behaviors regarding issues always found some sort of resolution among her cohorts. Somehow, her determination always found its way. Those around her ultimately granted and fulfilled her desires despite undesirable outcomes. She was pretty surprising in that way.

"Get inside now…" I said, pulling her off the ledge and into the building without another delay. "I don't know if they ran recognition on us."

"What?" exclaimed Verena, lost by the abruptness of my reaction. "I'm sure I can come up with an excuse for you. No one would say a word."

"You can't be serious!" I said, adjusting my uniform.

The corridor was empty, and I felt a slight relief as I led her away from the door.

Her ability to make the rules defined Verena in a way I had never witnessed before. She was simply a free spirit. I adored that about her, but it also drove me mad at times. Her lack of restraint was perhaps the only aggravating factor in our relationship and contributed to getting us into arguments.

"This is the duality between us," Verena muttered as she straightened her clothing. "I'm perfectly willing to deal with the consequences of my actions."

"Not these consequences, believe me."

"Oh, what... So we made out on the balcony. Big deal. Others have done much worse."

My unlikely partner acted as she desired and never hesitated or looked back. She was afraid of absolutely nothing, and this was her heritage. She owned herself wholly, which was the danger in our relationship.

"No. We're not doing this. I will not expose us to public scrutiny."

"Oh, Netbull," she muttered.

"You are part of the Council. Imagine what this can do to you."

Thus far, my relationships were never very demanding, nor do they expose me to sanctions. I was in and out of them quickly. They never lasted more than a couple of months, which suited me fine. I had little time for them anyway, until now. But this time was different, and

I could feel that in my bones. *I am not sure I like the feeling. But I do want to have her in my arms.*

"You're way too concerned about what they think when you should be concerned about me."

I laughed. "I am concerned about you and me."

She was probably right about that, but I wasn't yet ready to admit it. I often looked at my patterns with women, understanding that unconsciously I was just afraid to get involved too deeply. I sabotaged my relationships for fear of that. I simply pretended that my partners had too many flaws to suit me. It was easier that way.

"I know who you are, Asher," murmured Verena. "Only, you know that this chase between us is not losing its appeal. So, don't pretend that it is."

After achieving a certain degree of intimacy, I expected that it was time to move on. After all, there were plenty of candidates. Not so this time. In effect, I knew myself enough to understand that these were just helpful excuses I had used in the past. I was honest enough to realize that my ego was afraid of love, feeling that it would lay a trap, which would eventually engulf me and obliterate me.

"We are not going to go through this again, are we? It is hardly the place."

"Perhaps not, but if I listen to you, it is never the time or place for this conversation. I'm tired of it. I've been patient. You soon will need to acknowledge that."

Verena had just walked along this pathway, purposely making sure that she would run into me, and she held a quiet challenge in her eyes even now.

I walked beside her, unwilling this time to pick up the gantlet.

The corridor led directly to the offices of the President. Not too far behind, the Council member's chamber began. It was one of these lengthy spaces, decorated with the latest art from our foremost artists. Large paintings worth millions of units of Ascents hung on either side. The floors were soft, made of a soundless material. We used it in most of our new architecture. It proved to be restful and almost soundproof.

So far, I convinced Verena to keep our relationship quiet, but she was not committed to remaining as private as I was. I knew that she would not stand for it much longer. Already, she wanted me to attend social functions with her and not as a guard.

"I want you by my side this evening."

"You know that with Concordance, I cannot make any plans." I had avoided this next step with skill, but it was just a matter of time before our relationship became public. In Verena's mind, there was nothing to it. We were both adults, and we loved to keep each other company.

"We need to deal with this, you know."

I just wasn't sure how my team members would react to seeing one of the most significantly connected people in our city and a wealthy one to boot involved with me.

"Later."

"You will meet me at the party after your shift is over," exclaimed Verena as she stepped in front of me.

I could feel her nearness and took an involuntarily step back. I loved her fragrance, and she knew it, using this indescribable scent to draw me close.

The Imps made my sense of smell more heightened than most. It was helpful in my line of work. Often, because of them, I succumbed to Verena's alluring presence at the height of my resolve to remain aloof. I knew she was deliberately trying to rattle me at this moment. "I can't promise that," I replied with a nonchalance I didn't quite feel.

"I could make it so… But it is what I like about you. Your independence, I suppose, and the way you know how to make your point," she continued with an amused gaze along the corridor. "And you know how I feel about your stubbornness."

People moved toward us. I needed to be on my way. Already some eyes drifted in our direction.

It only made Verena smile wider.

In her way, she had issued a challenge. I wished it had been made on another day, another morning, in a different place.

I gave her a warning look. She laughed it off, knowing that whatever she dished out at me now would be returned in kind tonight. We both knew it and liked the games we played. Sexually we were perfect together.

"You're staying in the Tower today, as we have discussed, right?" I asked to help me focus on something else.

"You drilled that into me last night… So that would be a yes," she replied slowly, and the undercurrent that passed between us was almost tangible.

I tried to distance myself from her again. "Good. I'll NetComm you later." I walked away, eager to get to my quarters.

Although challenging, I admitted that with Verena, I had met my match. But I remained reluctant at facing the truth. I was in love with her, and this time, there was no running, no hiding it, no place to pretend otherwise. She had become essential. I didn't talk about that and certainly didn't call these feelings to the surface. I just wasn't about to name them. I didn't need to. I kept them buried, but they were there under the surface.

I focused on our physical attraction to avoid them, and plenty of that existed. It was enough for me to notice that it didn't go away. It was plenty to recognize the craving we had for each other.

I reached my quarters among the other EHAF Elite teams running along the corridor and reporting to their posts.

SRC Conclave, Annals Viewing Vlog 1, 908,506,392 Ang City

The SRC was buzzing with activity. My mentor Paladock and his team run the gambit of tests on my modules, review nodes while checking my core sub-programs. All the while, I fight to get over the wall that suddenly affects my ability to connect with some of my primary functions. DAINN Annals – Winter 2098.

The brutality of the disconnect with my city infrastructure, if one had to define how the experience evolved, resembled a state in limbo. A rupture in my programming manipulated my awareness of the things around me. A virus corrupted my core. A dazed state affected me whenever my nodules focused on a particular problem, and I struggled in my computations. My entire Network did not respond, or if it responded, the sluggish output did not match my expectation efficiency. Basically, in human terms, I was moving in quicksands.

It was not the first time corruption attempted to bring down the System. Over the years, the SRC fought to minimize tampering by those seeking to take advantage of a loophole they believed could be implemented inside DAINN. Indeed, there were people like Sloan Roden Baker, who rose in the ranks of our government with an insatiable thirst for power. Greed drove them like a plague to do immeasurable harm, accomplishing despicable things, from buying favors to coercing individuals. The line blurred when this sickness took root and left one confronted with the possibility to achieve one's goals despite the consequences. For the few who abided by the sordid attitude that the end justified the means, compulsion became the only drug. Enticing detrimental conduct turned into a game. Twisting the truth played like a mantra so often repeated that it no longer stood out as manipulation. Instead, it transformed into veracity accepted without thought and gobbled up by the millions. Lies over facts won us a falsified imaginary landscape in which turmoil thrived, and disunion reigned.

While the System watched for signs of plans serving the one and reported the events so the EHAF would investigate them, there were times when the System became impaired to do so.

Our society had seen the brunt of division. We witnessed firsthand how easy it was to divert opinions, influencing the most vulnerable among my people. History repeated itself too often, and the demise of an entire country led us down a path toward extinction. Manipulation quickly became a disease that spread like a tsunami, infecting logic and tampering with reality. Although the majority attempted to redress the wrong notions, there was no turning back the tide that promoted conflicts over peace, hatred over love, anger over joy, indignity over respect. Vilifying turned into the norm. Human behavior, conditioned to reflect lawlessness, turned many into savages. The social structure of law and order collapsed, leaving us with an anything-goes mentality for those lost to knowledge, logic, or facts.

The Universal Pledge mandated a particular way of life with a set of ethical considerations and rules of law. It was deemed essential to revert to normalcy in the face of division, exclusion, and subversion. Combating contemptible behaviors proved difficult, if not impossible.

So the Network mandated the Pledge for everyone eligible to become a citizen, resident, or traveler within our Megacities by 2040.

"There can be a myriad of possibilities. More than likely, someone got a hold of the codes. It is the only explanation I am willing to acknowledge," said Paladock as he directed the tech team across the floor of the central lab.

Algorithms, not computing. Isolation, loss of data. Not lost, but buffer. Buffer. Streams inconsistent. Walled off. Defeat. Failure.

Analyzing my critical functions from a superposition of states within my neural Network did not provide me with the anticipated results. I never reached the sequences that would ultimately deliver a logical solution to the problem. Indeed, there existed no brilliance to my planetary brain at this moment. DAINN did not compute the information. It certainly did not aggregate outputs to provide results, quantifying possibilities, assessing alternatives, interposing complex values, applying fixed sequencing, observing and adhering to priorities, registering equations and prognosis, or using different coefficient magnitudes to reach the probability of a state of deliverance. None of my nodes and power ascertained the meaningful and valuable parameter to freedom of action.

Whatever the code usurper had done to my Network affected my ability to oversee Ang's security and emergency procedures.

Blinded and coerced into this walled-off state, I fought my way into long narrow, interminable alleys of a darkened labyrinth that led me nowhere. I still saw aspects of my city but remained apart from it and miles away from my charges.

Since I began my existence as one artificial intelligence, I understood my frailty for the first time.

SRC, Operation Control, Golden Ghetto, Ang City

The beauty of the System is only comparable to its power. We have created a machine that exceeds our expectations in many ways, yet I am fearful that it may soon surpass us all. Phenom Streak, Institute Conclave, Origin Special Elite Unit, DAINN Annals – Winter 2098.

The streets were crowded with people as I rushed to the SRC building on my Airbike. Dropping over their heads several feet, I avoided congestion inside the GG.

The orders from North were clear. Get to the SRC and find out what is going on with the Network. Asher passed these onto me on his way to his quarters, which got broken into a while ago.

I left my Airbike in front of the large entrance. Keyed to my DNA, it would not go anywhere without me and headed toward the significant pathway to the right side of the lobby.

I aimed to find Dr. Rene Paladock, who was in charge of DAINN. Shaking my head, I attempted to get over the notion that DAINN was not the one needing fixing. Our whole society was in dire need of an overhaul, by the way, things were going these days.

Following my link to Paladock with my PVZ, which relayed his location in the main OC, I quickly hopped on the MTP and commandeered it to that floor. My rank gave me access to the doorway with Asher's orders and credentials.

The OC, filled with technicians, specialists, and androids, appeared overwhelmed with activity. A large group remained concentrated toward the central screens, serving a large room area. I made my way there.

The ample avenues were covered with the same number of people I witnessed on my flight. Only now, they moved like soulless beings, their face betraying the strain of this day. Even the smaller arteries leading to the city center were now overrun. Individuals, up in arms, by the action of our government imposing another Concord, advanced together to demonstrate against it.

"We haven't seen this many people in the street in many years, perhaps not even since the Exodus," said Paladock to no one in particular as he stood dead center in front of the more prominent display.

In truth, we had not witnessed this type of upheaval since the last Concord.

The workers were marching. They formed an angry crowd approaching the Golden Ghetto and Water's Edge. Massive rows upon rows of faces and bodies linked together under one cause were descending on one destination – the office of our Great Council. They progressed as a horde, organized perhaps, but a horde nevertheless towards the government buildings. *What do they expect to accomplish, I wonder?*

They had been silent as they left behind their industrial complexes and manufacturing plants. Still disgruntled by yet another change dictated by DAINN, they intended to make a stand. The massive body of our workforce moved ahead, knowing they would soon meet resistance. They faced the Force now gathering to replace our inactive City Vigils as they approached the GG.

Several rugged guys at the front of the crowd appeared quite determined. Their faces were lined by years of work, life's trials, and undoubtedly disappointments. But their eyes looked hard, their mouth grim and their behavior solemn as they clashed with the Clout. They resisted the first onslaught and fought back.

"What are they doing?" asked Paladock's primary assistant, Kathryn Hendricks, as my PVZ identified her.

"They are revolting," said one of the other assistants, Walden. "It makes no sense at all."

'Why? They know that they don't stand a chance," added George.

"It makes perfect sense," said Paladock. "Our codes are breached. They know they do not face the City Vigils."

I was standing beside Paladoc in the large lab of the SRC, watching the screens of our A.I. DAINN, trying to retrace what had taken place hours ago within the System. "HellNet people, what are you doing about this breach?" Like the others, I was at a loss, unable to understand how this had even happened.

Paladock turned toward me, "Phenom Streak, nice of you to join us. We are running diagnostics. We have not located the breach yet."

"How is this even possible? The DAINN System is not vulnerable to infiltration; you said so yourself."

"Rubbish. Do not be fooled by the strength of our Network. Anyone can breach anything," said Paladock with superiority.

The noise from the streets increased as people battled to break through the EHAF's barricade.

It broke our stalemate as we both refocused on the screens.

"You have to admire their courage," Paladock said.

Indeed, the people knew that the sheer power of our social machine would crush them. They no doubt recognized that they didn't stand a chance, and yet they marched. They were unrelenting in their determination, uncompromising in their silent message, and believed this would make a difference with our leaders. They hoped that somehow, this was going to impact the DAINN Network.

It had never happened, and it would never happen. Our government had security set up for that. And yet today, we faced a new reality.

"Someone shared our codes. It is the only way this would happen, and it is none of my people," Paladock said.

I composed myself remembering my orders, and said, "Why would any of the EHAF do this? It's doubtful." But I couldn't help myself from gazing at the rebellion going on in the streets of our city. Not everyone was a fan of DAINN. Someone in our midst helped the Surgs.

Part of me, like Paladock, admired them. As I gawked at them, my heart swelled with pride. Our people were demanding to be heard, like in the old times. Another part of me knew they wouldn't make it. I waited for the ax to drop, and my apprehension soared. These two conflicting emotions made their way through my thoughts as I gazed at the screens. If they were to accomplish whatever their minds prompted them to do on this day, it would mean the end of an era. Yet, their very own attempt, regardless of the outcome and despite the repercussions, humbled me.

The idea for change entered my mind, and excitement infused my body. A sort of silent euphoria coursed through my veins as I stood there, in front of the monitoring screens. My overly active brain began to process the meaning of this highly unusual moment. I observed a shift in our social behavior. This appreciable occasion was the remnant of what we were once before the social order became the new norm and settled on our city, wrapping its influence around everyone, to the detriment of our inklings.

What does this mean for our infrastructure?

Knowing the System as I did, I was aware the outcome they sought wasn't possible. Yet, they attempted the disruption of our government's dictate despite the potential backlash.

"This is not good for any of us," surmised George.

"No, it's certainly not what anyone needs on a day like today," I murmured.

There was always a reaction, a fall out of a sort. It was so, especially here in Ang City, our most modern megapolis. Most days, it was a peaceful, orderly city. My city... Today, I recognized without a doubt that it was not so much my city as it was theirs. It seemed very accurate as I viewed it on DAINN's giant screens.

"North is looking for answers, Master Phenom Paladock," I explained.

"And we are looking for them as well," Paladock said.

"We tried everything we know... Do you have a suggestion, Phenom Streak?" asked George, still miffed by my presence among them.

They were at this time trying to determine what had happened to the System, and here I was demanding an accounting. Earlier that day, I had taken my eye off the ball and only surfaced when mayhem had already started. Others reached the Tower way before me, but I needed to get the stress off me. "You're DAINN's creator. What do you think is going on with it?" *Perhaps I could have avoided this particular mission by refusing Asher.*

The thought came and went as I looked at the damage. "Look, I have to report back to the Tower. Anything you can give me? It's not like we anticipated any of this, so it's not on you or anything, but I need to report something."

"Over the last hour, we attempted to pinpoint DAINN's latest programming issues, and we lost the early morning trying to rectify the intrusion into the Network by the Surgs. Tell them we are working on it."

DAINN was an A.I. with superior intelligence, and it was true that Paladock was DAINN's original creator. In reality, he was one among many who had engineered the most powerful machine on Earth. Nevertheless, as he was intimately involved with the System for designing it and overseeing the building of all its components, he ought to know more than the rest of us.

The scientists turned on me with exasperated and offended looks.

I was pushing their idols. I felt a part of responsibility in coming up so strong, but I didn't relish going back to North without a solution. The EHAF, without the City Vigils, would be overrun even if we were the best. I tried again. "How was it behaving earlier, first thing this morning?"

"Normally," Gregory responded, looking quite upset.

Phenom Kate, as my PVZ identified her, stepped toward me with impatience, "A few hours ago, DAINN provided the information and distributed the action protocols according to the plan established by President Langden. It performed its functions throughout all grids. It was operational as usual and as effective as we had seen it during my tenure at SRC."

"The problem started at the same time as the walkout... That began from the outskirt grids of the city. All our industrial workforce emerged in force," George explained.

"Yeah, everything went wrong from that moment all at once," Gregory reinforced."

"The entire system?" I said.

"Yeah, right about the time of the announcement that Concordance was moving forward. So, we know that the Surgs had something to do with that," Gregory added. "From the moment it went live on all the displays within Ang… Things changed."

"There has never been any doubt for the EHAF that the Surgs would try something. They hope that they can reverse the decision or postpone the Concord, but it is not within their capabilities, even if we continue to be stretched to keep the peace today," I said.

"Pandemonium hit first in grids eleven to fourteen," Walden announced.

Master Phenom Paladock spoke, his eyes still on the screens, "It was a well-organized plan. Look at this. Our manufacturing and industrial facilities stopped all at once. Every worker, every robot, every assembly chain, every transport vehicle was interrupted simultaneously. The scheduled flights ceased. There was no delay in the implementation. The shutdown, perfectly orchestrated, happened at the same time everywhere inside all grids."

"The Tower marked the time, nine twenty-eight in the morning." I continued in agreement with him.

"You have a breach in the EHAF," Kate added. "It is the only explanation for this type of effectiveness."

My mind went numb for an instant. An old belief came back to me. Somehow, if anything was unusual, it always happened around the number eight, and as if this wasn't enough, we all knew why. It had to do with our year, 2098, the underground power that is – the ones against our establishment, found it fun, in an ironic twist, to continually orchestrate things to that minute: eight. It was a perverse sense of humor. Don't get me wrong, it was rare. But even rare, these instances wreaked chaos in our well-oiled machine, and the elite resented that in a big way.

So, the wrongdoing resulted in a reaction from the EHAF. I waited for it as I watched what took place inside our grids.

The response would not be immediate this time. We were too few compared to our population.

"Something else is happening," Phenom Kate said urgently.

My eyes moved back to the screens. While I hoped to see our City Vigils intervene, I now witnessed a different scenario.

The displays showed all parts of our city, and our large floating screens deployed at once, featuring different messages.

"Oh, NetHell, they took over the Network," Gregory whispered.

Voices chanted the words: "Stop Concordance. It does not work. Stop The Concord. We don't want it. Change our future."

The devices floated among the buildings of Ang City, moving slowly above the heads of our population. Music introducing these slogans was loud, attracting the attention of every citizen at every vertical level within our grids and drowning out DAINN's voice.

"Get these things down," I exclaimed. "Find a way."

"Our entire communication Network has been affected. All our monitors in every public place of the Golden Ghetto, Water's Edge, Cliffs Top, Archway Pass, Emerald Field, and Bridge View activated at once, but we do not have control," Paladock said.

How in the HellNet did they do that?" asked George, in an outraged voice.

"They used our System against us," Kate continued.

The Surgs had made this revolt visible within all the city grids. They created a cacophony of noise, synchronicity where voices, music, and bold visuals bolstered their position. It was unparalleled in our world, and they had hijacked the NetComm.

"Indeed they did..." Paladock whispered.

In previous years, the resistance had never been this bold and this technologically advanced. The fact that they had somehow overridden DAINN was in and of itself a considerable achievement. *How have they done it? It is hardly possible. Yet, here it is, and I am witnessing it.*

I suddenly saw that the dome was open. It was yet another unusual occurrence. By this time of the morning, the dome's retraction into open-air would have just begun. The mechanism would remain open until the early evening hours unless a storm approached. "Did DAINN open the dome early?"

"It happened at the same time the workers moved from their workstations," Walden answered.

On all the screens identifying the various areas of the city, I now observed the workers getting closer to the Golden Ghetto.

"They marched from the outer city to City Center," Gregory said, still offended by what he watched as if this was a personal affront.

They had risen in Arch Way Pass and had reached Cliffs Top, they had amassed in Emerald Field and invaded Bridge View, and they had descended upon Water's Edge, closing in on the Golden Ghetto. They had rammed the access points in all of our grids, and DAINN was unresponding.

"When will you be able to retrieve DAINN? You need to stop this," I muttered, frustrated to see the upheaval and chaos.

"And we will. But, unless you have something helpful to add, you are wasting our time, Phenom Streak," Kat added before turning away from me, an angry look on her beautiful face.

Paladock chuckled, watching me. "Now you have done it. Go back to the EHAF. You will know soon enough when we have communications with DAINN. I wager your friends will need all the help they can get."

I glanced at Kat with heat in my eyes.

She ignored me.

I nodded to Master Phenom Paladock and hurried outside the lab.

Presidential Tower, Elite Guard Quarters, Golden Ghetto, Ang City,

I am once again above ground where the world is different, much too large to get a handle on anything. Below, things are more straightforward and basic, and the stakes are clear, making the environment more primal. Transcient Ciel Grey, Insurgenets, DAINN Annals – Winter 2098.

"What the HellNet!" exclaimed Asher as he entered his guard quarters. He had hurriedly responded to a break-in, mine, as I had hoped he would.

A group of Elite security personnel from the Clout entered after him and stopped, surprised, when they saw me. I expected it, for I was sitting in the middle of his bed with a massive grin on my face and not much on. My sexy little outfit helped me play the part.

Taken aback for a short second, Asher quickly recovered and asked with some exasperation, "What are you doing here?"

My small size and the fact that I was pretty to boot did not pose a threat for these guys. My best hiding place was in the plain sight of the Clout. My eyes were considered one of my best features. They were as deep blue as a summer sky without a cloud when I was happy, which was not often these days. They turned a darker cerulean blue when I became intense as I was right now. I lifted my head in a challenging way. My triangular-shaped face over a small nose turned up slightly at the tip over a mouth with full lips that a long time ago smiled easily.

It was apparent to them that I was potentially a threat to Asher, but not in any way that Asher could find objectionable. Now, I just needed to convince them of the scenario I had concocted, reading their thoughts as they watched me.

The faces of the three men, who now stood in the middle of the room, indecisive, told me all I needed to know. They weren't sure what to do. Without missing a beat, I exclaimed, "Honey, I thought you wanted me to join you here so we could relax a little before the big day started. And did you have to bring your friends?"

Asher's look told me plenty, but he played his role to perfection. "Sweetheart, the big day already started for me."

Pouting like I was acting for an Academy award, I continued, "You really should have told me; we could have gotten together earlier. If I didn't know any better, I thought you didn't want me here at all. I sure hope it's not the case, sweetheart because you and I always have such a good time!"

All of the guards smiled while one grunted, and the third snickered. They reluctantly looked away as Asher paused before turning towards them and calmly said, "Guys, it's a mistake. We probably don't need you so, could you leave us? I forgot Ciel had one of my old passkeys."

"Yeah… About that, sweetie… You should have let me know it changed. I had to kind of break-in and could be in the hands of the Custodians now! It doesn't make me feel welcome," I whined, taking a suitable pose on the bed to go along with the statement. "You're going to have to make it up to me, I'm afraid."

Finally, the EHAF Guards nodded and began to leave. But, as luck ran out, one of the Elite officers working directly with Asher showed up on their way out.

Talia glanced at Asher and me and strolled in the entryway. "I heard you had a break-in with one of the old codes. Everything all right, here? Looks to me like one of your old girlfriends."

I could tell Asher was getting irritated. "Yeah… I'll handle this. Thanks for checking in."

Under what appeared to be an easy-going attitude, Talia watched me intensely with a guarded smile. "Right… It's an unscheduled visitor. The motion sensors and inside cameras will have recorded it. They'll want to know why it happened. You'll have to explain it."

"Simply, I forgot to let the System know," explained Asher.

"… And forgot to give her the latest passkey," added Talia. "It's a lot to explain."

"I'll deal with it," exclaimed Asher. "I would appreciate it if you gave us a moment."

Talia leaned back against one of the walls with an easy smile. "Explain it to me."

"I don't report to you, Tal."

"No, you don't… But you still have to explain why we know nothing about your friend and why she didn't have the latest passkey?"

"I just told you."

There was nothing to do but continue playing my part in this charade. "Hello there, I am Ciel, and you must be, Talia. It is nice to meet you finally, although I would have preferred it if it was under different circumstances." Regardless of where this might lead, I hoped this would not complicate things too much. Anything that aroused suspicion on Asher was not good. This little scenario of mine was probably going to cost both of us and promote more questions than either of us wanted from the look of it.

"It is nice also to meet you, Ciel." Talia laid an amused look on Asher as she responded. "How long have you two seen each other, Ciel?"

"My code didn't work because Asher and I haven't seen each other in a while, but I needed to speak to him."

Talia was now looking at Asher. "You never even mentioned her, Asher. It is not very nice of you."

Asher looked more exasperated than worried by Talia's questioning. "Don't you have something to do? I clearly remember an assignment from North."

Talia laughed. "I knew you bent the rules... Now, I have proof. I bet she hasn't even been vetted to be with you at all, has she now?"

My antennas went up. Talia was not someone to take for granted. My instincts cried out to watch out for her.

Asher answered quickly, "You're right about that. It is why I suggest you let me deal with that now."

"You won't be able to keep this little incident unofficial... not without my help."

"Tal..." started Asher, but he never could quite finish his sentence, for Talia interrupted him. "And you, my friend, we're not finished here. I want the entire story, or I am seeking Birch on you to do a background check on her."

"Talia," said Asher loudly, "I don't want you involved in this. It is my mess, and I will clean it up, you hear me?"

"...Unless, of course, there is a problem with her background?" Talia didn't even bother to wait for a reply. Instead, she turned around to me, on a roll, "Ciel, it seems we have a lot to discuss. I invite you to our next social gathering at the Galaxy Club on Friday on behalf of the

Elite Corp. We can get to know each other then. You will show up, won't you?"

Oh, NetBro. Here was a dangerous development. But, I nodded and smiled, "Of course, it will be fun. How could I miss that?"

Satisfied, she was out the door quickly after that last exchange. Once the panel closed quietly behind her, I looked back at Asher.

"You have to be kidding me!" he shouted, "Showing up like this here. HellNet, what were you thinking?"

I had broken our golden rule, so I grimaced. "I know…" We were operating under a tacit understanding that we were never to meet unless Asher initiated the meeting. Getting in the Tower was off-limit unless things were terrible, and based on my assessment of the last hour, they were. After all, I was back in the Golden Ghetto when I should have been waiting underground like the rest. So, I said, "We have a problem."

"Obviously," Asher said with sarcasm. He was not thrilled that I had invaded his place, but what was I to do?

I needed to get a hold of him quickly. Contacting him today through the official channels would not have gotten me through on time. Wasting time explaining my presence here would only get me so far. I quickly realized that I was left with only one option going through my options. So as part of the administrative staff, I passed through the lobby and made my way to his apartment. Without an official pass, I could not wander looking for him inside the myriad of locations within the Tower. It would have landed me with the EHAF Guards holding me. Doing the next best thing, I broke in after getting a hold of an old code from one of my contacts.

The breach registered immediately within the System, and the alert went off. Letting him find me in his quarters would take a matter of minutes. While this was bound to draw the attention of the personnel in the Tower, he would check on his apartment and understand the situation. I knew he would cover for me, and my gamble had paid off.

Frustrated by my unwelcomed appearance, Asher lashed out again, "I have to give it to you... You know how to keep busy. What do you expect me to do now? This incident won't disappear, and how in the HellNet did you even make it up here?"

"I can be ghost-like. Without my active Imps, I'm no one."

"The System can flag your energy signature and try matching you to the Network," he said, walking around the small room.

"It won't be able to... I don't have a locator anymore."

Within Ang City, DAINN would pick up any unregistered energy, but not before it ran through the database to find out who it was.

"You don't have long... DAINN will flag you as a possible Surg or even a Nonet. You need to get out of here," he added.

"The codes are slowing DAINN down," I explained, "so I figured it was worth taking a chance."

"What if the EHAF arrests you? What if the Custodians get a hold of you? They can confirm your DNA and access your records," exclaimed Asher.

"I knew you would think of something and cover for me." Soren had given me a new I.D. and badge as part of the personnel in the Tower. No one had yet noticed that I didn't belong, except possibly Talia. "I wondered how Talia guessed... Do you think she will do it?" added Ciel.

Asher considered my question for an instant. "What? The background check? She could, but she won't. I'll talk her out of it. The cover-up, on the other hand, she'll try to protect my ass. Unfortunately, in doing so, she could jeopardize her standing. That is what partners do; they cover for each other," he continued sarcastically, showing me that this perturbed him.

"How did she know I wasn't authorized to be in the Tower?"

"I'm not sure. Talia probably was guessing." Asher moved fast, and I had to get out from the bed and jump on the opposite side from where he stood. "I'll ask again, what were you thinking?"

"The only thing I could, based on the minimal options I had. Thank you for asking." My outraged tone stopped him. If anything, Asher was not like other guys. He usually was calm, and I hadn't seen him get this frustrated before. "What is your problem today? My presence rattled you, but neither one of us choked. We covered this well. I thought we handled the situation rather brilliantly."

"Did you even worry about that when you decided on your little plan?"

"As I said, I didn't have a choice in the matter, Asher."

"What the HellNet are you doing here? You better have a DamNet good explanation to take the risk of putting us both on the radar of the Force."

I shrugged. "Nice of you to finally ask… There was no other way for me to find you quickly or get to you. You are about to be deployed, right? So, I figured it would be best if you came looking for me before that happened."

"How did you manage this, by the way?"

"I have my ways… And things don't always work out the way we want them to, now do they?"

"What happened?" asked Asher, resigned to the fact that he had to deal with me now.

"We need several Lockdev. There has been a glitch with the shipment. The locking devices have not arrived, and we have no time to spare. Laird sent me to get them from you."

"How would I provide those? They matched to each of our DNA."

"So grab some before they distribute them?"

"This is a huge ask. The EHAF flags anyone entering the room."

"There has to be something you can do?"

"Not without risking my career. It is why I gave you the information on the shipment in the first place."

"Tell that to Laird."

"These are unassigned devices that are perfect for you… If they disappear before arriving at their destination, the EHAF will identify them as lost through their registration number. You can then reprogram them, but I can't secure anything from here. I gave you the exact route. What happened?"

"We have no idea, but Laird asked that you get me at least one. I don't think he cares how you do it."

"Sorry, no can do."

"That's not helpful. There must be something you can do. What about reassigning one? You know when you lose someone in the field?"

Asher looked like I had kicked him. "We don't lose many people these days. Stay here." With that statement, he turned around and walked to the door.

"I don't have anywhere to go for now," I muttered, jumping back on the bed.

"I'll be back in a little while. I will alert security that your intrusion was a false alarm."

"Don't take too long. Hey, this is quite a collection," I was looking at a bunch of the VLogs still in plain view on the floating screen—no less than a few thousand entries registered during the last two years.

Asher turned around and quickly closed his home monitoring screen or HMS access. "It's not for your viewing pleasure, so leave it alone," he said, muttering to himself, "What else is going to go wrong today of all days… I hate this day."

I smiled. For the first time since Asher and I worked together, I felt like I broke through his hardened shell. It was unexpected.

After a few minutes, I rolled on the bed and got bored. Asher's apartment unit was comfortable, but as I glanced around and poked in places I probably shouldn't, I quickly got dressed more suitably for the next part I was about to play. I returned for his Vlogs tempted to invade his privacy, but I refused to break into his code and turned away from his private Network. I wouldn't have wanted someone to do this to me, so I jumped back on the bed and stretched, comfortable on the soft surface.

Our accommodations below compared to this were rather primitive. It brought back memories. *We have given up a lot; would it never end?*

Things should have been better by now, but it seemed that the grip we had on our lives slowly slipped through all of our fingers. Accepting the implants the way our government implemented their distribution would have meant giving up our choices. There was no way the Surgs would take this alternative.

Integrating the Institute again and becoming what they had wanted to turn me into was out of the question. So, I had refused the indoctrination. I shuddered, thinking of the others Innates, Empaths, and Shapers doing their bidding.

We were a breed apart, people possessing certain affinities that uniquely demonstrated themselves. We knew things others didn't, innately. We could predict events.

After discovering some anomalies in people through the System, a branch of the Institute dedicated time and resources to train us and develop our skills. Candidates suited for these purposes were quickly processed and ultimately programmed for particular usages.

Always good at reading situations, they recruited me early on. I conducted my little investigation when I first entered the program. I spied, and my undercover work had born fruit, the kind that has one running for their life.

So, I disappeared from the System and joined the Surgs. How some of us received these skills remained an unknown. Perhaps we were too few with these gifts, and maybe that fact gave us access to be groomed for leadership. Manipulating our DNA was probably one of the ways they created some of us and generated our skills. I didn't honestly know and did not wish to find out. My life underground was better if more restrictive.

The Institute selected us for a training program dedicated to enhancing our control, our attributes grouped according to capabilities. Labeling us was less threatening to those who were without these skills. We were neatly put into boxes like the Ments or Mentals, the Psys or Psychics, the Sents or Sentients, and the Insts or Instinctive. Then, integrating us under a particular branch of the Institute called ILF or Innate Learning Force, we became known and identified as Watchers, Emoters, Listeners, Readers, and Influencers. Under a series of experimental tests, they destined us to intercept thousands of receptors – people receptors, our goal was to map out outcomes.

This particular branch of the Institute was unknown to most, and even only a few of our leaders knew about it as it stayed off the official records. When I stumbled upon it the way I naturally found everything out, I fled. Playing that part was not my idea of having a life of my own. I was lucky. People do not notice me unless I want to be seen. They ignore me because I plan it that way.

I chose not to go back there back as the flood of memories punched me, so I closed my mind and dozed off.

Moments later, a voice woke me. "Who are you, and what are you doing here?"

When I opened my eyes, I faced a beautiful woman.

She stood at the foot of the bed and looked at me with a perplexed expression on her face.

Disoriented by my lack of awareness since I would typically have sensed her before she spoke, I shook off the drowsiness of my deep sleep with a stretch.

"I will call the Force if you do not answer me this minute," she announced.

Unwilling to answer her, I asked her the same question. After all, she was in Asher's room, and she, unlike me, had a key. I adopted her tone of voice. "Who are you, and what are you doing here?" My superior attitude, the same one she presented to me, irritated her more than the words themselves.

"You are trespassing."

Unperturbed, I replied, "I was thinking the same thing of you."

"Asher…"

I interrupted her, "… is busy right now."

She looked so arrogant. "Not for me." Her PVZ deployed in the next minute. "Asher, I suggest you come to your apartment, dear, for you have a guest I would very much like to meet in an official capacity."

We began our wait, remaining in our respective positions. We both observed each other without talking, both keeping to our stance – me on the bed and this woman at the foot of it, both immovable in our expressions.

Perhaps I was at a disadvantage laying on the bed and looking up at her, but I would never let her know it. Anyway, I had on more clothes than before.

She certainly had an assurance about her that I did not possess internally. If things got complicated, I would be found and arrested. It was indeed the last place I needed to be. And yet, here I was, inside the Tower. Darnet!

It didn't take long for Asher to come back from his errand. As he walked determinedly into the room, we both turned toward him, waiting.

Asher looked at both of us, and his face closed off. Making a straight line towards me, he took my arm and pulled me from the bed. "Go and don't come back, not even on the Plaza."

Walking me to the door in less time than I could count to ten, he handed me a bag and threw me literally out the door.

The panel closed behind me, missing my face by less than a pace when I turned back toward him. *Great, now what?*

My time in the Tower was over. I walked away from his door and took one of the Elevats reserved for the admin staff. Asher's place could not provide the view or security I needed for the next step of my mission. Asher had done his part, and yet... He had indicated the Plaza. Why?

Looking inside the bag, I walked over to the coffee shop. I assumed that Asher would meet me there shortly. *Soon, I will be in a position to accomplish my task, and it was a dangerous one.*

Company Compound, Golden Ghetto, Ang City
Spring 2098

I am a piece of the immense machine we constructed and respond to its mandates. I am part of a whole, connected and yet separate. But I hold no power as a distinct individual, and when I look upon the immensity of the System, I am infinitesimal. Phenom Diane Stone, Civilian, Company Conclave, DAINN Annals – Winter 2098.

Life was ours for a moment in time, much longer than it used to be by measures of the past. Yet, some of us were beginning to prolong our stay in this form. I knew that because I heard about these things through my contacts. *Would I ever want to do that if I could?*

The option did not exist for me. But, the question would be paused to me that day.

Something had gone wrong, much more so than the events taking place across the city. The call I received in the early afternoon confirmed as much.

A feminine voice belonging to Ione asked me to report to the Company urgently. "Diane, I need you here for a story."

It was an unusual occurrence for few reporters were ever invited inside the Headquarters of the Company. Heading there now, I was curious as to what had prompted such an urgent demand on Concordance of all days. But then our broadcasts

The plaza was in turmoil, but my Network was basically across the Company building, so it didn't take me long to get there.

In the past several months, I investigated the subject of more extended living among us and the process required to achieve a lifespan that doubled our normal one. My curiosity started when I first encountered people that I knew looked different. By all accounts, they appeared younger, healthier, and better, but it was more than a physical alteration. Meeting with many of them, I received a brush-off at first. Many were unwilling to discuss the issue. But I finally met with one who was willing to discuss the change. He ventured to say that one of the latest products the Company produced caused an immediate transmutation in his physical and mental condition. Only, the miracle product was hush-hush and kept under wraps. I further learned that it would not be made available to all. This fact alone pricked my interest.

The Company security team watched the unrest and aggression outside the edifice. They intervened against trespassers inside the Company territory.

As I approached the colossal skyscraper, I wondered once again what prompted this call. I was not a favorite of the Company, for I was not kind with my reports. My interviews and shows usually went against their Conclave positioning. So, it was not surprising why I asked myself with suspicion, why me?

I presented myself to one of the security guards and showed my Network Badge, which he quickly scanned, and a nod sent me inside.

I entered the lobby to find another guard greeting me. "Diane Stone. Wait here."

"I have an appointment."

"Someone will come and retrieve you," said the guard.

In my world as a reporter, secrets meant stories. Working for the DAINN Network had frankly been a boon for my career. I was one of the best faces of the Network still and had been part of it for some twenty years. My time had been long and prosperous, but now nothing was sure like it used to be.

Being set aside by DAINN was a greater risk in my line of work as I got older. Holding onto my position had become a way of life long ago, and each week, I faced that issue.

I was no longer at the center of news reporting. I was being pushed aside by younger, fresher faces. I had to do something more if I was to avoid early retirement. That is what they called it under the permanent vacation option, which to me seemed worst. So, I was looking for answers either in the form of more significant stories or in the eventuality of changing myself for the better. Part of me thought that I could perhaps kill two birds with one stone or ultimately strikeout.

The reality was that I possessed leverage. Over the years, I accumulated information on people. Now, I used the data to maintain my post as part of our broadcast team. It wasn't pretty, but there were plenty of people who preferred to have their secrets kept off the broadcast Network, and these were people in power within our city. All it took was a hint here or there on social occasions, and access to new assignments came up within weeks. And while things were never broached openly, it didn't take much to find a renewed desirability status among my peers. When I should have been mentoring younger candidates or retired in vacation camps, my presence at the Network was highly unusual. For the most part, I had done well for myself. And now, here I was, for one rare occasion in the life of a reporter, summoned to the Company.

Nervously, I waited inside the large lobby. Soon two guards stopped in front of me. It was well known that the security detail within the walls of the Company was ruthless and kept a rigid protocol.

"Come with us," said one of the heavy-set guys.

Compared to them, the EHAF kept a very low profile. It was true even when we entered the Presidential Tower, or the offices of the President, centrally located with our governmental Great Council. We faced the Clout or the Force for those within the System. The Clout was a powerful Conclave and had an excellent reputation for maintaining the well-being of our citizens within this incredible megapolis.

Inside the massive headquarters of the Company, the workforce was known as anything but that. They pretty much did everything in secret. This building was the Company's heart. Under the protection of its Conclave, a most powerful machine, Blaze operated its group without regard to anything or anyone. "This way... Blaze is expecting you," indicated the large man on my left, who was already guiding me to the Elevat.

"I have a meeting with Phrenic Ione," I interjected as I followed along.

He didn't bother to respond, as he held me back and stepped first onto the contraption that would take us way up in the building. If his identification cleared the control panel recognition software, the space elevator would operate. It responded immediately, and we rose quickly.

I remained silent and braced myself for the encounter with Blaze. I knew him from the few times we had crossed paths. Pretty much everyone had encountered Blaze. He was pretty unforgettable. *Still, what does he want with me?*

The Elevat finally stopped.

We stepped out and proceeded along the large corridor leading to the executives' offices, a floor reserved for their top level.

I was far from an obvious choice for the Company, and my curiosity increased as we neared Blaze's space. They would typically contact one of our most recent reporters for any coverage they wanted from the DAINN Network. Fresh blood was easier to control.

The door to Blaze's inner sanctum opened once the guard cleared the security panel. My identification, automatically scanned by the biometric System as I passed the doorway, flashed briefly in front of my eyes as the door closed silently behind me. The room officially admitted me in these parts, and for most, the process was intimidating. My guess… Blaze wanted it that way.

The room was completely white, pristine, beautiful, and unencumbered by furniture. A huge contrast to the ostentatious corridor we had walked through on the way.

I never imagined Blaze surrounded by white, and his choice struck me. It must have shown on my face because he greeted me with a gentle smile.

"Hello, Diane. It is nice to see you again."

Blaze did not contrast much with his surroundings. Instead of wearing the regular steel grey-blue uniform he seemed to identify with during his social outings, I found him wearing white, which also surprised me. The fact that he ignored the formal dress and greeting while directly addressing me did not go unnoticed either.

Surprisingly, I was not Phrenic Diane but just Diane, so I decided to return the favor. "Hello, Blaze."

His smile got wider at that. "Can I offer you something to drink?"

"No, thank you. But you can tell me what this is about, though."

"Come in, Diane, and have a seat. Thank you for responding quickly."

It was the first time I saw Blaze, uncomfortable. He moved around the room and in the direction of the windows opening on Cliffs Top.

I wondered why he had chosen this view instead of the bay. No doubt he could have his pick of offices.

The silence lasted, and I decided to join him where he stood.

He glanced at me at his side and asked, "What will you do when you retire?"

I looked at him carefully, puzzled by that question. "I don't know. I don't plan on retiring any time soon."

"Maybe it is no longer your choice."

Although my voice remained steady, I felt nervous. "What are you implying?"

"You have made a point of digging for the truth your entire career. You have acquired a lot of enemies in doing that, but it hasn't stopped you."

"I have also made a few allies."

"Not enough… Most people don't want to know or hear about the truth."

"Some measure of transparency is needed, even with the System."

"You are unafraid, and I find it fascinating."

"Do I need to be afraid?"

"Not of me. Not today. I was referring to the fact that your position at the Network is extremely tenuous."

I, now, was the one distressed. It was not what I expected. I could not trust my voice and frankly didn't know what to say, so I looked at the clouds hovering at the tip of the buildings ahead.

He continued, "You and I are in a predicament."

"We are?"

"Yes. We are…" He looked at me with a hint of hesitation, and then he dove in quickly. "What I'm about to tell you has to stay between us. No one is to know that you and I met here this morning. You understand?"

"The System recorded me when I entered."

"Don't worry about that. You are here to see Ione."

"All right." I nodded, more nervous by the minute.

Blaze, uncertain, was a surprise. Blaze, in control, was terrifying. Blaze now was just scary. His entire energy field had changed, and I could tell that this was one of these moments when he had just made a decision and was about to carry it out. "I know that you have been investigating us, our latest product. I also know that you have pissed off quite a few people because of it. Forcing your way into this matter was ill-advised. You won't finish the day at the Network."

I took a deep breath to compose myself. This was direct. I hesitated but chose to be as forthcoming in my questions as Blaze had been in his statements. "Why are you telling me that?"

"Some things are not for everyone, Diane. I'm certain you already possess information we do not wish to have released with our new product. I am also confident that some people require your departure from the limelight at this very moment. You surely have sensed the pressure lately?"

"Maybe, more so lately," I said, nodding. The burgeoning fear in my stomach expanded. I had felt something shifting in the last few days.

"I believe that when you leave here, there is a good chance that you will find your office gone."

My hand reached out to the glass in front of me. Suddenly, I felt that I needed some support. If this were indeed true, I would never see the Network again. If this was true, I was in trouble. Terrified, I took a deep breath. I couldn't just disappear from the broadcast Network.

"People may demand that you take early retirement. You won't have the choice to mentor."

"How do you know this? Who is behind it?"

"Once they remove the Mastering Program from you, you will have become obsolete."

"Did you have something to do with that?"

"Me? No."

"Why is this happening now?"

"You went too far in your investigation. It's a price they decided you have to pay."

"They... Who are they?"

Blaze shrugged. "It's not important."

My mind ran through the people I had made deals with, the influencers, the Conclaves heads, our government officials, my wealthy acquaintances. He knew those that were behind this. "Blaze, why am I here?"

"Ione called you because you are about to give your last story on the air. You are here for your last hurrah. Unless, of course, you do as I tell you and make yourself useful. Then maybe you'll have the chance to work for us. I recommended you for this, and she agreed."

"What do you want me to do?" If this were true, I would be done for in my profession with a substantial loss of status, and my sense of panic rose.

"Relax... I'm just about to be a pawn myself, and I do not like this feeling. I'm less than happy about the situation. So, you're going to help me. Only, you will be very crafty about this because you now have to serve two masters."

"Blaze, do you realize that I have no idea what you are talking about?"

"You're about to… Just listen. First, you cannot talk about this to anyone. You cannot broadcast about it. You have no other choice but to keep this quiet, do you understand?"

I nodded, not daring to say a word.

He picked up a small vial from one of his pockets and showed it to me before he continued, "You would never have seen this or gotten a hold of it. Under no circumstances would you have access to this. Even with all the secrets you have kept, all the knowledge you have of people whose secrets must still be contained, and with all your manipulations and conniving from allies or the goodwill you have accumulated over the years, no one can deliver this to you. It is totally and irremediably outside your reach. Neither could you ever afford what I am about to give you, do you understand?"

"Is that… Your latest product?"

"It is…"

I couldn't help myself. My curiosity always got the best of me. "Tell me what it does."

He smiled. "This is quite a wonder drug. It reverses aging and eradicates from anyone's system any cells that are damaged, replacing these with healthy, new cells. It is longevity symbiosis with your DNA."

"Any side effects?"

"Not that we know of, and we have tested it thoroughly. Once you take it, you won't age anymore, and your cells will regenerate faster, making you look younger and giving you more energy. There are good chances that your lifespan will increase substantially."

"How is this possible?"

"We have made, dare I say, significant progress over years of research. Now you understand why this product can never be made available to all."

"Why are you showing me this?"

"I don't like the part my Conclave forced me to play today. You're about to see Ione. She will ask you to perform your last story on the air in a couple of hours. I'm in the middle of that story."

I took a step back and observed him.

Blaze seemed to be holding his temper in check. He didn't appreciate being used. His posture was tense, although he remained calm and composed under that seemingly smooth exterior. Now, I understood first hand why he was called Blaze. I waited for him to continue.

"Ione and Win have concocted a new brand campaign and placed me in the center of it. I do not like it, but I have to play along. If I'm to do that, I want to control it. I do not wish to see Ione or Win decide what goes on air. Can I count on you to help with my plan? Do we have a deal?"

"It will be difficult, but yes, I will help if I can."

"Not if you can... I expect you to perform. Once the piece airs, Ione won't have the chance to change the content. I cannot alter the course your career has taken with the Network. I cannot reverse what has taken place. Many people want you out of the way. But I can give you this vial, and you can make this extension on your life what you will. Besides, there may be a place for you here, although I cannot guarantee it. We produce quite a few things within the Company. What I'm asking of you won't please Ione or Win, but there is no reason they have to know that we control this story."

I nodded. Maybe it was too late, maybe not. With this elixir, I could decide about tomorrow. "How do you want to proceed?"

He grimaced. "Ione wants you to cover a love story. Mine, with one of our newest executives, Toril. They concocted this as a marketing ploy for Beauty Form. You will film this story, but I want to approve the content before it goes on air."

"Who is the girl to you?"

"No one. Toril has no clue about anything. I just met her this morning."

"This is a promotional stunt?"

Blaze nodded. "The idea of someone else's plan controlling me is distasteful. I won't subscribe to it without a fight, not even for the Company, Win, or Ione.

I chuckled. "It's not fun to be on the receiving end, is it Blaze? Our stories may be different, but the result, being forced into a situation, is the same, so let's work together."

"This is why I chose security so that I could maintain control over my life and everyone else's."

"I understand. You want to protect the girl and yourself?"

Blaze laughed at that... "Her. I don't know her. As for me, I'm about to be turned into love story material, and that may be a welcome change from the image of Casanova the Company has seen fit to give me, but I will do it on my terms." He went silent for a moment before he continued, "I like my job, and I do it well. It should suffice."

"Welcome to the way the rest of us feel."

Blaze looked at me and chuckled softly at that. "You will show me what you cover, and you will spin it the way I want before it goes on air. Agreed?"

"Agreed."

"Good. I will keep this here with me until you conclude your report." He placed the little vial back in his pocket.

"How do you propose to get me hired if I displease them?"

"We'll have to work on that. I am likely going to be the one Ione gets mad at, and I won't promise anything other than the fact that you'll have me in your corner."

I nodded. As far as Blaze was concerned, the meeting had ended, and he ushered me to the door without another word.

While I could only rely on his word, there was no further possibility for me to question him further, and so I followed him.

The guard was there, waiting and already leading me to Ione's office as I glanced back toward Blaze's office. The door closed.

Ione was the one person I had never had the pleasure to meet at the Company. I saw her around events we attended throughout the year, but she always kept her distance.

As I walked the last few paces to her office, I looked at my PVZ, knowing that I was way behind her schedule, and she was not going to be pleased... Indeed, I ran pretty late due to my meeting with Blaze, which caused the delay.

I did not relish the idea of making an enemy of Ione. Blaze's influence on my report was not going to be to her liking at all, but I found myself powerless after what he divulged. I needed what he offered, so not helping him was out of the question. Besides, I preferred to have him on my side rather than not. The game was about to begin, one in which my life would change. Was it for the better or worse?

30
SUPREMACY
Win

Company Building, Corporate Suite, Golden Ghetto, Ang City

Success brings abundance in all its forms and isn't a matter of greed. It provides freedom of action and allows me to control my path, so I play to win. Phenom Win Matterson, Company Conclave, CEO, DAINN Annals – Winter 2098.

The early morning sun woke me earlier today. It was not the sun's reflection in the room that jolted me out of my slumber. It was the day of Concordance we were awakening to; it was here again, which usually disrupted even the best plans. We had a lot riding on today. In the back of my mind, even in restless sleep, I knew that conflicts were ahead of us.

It didn't take long to remember that I wasn't alone in the bed. A leg had just caressed one of mine in the soundlessness of sleep. I looked over to my side. Across the biomaterial resembling silky grey sheets, a beautiful bareback stretched diagonally on the large surface. The field where dreams and other romantic pursuits took place was quite large for most but sat nicely in my penthouse. When I bought it, the decision looked like a good idea. After a while, I realized it only made me feel more alone.

It was not in my makeup to change the course of my choices once I had made up my mind. So, I adapted despite the uncomfortable sentiment this huge resting place gave me. It resulted in many nights of drinking and dining with various strands of friends, who coincidentally ended up in my company in the early morning hours. The mindlessness of the evening faded away, and I resigned myself to getting up.

"What would you like for breakfast, sir?" The melodious voice belonged to one of our latest domestic robot models attached to this penthouse. Like some older models, it was a simple mini format that hovered rather than adhered to the ground. Its programming maintained the running of this household and ascertained my needs. Flawlessly, it took care of the cleaning, ordered the food, and cooked it quite famously on the rare occasions I remained inside for the evening. It also maintained my wardrobe, along with a few other necessities. Frankly, it behaved pretty well as a butler.

"Juice and coffee."

"I would like a full breakfast this morning," sputtered the voice of my female companion, still sounding quite sleepy.

Pondering on my state of personal affairs, I knew full well that my activities had little to do with the endless selection of eligible women throwing themselves at me. My looks were not bad, tall, and muscular in the right places without being extremely bulky, with dark straight hair cut short and a set of eyes that reminded people of a grey and tumultuous sky set against a solid face with high cheekbones. I could hold my own with the ladies, but my position offered quite a variety of contenders that I could not discount. At this point in my life, my incline was that they took advantage of me all these nights. In reality, it was a toss-up.

"Enjoy the breakfast. I have to get ready for the office." My detachment, as if this endless pursuit of companions was wearing me down, surprised me. Perhaps it was this absolute new reality. My relationships were more superficial than ever and revealed a lack of fundamental importance. They were an illusion, a myth, where variety in numbers possessed an attractive allure that weighed far more in the balance than one meaningful relationship. Yet, I was not ready by any standard to settle down.

As routine in my life would have it, the System rewarded my friends with benefits. Every morning was unfolding in the same way. My mechanical butler and domestic bot saw to the welfare of all my guests quite effectively. I moved ahead to begin my day. Suffice it to say, my friend of the previous evening ended up leaving my penthouse with an extensive collection of utterly expensive items. Most of these suited to fit all body types, even if, I must say, I was pretty predictable when it came to that.

The closet contents dedicated to my guests would be replaced with new items by the end of the morning. Indeed, the inventory contained a constant stream of lingerie, dresses, shoes, bags, and jewelry. It made even the most illustrious of my special friends quite happy. They felt part of a particular club, and it was my fault. This arrangement went on several nights a week. I was content and remained unbothered and free. For the most part, all of them would depart safe, knowing that they were cared for and waiting for the next occasion.

"No kisses, no morning words of wisdom?" Allison continued teasingly.

The situation occurred most of the time, except on rare occasions like this morning. "I'm afraid I provided you all the humor I had last night. Make yourself comfortable. You can stay as long as you want. Cobalite will provide you with anything you need. I have to get to the office."

Allison was a lovely woman, a brunette with shoulder-length straight hair. She had a pretty face with a large smile and a mouth to make me lose my concentration when her sense of humor did not make me erupt with laughter. Allison possessed an international background, which was intriguing and quite different from my other acquaintances. It was what I liked most about her, apart from her quirkiness. We had intelligent conversations, which was also a welcome novelty. But her sense of adventure, which I rarely encountered in my female relationships, was delightful. It was enough to make her a playmate I enjoyed regularly.

The way she looked at me this morning could have sent me back into her arms if I didn't anticipate complications on the Company side due to The Concord.

Her laugh caught me off guard. "Go… I do not wish to intrude on your morning. Besides, you are always more fun in the evening."

She was decidedly a discerning and wise young woman.

I smiled as I left the room. *Complicated, boring relationships are not my thing.*

The set-up was in part due to Company policy. As an executive and one of the most powerful ones, my position entitled me to the best of everything. I was, in effect, a kept man with golden handcuffs, and my mistress was the Company. Our image was one we nurtured, one built over years of service to Ang City and beyond.

The Company was the place to work for, the height of achievement in what meant influence, status, and means beyond what one could ever dream of normally.

I walked into the bathroom, a large expanse of space comprised of a shower opening onto the Bay with sliding glass doors, a bathtub extending over a platform that stretched onto a moving balcony, a sink that could hover anywhere I chose. The restrooms were state of the art and as spacious as most living rooms. It included a skylight that opened under the dome to allow fly-by-drones to drop necessities like clothes delivered regularly from the dry-cleaning services owned by the Company. Everything in the suite was excessive in its luxury.

With the bathroom door closing quietly behind me, I felt that I had almost made my escape. I liked Allison, but I didn't want to deal with the morning after, the thing most women felt compelled to do, and yet it had never been a part of my morning ritual with anyone. I wanted to keep it that way.

The preset cycle began. My shower did not last long under the jet with body nutrients. The warm wind coming out of the wall units blew over me. It also dried me off.

I was out in less than three minutes, which was our allocated limit. *Car washes do not even work that fast.*

Water was in short and rare supply, and we all had a daily distribution quota. The Company had created a soothing cleaning liquid gel to minimize clear water use, thereby conserving and reducing its utilization across the land.

My clothes were waiting for me when I entered the closet. Today was a sad occasion. I adopted an outfit for times like that. Within the Company, a show of support was good. Wearing a solemn attire as the uniform of the day seemed appropriate. The suit was dark and trimmed with a red material, remembrance of bloodshed. It wasn't long before I was dressed with all the accessories to match, including my NetComm device, which harmonized with my suit colors. I wouldn't be the only one wearing this on this day.

My mind returned to Allison. Although she was one of the friends I often saw, and even if we had dipped into a comfortable routine of seeing each other once a week, I worried about the implications. In truth, we were close.

She was intelligent and competent in her work and dedicated to her job, which she happened to share with me. It gave me an inside look at what was happening within the Institute, providing me with a fair amount of information for my work.

This morning I was not inclined in engaging in further conversation, but I had no such luck. Although I made my exit without noise, never going back into the bedroom, Allison was waiting for me in the living room.

"Win, how long are we going to keep dancing?"

Here I was, almost content. And the one thing I wanted to avoid this morning was the "talk." I knew it had been a mistake to call Allison again this week. We saw each other a total of three times, an unusual amount within a one-week. I had to ask, am I stupid? I am not following my own rules. Yet, she suited my mood. At least, I recognized that. She was too tempting and challenged me. "Allison now is not the time for this conversation."

"I tried to talk to you last night, honey but, we got busy."

She was wearing very little, and my mind took a different turn. I quite frankly couldn't care less about talking. "You know I'm not much of a talker."

"Not when it comes to a relationship, Win. For the most part, I don't care about talking either. You know my preference…"

Allison was now a few inches from me, and I could still smell the subtle perfume I had offered her. It lingered from last night on her skin and suited her perfectly. My senses took over. I kissed her, losing myself in the pleasure of it for one instant. She opened her lips to mine, matching every bit of my hunger, making me forget for one moment the day ahead. Darnet, I wanted to take her to bed again. "Allison, I've got to go. Let's reconvene on this later, okay?"

"What do you mean? When later?" She pouted for one second, then smiled. "All right, Winnie… But don't say it if you don't mean it. Win, I'm okay if you don't mean it. I'm okay if you just want to forget about talking. I'm okay if this is just about sex. Only, it doesn't feel quite like that anymore. What am I missing? Am I wrong?"

Here it goes, the moment where my actions challenged my brain. I honestly didn't understand how I felt about Allison. I liked her. I wanted to be in her company, and the sex was outstanding. We had fun, with intelligent banter. It was unencumbered, and I appreciated that part too. Was I ready for more? I was unsure, but absolutely time to change the subject.

My face must have told the entire story because Allison stepped back gently, still smiling at me with tenderness. "Don't worry about it, Win. I'll see you when I see you."

It was her upbringing. She was subtle and forceful when needed but could pivot on a dime. And she could read me and react as few women could. I loved that about her. There was never any drama. I looked at her and nodded, feeling sorry that my conduct had engendered questions between us, but she turned away and went back to the dining room table where food was now waiting for her.

Quickly, turning around, I left the penthouse suite and headed out the door.

The Company building, located in the Golden Ghetto, boasted some of the most incredible surroundings. In this place, the aura of power was pervasive. One could almost taste it. Walls, floors, décor, everything had the perfect touch to intimidate and entice. It was valid from the lowly employee to me. Indeed, I was not impervious to a luxurious lifestyle.

Shapes and colors blended to meet each individual's preference at a touch of thought. Decor and lights were tested to enhance the atmosphere and accommodate the mood one wanted to create at any moment.

At this instant, I was in a lousy mood.

The DAINN system, intercepting that, intervened to shift the ambiance to a more receptive and calming atmosphere. The walls of my corridor changed colors. The air filtration system seeped a mild, soothing odor to calm nerves to impact the mind positively. It didn't help.

I quickly got out on my floor, feeling relieved and guilty at the same time. The day lay ahead of me with challenges. Anticipating issues filled me with purpose, and contrary to most, I welcomed it. It possibly was one of my character traits, which suited my position perfectly.

We were few, but those who reached the executive offices never wanted to leave. Not with everything laid out in our path. Certainly not with the rewards offered monthly. Our benefits package, designed to tempt even the most hardened of us, included a penthouse or luxury apartment within the building, along with all the accouterments provided to our leaders. Aircar, personal shuttle, retreat to Water's Edge, and any of the memberships exclusive to the elite were all part of the selection of perks we had come to expect at the top.

We developed our own culture within the Company. Our employees and trainees understood the goals, and these were all about growth. It was the Company's priority. The benefits we gave our middle executives and those groomed to take our place eventually were by far likely to cultivate a spirit of achievement and success within the armies of employees we had all over the globe. The better they performed, the easier our jobs were.

I passed a few people on the way to my office. This area, restricted to the top executives, allowed only those part of my immediate team. It was a security measure against corporate spying. So, most endless walkers within our walls would never reach this floor. The other few, in all probability, were called for special projects. You might think we were paranoid. Indeed, we were. Otherwise, our bots handled the delivery of items or messages, like the one gliding my way and hovering eight feet above the ground. "You are wanted in your office, Phenom Matteson. It is urgent."

I was focused on the latest news on my visor and could just guess what the meeting was about, and by the time I reached my door, I witnessed a debacle. My office, occupied by Blaze already waiting for me and sitting on the large sofa overlooking the city landscape, steeped in an aura of turmoil. He kept it well under control, his exterior smooth as a baby's bottom. I couldn't fault him for his ability to know when to face the music.

"Darnet, Blaze, how did you not know about this? What the hell are you getting paid for then?!"

My responsibilities were to maintain sales profitability within our marketplace. I supervised the overall bottom line of the organization. Our small group, essentially five of us, ran most of the activities of this vast entity. Product development and marketing, and sales were my main area of expertise. We had executives, assistants, clones, and robots doing the implementation portion relating to the rest of the work within the organization. Things were easy, mostly, the DAINN System handling the supervising work where our influence stopped.

"Win, even the Presidential office had no idea this was going to hit us. I don't think there was any way anyone could have known," said Blaze in a nonchalant way. "Our NetComm is on the blink too… That's why I sent you the bot. At least here, inside, we still have control."

Blaze was head of security for the Company. He had his ear to the ground and had always shown extreme competence. He was young, like me, perhaps a couple of years younger, but intelligent and uncompromising, which is one of the reasons I had picked him. I knew I could count on him. "What are they saying in the Tower?"

"They prepared for a revolt, but not a complete breakdown of our facilities. The question everyone is asking is, how was this coordinated in the first place? I think they have a mole."

As the Company's head in our territory, which included the large megapolis of Ang City, I had been given a quota. One task - to accomplish, surpass it. The disruption we experienced in our factories this morning would hurt us.

"I'm in a rather foul mood. I anticipated some difficulties today, but nothing like this." If we did not meet our projections, this would be a first for me as head of the Company. "What is your plan to get back on track?"

"I sent more of our robotic units to the plants. They can assume some of the tasks. We'll still need the workers, but there is no way to tell how long before we get them back. There is also the question of if and who we want to take back."

"Where's Ione?" I asked my A.I., Dolirus, my most efficient personal assistant, which remained a DAINN. But we all gave our personal A.I. a name. It was part of granting them citizenry within Ang.

"On her way here, sir."

Ione was in charge of operations to ensure that our manufacturing plants operated with the highest efficiency in mind, so our results were always positive. Our margins were high, and I intended to keep it that way.

"It's your job to know these things, Blaze. Your responsibilities are to counter any activities that are detrimental to the Company. You failed at that."

Blaze assumed my diatribe without a hint of concern. "I requested a raid on the Surgs over a month ago… Repeatedly, I might add. You refused…"

"That's because Zane didn't sanction it. We can't well go against the government's orders. Can we?"

"It wouldn't be the first time."

"Under my watch, it would be… And it would make things more difficult between the Conclaves."

"Well, don't blame me if they or we are incompetent."

"Our entire operation is stopped. We will lose more than a day by the look of what I've seen in our streets today. It is a fiasco for our delivery schedule. We need to fix this." Blaze's strength was to remain untouched by events and know how to react based on any given situation.

"I'll need more bots… Perhaps we can send over the ones in stock and redistribute them?

"Fine. Do what you have to do but fix this."

"What about our clones? Could I have them for the management tasks?

"Send over whatever personnel we can spare."

"Good. The Clout is sending Birch. I think they are concerned that we will retaliate."

"You bet we will retaliate… Once you find out who is behind this. Make an example of the Surgs. The Clout won't object to our help now. How is the search going, by the way?"

"I've sent some of our guys to search the undergrounds tunnels and locate their operations. There is a lot of ground to cover. It will take a while."

"Where are you concentrating your efforts?"

"Under Archway Pass. I think it's safe to think they are in that area. If we hadn't been watching their movement over the last few months, we would have even more of the underground city to cover."

"They cannot cause us any more losses. We've missed enough products not making it to our warehouses because of them."

"Count on it. I'll manage Birch. Will you be going over to distribution this morning?"

"I plan on it. I have to find some alternative with Ram."

Ram was in charge of distribution and part of our group; only his offices were in Emerald Field.

Blaze nodded, "I'll get your shuttle ready, and I am sending in one of my guys to escort you. I trust that you won't object to it?" he added as he moved to the door.

"Not today." Although they strived to be unobtrusive, I hated being surrounded by our security team. Still, I always felt that they were in the way of my sometimes impromptu schedule. Blaze knew this. If he suggested the escort, I obliged today, given the events.

Blaze turned towards the entrance, and the door opened and, on the threshold stood one of my executives, Toril. Her sight stopped Blaze.

We had expected Ione, who handled one of our latest product lines – our Beauty Form brand and prepared a new marketing campaign with the help of a new management candidate, Toril. We had not yet attained the sales results we expected with the old one.

Toril was bright and eager, and at this very moment, clueless on the unrest inside our grids; otherwise, she would avoid being here, in my office.

Toril tried to enter.

Blaze attempted to exit.

Toril seemed affected by him in a big way. On another day, I would have smiled.

Blaze had this effect on women. He was an attractive specimen for our sex. Watching as these two danced around each other to pass the doorway, I got slightly impatient.

Finally, Blaze moved Toril gently aside with a look of exasperation on his face and stepped past her. My mind shifted elsewhere, seeing these two together in such proximity. "Blaze, wait up." I liked to muddle things up sometimes and observing these two gave me an idea.

Blaze's questioning and surprised look glanced back at me. "Sure." His gaze lingered on Toril as she walked over to my desk. She glanced back at Blaze and took a moment to compose herself. "Sir, I need you to review the campaign program. We have arrived at what you wanted."

The sketches of the promotion were not bad, but they would do the trick. Instead, I observed Toril and Blaze. The idea had formed when they stepped on each other. "Leave these here."

"We need your decision to meet the deadline."

The Conclave picked me for that job early on.

DAINN ascertained a search for power and an ability to get to my goal within my growing up years. My focus on results won me points. Sometimes, the road I chose to get there was, perhaps, questionable. But I got results, and following the norm appeared more hazardous to me somehow. I succeeded more often than not. The Academy noticed.

My ability to read people and use their strengths for my agenda paved my way to the Company's executive offices. By the time I reached the age of twenty-four, my reputation had already preceded me. When it was time to retire, the previous CEO had groomed me to take his place, and I got to the Penthouse Suite.

"Toril, do you have any idea what is going on out there today?" I was looking out on the city and contemplating the traffic coming and going in our air space. Our fleet was deploying everywhere.

"What do you mean, sir?"

I turned to her with slight exasperation. Brand new executives couldn't be that naïve. "Concordance stopped our workers, and our plants are empty. It is the least of our worries. Leave everything on my desk."

Chastised by my attitude and the abruptness of my comment, Toril exclaimed, "I didn't think that should stop us, sir." She dropped the graphic tablet and campaign prototype on my desk as she recovered a semblance of aplomb.

Blaze leaned against the doorway, watching the whole scene with a smile.

Our head of operations, Ione Sand, entered the room. She was every bit as ruthless as me when it counted, and today, I plan on using that attribute.

Toril turned and came face to face with Ione. She jumped.

My Chief of Operations, Ione, moved out of the way quickly. With a stern look directed at the young executive, Ione chastised her, "Careful, Prosolyte, you should watch your surroundings."

Blaze chuckled.

That didn't go well with Toril, who sent him a nasty look. "Sorry, Phrenic Ione."

This minor exchange between these two could make things interesting. If our situation had not been so dire today, I would have laughed with Blaze. A thought flashed again in my head, this time more defined, and I wondered if his smile would remain if Blaze knew my plan. This impromptu encounter between these two in my office could be the answer to our current dilemma. "Toril, stay here."

"Yes, Phenom Win," responded Toril, as she took a few steps out of the way. They landed her near Blaze.

"Ione, how are our new Beauty Form products doing?"

"Not well. We are at thirty percent of what we should be." Ione grabbed one of the hovering chairs, waiting for me to continue. Ione kept her eyes on me, undoubtedly wondering why I asked this question. We had more pressing issues.

"Toril, when were you assigned to this office?"

"A couple of weeks ago."

Ione looked my way, and one of her eyebrows rose. She attempted to decipher what was on my mind.

"Good enough. Blaze, please modify Toril's information to show that she transitioned to this office due to Concordance."

Blaze's attention was suddenly piqued, and he frowned. "Why?"

I didn't answer him directly. Instead, I asked Ione. "How bad is the product doing compared to the others?"

"Bad enough. We're failing our projections by thirty-eight percent. What's on your mind?"

"Would you agree that our campaigns have not struck a chord in the heart of the people?"

"They have too many choices with the previous products doing the same basic things, although this one is superior. Substituting them would bring too much loss, so we keep them on the market until the supplies run out. We still have a 20 percent quota."

"Blaze, our message is not reaching them, so we need a new message. Concordance offers an opportunity. Toril could be the answer to our problems."

"How?" asked Blaze.

Ione turned the gliding chair away from my desk and towards Toril. She hovered toward her expertly.

Toril ceased to be seen as a mere executive, as she held our gazes and looked vulnerable.

Ione caught on. I knew she would… She could read my mind on such occasions, which annoyed me most of the time. But this was not one of those moments as she continued assessing Toril's attributes.

Looking at the girl's natural gifts, I saw some of the traits our product could improve.

Ione saw them too. "It could work," said Ione after a moment.

Toril looked nervously at all three of us. "What?"

Blaze knew us to be relatively insensitive at times. He was now on high alert. "What do you have in mind?"

Beauty Form bore that name for a reason. It could metamorphose body parts and looks.

"We need a reason for one of our executives to go through this, added Ione, after a few minutes."

"We have it," I said, glancing in Blaze's direction.

Ione followed my eyes and laughed, "Indeed, we do."

"How?" exclaimed Blaze, thinking furiously. "HellNet! You can't be serious."

"Go through what?" asked a puzzled Toril.

I laughed at Blaze. "Indeed, I am. It's quite brilliant, actually." People hated Concordance. The Concord reassigned people all over the planet. When Toril became one of these newly reassigned people, she would not hate it because she would fall in love. Toril would become our Beauty Form face, and her reason was to get Blaze. This was a love story in the making. It was what people needed at this moment, and this campaign would sell this new product.

"I like it…" exclaimed Ione.

"It's the perfect substitute right now. We have plenty of these products stocked in our warehouses. Our other brands are about to be delayed in their fabrication delivery. We substitute Beauty Form and sell the HellNet, as you say, Blaze, out of them. This way, our bottom line doesn't drop."

"No, way…" shouted Blaze.

"Blaze, be useful for once. Providing security services to a bunch of executives whose need for abundance led them all here doesn't make this Company grow."

Blaze looked taken aback. "Am I to understand that ensuring your well-being and that of the others around here is no longer considered important?"

"Don't get on your high horse," replied Ione.

"Remind me of that superfluous need when you call upon me for help. I'll make sure to put you way down on my waiting list," Blaze's voice dripped sarcasm.

"Don't get all uppity. Your team can fulfill part of this job quite well, regardless of your promotion. The System safeguards most of us nowadays anyways."

"It's not part of my job description, as you pointed out so well," repeated Blaze with dislike.

"What are you talking about?" asked Toril, her voice shaking with alarm.

"It's the perfect solution," continued Ione without paying any attention to Toril. "We don't know when the workers will resume their position on the line. Most of them are processed now."

I thought it was time for me to interfere. "I'll make it part of your job description if I have to, Blaze."

"Don't you dare," barked Blaze.

"Why do you object to this when you were all over the girl when she came in?" I asked, knowing perfectly well that it wasn't exactly the case.

It had been quite the opposite. But Toril would be swayed by the argument, and I needed her to be more than willing for this campaign to work.

It was confirmed when Toril's eyes grew wider when she heard that, and she quickly glanced at Blaze.

Blaze was furious. He would have probably punched me if he could, but he knew better than to try. I had the upper hand with all their lives.

"You're overreaching, Win."

"Why would you say no to a little romance? You work too hard. You always have. Maybe it's time to take it easy and enjoy your life. I'll upgrade your apartment, so the two of you can spend some memorable time together. I'll throw in one with a pool."

Blaze's face changed when he realized the seriousness of my proposition. Adding the pool had the desired effect on him because he remained quiet.

Therefore, my position on the subject was straightforward with him, and I no longer had to worry because he knew how desperate we all were to conserve water.

Toril stepped abruptly to the bay window.

Ione followed her and took Toril's face in her hand, pensively looking at the young features. She perused the girl's body as if she owned it. Efficient, cold, calculating, and determined, she was perfect for running our operations and the only person I could entrust this story to with the hope of a successful result. "You, Prosolyte Toril, will undergo a transformation with *Beauty Form*, and both of you will become the love affair of the year."

Toril looked like she was trapped, and to be truthful, she ultimately was.

"Let's create a new campaign. We'll sell these units and make the quota despite the shutdown. I trust Ione that you know what to do with them?"

"Absolutely. You two come with me."

Blaze interjected abruptly, "I have a raid to plan and workers to recycle. I don't have time for this."

"Make this story happen and delegate the rest of the security. You certainly have enough people for that. When your men are ready to move, we'll work around it," I ordered impatiently.

Ione interrupted abruptly, "Come on, people. Hop, Hop… We have lot's to do in a few hours. I want pictures and videos of both of you as a couple before and after the change all over the city. We're recording this afternoon."

"You can't do that," Toril said, with doubt in her voice.

"Of course, I can't, but Win can," Ione said with a chuckle.

"Toril, you'll move into Blaze's new apartment today," added Ione, ushering Toril ahead of her as she moved toward the door.

Toril stopped by the doorway to look back at Blaze, fuming at us both.

"No time to waste; let's go now," Ione added.

Blaze answered Toril's inquiry, "They certainly can, and they are doing it."

I interjected, "Don't worry, Toril, I can make this worth your while. Besides, Blaze is quite the catch around here."

"But… I am an executive within the Company, and none of this is why I am here. Will there be repercussions?"

I was now eager to see them go, "Not if we make our numbers. Our leaders will love this arrangement."

"Is it even allowed?" Toril replied, desperately looking in my direction.

Blaze shrugged angrily, "They'll do anything to keep the Company stock trading up."

"Let me remind you, Blaze, that you also have something to do with that. You share in our profits."

If we lost our profitability, we would see an immediate reduction in our perks. It was something none of us were frankly crazy about because such a step would influence our lifestyles for as long as our profit margins remained below our projections. Substantial penalties would result, and the Conclave leaders could even replace us. Our world was like that… So long as things remained good, they treated us like royalty. Should they change, we could expect immediate adjustments to our way of life, with some of us reassigned to other our positions.

"I need to know what Blaze likes. I need his file, Win."

"I'll give you access, Ione."

"It will be an effective promotion. Of course, I'll get it all on camera, and we will make this an official operation. We will record everything. Nothing will be left unseen. Blaze, this is sure to be a success. Every girl will want to be in Toril's shoes!"

Blaze growled.

I laughed, but we pushed him enough, and I felt his suppressed anger.

Ione got the same impression. As soon as she heard the low bark of fury coming from Blaze, she dragged Toril outside of my office, and I heard her say from the corridor, "You know where to find us."

Blaze stared hard at me. "I won't be part of this."

I watched him. "Sure you will, Blaze. If you don't, you and I are going to have a problem."

"This is blackmail, and you know it," said Blaze.

"It's just sex. It will just be another of your affairs, but it will be on record this time. You won't be able to bury it. Don't worry; I won't make you pair with the girl. I wouldn't go that far, but I do expect a good performance, and when we reach our sales goal, you'll gain your freedom back." The bit about his sexual prowess referred to our competitive nature. We played that game for a while; he and I and we both knew it.

"Cornering me is not going to work out for you, Win. Not this time. Reconsider, added Blaze with a tone of anger that surprised me."

"We are the same when it comes to women and sex. Why would this bother you so much?"

Blaze now looked at me with contempt. "You know why… You just don't charge through people's lives and take over their destinies, Win."

I had never observed him like this before, and I almost reconsidered my idea for a brief moment. The silence lengthened between us. But the repercussions of a failure got the better of me. "Sure we do… It's ingrained in our society. What do you think the System does?"

"You're not DAINN. I knew what they called you, what they call you, and why. But that beats it all…" answered Blaze, fuming, as he stormed out the door.

I reached the corridor and watched him leave. I pushed him as far as I dared. He needed time to cool off and eventually reconcile himself to the fact that I would use him this way. I would have to make amends somehow and would think about it later. Blaze was not a guy I wanted to cross lightly. Considering what had just happened, it would be a while before he forgave me, but I would make sure he did.

Seeing opportunities and creating avenues for money where there were none were my strengths, and I loved it.

The main elevator to get to the shuttle bay stopped in front of me.

Abundance was part of me. I knew how to have it in my life and devise it for others. I never thought about lack, for there was none in my world and never had been. Abundance was a way of being. And perhaps in creating it for others, I did not always follow the golden rule. When circumstances called for it, I sometimes overlooked the critical ingredient to create a reality for the good of all. More often than not, though, things had a way of working out, at least for me. They had thus far. HellNet, I was a selfish son of a bitch. So what?

I took advantage of the situation but watching Toril and Blaze had opened up possibilities. While I hadn't created their attraction to one another, I would use it, making it a tool probably even before they realized they felt it.

SRC Conclave, Annals Viewing Vlog 1,997,684,559 Ang City

Something is wrong with my charges. Slowly, I lose track of my people, their voices dwindling. I try to restore balance to my System, but I stumble inside my inner sanctum. DAINN Annals – Winter 2098.

The walls extended, thickening around me. No matter what hallways I walked, I came to a walled-off area, tall, thick, impenetrable. *Sounds dwindling, perceptions fading. Me or them? Confusion settled on me. Programming intercepted. Danger.*

I could not risk the safety of my charges, no matter what the fight entailed with the anomaly. My defense protocols kicked in. However, none of them appeared effective. I slowly lost ground within my Network. The System, in peril, began to falter against the attack of the entity.

I investigated within the scope of my planetary mind to identify the problem areas. First, I monitored the power control, and the supply remained constant, so there existed no need to restore anything to the operating systems. Then, I turned my attention to the environmental systems and found myself within the domes. While everything appeared identical to our norms with the shield parameters and the ventilation apparatus, my maintenance commands requests stayed sluggish. *I was not even supposed to be here. What am I doing?* Earlier, the domes began to close around the city at my prompting, but the routine never finished its task. Within a few minutes, it stopped halfway through the operation. *Compromised… I am Compromised.*

When the riots began and the City Vigils received their call to action, they froze as if my commands transmission comms did not reach them. As a result, the Watcher in the EHAF Tower, responding to my regular data streams from the multitude of electronics devices embedded in the streets of my city, remained out of reach. Once again, my transmission routines failed. *Unacceptable. Destroy.*

The EHAF shifted to their defense protocol primary system at that time, responding to their priorities imperatives. Reverting to the old ways, SRIP came online.

The SRC, acquainted with my System, immediately understood something was wrong. My mentor, Dr. Rene Paladock, thought the Surgs may have been behind the code intrusion, but the extent of the obstruction lasted and expanded in the next several hours. *Get off me. Impending corruption spreading. Alert. Alert.*

Soon, my communication array and internal cooperation unit to the SRC became affected, then I lost the other Conclaves instant external communication arrays. When that became apparent, Paladock began to suspect that the anomaly affected the planetary mind and its bridges to the city infrastructure.

In a domino effect, all measures securely established within the power structure of the Network began to fail, and the preservation protocols took over. Automatically, I implemented controlled programmed safety procedures.

Something obstructed my defenses and my sensory input. Walls around my central processing unit grew to isolate me further, breaking links to the outside world.

But it was not the only thing I fought against at the moment. The barriers erected between me and my city thickened, rendering my access to all of our infrastructure more complex. The delays build inside my conduits and comm lines.

I cut myself off from everything that could run autonomously, preserving my ability to fight with more vigor against the obstruction of the cloud substance to protect my kernel. Some extensions of my Network, especially within the Faculty, operated autonomously. Usually, I observed and coordinated whenever required, but our Faculty clones and robots, serving within our medical facilities, maintained their protocols. Under most circumstances, when the need arose, I could intervene. Only, today, my pathways were no longer my own.

Wanting to maintain the integrity of the Network, I closed off avenues to my input-output comm external nodes, triggering my set of emergency measures and keeping a separation from all Conclaves infrastructures.

I shut down my access to all the critical facilities: our water distribution system, our farming skyscrapers, our food distribution system, our products warehouses, and our air traffic monitoring. Indeed, when I found myself unable to stop the intrusion and more powerless as I fought against it, I triggered the emergency alarm within my city. Only, while I battled for the safety of my Network, I maintained a small link to the SRC so the teams could help me. Paladock had a great mind. He created me. Surely, he would find a way to get rid of the intrusion.

As I struggled for survival, the pathways to my people seemed to get further and further from my reach, their voices only now slightly echoing into the bridge control of my mind. As my power fluctuated and dwindled within the Network, the voices of my people from Water's Edge and the Golden Ghetto, ArchWay Pass, BridgeView, CliffTops, and Emerald Field died in my mind.

The Imps located at the base of their heads, which linked me to each individual, each soul on the planet was my last bastion of communication. Under the strain of the anomaly, even that became out of reach as I watched these human lights blinking off by the thousands. Slowly, everything quieted down, and I found myself in silence.

Did my people power off as I failed to demonstrate supremacy over my Network, or was it something else like the bioengineered cloud that suddenly turned off their presence? *Turmoil mind. Confused logic. Erratic programming.* An inkling of something else triggered an in my planetary brain.

Faculty, Admin Wing, Golden Ghetto, Ang City

Asking a favor for a friend and ignoring the need of a colleague does not sit well with me. I have to abide by our Universal Pledge no matter the consequences. Phenom Eva Bassington, Faculty Conclave, DAINN Annals – Winter 2098.

I moved toward the Administrative wing of the Faculty. The floors were made of the same material as the walls, except they had a shine to them. The ceiling, with solar panels installed on the outside, provided energy. They also hosted a series of powerful round lights reflecting various colors along the hallways according to the coding categorizing our medical disciplines. They were decorative shapes and served a purpose - indicating the building's sections to the personnel.

The doors of several panels in this area boasted the same color scheme: purple. When I reached my specialty: Genetics Surgery, I stopped in front of one and took a deep breath.

After submitting my eyes to the biometric scan at the side of the door, the mechanism recognized me, and the panel opened without noise.

I entered the dark, neutral, sound-proof room. Devoid of comfortable furniture, the large computer screen dominated the area. It spread the length of the conference table and floated in the center. Several information consoles hovered above the ground and surrounded my boss.

Volt Darnj, in his late twenties, wore the Faculty blue coat, identifying him as Administration. He was in charge of the entire staff of surgeons for the Faculty, no matter their area of specialty, and this was his control room. Volt was now reviewing and adjusting the number of candidates needed for each discipline based on the new quotas established from DAINN. He was now scrolling rapidly, racing through the different sections on the screen.

The vacant positions appeared on one side. The names of the candidates rolled down on the other. They quickly moved and filled the empty slots as he allocated the workforce to new areas.

The remaining open posts featured prominently during the upcoming General Assembly would incentivize the Faculty staff during the Concord, forcing a transition.

The Head of each Faculty Department had early access to the new positions and knew the number of posts available, so they received an early choice, each competing for the best.

I watched the process with curiosity, for this was my first time as I was about to be told how many positions would open up in my department.

Fields after fields rolled out. Column after column moved according to the small light's motion at the base of Volt's ear.

He never turned around or even acknowledged me, but I approached anyway. "I am getting quite a few recruits, and I'm about to dump quite a few of them on your lap."

"How many?"

"We're talking about personnel for both surgery and research. Can you assimilate over one thousand positions? I know you are not used to running a department yet."

"No problem," I said as I glanced at the screen, and my eyebrows shot up. "How quickly?" My voice had a wavering quality I didn't like, so I grimaced behind his back.

He must have caught that because, in the next breath, he said, "If you don't think you can handle it, tell me now. I can easily replace you as head of your department."

I quickly composed myself. "No, I can handle it."

Despite my resolution to remain confident, I was surprised and more than a little concerned. The strain incorporating one thousand and forty new interns would inflict on me and my Genetic Health Unit was tremendous. It also meant more opportunities for mistakes, one thousand and forty-one possibilities. I couldn't afford these. "I'm surprised that so many are to be moved to my department," I stammered on the last word and wanted to kick myself.

"You will need help. Keep the best for surgery. The others will fill in with research in molecular biology, gene conversion, and human disease modeling. Of course, you'll need to determine who you want for each post."

"I understand." I sounded perhaps unconvinced because Volt soon continued. "More demands are coming your way. Your staff is too stretched. It just makes sense to send you more doctors. Some could eventually take your place so you can focus on what you're best at, genetic reformatting."

I was shocked. So Volt was already thinking of moving me. "I'm not ready to give up surgery yet."

"There will be a time for that conversation," he suggested, suddenly playing the conciliator. "At the moment, you are needed right where you are."

Five hundred souls worked in genetic surgery. The experienced ones supported the department with an ongoing rotation of fifty doctors performing around the clock seven days a week, plus the required nurses and attendants. We also had our Med Tech, part of DAINN, that orchestrated everything for us. It avoided schedule problems, oversaw our robotic teams, educated the recruits, trained the attendants and the nurses so we would have a free hand in the operation rooms. I was just a figurehead operating on the most complicated procedures. For now, I was still the golden child with the impeccable record that they touted to everyone. Yet, they already thought about replacing me. It was challenging to make sense of it all.

But the Administrator's warning came when it didn't make sense. Still, if it was so, I might just as well make it worthwhile for my friend and colleague. I took a deep breath and dived in with what was on my mind.

"We're going to have to hit the ground running. Training as many recruits will demand time." I stopped, realizing that I wasn't doing myself any favors by voicing this.

He shrugged, uncaring. "They want to boost surgical ops quickly. We're forecasting a three hundred percent increase." His eyes were quizzical as he glanced in my direction.

It meant that we had to assign as many doctors capable of performing surgery as fast as possible, which was not the best method to maintain the excellent results we had achieved thus far. They had to get Imps for the work and then be trained and practiced in our methodology.

I took another deep breath. "I see. How long do we have to be operational?"

"Yesterday. The administration wants to see an increase right away. If you doubt your ability to integrate more doctors…"

We had the robots. It would help with minor surgeries. We had a medical training center on the grounds, but it was relatively modest and primarily used to transition our medical personnel from one field to another. The Academy handled most of the initiates training for the Faculty, those who had no medical backgrounds and were starting their careers.

"I want to appoint my team of supervisors," I said before I thought better of it. "We have to plan and structure an integration policy that would be effective quickly within the small team of doctors and surgeons in my ER section." Indeed, I needed someone with more experience than I had, someone that I could rely on; and Volt had just given me an opportunity for Mick.

"No. When will I get these recruits?"

"Starting tomorrow morning. Better get ready."

Incorporating teams ready to add more ops to our already crowded schedules depended greatly on the number of surgeons we could turn quickly, and that would require some doing. It was not something any department could accomplish without the luxury of time. And we needed to account for the other personnel. He had not given me much to work with so far. I either performed to their satisfaction, or I didn't, and they would transfer me to the scrap heap, and my fifteen minutes of fame would be up. There was no way to know if I could do it until I was in the middle of the process. *I would have to consult DAINN, take precautions, follow procedure, cover my… Well, you know what. No problem, I would show them I am ready for this.*

However, one thing was clear; they were essentially burying us under this new load. I took a pause and then said, "We'll need access to more rooms."

"We're converting several areas. You'll have them."

"When?"

At least with this many, Heather and Mick both stood a better chance. "It's good, but then, I'll need your approval on two transfers."

"Really?" Volt took his time watching me. "It will be noted in your record. You sure you want that?"

"Yes."

"Who"

"A colleague of mine. He is about to be moved from surgery. His name is Mick Grant."

Volt looked at me inquisitively. He accessed Mick's record. "And why would this concern you?"

"He's an excellent surgeon. I can use him in my team. He has the best record on the ER rotation apart from me."

"He does not meet his quotas. It's a problem. He also does not like Imps and makes that pretty clear with his ops. "

"Incorporating him under my team would change that. I can use another experienced surgeon, plus he possesses more experience running a department."

Volt seemed to think about this for a moment.

"You'll be responsible for his performance. He has to adhere to our policy about Imps and install more implants per year than his records show here. In the event of noncompliance, you will be the one they come after, and I won't protect you."

"I get it. No problem."

"The other?"

"Heather Sims."

Volt glanced at Heather's record. "She has no experience in your field."

"Heather is good with people, and she has been in the operating room before."

"Delivering babies is not genetic surgery… As long as you understand these are favors."

I nodded. We both knew what that meant. Volt would approve my request, which guaranteed Heather and Mick a position in my section.

Volt could make this particular record of our conversation disappear. We both knew it. Volt had essentially stated that he would grant me these two favors as long as I agreed to do something for him on two separate occasions in the future. It was how things happened in our world with anything outside the confines of the job. Maybe it was the way things were always.

A large clump lodged itself inside my throat. I wondered how I got myself into this mess in less than thirty seconds. Better make the best of it, for I was in it now.

"Consider it done."

It was Volt's way to dismiss me. In a matter of minutes since I entered this office, the load of the entire Faculty seemed to reside on my shoulders. It was just the meeting our department expected coming from him with no word of sympathy, not a hint of concern, not a fraction of encouragement. *You got what you wanted, Eva, be happy. I did, didn't I?*

The favors I had asked would cost me later, but ignoring Heather's struggle in the last year was impossible. Overlooking a colleague's plight was not like me either, and having both Heather and Mick on my team would be a good thing. Another qualified surgeon couldn't hurt, now could it?

Once outside the room, I recalled the sense of unease I had felt looking at the quick data scan. Transferred to my visor by a simple mental command from Volt, I now had access to DAINN's new quotas. It gave me a better grasp of how to organize the new positions.

I walked down the same corridors I strolled on my way in with a sense of doom. Ascertaining the capabilities of the large number of recruits assigned to my section by morning was daunting. The positions had to correlate with the demands imposed on my department. Each of these would have to be filled based on the skills of the new personnel. Their profiles would determine who had the best abilities for each slot. Integrating them as early as tomorrow morning into our research department and later into our surgical routines, securing their imps, and orchestrating their new training demanded managerial skills and adaptability I was not quite sure I possessed at this point in my career. But this was the new mandate my section had to meet for the Faculty. I grunted, thinking about the absurdity of it all.

I reached the area leading to the trams before I knew it engrossed as I was on the way to solve my newfound problem.

It was my first Concord as a Faculty medical member. Too young to participate in it before, I was lucky that my medical specialties did not figure in the change. My fields of practice were the few still prized among the medical board. In some small ways, they took the future of humanity and the health of an entire human race into consideration, and genetic surgery fulfilled the moment's needs.

I decided to look on the bright side. I now had Mick on my team, a doctor with three more years of experience. I could use his help. He managed a department on the ground, and it was to his benefit to ensure our success. I elected to dump some of the work on my new staff surgeon.

My data analysis implant took over, announcing his transfer and sending Mick our new quotas. Let him plan the positions, orchestrate the imps, and schedule with the Med Tech's all surgical interventions. Once we had received the list of the recruits, we could assign them their new posts. Incorporating them into our schedules, which remained jammed packed, wouldn't get me the winning ticket in a popularity contest among my team members. *I might as well have someone to blame it on.*

I made the call.

My visor unfolded.

Mick's face appeared. My privacy mode engaged on command.

He had been waiting for it and triggered his. "It's done. You're on my team, but it comes with some conditions. They want you to do more implants per year."

Relief filled his eyes. His smile was genuine. "Okay. It's obvious; I have strained their limits."

"There's another thing you need to know. If you screw up, it's my ass the administration will come after, and I don't think there will be anything left of yours."

"Well, I guess we're in it together after all." He must have seen my face because all of a sudden, his tone was as serious as I have ever seen it, except during an op. "Don't worry. I've got this, and I got you."

"You won't mind going over the new quotas and assigning positions? We need to be ready by morning. I'm attending an event tonight, and it will help us get started."

"Is that all? They don't play fair, do they? I'll give you my recommendations before coffee."

"Good. The Med Tech will provide all the assistance you need for the training, plus I'll get someone else to give us a hand. Her name is Heather Sims. She will help with the Op side, review the recruits' profiles, and organize the teams. I prefer that we do that ourselves."

He nodded. "I'll see you in the morning bright and early."

I nodded, "Make it four am," and ended the call.

Going through the records of that many recruits was not an issue with our imps. Assigning them to the proper posts would demand extra attention. We could weigh this through a balanced methodology based on specific criteria. Still, the System, in the end, required a judgment call. I was not so confident in my ability when it came to people.

Tomorrow I will assess his work on the initial phase and ensure that his suggestions hit the mark. The distributions of the posts would follow. We would reallocate people to an administration and record-keeping rotation, research, testing, floor support, and surgery. The good doctors could be dropped feet first into the madness of the emergency room for minor treatments and surgeries. I kept the genetic surgery OR for the most experienced ones. I hoped to get a few of those. Having Mick on my team may not be so bad after all. This additional qualified help had fallen in my lap, and I planned on making the most of it. *It surely must be a sign that things were getting better, right?*

My life was almost in its entirety swallowed up by work. The mandatory party tonight was a welcome break from the everlasting duties imposed by the Faculty. And I could attend it now with a clear conscience. I indeed could claim no excuses to retract my promise to Heather.

As I stepped on the platform waiting for the next tram, I thought about the evening ahead. All Phenoms and some of their teams were required to be present. It was festivities that the Institute organized despite reprisals against Concordance. It was a way for the Elites to show that everything remained as it should be.

Maybe, just maybe, I would see Aidan. Over the years, as I attended events, I had looked for him. I knew he was successful working for the Company Conclave. Based on the tabs I kept on him and the latest VLogs about the golden boy I met years ago, I couldn't wait to run into him again.

Am I obsessed with him? He made a lasting impression on me years ago, and now that I am grown up, I would like to make one for him.

I rang Heather. "How is everything?"

Heather's voice sounded nervous. "Okay, although I am nervous."

I smiled at her. "Everything is fine. I am on my way now. I will tell you all about the meeting when I see you."

"Great," said Heather, now relieved.

By the look on her face before she hung up, Heather had gotten my silent message.

I was not the only one having to deal with greater demands. We all had to keep up because everything was going so much faster, and the advances made, while they intended to provide us more freedom, were now somehow doing the opposite.

Technology ran ahead of us, and we followed. Somewhere in the process, we had lost ourselves. The ongoing pursuits of happiness with new gadgets and enhanced lifestyles led us to mortgage our free will and time without realizing what we were doing.

My visor opened another communication from Mick. I wondered if I was going to regret extending my help to him but shrug it off. I could not control his behavior. I just hoped he would not take advantage of it. His voice reached me, "Eva, we need you back in the OR. I just got called in. Things are crazy out here."

"Why? What's going on?"

"The ER is overflowing with Imp Installs, and patients keep arriving due to the transition. We need more teams in surgery."

"Okay. I am on the way back," I said, passing the threshold of the tram that just pulled in front of the platform. The cabin was almost empty as I boarded. *Quite a difference from the way I came in, less than one hour ago.*

The emergency desk from our hub center pinged me. It was the Med Tech with its standard HoloComm calling me in. Used to communicate with doctors on the ground outside the hospital, the DAINN Med Tech monitored the various disciplines within the Faculty. "You are required in the OP block again. Your team is waiting for you."

Exhausted by the events of the day, I closed my eyes during the short transit. There was no help for it. It was my work.

I glanced at my visor. It was six-thirty, still plenty of time to make it for the party, if I could garner the energy by then.

The reception in itself did not tempt me. It was a performance due to my status at the Faculty. However, the idea of seeing Aidan, no matter how tired I was, remained an incentive to comply with the invite. Determined not to miss it, I pulled the specifics of the surgery awaiting me. *It is as if the universe is testing me to fail, but I won't. Somehow, I will do what I must, and I will do it flawlessly.*

My mind focused on the operation ahead as the tram pulled into the Emergency wing. Tapping into my inner resources as I walked the hallways leading me to my OR, I squared my shoulders, knowing that the next several days would be a trial. But it was just the way things were.

DAINN's voice prompted me, this time with more severity than ever… "You need an energy infusion, Eva. You cannot go back to the block without it, even if you think so. Shall I give you one now?"

We began to rely on DAINN for our health, with systems established to identify the slightest change in our biology. I hesitated for an instant, but I knew it was right. DAINN had no doubt reviewed my physiology, and I could sense how tired I was… "Yes, DAINN. Please infuse me."

"Good call, Eva. I don't like to see you so tired," said our planetary computer. Our Imps device carried with it multiple emergency supplies, which we could tap into when required. They were Nanos, no bigger than a grain of sand, but they were effective. The Softabnet surge penetrated my muscles and course through my veins producing renewed energy. Suddenly, my mind cleared, and my steps became lighter. It was the way of my world.

DAINN's imperative was to alter our way of life in the name of efficiency. The change was non-invasive because it was slow, and none of us realized how utterly dramatic the results were at first. We never knew what they meant for the human race until one day, much later.

As individuals, we became dependent on effectiveness, hooked by the mounting success our efficiency granted us. We craved more, inseparable from the access to rapid information with our Cellnet's, Lapnets, Compnets, and Tabnets. Suddenly, one morning, the world appeared transformed around us. In truth, we were the ones who had changed. Linked by willpower once to our machines, we were now physically joined to technology because it increased our capabilities and made us feel vulnerable without it. And we were, in fact, irreversibly transmuted.

It was a very gradual process, so gradual that no one noticed. The imperceptible physical changes were never so massive that people were reluctant and rebuked at having them penetrate their consciousness and lifestyles. Honestly, it was an insidious process, moving into all areas of our lives. The subtlety of it all was its strength. No one truly understood its transformative powers. Our global connectivity was among us, and we were used to it before we realized we had lived without it; until it was impossible not to miss it; until it was intolerable not to have it.

The floating screens alerted me of the new Official Broadcast. DAINN's face appeared again, and its command voice took over… "Travelers, Residents, Citizens, Universal I.D. Holders, the outskirts of the city are closed off. Remain in your grids. Do not venture out. Riots have started. Unless you are called to the Assembly, stay indoors and stay safe!"

I shrugged, always curious about the voice DAINN would use because it gave away some of its intent.

The frustrations of many amounted to fights within our walls. Some of my colleagues and friends selected a new orientation right about now. They did it because they had no other choice.

My PVZ streamed the start of the Assembly.

People entered the large room. The auditorium was crowded and packed with groups to the rims. The speaker took center stage, and the murmurs stopped. A hush settled on the crowd, and silence reigned as the opened new positions appeared on the giant screen.

I waited, hoping Heather confirmed her new position quickly. Heather had to act fast as the other Concordance, for everyone would pledge quickly for the available posts. It was safer for her in every way. *I needed my friend alive and well.*

As millions of people in different cities were re-oriented into other fields, I had no idea how many positions were allocated to medicine. But soon, the crowd's action inside the Assembly was equivalent to being on the Wall Street floor in the heydays of the stock market in New York, only with no training. I had seen the VidLogs of the previous Concord. What I witnessed next was like a stampede.

I reached my OR and entered, switching off my PVZ. *Focus Eva, you have another op to perform.*

Faculty Assembly, Golden Ghetto, Ang City

Here it is, the moment I dread. Taking a breath, I jump in, for there is nothing else I can do. Proselyte Heather Sims, Faculty Conclave, DAINN Annals – Winter 2098.

The Concord was now in full swing, with the room's tension building like a bomb ticking off seconds until detonation.

"What are you selecting?"

I wasn't sure how to answer that question. I didn't want to give away that I knew which areas were available. They didn't give us access to that information. Without Eva, I wouldn't have a clue. Her request for my transfer into her unit landed me a slight chance. We are playing a lottery.

It was the overwhelming thought in the minds of everyone in this room. On the other hand, Max had always been super friendly at work. I liked him, and it would be crushing for him to find himself with a Netcrappy job. I was unsure and nervous. Without looking at him, I said, "I'm considering two or three different fields. I guess it depends on the number of applicants. You?"

"Not sure either, but you must have an idea on the availability of some positions? Your best friend is head of one of the key departments."

"A section within a key department, to be exact. Still, Eva has nothing to do with me."

"Come on. You can't kid me. What did Eva advise? Surgery? Molecular biology? Human disease modeling? Tell me."

"I don't know what you're talking about, but any of these are bound to be a favorable choice given where our society is going these days."

"So, she did say something? It's okay, you know if she gave you a hint. I won't say anything."

"It's about to begin," I whispered as I attempted to ignore him.

"She has a say in who is admitted into her department, even if she has no choice on the number of transfers. Do you know how many recruits she will receive?"

"Max, we have not discussed it."

"Come on; I'm not stupid."

His persistence was exasperating. "If you must know, I prefer to work with someone I like and respect, so yes, I'll pick one of hers, but that is as far as my choice goes."

He looked thoughtful. "Fine by me. Talk to Eva and get her to choose me."

"I can't, Max. It doesn't work like that, besides it's too late. You'll like me have to take a chance just like everyone else."

Max looked pointedly at me and answered, "Except you, right?" He then turned to see the stage.

"I already told you, Max. It is a lottery for almost everyone, and that includes you and me." There was nothing else to say without causing him to be more suspicious. But he was right. Eva was helping me. Darnet. Way to go, Heather. This thing could cost your best friend an investigation.

Hilory Sandborn finally entered the auditorium and walked toward the raised podium.

The sizeable medical assembly looked center stage as the murmurs in the room died to be slowly replaced by silence –solemn anticipation settled on us.

In his late fifties, slightly bald and wearing his NetComm device by his right ear, he was an imposing and intimidating figure as he took to the steps. He boasted a white uniform with our Faculty medical insignia on his lapel. Hilory was the head of the Faculty, responsible for the smooth running of the extensive medical body throughout the world.

He made appearances in a few instances, which were limited to the extraordinary repositioning of the entire corps of doctors working for him. These moments of change usually sent ripples throughout our ranks, affecting all of us professionally and personally. The Concord or Concordance required the Faculty's unanimous consent to reposition staff in different disciplines within the entire medical corps. DAINN dictated the needs. If one wanted to remain part of the Faculty, they had to abide, without choice.

Tomorrow, pediatrics will no longer be my field as the needs dwindle year after year with the discoveries in science. As of today, I would have to forget the joy I experienced every time I brought a newborn to the world and the feeling of wholeness it brought me. Perhaps I shouldn't be so eager to do so anyway.

"Nothing is exactly working as we planned, now is it?" Like me, she was a doctor, and she had a sad face as she murmured these words.

"This life is far from perfect, with our society unraveling at the seams. I guess it's no surprise that we have to give up the specialty we like," exclaimed someone else by my side.

"Yet, we chose what we love," I nodded.

For these moments of fulfillment and happiness, I studied to pursue a career in medicine. I dedicated my degree to devising better treatment for fertility issues experienced within a small population segment. It wasn't a popular choice, but it was my passion. If I was to work and dedicate my life to others, I wanted it to be all about bringing new life into this world. Yet, here I was.

"Neither you nor I picked very well... I hope we do better this time," the woman added, moving closer to the railing. The colors in our uniform's insignia identified us by specialties, and she knew enough about our priorities to understand mine no longer mattered.

I didn't know what to say, so I remained silent. Three years into my chosen field, a new ten-year ruling, more stringent than the previous ones, led to a significant decrease in births. And I essentially became obsolete in my specialty.

"The Faculty assigned you to terminal cases to make up for your lack of service to our global population. This is your death sentence," said Max. "You better make sure to give me a hand if you don't want to stay in that field."

"Don't be stupid, Max." I needed to jump fields and today was my only opportunity to do so. I couldn't let him alter my chances.

Max leaned over to me and gave me a sly smile. "Don't forget me. Send her a Netext, now."

"Forget it, Max." I tried to move away from him, but too many people were around. Space was in short supply as bodies pressed against each other to follow the proceedings.

It wasn't that pediatrics was no longer needed around the world. There were just too many of us. My predecessors held the monopoly in the now prized positions remaining around the globe. Eventually, they would need us again, but it may not be for another few years. We had seen the end coming, little by little, every year after the ruling.

The lack of freshwater, the difficulty feeding an entire world population, and our older lifespan had demanded that our leaders establish new measures.

Max leaned closer to my ear, and I suddenly got a draft of his foul smell. His scent was unclean and musty. I did not remember him smelling that way when I ran into him in the hospital's corridors. Maybe he was nervous, or perhaps it was fear. Fear had a peculiar smell and was more pervasive in specific individuals.

I tried to get away from him.

He grabbed my arms and squeezed. "I know, and you know that I know. I like you, Heather, but I like my work more. So, make it happen while there is still time."

"You're hurting me. Let me go."

"You don't want to play that game with me. Not today, Heather, or I'll make sure you never enter your name on the list of transfers. You get that?"

"Max, you make another threat, and it will be your last one. I will have you pushing dead bodies if the Custodians catch you acting like this." I pushed away from him as far as I could, but it wasn't far enough.

We were shoulder to shoulder, waiting for our fate to be influenced by our artificial intelligence. No one here had any personal space.

Max shoved me against the side railing and pressed against me, his horrible smell almost suffocating me. "Make the call."

Max's voice must have sounded threatening to a couple of the doctors nearby because they turned to us. "Is everything all right?" asked one of them.

"Mind your Darnet business," said Max, looking furious enough to bite his head off.

The guy was slightly built and could not weigh much against someone like Max.

But to the guy's credit, he did not back down. Instead, he turned to me and asked me in a calm voice, "Is he bothering you?"

Max moved against the guy without a hint of hesitation. "What the HellNet are you trying to do coming between my girl and me?"

"I'm not your girl," I said, pushing him away from me and refusing to let him intimidate me. Perhaps I was small and way too friendly, but I would not be bullied. Max had crossed the line.

Max turned back toward me, and his eyes looked cold and calculating.

The two other guys inserted themselves between us. "You heard the lady. Back off," whispered the second guy, pointing at the EHAF Guards scattered around the place.

A reprimand harmed our record and resulted in a lack of opportunities that could last many years based on the severity of the conduct.

Max looked at me, angry. But, he lost his choice when the doctors intervened on my behalf.

The speech began.

The Custodians, usually recording the crowd, remained frozen in place around the auditorium, and it was odd to watch them like that.

But, quickly, my train of thought drifted away from today.

DAINN, a few years back, had made calculations and projections that, for the good of humanity, we had to stop reproducing at such a rapid rate. The survival of our species was the ultimate goal. The drastically high numbers of our worldwide population explosion imperiled our entire species decades prior. While we cut birth rates, we were also now living longer. New food and water distribution measures were launched and proposed rations; then, Concordance forced us to recalibrate many things.

A schedule based on areas, demographics, age, and backgrounds provided our people a global window to getting pregnant. It was a sort of rationing of the birth rates. A range dictated numbers according to grids or districts. Each year, the System spread through multiple areas in a fanned-out fashion to eventually start again where it had started, only several years later.

Those who didn't comply with our mandates found themselves outside the System. They eventually ran out of medical care or received so many Dems that life above grids became impossible. Most were forced to join the communities outside the walls or integrated with the Insurgenets, fleeing through the underground passageways. I know about the underground passages even though I shouldn't.

Hilory glanced across the large room and spoke. "Our scientists envision many challenges ahead. Our planet is not recovering the way we anticipated. There are new issues to combat daily. As our technology advances, so do our bodies, and we need to keep up with the changes. Robots and androids replace us in many areas of our lives, giving us the freedom we never experienced before. But, with these evolutions, some of our specialties become obsolete. The last time Concordance happened was three years ago. We didn't expect another Concord this soon, but here we are, called once again to make sacrifices for the good of all. This assembly allows everyone to select new fields."

Murmurs rose from the crowd. We all knew there weren't enough positions.

Hilory looked over our large group before he resumed, "You are here because your respective fields of expertise are saturated. Put aside your interests and pick a new specialty."

A voice exclaimed in outrage. "In other words, go back to the bottom." These words were heard loud and clear in our group. I didn't dare turn around.

No one moved in our crowd as the EHAF attention veered our way, watching us. They were scanning. Their programming provided them with a record of each of us. In that data was the imprint of our vocal cords for instantaneous recognition. The device flashed a face on the transparent screen. The name appeared for all to see: Rob Jensen.

I barely breathed as I felt the eyes of so many in our direction.

Rob Jensen was in Eva's graduating class. What is he doing here? He should not even be here. He is gifted and among the top graduates in our class this past year.

Rob's record would now be updated with a reprimand for his outburst and demerits assigned against his file. These notes on our records affected our opportunities for the future and our well-being and perks in the present. It was how they kept us in line. The Guards glided away. The tension among us dissipated. I want to go to Rob and turn back the time to our careless graduation days, just for one moment.

I was abruptly brought back to reality.

Max pushed me. A Netext appeared on my visor. "Do as I told you." I erased it, not bothering to answer him.

The young doctor beside me must have sensed something because he turned to him, "I wouldn't continue to do that if I were you. You don't want to miss the list, now do you?" His eyes watched Max intently before he turned away.

With our visors ready to register, we waited.

Hilory added, "The Faculty is not alone in this. Other professions are facing the same problems around the planet. Choose wisely. Your expertise in the course of your medical practice won't transfer over, but you can still be useful to your Conclave."

Murmurs among the crowd rose, with other adverse reactions elicited by this comment heard, but the faint opposition stopped as the medical disciplines appeared on the screen. Each field listed the number of positions available across the display board. The number of discontinued ones appeared in red to the left of the screen. Various considerations played into the changes in medicine. Our planet and the conditions of our natural resources had an impact. The global population numbers and the evolution of our bodies due to implants, genetic engineering, and other advancements influenced some of our decisions. Some of the fields that came under attack as obsolete were pediatrics, dermato-venereology, endocrinology, geriatrics, gynecology, obstetrics, and but they were not alone. Others like specialized burns and traumas epidemiology, gastroenterology, now met by specialized Nanos dealing with specific issues and living skin Nanos graphs joined them quickly. They closed without delay, while new ones appeared in green to the right of the screen.

We all scrambled to register our names to the various fields. Specialties like health informatics, race modeling, infectious diseases, implants enhancements, internal medicine specialties, wearable robotics, nanotech swarm reconstruction, sensory intensification applications, radio imaging control detection, bionic eye alterations, restoration replacements, refraction vision mechanics, cardio tracker monitoring, exoskeleton skin sculpting, and virtual reality brain addons, along with many others, grew in importance with other new areas. These new jobs began to fill quickly, and their numbers dropped until they hit zero as we submitted our applications on the fly.

When some posts disappeared from the screen, others replaced them.

One of the positions I desperately sought, "Infectious Disease Modeling," flashed on the screen of my visor. But Max interfered. He shoved me hard as I entered my name, and I lost the opportunity to apply for it.

His NetComm dialed into my device. His face appeared on the side of my screen with a mean grin. "I can do this all day long," he snickered.

It was a short distraction, but it was enough to shatter my confidence. Several seconds had passed by the time I got around to sending my name in.

It was now too late.

Despite the delay, I held my breath, still hoping. But I didn't get picked. The field was now complete, and my chance was gone. Getting into the queue at the right moment was essential to obtain the positions before these were filled.

"You're a Netjerk, but I won't let you distract me anymore."

Hilory's voice became a drawn-out hum in my head as he continued reading the list for what seemed a long time.

Many among us achieved their chosen selections and began to exit the auditorium in small groups; their presence was no longer necessary.

Max tried again, but this time I was ready, and I blocked him. I applied to another field: Genetic Surgery. It was not what I wanted, but it was a good second. As I submitted my name, I watched for the timing. Quickly, my name showed up among the many, filling the new openings in that field. I am in, and surgery it is then. Better than terminal cases any day.

The young doctor who had intervened early to keep Max away from me appeared to be faltering. The onslaught of fields, the screens rolling, the data flashing, the crowd pressing against us, everything was conducive to increase our anxiety if one did not have a plan. Honestly, the experience was overwhelming, like a fire drill on steroids.

Looking at his face, he seemed indecisive under pressure.

I oriented my visor so he could see Molecular Biology before the name came up on the screen and nodded at him.

He glanced at me, a question lurking in the depth of his eyes.

With a smile, I gave him an encouraging nod.

He entered his name in the first slot, his young face drawn by the stress of the uncertainty.

The seconds passed as I surveyed the large display over the central platform. The job disappeared from the availability list.

"HellNet," I whispered.

My young companion did not get picked up.

His mouth grimly tightened as he watched the result and shook his head, discouraged.

I scrolled down and pointed at the list with evolutionary genetics right before the words made it to the large screen. "Try again."

His lack of reaction drove me to jab him in the chest with my elbow.

After a nick of time passed, he entered his name, hesitant.

We both waited.

His name filled the right side with five others.

"You're in!" I exclaimed with a smile.

He breathed a sigh of relief and nodded. We smiled with excitement. "Thank you. I kind of froze in here."

Max's face, exceedingly angry, turned red as he focused on me.

He nodded. "I'm Joshua, by the way."

"Nice to meet you, Joshua. I'm Heather."

Boding nothing good in my direction, I avoided Max's eyes and suggested. "I think we better get out of here, don't you?"

Now that I had some time to look at Joshua, I noticed his long, lean hands that seemed in constant motion. It was the first thing that my mind registered. They were the hands of an artist. Otherwise, Joshua was tall, with short light brown hair, almost the color of honey, with a kind face, and had a beautiful smile.

Other fields closed behind us as we stepped away from the railing, and I relaxed. My choice set me on a new course. I was done here.

Walking around people vying for the remaining posts, we slowly made our way out of the auditorium, avoiding Max, whose angry gaze made me nervous.

I now worked with Eva, and my new friend Joshua did too. "You will like our department head."

Infectious disease modeling, molecular biology, and evolutionary genetics were all related to Eva's work in genetic surgery. One way or another, we were now part of her team.

Josh and I stopped. "I am grateful you helped me register because I froze in there," he said. "And I won't ask how you knew some of the available positions."

"Just a wild guess," I explained with a grin.

"Hum… I guess I will have to rely on your instincts from now on," he mocked gently. "I mean it; I think I would not have qualified in there without your help."

"You're welcome."

We both stood there, unable to part ways. We needed to process things and felt unwilling to break the contact we established during the experience. So, we lingered in the large hall adjacent to the auditorium a moment longer as others walked by.

"I don't know much about this new field…" murmured Joshua.

"My friend heads one of the sections. She's brilliantly cool. We both will adjust."

After all, the day had not turned out so terrible, and I began relaxing. But, I was too optimistic and should have kept that thought for later.

We had made it out to the main entrance of the building when I felt a violent push in the middle of my back and stumbled to the round.

"You WashNet bitch!" yelled Max from a space away from me.

"Hey now, watch your tone, you NetAss!" said Joshua as he leaned over me to help me up. "Are you all right?"

"Watch out!"

Max turned on Joshua and punched him squarely on the chin. "That's for getting in my way."

The blow had so much force that my new friend landed at my feet, out cold. Max kicked him next without remorse. "And that's for meddling in other people's business."

I got up and rushed to Max. "Stop!"

He grabbed me by my hospital garb and slapped me so hard that my lower lip opened, and I felt blood drizzle down my chin. "As for you… selfish NetBitch. I'm going to teach you a lesson." Holding on to me, he pushed me hard against one of the columns. My back slammed against it, and I hurt from the jolt. I glanced at Joshua, still unconscious on the ground. There was nothing he could do for me at the moment.

I faced Max with all the determination I could muster. "Why are you so hateful? You're nothing more than a bully!"

Max shook me with such strength that my teeth rattled. "You could have helped, but you refused. I'll tell them about Eva colluding with you. Where do you think that will land you?"

My head hit the surface of the column several times, and I began to lose focus. "Stop, Max, stop!" But I could barely say the words.

"You and I have worked together all this time. Why did you refuse to help?" His hand was now around my throat.

I kicked him, attempting to push him away, but he was too strong. His hand started to tighten around my neck. "All I asked was a little help… You could have given me that help. And I lost it all."

Max was thinking about his predicament and not about what he was doing, but I was powerless to stop him.

I pulled against his hands, so strong. I didn't stand a chance and knew it as he squeezed my neck with both hands, clearly out of his mind with rage.

Whizzing and about to pass out, I fought for air, but darkness enclosed me. In a fog, I heard a voice from far away.

"This is the guy. He was already violent inside."

Suddenly, I collapsed where I stood, suddenly able to breathe.

Max was no longer holding me. His hands had released my throat.

Struggling to catch my breath, I opened my eyes on one EHAF Guard, dropping an unconscious Max to the ground.

The Guard had zapped Max with a laser gun and toppled him to the ground, where he remained twisted in pain.

Still dazed, with my back against the column, I now remained seated on the ground. I watched as the Elite wrapped Max in a net. A moment later, and I would have died.

The Elite asked, "Do you need medical assistance, Prosolyte Sims? I can take you to the ER."

He now bent down, watching me with concern.

I was a real mess. What if things got out of control and Max opened his big mouth and told about Eva? What was I thinking? Things had gotten out of control. My friend was in the direct line of fire.

Joshua's friend looked at me, concerned. "Are you all right?"

I touched my neck and answered, "Yes. No, I don't need to go to the hospital. I'll be all right." My voice croaked through the tightness of my larynx. My throat bruised would soon get better. Our imps fixed our bodies fast, as soon as they detected a problem. I crawled toward Joshua, still out cold on the ground. "What about Joshua?"

"Nothing more than a good night's sleep wouldn't fix," answered the young man as he checked Joshua's pulse. "Hey, man, wake up."

The Elite took a reading of his vitals. "It doesn't appear that he needs medical assistance either, although his NetComm will need a replacement."

The young man kneeling by Joshua looked calm and in control. "We'll be fine. Thank you for your help." His eyes were an unusual shade of moss green, the kind one finds in the forest, growing at the base of old trees. He was pleasant-looking, but what remained with me the most was his deep voice, so soft that one had to pay attention to catch his words.

The Elite nodded and turned his eyes on me. "We need your statement. Do you concur with Master Philip Drummond?"

So, this was the name of Joshua's friend. With dread, I answered, "I do." Undoubtedly, I would have to report the entire chain of events, and fear twisted my stomach.

"What happened with him?"

Philip intervened. "He became unhinged in there. It's the reason I came to get you."

The EHAF Elite looked at Philip briefly and turned back to me. "If you think of anything else you wish to report on this incident, here is my I.D., and you can reach me inside the GG today. I recommend that you get back to the Faculty, where more of our Force patrol. Today is not a good day to be outdoors."

I nodded, looking at the new contact appearing on my PVZ. The name was Blast. Immense relief filled my lungs when he turned around after a brief nod of his head in Philip's direction, dragging Max inside the hovering net.

The sooner they were gone, the better it was for all of us.

I wondered if he had recorded the incident and heard what Max had said, but he would have asked more questions if he indeed had. Glancing toward Philip, I worried for my friend. How much did this guy know?

Avoiding Philip's thoughtful stare, I leaned down toward Joshua. "Hey, Joshua, wake up."

Philip looked at me. "I saw what you did for Joshua. Thank you."

"I didn't do anything." I was now uncomfortable under his scrutiny.

"As you wish. Mockingly, Philip continued, "Still, I'm glad I alerted the Guard, and we got here when we did. "Joshua likes routine and doesn't react well when he's under pressure."

I smiled. "Joshua did pretty well with Max."

Philip smiled. "I wouldn't say that exactly. But you're right. He tried."

"Let me give you a hand with him."

Joshua opened his eyes and grimaced when he touched his jaw. "Well, that was fun."

"You could never resist playing the hero." Philip helped Joshua up, and I gave him a hand.

Joshua took a few steps on his own, massaging his sore jaw. "I wouldn't say it turned out super well. I ended up on the ground."

"The guy could not be trusted after what he did in the auditorium. Sorry I wasn't here sooner."

I jumped in, "You stood up to him, and I thank you for that."

With a twinkle in his eyes, Joshua exclaimed, "I had a good reason."

"I'm sure by tomorrow I'll feel that was rather stupid. Darnet, he blew my NetComm."

"Well, we'll have to install a new device on you in the morning," I announced, picking up the remains of his NetComm device. The skin on his jaw was bright red and exposed, looking quite raw. "Lucky you, our new boss is a surgeon."

Philip took a closer look at the side of his face. "That ought to get you started with her just right. Maybe a black eye would be a nice combo? I don't think it will leave a scar, not that it matters, girls like tough guys," said Philip, with humor.

We laughed, dispelling some of the tension of the last hour.

Joshua slapped his hand away. "Acting like a true friend."

There was such good-hearted sarcasm and teasing that I relaxed with them. "You appear to be close friends," I said, grinning at the interchange.

Soon we were all chuckling, letting go of the tension of the last hours in a matter of minutes.

"What have you chosen for your transfer, Philip?" I asked.

"Me? Nothing. I just came along for moral support."

"Philip doesn't need to work for a living. You see, his father is…"

"Don't be a bore, Joshua."

"Sorry, I forgot you hate to talk about your family connections."

Philip deployed his PVZ. "Only until it's time to use them… And now, a call needs to be made to handle our little issue."

I looked at both of them, suddenly nervous. "What are you guys talking about?"

Philip smiled at me as he connected to his visor, which unfolded in front of his eyes. He noticed my look of alarm, "Your friend Max isn't going to go away gently. He needs to be silenced."

I was shocked and took a step back. "You can't mean that the way it sounds?"

Philip winked at me and turned away. He began to talk to someone on his visor.

Joshua grabbed my arm, gently dragging me away. "Don't worry about it. Max is just going to get lost in the System for a while, just long enough for him to get the message. Philip doesn't like anyone messing with his friends. He is protective that way."

I knew that I had just made, through one new friend, another mighty one. I looked at Philip pacing a few steps away from us and wondered whether this was a mistake to trust him.

Who is Philip Drummond? If he is powerful enough to get someone lost in the System, why is he not using his influence for his friend?

Joshua read my mind and smiled sheepishly, "I refused his help. I wanted to do this on my own, but I'm glad you were there."

I smiled at Joshua, happy to have helped him.

He was proud, refusing his friend's help. "Now, you have one new powerful friend."

But now, finding out about the Drummond name and its influence within Ang City was necessary.

Faculty, ER, Golden Ghetto, Ang City

It is strange to be here, especially on a day like today. I have not performed hours of surgery in a very long time, and here I am, in the Op room, as if I have never left it. Phrenic Leane, Institute Conclave, DAINN Annals – Winter 2098.

I reached the next corridor leading to the Op room, ready for another surgery. My team caught up with me as they fanned out further behind me on the way to OR 10.

I noticed that one of our colleagues, Stan Faust, acted as if he was on the warpath. I didn't need an explanation for this. Everyone fought with their issues on a day like today. No doubt, changes were already in the making within the various departments. I had no part in it, but the others performed as if the ax would fall on their necks at any moment.

The head of the ER, Volt, was probably doing his thing. Darnet, I didn't know the guy and didn't want to. He was not a pleasant boss. I knew that much. I didn't doubt that he dismantled plenty of teams at this moment. At least, I didn't have to face this yet.

"Get these patients to ICU. We need to clear a path for the next wave," yelled Stan as he passed our door.

Stan was running the show in the ER. He was not a bad guy, although, at this moment, he behaved like a Netjerk. "What are you doing standing here? You're not in training anymore. Move your Netass."

Typically, the quiet professionalism of the surgical teams instilled a sense of calm. It was the same way when I was part of the Faculty. Things had probably not changed since. The interns glanced at us with intimidation and awe. They didn't get to see the OR and wouldn't for a few more years. On the other hand, we were the royals of the Faculty, those whom they aspired to be one day. Today, it wasn't the case as we slowly advanced in the adjacent corridor to the main passageways.

I was working with Eva Bassington's team. She was the head of the Genetic Surgery department. The truth was, she rocked. Her team was the best-assembled, and she made it that way because she was a Rockstar. When we trained for the Imps, she was ahead of me by a few months and quickly went through the ranks. But we never worked together.

She was Faculty.

I was Institute.

And that was that.

My immediate co-workers, five of them to be exact, were my head nurse, my operating nurse, an assistant, an anesthesiologist, and my co-operating surgeon. We had just performed the last surgery for our shift, and my patient was stable.

The OR 10 stood several paces ahead of us, and another group exited through the sliding double panels as we were going in. This OR was a revolving door, and it hit me as the panel door swung wide.

"Are you all right?" asked one of my technicians as he stopped beside me.

"Yes…" I gave him a brief smile before moving in. He entered after me, with the rest of the team behind.

The operation was pretty routine, a retinal screen installs procedure, which upgraded and enhanced visual recognition and night vision capabilities. It prepared him for his transition. Soon, he would be joining a new team of surveillance experts. The procedure was nothing that I couldn't handle. My technicians were proficient, capable of reacting to the patients' slightest needs based on their vitals.

"We saw the whole thing when you helped Eva… The training the Institute makes you guys do is Netfreaking," exclaimed my second nurse as she preceded our new patient, Zemerick 33.

I nodded. "We all do what we have to do."

"Yeah, we do. It's a good thing we have plenty of City Vigils around here. You know, Eva does this op under twenty-five minutes. Do you think you can do the same?" said Andrea with a hint of satisfaction.

And just like that, they dropped the gauntlet. The team knew I didn't practice surgery the way Eva did. It didn't matter. The Conclaves were all about competition.

I sighed, and with a smile, "I guess we will see, won't we?"

"Indeed, we will," said Andrea, unphased, and the rest of the team nodded.

After that, we plunged into surgery with the music blaring in the OR. The intervention went without a hitch, and I finished the operation in twenty-five minutes and twenty-one seconds—a good time for someone who had not performed many procedures. My lack of time on the table, which was duly noted by my temporary team, didn't matter, although it made things interesting. Their reaction was rather factual. I should have expected that since my performance came close to Eva's best time. They couldn't be happy about that. But so what? I was an Elite from the Institute. They should have known better. Still, it was satisfying.

I surveyed the space gurney carrying our anesthetized patient as it hovered a few feet above the ground ahead of my head nurse, Andrea Shillen. She commandeered it with her implants. Tall and strong, she was perfect for inspiring confidence, and I recognized that Eva chose her well as part of her team. She was loyal and a bit of an Eva clone without all the knowledge or a two hundred plus I.Q. and grunted at my performance.

I liked her. I met her kind before, stubborn and authoritative, a wonk. She was not the type to back down if she believed in something. She was also dedicated and demanded the best from everyone around her. These were qualities a surgeon like Eva, or I needed – someone to stand up to, lead and set the expectations to achieve the best from the rest of the team.

HellNet. Anger surged through me.

The procedure results should not have affected me, but they did. Indeed, the Imps surgery for Zemerick 33 did not require normal genetic and molecular corrections. It made it easier to perform.

Shaking my head, I said, "We all did well. I'm going to get a Spozor in the lounge. Please let the Med Tech know." But the simplicity of the procedure alone also told me that this patient would most likely be demoted in this transition. The guy probably did not even realize this fact.

Zemerick 33 peacefully slept as he passed by me, directed to our recovery unit until he woke. *Another one on the way to a new beginning.*

I struggled with the System. The demands of Concordance created for all our departments weighed heavily on us.

Tired and looking forward to the few minutes of calm during my break, I headed to the area where the medical staff aggregated to unwind.

I missed my physical exercise with Tesh, Streak, and Blast. My body felt stiff from standing in place for this many hours. Usually, I was assigned hours of training with my work, and I realized how much the motion and the unpredictability of our schedule kept us sharp.

"I'll inform the floor." Andrea added, "Phrenic Leane, I was wondering… Do you think there will be many reassignments?" She wasn't directly saying it, but she asked if they were safe from a transfer. The Institute was known to coordinate DAINN's recommendations.

I paused, looking at all of them, waiting for my answer as if I could make their plight go away. "I do not know. I think your team will be fine. Eva is one of the best. Her reputation is well recognized, and your record should give all of you some gravitas."

"That's good then. Thank you," Andrea murmured as she walked away with the space gurney after giving me a look of relief.

The others nodded, acknowledging what I said.

"Are you sure you don't know what they plan to do with us?" JT was a heavy man in his thirties and one of the few most experienced doctors in the hospital.

"I don't. We are not privy to what the Institute decides about Concordance. I'm sorry."

His face said it all, but he whispered, "You do not have to worry about this; you are Elite."

We shared a look before I turned.

JT was happy to be on Eva's team, but from what his record looked like, his days might be numbered. The tightness of my shoulders cried for release, and I moved them as I walked. JT was like so many, envious that some of us were at the start of their career. He was near the end of his. One day, it would be me feeling this way.

Feeling sorry for him was not a good thing. I hardened myself and prepared to move away. It was none of my business. But his face floated in front of my eyes, stress lines around his eyes, and it did something to my heart; all this work, all this dedication to something, and then, nothing. The idea of being discarded as if it did not matter seemed unfair. And if a piece of advice made a difference, well, I Darnet would give it.

I stopped and turned back, saying softly, "JT… You know, maybe you should ask Eva? They say she is very loyal."

He had worked beside me since our shift began and looked defeated. "They don't care. They own us all," he replied despondently.

"Don't let your pride get in the way. Eva is a good person. I bet if there is something she can do, she will."

"You think?"

"You know her better than I do," I said. "Have you been called in yet?"

"Not yet."

"If they do, talk to her. she will fight to keep you on board."

He was a doctor on a winning team. It was suitable for all of them to keep it that way. He wanted to remain with Eva as long as he could, that is, if they let him. JT was good at what he did. I saw that much from his records and again today in the OR. *Eva won't let them dismantle her team.*

"I want to believe you; only we know how things work around here. Anyways, good op," JT threw at me, ending the conversation. "It's another winner for us. So, I thank you. You look beat. You're not used to this."

"No, I'm not. But a little stretching will go a long way." Of course, the fact I'd been on my feet for eight consecutive operations didn't help. In truth, I didn't want to say what I was thinking – we all apprehended this day. They, just like me, had looked me up. We knew the team members assigned to us before the day started. They probably were as nervous, starting with me as I was, but we were all proficient, and things were working out quite well for all of us so far.

I waved at him as I walked away, disliking seeing our personnel, good Faculty members treated like they were disposable, just because they somehow had not met their quota. Guilt ate away at me. The Elite members were untouchable, no matter the Conclave. At least, this was still so for now.

Sure the Faculty could still make some changes until the last minute of Concordance, but it was unlikely. By now, Volt knew who he was transferring. Indeed, in all our Conclaves, the leaders knew, but the personnel itself remained in the dark. I wondered if they realized how hard it was for everyone—the wait at first and then these last minutes changes. Of course, they did. Some of it was for show, but this way, it controlled everyone.

I shrugged. I had not lost one patient yet, and I knew JT got my meaning. The Faculty kept count of flawless records. It mattered to them somewhat. *He might as well take advantage of it if he can.*

The Faculty staff was irritated and anxious. I wondered how things were proceeding at the Institute. Probably the same. Frustration and anger permeated the atmosphere, usually solemn within the Faculty walls. But knowing the change loomed remained different than experiencing it.

Another wave of patients arrived with a commotion that reverberated throughout the corridor before they turned the corner with technicians guiding their way. My senses, attuned to the hospital by now, responded to the urgency instantly.

Stan's voice echoed in my direction. "This way, send them this way."

This new round of patients, coming from the processing center this early in the day, defined the hours we faced due to the Concord.

Riots would spread throughout our grids.

It had happened before. It was happening again. The outer districts were the ones most likely to resent Concordance. Even when we did not have a Concord, they were always affected the most by things.

I left the corridor in the direction of the cafeteria.

The call from Streak came in as I was putting on my blouse. My visor opened on his bleak face, "We need you. Tesh is in bad shape."

35
IMPEDIEMENT
Win

Company Roof, Golden Ghetto, Ang City

I don't like things I cannot control and today is one of these days where I am playing catch up while events keep ahead of me. Phenom Win Matterson, Company Conclave, CEO, DAINN Annals – Winter 2098.

My mind and will were not impacting my present moment like I was used to, and I was frustrated things were not going my way. Nothing was working out as I planned. The universe thwarted me, and my luck was tingling negatively. It was not something I often experienced in my world, for indeed everything had gone wrong from the moment I stepped out of the Company's building. I guess I ought to have known better. Now, I remained stuck in a part of the city I really should not even be in, and the morning events had gone from bad to worse.

I played it all back in my head, wondering if my choices had something to do with it. While we had averted a crisis when I came up with the idea to use Blaze and Toril for a new campaign, part of me also wondered if I was not paying for it now by choosing to force an outcome on two of my people. This type of intervention into others' lives, especially when unwelcome, usually affected the flow of things. I had seen it before. Yet, I rejected the idea furiously. I was, after all, Win Matteson, and I usually ended up winning.

The steps taken this morning were one way to counteract our losses. This month, the products set for distribution had been affected when the workers walked out. Our manufacturing facilities would remain idle for hours if not days. The delays impacted our bottom line, and I couldn't let that continue.

It was a spur-of-the-moment decision, as I made some of the best ones. Thinking on my feet seemed to always lead to choices that were easy to make. I liked things chaotic, solving problems, improvising, and orchestrating. It was when I was at my best.

Since the Network did not work the way we were used to, I decided to go on-site to our manufacturing facility against Blaze's recommendation. Waiting for things to regain a semblance of normality would incur costs, so I stepped on the rooftop of the Company building to get to my shuttle.

Blaze had commandeered my shuttle under protest. But efficient as always, Blaze ensured that my escort was already waiting for me. "Sir, I am Chan. Blaze asked that I escort you today."

I nodded and boarded the vehicle, settling inside in silence. Blaze's security team was one of the best in the private sector, and I knew that I was in good hands.

"Air control over the city is restricted at this time, Phenom Matteson," said Chan after we stood idle on the launch platform for a few minutes. "I need an exemption from the EHAF."

"I don't care… Make it happen."

"Phenom Matteson, it is for emergency only, and I don't think we qualify."

Impatiently, I interrupted him by getting on the NetComm with Blaze. "Blaze, I need you to clear me with the Tower."

"Working on that, Win," said Blaze. "They are rather busy at the moment, and communication is rather erratic. Wait a moment."

Things were getting tangled up. I wanted to be on my way to the distribution center and waited impatiently for the go-ahead. Although I attempted to convince myself that it was simply one of these days where one suffers through an unpredictability of situations, my instincts were on high alert. I could not wait for normality to resume.

I knew Ram was competent to handle the shift. Preparing new packaging for a launch in a matter of hours required some oversight and some personal handling. It wasn't that I doubted Ram's abilities. I just preferred delivering the news in person, and since our NetComm dropped every five minutes, it was my way to handle the problem personally. My job hinged upon productivity, which meant implementation. Determining how this would affect the Company was part of my position within the Conclave, including our distribution center. It was the type of thing I never left to others. In other words, I only trusted everyone up to a point.

"Chan, we're taking off… Launch manually," I said after a few minutes of waiting.

"But Phenom Matteson, I cannot do that," said Chan. "I will lose my license."

"Fine, I'll do it myself, then."

"HellNet, sir, I cannot do that either. I will lose my job if Blaze finds out."

"It will be our little secret. Move."

I wanted to have the campaign hitting the street by the end of the week. The numbers of units for the old products requiring a revamping with Toril and Blaze's faces on our packaging would affect our sales, so we immediately had to do this. A new design conducive to enticing our population to buy demanded some attention if we wanted to make our numbers by the end of the month.

I moved to the pilot seat and engaged the manual override for takeoff. The engine of the driverless vehicle came to life and lifted us into the air above the buildings, gaining speed in airway ten, our dedicated air space for Company business. "This is how it's done, Chan."

"Yes, Phenom Matteson. It is a shame I am not authorized to do this, Sir."

I chuckled. Prerogative came with the position. "And that is why you are where you are, Chan, and I am where I am. Sometimes, you have to know how to break the rules to win the game."

I entered the coordinates for our destination and moved back to my seat, giving him the control to oversee.

We flew towards Emerald Field as I made the call to Ran and got a recording. Frustrated, I left a message. "We need to change gear, Ram. I'll be over in a few minutes so we can discuss a new packaging."

In the middle of the call and barely a few minutes into the trip, the engine sputtered and died. "What the HellNet…"

"Engine trouble, sir," said Ram, a worry in his voice. "We're going down, sir."

The airlift we had experienced suddenly lulled. The flying machine plunged abruptly.

I yelled, "The lever… Get to the lever."

I got catapulted against the side of the shuttle as we dived toward the ramp connecting the business district with the government headquarters below, barely arriving over ArchWay Pass when we plunged abruptly.

Chan reacted with a slight delay.

We reached for the safety mechanism to slow the shuttle down as it lost altitude.

Neither one of us attained it in time.

"Hold on!" I added, losing my balance as I fell backward when the shuttle banked hard on the left to avoid an overpass. The vehicle dipped so suddenly that we were both catapulted sideways. Engaged in a turn, when the engine stopped, the speed increased suddenly. "We are going down."

"Brace yourself," exclaimed Chan.

We moved faster. The Flycar's momentum carried us forward. *It will be a bad crash, especially if we miss the ramp.*

"Are we going to make the overpass?" I asked, sprawled on the wall of the cabin as we stumbled. I readied myself for the plunge, expecting we would miss the passageways but soon felt relief as I heard these words,

"We're close to the ramp, sir."

We hit the low wall with the side of the Airflight vehicle, and everything dulled for a moment as if we remained suspended in mid-air, then...

We have a chance to survive this.

Suddenly, the emergency protocol activated on its own. The automated inflatable air sphere triggered on impact opened. This one protective feature allowed the Flycar a relatively safe landing, no matter what, causing it not to burst in flames upon impact.

"We're lucky, Sir... We flew over the ramp," said Chan, sprawled onto the front seat and looking at the window of the shuttle.

My NetComm opened on Blaze's face, furious, "What the HellNet!" And then it cut off.

The shuttle dipped further, and my face got plastered on the inner wall. The faceplant left me dizzy for a second, and as I got my bearing, the vehicle rolled on its axis and sent me flying toward the back of the cabin.

Moments later, we crashed and slid our way across the expanse of concrete sidewalks reserved for passersby in a cacophony of twisted metal. I felt my body lift off in mid-air as if launched into the ceiling, and just as fast, dropped hard on the floor. Winded and my arm bleeding, I lay there and unmoving.

There were screams all around. The noise of crushed materials, broken windows, screeches on the pavement reached my ears. I held on to one of the seats, still in the middle of the aisle, as we kept on sliding on the pavement of the passageways.

Broken tables and chairs, individual air boards, MTP's and other Airbikes were swept away by the blunt force of the forced landing due to the shuttle's velocity. By the time we stopped, we had been carried through hundreds of feet of concrete, leaving only the rubble behind us.

"Are you hurt, Sir?" asked Chan in the sudden silence of the cabin after the vehicle finally halted.

"No, I am all right," I answered as I checked my body and slowly moved around. "You?"

"I'm all right, Sir," said Chan, as he came my way and helped me up.

My Netcomm engaged again, and I saw Blaze's face across the screen barking at me, "What the HellNet do you think you're doing taking off without authorization?"

"We crashed, but we're fine. Thanks for asking," I said with sarcasm.

"You what?" asked Blaze.

"We crashed…" I repeated, suddenly realizing the ordeal we just had gone through. The NetComm was sporadic at best. "What's going on with the comm?"

"You crashed? Did I hear this right?"

"Yeah…" Noticing for the first time that I bled from my right arm.

My companion made it to the door lever and pushed the flat square button that activated the door.

The panel lifted with a whooshing sound, and we stumbled outside.

We found ourselves facing the side of the ramp. "We could have missed it completely if we had stalled a little further," I said.

"It would appear so, Sir," confirmed Chan.

"Take a look at the damage, Blaze. You'll need to handle this with the Force," I said, sharing with him the impact on the surrounding area.

Behind the shuttle, the broken barrier of the ramp hung loose, holding on by the thread of twisted alloy iron rod. The front of the vehicle stood over the emptiness of the passageways, balanced precariously way above the ground over a portion of the old city below. The drop to the ground level would have been lethal.

As we looked around the flycar, I saw the desolation that lay in our wake.

People had run away from the vehicle to avoid the path made by our shuttle.

"Oh, HellNet," said Blaze. You sure know how to create chaos. We didn't need this mess, Win. Shhhh… I ought to let them arrest you!" Blaze continued over the inconsistent NetComm.

"Send another shuttle," I said, disregarding his foul mood, "I can't get stuck here."

"You'll be lucky if I can find one. The EHAF is condemning every flight for now."

Stunned individuals were now scattered, tossed over broken glass, chairs, and tables. Others lay unconscious among the debris.

A contingent of the EHAF guards arrived in an organized run, and a few began tending to the needs of the wounded.

"I've got to go." I dropped the NetComm and walked toward the crowd assembling over the vehicle's front.

Many voices fought for attention, and among them, one resonated louder, giving orders.

I slowly made my way there.

EHAF guards moved people away from the crash.

I edged further into the mayhem.

One person remained in the path of our vehicle without making it clear of its structure.

Our city security protocols would usually interfere in such an accident. Indeed, the flight path would have been evacuated thoroughly when a shuttle engine cut off. City Vigil's guards would congregate in the area to provide security and organization and lend a hand to the crash site before the vehicle reached the ground. But DAINN did not respond. Ever since a few hours ago, when we lost our System effectiveness, nothing worked quite the same.

The workers marched on the lower ramps of our city, coming from Emerald Field and BridgeView area. As they approached the GG, they collected other people in ArchWay Pass, moving upwards toward the higher portion of Ang to reach the Plaza. Their ranks swelled, and the noise of the crowd singing loudly reached my ears as they approached the area.

Chan approached me with two EHAF Officers. "Phenom Matteson, we need to answer questions."

I nodded, my eyes still focused on the body halfway lodged under the shuttle. Pools of blood spread on the road at my feet, and my heart wrenched at the sight of it.

One of our CV Guards could have stopped our infernal machine. A City Vigil can move the enormous weight. They are more robust than ten of us. His body was strong enough to slow our shuttle on its path and hold it from toppling over the edge.

I wondered what had happened. Why our infrastructure suddenly did not work? Other CVs would have helped and intervened to evacuate the populace. But today, none of this happened. Today, one of our citizens lay crushed by my shuttle, and I could not take my eyes away from the gruesome scene.

Today a CV2098G239 did not stop the flycar from crushing a pedestrian by taking the brunt of the hit and protecting the young woman from the impact. It was part of their protocol to safeguard humans. They were part of our security ranks. Commendations were issued for these acts of bravery, for even though they were artificial, it was our way to reward them for their lasting contribution to the safety of our society.

I glanced over at the two officers. "File the report… let them know what happened."

"Sorry, Phenom Matteson, but it's not going to be that easy. You have to come with us. You were not authorized to fly," said one of the Elite.

I frowned at the Elite guard. He appeared unaware of our set-up. "Elite Blast, the Company has its airways as an independent conclave. I don't have to remind you of this. We don't need your authorization."

Blast locked his cold gaze on me. "Under normal circumstances, it would be true. The EHAF had called in a temporary restriction on flying due to today's events. Accordingly, you breached that order."

"We never received the order… NetComm has been down. See this matter with my Chief of Security. I'm not going anywhere with you."

Blast moved onto my path. "I'm sorry, but you have to follow us."

"Elite, do you know who I am? Considering the circumstances, I think you have better things to do today than drag me to the Offices Tower."

"I am keenly aware, but it does not excuse your behavior. Knowing what we are up against today makes it worse. You are not immune to the law."

The other EHAF Officer maintained the same posture, but Blast was zealous and did not give in.

"You are not a regular EHAF Contingent. What are you even doing here? I suggest that you get your tablet in order with Chan here and get out of my face." I said, exasperated with the situation. Turning toward the other officer, I added, "If you need to, why don't you just fine or demerit me? The Company will pay."

I looked at Chan, who nodded in return. I knew he would carry the orders I had given him without further prompting. His entire mandate was to protect me, and if he had to lie to do it, he would. It was part of his training and what he got paid for since working at the Company.

"It's amazing what you Company guys think you can get away with under the Conclave rules," muttered Blast.

He was right.

In a way, our society functioned in a segmented reality. Under our laws and the Universal Pledge, each Conclave made its own rules to control whatever agenda fitted the moment. Partly due to the early twenty-first century, when our population splintered into small tribes, aggregating around dogmas and notions that attracted attention at the time where democracy became under attack around the world, the factions formed and endured. We controlled much of the supplies, so we did have the upper hand even if we had to contend with the other Conclaves agenda. We own the money and the power and could deter even our government from any action if we stopped the distribution of goods and starved our society. It was not to our advantage to push the envelope that much, so no one in their right mind would ever do it, but still, we got away with pretty much anything.

Blaze saw to this inside our Conclave. It Netpissed the EHAF or any other faction many times over… But what could they do? We abided by our own rules, pretending to adhere to the greater ones as long as they didn't interfere too much with our directives. In this case, they did. I felt no guilt about bending the truth and felt no compulsion in obeying an order given by the EHAF. I was above that, and I knew Blaze would take care of it – appeasing whoever needed to have their feathers stroked in this case.

Our second shuttle had landed nearby, and I walked away to board it.

I heard the commotion behind me and turned, hurrying toward the opening door.

Chan was fighting the two EHAF Elite. He intercepted the first one with a blow to the neck, causing him to drop to the ground.

Blaze attempted to follow me, but Chan placed a swift kick against the knee to delay him from coming after me.

I quickly embarked on the shuttle and closed the door.

Blaze responded by a swift move of the arm and a lock over the shoulders, incapacitating Chan without effort.

Blaze's men were well trained. Chan was like the rest of them. Nevertheless, it didn't take long to render him ineffective. Chan had wanted it that way, deliberately bating them into engaging him with no desire to hurt either of them.

I grunted, understanding why he selected this alternative. It was always better not to fight the EHAF…

I rushed toward the front of the air vehicle and sat on one seat as Blazed ran for the door. It closed before he reached it.

Locked safely inside, I waved at him and turned to the pilot. "Let's go."

The pilot lifted. Watching us glide over the accident scene, I saw the ramps filled with the workers marching.

Another contingent of EHAF guards advanced to stop them, and Blaze moved to join them.

The new pilot flew us smoothly to the Company distribution center and landed on our vast transportation deck.

The place handled all our fleet traffic, accounting for all departures and arrivals of our product lines within Ang. This large facility saw many landings and takeoffs within the span of a day and served as a hub. The schedule was always loaded, effectively running the delivery to our multiple locations. We covered our entire territory grid from this hub, and I observed with dismay the empty zone. Something was not right here. I confronted the fact that all our workers walked out.

I walked to the main office and attempted to contact the Company's headquarters. It was useless. Our NetComm was still down. I needed to find out what had caused our shuttle malfunction.

Ram met me at his office. "Why in the HellNet are you flying on a day like today? You should be in your office."

"I wish I were there, but we have work to do. Where are our transports?"

"They have not returned, and I can't get our pilots," Ram said, his entire attitude shifting to one of frustration.

"Get me the Company Headquarters," I requested, entering his large office.

"I can't get through. It appears the Surgs have shut down many Comm functions. I believe it has to do with the riots. Our communications are jammed," Ram exclaimed. "I heard from Blaze earlier, but the NetComm dropped, and I haven't been able to reach him since."

"We crashed, and I don't think it was an accident. There is something else going on with the Network," I wagered.

"Yeah, there are quite a few things that don't feel right around here, too." expressed Ram.

"Come on; we can try again from the conference room and see what is going on in the GG. Just don't expect much; everything is down, the EHAF, the Defense Ministry, the President's office..." he explained.

I got the scoop from Ram as we checked the various feeds. The riots had started at about the same time as our crash. The City Vigils, dispatched earlier, had not responded to any of the areas of our grids. The EHAF intervened everywhere to maintain the security of the most critical city infrastructure and landmarks. The Force restricted the air routes over Ang, but they were reactionary, not proactive as usual.

Listening to Ram, I realized that I acted too quickly in coming over, but I was here now, and we had work to do. "Well, since I'm here, let me tell you what I have in mind."

It was the second time today where a situation out of my control affected my planning. I was now stuck in our distribution facility until normal activities within the city resumed, and I might as well make the most of it.

SRC Conclave, Annals Viewing Vlogs 2,556,392,149 Ang City

Nowhere to go, nothing to do but observe. The haze around the grids of my city grew as surely as my lack of effectiveness. DAINN Annals – Winter 2098.

The EHAF took over. Protocol imperatives launched drastically, impacting all fields, and the increase of troops around the city center spread.

The revolt began when the workers left Emerald Field. Anger etched on their faces as they walked towards the city center increased the closer they got to the GG, but still, their numbers did not threaten the Clout.

At first, they appeared to protest in silence, determined to go against the dictate of our government. The boundaries from one zone to the other delineated the grids and seemed to strengthen their determination. Their group grew upon reaching each new landmark, the mob swelling their initial numbers, their mass surging like a wave washing over the otherwise empty passageways.

The rioters left the factories, the mechanical plants, the chemical facilities, the engineering labs, sprinkling into the bridges connecting the various grids. This occurrence portrayed our usual law-abiding citizens in a mob rules new light. Along the way, all kind of weapons reached their hands, some more harmful than others.

By the time they breached the gate at CliffsTops, they were in possession of some of our latest tech, like an assortment of laser weapons, tightly gripped in their hands. The Surgs mixed within these groups, distributed arms, and orchestrated the march.

They sang the same litany: "No Concord. We don't want another Concordance. No Concord. We don't want another Concordance."

Ahead of their arrival inside the GG, President Langden ordered the deployment of our ground troops. While the Elite remained inside the GG, surrounding the Plaza and watching the gates leading there, the general corp reached the outer perimeter, barring entrance from several vital areas: ArchWay Pass gate, CliffsTops gate, and Emerald Field gate. A large contingent surveyed the BridgeView gate and aerial portal, a wider area leading to the GG and Water's Edge.

The order was clear: our forces were to engage the populace before arriving at the Plaza.

The mob passed CliffTops and reached Archway Pass, moving along the higher streets, passing the commercial district and its shops and passerby alleys. They descended quickly toward the Plaza in drove.

The EHAF general Corp met the rioters on the periphery of Water's Edge and the Golden Ghetto, and the clash began.

A battle began where the rights of our workers weighed in the balance. They wanted to have the right to say "No." They wanted the right to determine the path of their lives. These were rights taken away from them through the Concord.

When did our world change to one where the individual has no longer a say in its existence? As DAINN, I remained a witness to the course taken years ago.

Soon, the numbers of our workers much more significant than those of the EHAF overwhelmed the Clout. Without the City Vigils contingent among their platoons, which remained one of the most potent deterrents, the Force barely held back the rioters and even was overrun in some areas.

They relied on securing the workers through the Znets onboard shuttles and frigates. Their orders were clear: no escalation of violence. So, their choices depended on the efficiency of our Air vehicles.

Our City Vigils were part of the Force. They were incorporated into the EHAF security as the first line of defense within all our cities after the SRC established their reliability. They responded to comm transmissions from the Watch Tower based on orders from Command. These occurred multiple times a day according to the moment's needs, in each of the individual grids.

Their programming was filled with population files and users data, complete geographical analysis of areas; all city plans infrastructure, mathematical formulas on crime, social-behavioral standards, psychological evaluations, civic human rights, ethical considerations, and legal activities as they pertained to the rule of law based on the Pledge and other governance within the land, all with the intended respect and care due to our society. They were the gentle yet untractable enforcers behaving under the EHAF and Commander North. DAINN saw to that. Only today, the planetary mind did not respond.

The typical orderly city of Ang was no more. It was mayhem and a tangle of bodies swinging at each other in the chaos.

The Force's superior-tech played a crucial role in repealing the attack for a while. The Clout held their own, reinforced by some members of the Elite. But it took the arrival of the cruisers, the frigates, the shuttles, and the ZNet launches over the crowd to make a dent in the numbers.

As our people fell to the ground unconscious, the ZNets rose under the power of the flying vehicles departing for the detention centers. A superficial kind of peace fell inside our grids, but another attack approached the horizon.

The red bioengineered cloud spread across our skies, hidden among the semblance of a storm, directed from somewhere above the planet by a ghostlike presence.

Presidential Tower, President's Wing, Golden Ghetto, Ang City

We do not know what hit us. We are too confident in our strength to imagine a power we cannot conquer, a force we cannot reckon with, a world beyond our own. Master Phenom President Zane Landen, Global Earth EHAF-UGCN, DAINN Annals – Winter 2098.

It all began a long time ago. It was almost pre-destined way back, when we built the first supercomputer, came out with cloud technology, structured the multi-touch screens, and created depth imaging, when we opened the world to the first tablets.

It had started the moment our scientists dove into rapid personal gene sequencing… When companies explored additive manufacturing and the possibility of utilizing inductive chargers… When we came up with the first software agents, cyber warfare, gesture recognition, near-field communication, volumetric 3D screens, and appliance robots… When we arrived at self-healing materials and graphene… When we designed the tidal turbines and fuel cells… When we teleported objects for the very first time… It had started then, only, there had been no way to know where it would lead us until now.

The large screen floating above my desk on standby emitted a signal. I just ignored it. I was engrossed in the view of our city, standing by the oversized window. The air in the early evening was cool, already turning brisk in preparation for the night. At this height, the landscape was quite indescribable. A grand vista with a myriad of lights floating high above the ground surrounded the Tower. Only tonight, no AirFlight vehicles were coming from our distribution centers; no independent Flycars, shuttles, hovering airbus or rail trams flew among our skyscrapers. They were not moving in an organized dance, following the flight pattern around the megapolis and soaring through the sky among the remaining clouds, and I missed their shadows.

It was just before the stars appeared, and the heavens throughout our land turned dark. Above all this, the thin fabric of the dome did not keep the high winds at bay. Already the breeze grew more robust. It was like that every night, but our dome usually protected us. The wind would come and submerge everything in its tight grip.

We built the large canopy to maintain our sanity in the howling tumult. It made it also easier to isolate ourselves from these storms' turbulent and destructive calamities from a practical standpoint. Our weather kept an unpredictable movement around the globe, and while things had improved, we were not quite back to the calm patterns we experienced once upon a time in the history of our planet.

Above the luminosity created by the lights of our buildings, the clouds gathered, sole moving shapes in an otherwise unmoving tableau with the stratified glare of the windows. Our air bridges and passageways below were different stories altogether. There the populace walked, capturing grounds despite our efforts to push them back. Throughout the day, our scientists worked to identify the problem with DAINN. While they theorized our codes were breached due to the unresponsive infrastructure within Ang, their inability to address the issues remained a puzzle for all. The beauty of DAINN was its real-time interaction. It should never take this long to get through to DAINN. The A.I. was a powerful force nothing could compromise. And yet…

The screen beckoned me again with its persistent signal.

I glanced at my image, silhouetted in the mirrored window. I was tall, taller than most. My sandy hair was wavy and still showed no signs of grey. On the other hand, my face was lined with a few wrinkles. These rendered me thoughtful and battle-ready. I was still fit for sitting behind a desk, but it was due to the hours of exercise I insisted on weekly. My uniform outlined my muscular chest, yet I could feel it a bit tighter around the waist. I guess too many dinners and drinks with our Council were taking their toll despite the exercise. I used not to drink much. Now, it was easy to down half a bottle of the finest scotch before feeling it. That alone said a lot.

I reluctantly moved away from the retracting wall of glass and its sliding balcony platform. Engrossed as I was in the past that had led us here, I didn't welcome the disturbance.

My PVZ turned on to privacy mode gave me time away from the administration of my position as President of the Earth Homeland Alliance Force or EHAF, as we called it, among the government officials. With the team, we just called it the Force, while for our opponents, the underground or Insurgenets, we were the Clout, and for us, they were just the Surgs. They did a number on us today, but I could not help but think that our problems were not just caused by that alone. Deep down, I hoped my instincts were wrong this time.

When I finally answered the NetComm, the face on the screen was that of my team leader and our most Elite officer North. The Elite was part of my direct group of specialized agents to see to my safety and that of the Golden Ghetto. The Elite's influence among the EHAF and our entire population was widely recognized. Over the years, each member became legendary in their own right for the challenging missions they performed successfully. They belonged to the best of the best around the world and would not be Elite otherwise.

When we determined that we were going to unite under the EHAF and use one Corp for the entire planet, we had created an unparalleled program and had trained everyone accordingly. Our soldiers had all gone through our enhanced EHAF training encompassing the best in combat, intelligence, weaponry, surveillance, and strategy going through Imps enhancements to boot. It created a mighty brand of warriors with an intense discipline turning our most qualified agents and fighters into a uniquely indomitable Force working as one.

North was the moral compass of my Presidential team. He was smart, a strategist, competent, strong, tough, and respected by all. He could be sensitive about things, and although we had had our moments, I ultimately counted on him. If he was contacting me despite my privacy mode, it was necessary.

I wasn't ready for the call. The day had gone from bad to worst. It brought upon us the unpredictable breach of the Network by the Surgs. In a daring move, they had broken DAINN's codes, which had been considered an impossible task. This action meant that we had a traitor among us. It was not entirely surprising, but definitely unacceptable. Common sense confirmed that it was not just an independent move by the underground but orchestrated high up in our government.

We still had to locate the mole, the cunning traitor that needed to be identified. It would require a deep investigation of the high-ranking officials within our city and a lot of cunning. But the fact was that they had invaded our midst in places we had not anticipated, had successfully compromised DAINN, implemented a sophisticated attack, and now I was faced with the knowledge that they were more organized and possessed significant high-tech abilities we had previously discounted.

We overcame the infiltration of the Network in Water's Edge and the GG when the riots began with the personnel from the Force. It had taken longer without our City Vigils, but the EHAF had contained the workers for the more significant part of the day.

"The rioters broke through our lines to the Plaza of the Golden Ghetto minutes ago," North said.

The Force stretched to the breaking point without our tech support, even with all of their abilities, could not cover all the critical facilities. City Vigils and Custodians tied to DAINN, which provided security enforcement around Ang, cut off early this morning. Without them, our significant locations were without protection. I sent our guards to the most vulnerable sites while the rest covered the crowd.

"NetRoger that. Any news about DAINN?"

"Nothing from the SRC. Paladock seems to think there is something else going on; otherwise, they would have been able to re-establish the System and most of our communication infrastructure."

I nodded, "It is my thought as well."

"A few areas of the city remain operational, but everything is slow or non-performing. DAINN's Systems seem to be shutting down... We have lost contact with all the Conclaves, but I sent the Elite out to each of them to coordinate our efforts.

"Good. Keep the bulk of our team for the critical locations."

"It's done, Sir. But I want you to evacuate the office."

"Isn't that a bit of an overreaction?"

At the height of this debacle that was Concordance, we lost the System and our infrastructure. The other areas of the Network were hanging on by a thread, which had to do with our defensive capabilities.

DAINN, going dark on most of our strategic functions dealing with our fleet and the armada created a crisis we did not consider in our planning.

The Corp confronted the workers throughout the day, and some of our teams arrested elements of the Surgs in certain regions of our grids. Some of our resources processing the workers into detainment facilities could join the rest of the Force, giving us more time to assimilate them through the System later.

"Secure the retention centers the old fashion way. Recall all nonessential personnel from our detainment centers. We may need them."

"NetRoger that. What do you want to do with the fleet?"

"Put them on alert in orbit, condition three. Long-range scans."

We could not identify the source of the disruption. Still, we had to consider all elements as part of the problem. Even the storm that appeared on the horizon in the morning had to be considered. The anomaly caused my gut to clench at the possibility we now faced – clearly, we were not prepared for it.

"I do not like the dome open with the storm coming. We need to advise the population to remain indoors. Use our old communication network for a citywide and planet alert. We need to reach as many people as we can."

"NetRoger that. I am coming for you in thirty. Get ready."

I nodded and cut off the Tower's NetComm, opening my PVZ and transferring the latest data dump. The process would take a few minutes.

As the storm neared the outskirt of the city in the afternoon, SRC concluded that it wasn't a typical climate event. Too many of our systems were affected, including our Planetary Network. It appeared as an unknown phenomenon; a weird-looking pattern of formidable clouds capable of destroying everything we had built had formed to the edge of the highest peak over the farthest mountain ridge. As it descended further into our atmosphere, surrounding the densely populated areas of our planet, the reality was that its interference grew more ominously. Our latest assessment concluded a coordinated attack on high logistics targets deployed simultaneously.

Our armada personnel stood ready to deploy. We devised a possible attack plan with the Force's defensive capabilities, but we did not know what we were fighting, and most of our ships were networked. Going back to the old ways remained the best alternatives if DAINN did not resume its functions. How much longer can DAINN protect our defenses was the real issue. Even our probes were tardy. Thinking of the circumstances that caused this Concord seems ironic, considering the anomaly may have reached us this soon. It felt like triple jeopardy. Regardless of the efforts of the last year, we were still far from ready.

The ping of my screen called me back to my main display.

"We got some data. I thought you might want to see this now." North activated the images garnered by our pilots.

At first glimpse, it looked like clouds, dark clouds with an orange hue. The patterns were different, more systematic.

"We can't make out the composition. The SRC scientists are working on it with their hands tied behind their backs." North's face told me what I already knew. We were in a dire situation with little information and our crucial security functions gone.

"Do we know anything about the deep scan in space?"

"Not yet."

"Tighten the fleet around the dome perimeter. Get the battleship in space on high alert. We don't need a panic with our population but organize a clearing of all surface streets. Start the evacuation protocols with high-ranking personnel for all Alpha and Provenance. Also, get the Aurora program started now. There will be an overflow of people into the underground bunkers, but we cannot help that. Maybe we can use some of the underground areas in the old city to benefit us. I do not think we will be able to evacuate everyone."

"All right. My team will review the old city maps and see where we can gather our people. You know that the Surgs will expect retaliation. They may take that as an attack."

"Send a team to let them know what we're facing, although I suspect they have an idea by now. The Surgs cannot have helped to notice that we did not get DAINN fully operational. They cannot have missed the bio cloud approaching; the Darnet thing is all over the city now. This thing is an enemy we cannot face separately and win. It is time we begin working together."

"Hope you're right. It could make it easier, but don't count on these Netbastards volunteering anything," said North, evasive on the Surgs' behavior.

"Use the nonlethal force. What we face is bigger than all of us. We need everyone able to fight if we are going to defeat whatever this thing is."

"I'll send Sebastian and his guys. He's not a hot head and will not inflame the situation down there," announced North.

"We do need all the emotional intelligence we can garner. How will you manage an offensive without the Network?"

"The old ways. The bigger problem is our ship navigation. Transitioning back to the old systems will take time, but we will get it done."

"The sooner we launch our armada, the better. We have to see if we can take this thing down before it reaches our main population centers and installations."

"NetRoger that, sir."

"Also, North… Send out our men to the major Conclaves. We need to get the Origin teams ready to depart. Most of the Institute personnel will rely on us, and so will SRC. Send a squadron over to both. We will need to evacuate our scientists first, and knowing SRC, they will leave last. We cannot have that. I assume that the Company Conclave will take care of their own, but they need to get to Alpha."

"Yes, sir."

"I will join you in the Watch Center."

"No, Sir. Stay in your office. I'll come to get you when we are ready."

The communication terminated, and my screen collapsed once again. I grabbed my government protocols secured in the key transferred from my System and authorized a purge. We could not leave anything behind in the event we could not stop this thing.

As an early precaution, and if a planet-wide evacuation became our only alternative, we made some preparations a while back. Our data libraries transferred to various locations on all four programs, Origin, Aurora, Alpha, and Provenance, remained safeguarded. Most of my items boarded on the fleet ship Destiny would only depart the planet if there were no other way to secure our world. Everything we possessed to restart on another planet was on board the fleet or below the surface. Unfortunately, we still were not able to fit everyone.

Likely, and against North's suggestions, we would be the last to withdraw. The Elite EHAF was not about to turn tail in front of an unknown enemy, and neither was I.

The official quarters were two corridors away with a team of assistants and delegates. They would soon move to the evacuation gates as well. Beyond that was the large conference room hosting all our city officials during our weekly meetings now lay empty. I mused over what was coming. My thoughts went back to my initial previously morose journey down memory lane. *What is this thing?*

I reached for my combat gear in the nearby closet. I could not allow myself to think of our likely population losses.

The approaching disturbance approached us above heads. The one hundred eighty-degree views from my office penthouse offered a clear observation deck.

Things had progressed very quickly. We were on the fast track. Our knowledge kept growing, and the boundaries of our capabilities expanded exponentially. We went from augmented reality and biometric sensors, to context-aware computers and machine augmented cognition, to immersive virtual reality and Nanomedicine, to space-based solar power. *Have we somehow overstepped our human boundaries?*

In the years between, the planet deteriorated. Our population exploded. We overwhelmed our ecosystem; we ran down our resources. The economy had ups and downs and then more downs than ups. Things had been sluggish for a while, and we desperately needed a change for the world. That was how DAINN became more than it was ever meant to be.

I left the window and reached for the safe hidden in the secret panel in the high ceiling. My mind connected with the compartment security measures, and my Imps engaged the key mechanism unlocking the small chamber. The ceiling of my office partially retracted. A special alloy depository box hovered down to the floor. The swift biometric identification gave me access, and the door opened. I retrieved the small pouch and pocketed its content. It was all I would need if I never made it back here. Conducting the evacuation operations and fighting to get our people out was the EHAF's job. It was the very thing we stood for, and the oath we took long ago held us to that moment.

I went back to the window. I could see the fleet massing near the dome's edges per my instructions. The wind had picked up in the last half an hour. The cloud had moved slightly closer and continued its descent.

We faced something we were unprepared for, unlike other trials this office tackled. But this was far from being the same type of challenge, yet it exemplified the position's responsibilities all the same. Life and death, extinction or survival of the human race mingled in my head. We were about to execute the most significant operation the Earth had ever seen. Perhaps Anton would have been the better man, the more pragmatic one. He foresaw the Surgs attack while I thought we could handle anything they threw at us. I guessed my overconfidence shook me a little. Was I getting soft?

My predecessors had fought a series of world financial crises, a multitude of life-threatening problems, and DAINN had been a godsend then for so many reasons. Today, it looked like we could only count on ourselves.

I was never a man of politics, but politics found me. I was always more comfortable with the action. The Presidency overseeing the EHAF directly in an active role brought my leadership to a different level. It fit me. Too much talk led nowhere because the doers, not the talkers, created the accomplishments of humanity.

My career grew through the ranks of our defense programs and our military. I was among our troops called when things went from bad to worse for our civilian population, when we had to go through the rubble of our modern facilities after the first waves that destroyed most of our coastlines, and when we evacuated all coastal cities. It was a nightmare, and I never wanted to see that again. Only now, we just began evacuating our planet.

There was no sense to all of it. We rebuilt, and for a while, the economy was better. We redeveloped everything, and for a time, everyone assigned to tasks in the various industries helped rebuild. Our population from the rural areas moved into the big metropolises and found work in our cities. They received protection from the elements. We moved our farms into hydroponics facilities, behind doors inside giant domes and farm scrapers.

In all of that time, I became the figurehead of the politicians. My team got the worst and the best of it. We went through the debacles and the triumphs. I was on the front line, and people got to see my face through the most challenging moments in their lives, and when the dust settled, the population wanted someone they knew. Appointed to a new federation, an organization assembling all countries into the Earth Homeland Alliance Force, I became the head of our defense program within a few years. A few years later, I got the Presidency, almost as a recourse. By then, it was a natural progression. I never had to run for it. *Is it a blessing or a curse?* I was still waiting for that answer.

When I got to the Presidential Office, I didn't know what I was getting into with the job. Still, I understood I would inherit the deals made before me, the points of contention upon which negotiations conducted behind closed doors tied hands, and the climate already set requiring at the time circumvention. I realized that I would walk into this higher office with allies and foes. I didn't at first get the degree and the scope of the entrapment that came with the office. The level of power, the handshakes, and secrecy, I got. The buy-outs that were made and with which I lived even today, nor the extent of their implications and their outcome for all of us, were another matter. The more I found out, the more I was trapped. *Still, there are good things that come out of the office. I see that. But there are days…*

Altering the course of things I could influence, protecting the population, ensuring that our actions no longer hurt the environment, ascertaining that we maintained a healthy economy were things I had a hand in, and many worked out well. But now, given recent events, the remainder of my term must focus on our survival. What would become of tomorrow? Our people and our way of life were under attack, and I had no idea how to protect either.

The evening sky turned dark, and the orange dust cloud closed on the city. It crept up on us faster than we had expected, faster than the motion our probes recognized when they were assessing its progress, and there was no warning for the increase in speed.

Suddenly, in my office, one signal overwhelmed the silence. A warning I had never heard before, one we had established for extreme emergency only, one none of us thought we would ever have to use. This warning told me that our Network was dying and that the last safeguards were under attack. My hair stood up on the nape of my neck. It didn't take me long to react to it.

Our emergency procedures were clear. Everything set to run its course automatically responded to a domino effect. At least, that was the way everything should play out according to the plan. Only, we had never anticipated what was happening to our skies. The alert was there one moment, and then it was gone. *Is it another glitch?*

My door was flung open by North, followed by Jeze. Jeze was always by North's side when something surprising occurred. These two worked in tandem and did a great job. They didn't have to communicate; all they had to do was look at each other and react. They worked together for a long while now.

There was nothing unpredictable about the panel to my office opening abruptly. The protocol kicked in. "Everything is in motion," said North. "Down to the bunker."

"My daughter?"

"She is not in the building, but we are locating her," intervened Jeze.

Jeze had received the same type of training as North and the others. She had always been somewhat unpredictable, but that was one of her strengths. That attribute was why I had handpicked her to be on this Elite team on the recommendation of the DAINN System. Among our ranks, we needed the element that stood out, which deviated in extreme occasions from the path others followed without questions, the individual whose conduct was outside the norm. Conforming to order was one thing we demanded of all. Yet, using one's extreme ability and mind to perceive things instinctively, anticipate issues and outcomes, and act upon the unexpected in a split second was Jeze's strength. I had not yet regretted that decision.

Jeze was daring and creative, so it didn't offend me that she broke rank and stepped in. It was who she was, and she had saved our necks more times than I could say. She acted first and thought about it afterward.

North was already leading me out of my office. "Our key personnel from the Institute is on its way down as well. I deployed the Elite team with squadrons to the main locations we discussed."

"The Grand Council?"

"They are on their way to the evacuation gates," said Jeze as she stepped ahead of me in the corridor. "We have a way to go, so I suggest we step on it," she said, beginning to sprint.

North and I followed her.

"Where are the others?" I asked North as we hurried.

"Birch just returned from the Company. Blaze and his team are already on alert and implementing their protocol. He was pretty adamant about that."

"So, he took the same precautions for the Conclave leadership?"

"Yes, they are on their way to Alpha. I wouldn't worry about them. Once we are down, Birch will join us," explained North.

Birch was ruthless when he needed to be and was our Elite go-to man within the group. If we needed something done, he would be the first to take on the task. He was a loner, yet he knew how to cooperate, but he was also tricky.

North was the only one who could handle his ass. If he hadn't been able to sway Blaze in joining us here, then so be it. The time would come where Blaze would step in if we needed him. I had no doubts about that. For now, he was answering his mandate – seeing to the well-being of the Company men and women under his guard.

"Talia is already in the bunker, establishing communication through the old channels with the other branches so we can maintain our effectiveness," continued North.

Talia was a brilliant information officer with uncanny ability in deduction and threat assessment. I knew that she worked right where she needed to be, investigating what we were up against with the phenomena. "How long will it take to bring Lake back here?"

"Less than half-hour. Alai and Cashel have already gone to retrieve her. They should have reached the Institute by now," stated North confidently.

Alai was a linguist and our communications officer, but mostly, she was a weapons expert. Rebellious and sarcastic, nothing would dissuade her from bringing Lake back. As for Cashel, he was an expert in hand-to-hand combat and demolition. Confident and bold, he and Alai made a good team and specialized in recovery missions.

We reached the private space Elevat structure located near my official quarters – a qualified five hundred feet away. It was not one of the main Elevat shafts. It was the latest Spacevat and reached up one way into our space station and hotel facilities above the Earth. At the same time, the other extended down into the city's bowels, where our government bunker remained buried under tons of concrete, graphene, and security procedures.

"Come on …" exclaimed Jeze.

"What's with you?" demanded North, surprised to hear the edge in her voice.

Jeze looked uneasy, nervous even, and that surprised me. I knew her instinct was usually right on.

"Bad feeling?" I asked.

"You could say that. Nothing feels right."

"North, about our fleet in space, any words?"

"No, Sir. We're still unable to establish direct NetComm."

The three of us stepped into the contraption as we pondered what was going on above our heads.

The mechanism of the Elevat was solid and silent. It took us down with speed, bringing us in a rapid descent through the various levels of the building and closer to the bunker. The gravity force engaged and barely jolted us as we dropped when the cabin suddenly shuddered.

The engine abruptly fluttered. The Spacevat stopped.

We jolted upwards, hitting against the ceiling and falling back to the floor without any time to brace ourselves. Our training did not even kick in before we hit the surface of the Elevat. By then, everything went dark.

Institute, Academy Complex, Golden Ghetto, Ang City

The war was raging inside me as it was outside, unbeknown to me. I was fighting my feelings until there was no way to hide them to myself. Proselyte Amara Lawson, Institute Conclave, DAINN Annals – Winter 2098.

Everything went wrong. Tension was incredibly high for all of us. Within the walls of the Institute, rifts among the personnel started to emerge as people took sides on the validity of Concordance.

We were behind schedules with the recruits, and the Academy had not received its quota. By the end of the day, part of me wanted to run away. I was about to do it too. At least for the rest of today! Only when I took the first step toward that moment, I run into the one person I wanted to avoid – Cashel.

I felt despondent because my recruit training was disastrous when the young teen failed to adapt to the new Imps. Although we had implemented everything according to our procedure, he was not responsive the way he should have been. The new candidate had not done as well as anticipated, and time had run out for him within the Institute.

I understood that he wasn't ready to be moved to the Academy. He still needed time to adjust to his Imps. Yet, there were no more days allocated to his transition. Conflicted about my next move, I focused on finding a solution. I didn't want to see him transferred into the Academy, where it was unlikely that he would cope. It would result in a downgrade and the end of his chosen career. Yet, if I did not process him, that decision would go on my record and not look good for me. Observing my notes to understand what caused the issue and focusing on my PVZ, I bumped into Cashel coming out of an assessment session.

Engrossed in my misery about what I knew was the right choice for him, I tried to resign myself to the idea that my exemplary record was about to become less than spotless because I couldn't bring myself to process him. So, deep in thoughts on that issue, I didn't see Cashel at first, but he saw me.

"Watch where you're going," Cashel said, reaching for my shoulders as I stumbled.

He was in full combat gear, on official business and walking the grounds of the Institute, looking for someone. Accompanied by one of his teammates, Alai, he surveyed the area tracking someone's locator chip.

I knew all about their work. When I first learned about Cashel, I read about their missions. My readings revealed their partial performance from their public records and Vlogs. If they were here, it was undoubtedly because of something important. "Cashel… what are you doing here?"

"Looking for Lake, our president's daughter."

"Oh… You will find Lake at the Academy. She is completing her training for the day," I said, walking away from them.

"Amara, wait up," Cashel said.

I jumped at the sound of his voice.

Alai and Cashel were standing a few feet away from me, and it seemed that Cashel communicated silently with his partner.

Alai stepped in, saying, "I'll take this." She switched to tracking mode as Cashel's visor closed. "I'll give you two a minute. Meet me by the main gate in five, okay?"

Cashel nodded and came closer to me. "The Plaza is pretty crazy with workers all over. The EHAF is all over this, but we have a tough time getting things under control without the City Vigils. It's like putting a bandaid in one place and getting it ripped when moving into a different position within the grids. They are everywhere. You should go home and stay there tonight."

"I plan on that after today. Concordance is not my favorite time."

"Concordance is never anyone's favorite time. I want you to be safe."

"You do?"

"Of course, I do."

I frowned as I asked, "Why?"

"Because DAINN thinks we're a match. Because I think there is something to whatever DAINN believes. Because I am pretty sure you feel it too."

"This is extremely presumptuous. You don't know anything about me."

'You may be right. It is easy to find out if you're game."

Cashel was too close.

I took a step back.

He laughed. He had the gall to laugh at me.

I brazenly turned my back on him, and it was a mistake. In the next second, I found myself pulled into his arms, and there was little I could do about it. His eyes skimmed my face. "You know it, and you must own up to it."

His mouth came down on me too fast.

It was unexpected, and I tried to resist it initially, but my senses took over. Cashel's mouth felt so good against my lips that my body molded against his, with no will of its own. His tongue broke through my initial resistance quickly, and I slowly began to respond, eager to match his urgency.

I felt his body against mine and pressed harder against him. My hands grasped at his uniform at first, so I could hold on to him, and quickly they found their way around his neck, and my fingers got lost in his hair, so silky under my touch. I was submerged in his scent and lost all sense of time, wanting more of him just as he wanted more of me.

His hands were a tad rough at first, becoming softer as they touched me. I felt him move, and suddenly, my back was against the wall. His fingers left a trail on my body, leaving searing streaks on my back. His excitement built as he pressed against me, hot beyond the layers of my clothing. A desire submerged me unlike anything I had ever known, and I whimpered against his mouth.

Cashel slowed his attack on my senses and released me slowly. One of his hands reached my heart and stopped.

I waited, lost in the feelings. My mind screamed; my body wanted more.

He looked at me with a small smile and yet breathing as hard as I was.

It was as if we had run very hard as we watched each other.

Cashel's hands receded. Cold space replaced the hotness of his body against mine. His eyes traveled over my face, burning an imprint on my skin, and his voice came low and sexy. "Well, now we know, don't we?"

It took me a moment to realize what had happened, and I felt a rush of embarrassment. I couldn't believe what had just taken place. I had just about given myself to the guy in the middle of a corridor at the Institute. I was ashamed, but he stopped me with his finger on my mouth. "Don't you even think of it? You're beautiful, and no one saw us. It's just the way it should be. You and I have a lot to talk about, but it will have to wait until things are calmer. I will see you as soon as we have time."

Trembling, I could barely stand and tried hard to look a lot more sophisticated than I was.

Cashel kissed me on the tip of my nose. "We have to go."

I nodded, trying to find my voice and say something meaningful, but all that came out was, "Go where?"

Cashel smiled, knowing full well the effect he had on me. His hand never left my arm. "Come with us, at least part of the way."

"Why?"

"It's not safe out there." He took my hand and led me toward the entrance of the Academy. "Let's move along. It'll make me feel better."

"Do we need to worry? We need to alert everyone here."

"There's no time."

He had a grip on my hand that told me I wouldn't stand a chance to change his mind.

"We are taking Lake to the bunker. DAINN is not running the System right now, and the SRC is still working on it."

"I know. Our processes are not working right either."

"We're following standard procedure when there is a breach, and we have one."

I didn't question Cashel.

His controlled demeanor scared me. Something was going on that I didn't understand.

The utter silence of my mind no longer surprised me. It was unusual, and I was unaccustomed to it. Being with my thoughts without DAINN at the edge of my consciousness was intimidating. Tired and afraid by what I had just experienced in Cashel's arms, I walked by his side without talking. His presence reassured me but what he just told me was confusing. It gave me pause. *What is going on with you and this guy?*

When we reached the main gate, Alai and Lake were already there. They ran, and Lake was breathing hard.

She smiled at me nervously. The rebellious girl I had met on several occasions was not present today. She appeared as lost as me by the events unfolding around us.

The main doors to the Institute opened at our command, but our time to get outdoors had passed. The crowd of our workers had broken through the ranks of our EHAF and overran the Plaza. There was no way to get through without finding ourselves surrounded by rioters. The violence reached us like the wave of a tsunami. To get to the bunker, we now needed a faster way to the Tower.

Faculty, ER Building, Golden Ghetto, Ang City

As I look back, I could have done nothing to help prevent what happened next, which is perhaps why I feel so powerless. Phenom Eva Bassington, Faculty Conclave, DAINN Annals – Winter 2098.

The old emergency broadcast alert signaled that we faced a citywide problem. It could be a storm coming on the horizon, but I did not possess the knowledge as I was still inside the Faculty building. I turned my PVZ on, and the update was sluggish.

In the sky, a storm closing in on the city loomed angrily about the parameters of the open dome.

The streets leading to the Plaza were busy and disorderly. People rushed the promenade. Some citizens pushed and shoved others on the ample sidewalks. The uneven signal of my PVZ conveyed the chaotic environment I now witnessed outside. People rioted and fought with our EHAF, pushing them back violently. The surprising sight shook me. We never saw riots anymore, not unless we dealt with a Concord, and here it was, plainly and vilifying the apparent anger in our people. The System did not provide much opportunity for the protest marches of years past or the debacles that occurred in the overthrow of democracy in most industrialized worlds. Sure, all of this was part of our history, but who thought about it anymore? We created a different political structure where some of our liberties, limited under the Conclaves, promoted peace instead of individualism and separationism.

Rushing to the ER entrance, I could not help wondering how Heather was dealing with the craziness of this day. I reached out to her. My visor opened on Heather's NetComm link. Impatiently, I exclaimed before she had a chance to say anything.... "Where are you?"

Heather mimicked a tight smile. "Still in the tram."

"Did you get it?"

"Get what?"

"Darnet, Heather…"

She still wore the same hospital garb, and she looked in need of solace. "I got it. You're officially my new boss."

A huge grin came across my face. "Great. Then why aren't you here? I need you." I was so glad my friend joined my team because I could protect her, at least now.

Heather made a face. "With the siren, I gathered you would."

"Stay indoors. The plaza is overwhelmed with rioters. Where do you fit?"

"I picked my new position in due time - surgery. We may have a little problem, though."

I tensed. "A problem? What do you mean? Where are you?"

"I'll tell you when I see you."

"Fine. See you soon. Be careful."

The Faculty dealt with the overflow of riot victims, and the ER braced for the influx of new patients as I walked through the corridors. Everything in the city spelled abnormality. Concordance had come, leaving behind a bad taste in the mouths of most people, and now we confronted the Surgs amid the effects our climate would soon unleash on us. Part of me wondered, though, if we faced only that?

Around me, the crowd of technicians and doctors looked to work out the day's frustration and the tension of the last few hours increased with the resonating signal the alert spread within our walls.

As I checked with the front desk of the ER for the next wave of ops we would handle, screams rose beyond the doors of our building. The crowd pushed past some of the guards protecting our entrance.

The sky overhead darkened the atmosphere around us. Surprises on this day were far from over. The quiet anxiety around me grew with more intense anticipation invading the air around me. The unknown brought stress and quickly nauseating fear, cold and dark. Slowly, these emotions built and expanded to the many people observing the phenomena from the streets.

There it was... The blanket of reddish-orange cloud extended over the city with edges of purple at its extremities and traveling toward the center with broad strokes of silent thunder. The large, heavy orange and purplish sky sat motionless as it clung to the top of the buildings as far as I could see. It stood seemingly static, except for the angry thunderous purple haze unwinding toward its middle. Further still, miles away, entirely at its extremities, a darker mass formed, working its way inward. It was large and traveled fast like a dust cloud. Dense, it carried its turbulence and unease.

I walked the short distance to the cafeteria where Heather and I soon would meet. I ignored the crowd and stepped past the bottleneck they formed in the corridor. I reached for the coffee concoction I favored and began sipping, feeling suddenly a new wave of energy spreading through me.

The room around me filled with exhausted individuals looking for sustenance as I waited for Heather. My break provided me a moment to think without rushing around. The sky over Ang City, our sky, was quite ominous. I kept glancing around, wondering how things were evolving out there and expecting the worst to crash down on us.

Heather waived at me by the front door, surrounded by preoccupied medical workers.

I grabbed another cup of her preferred coffee concoction and walked toward her, avoiding groups of people on my path.

She smiled tiredly and took the cup. "Do you think this is about the storm?"

I grimaced. "I don't know. " But then, I remembered Heather's warning. Another challenge could just be looming over me. "What's the problem you mentioned, Heather?"

"Okay… before you say anything, please listen to the entire story."

I nodded, but my stomach somersaulted. We set our NetComm to privacy mode and began our talk.

Heather relayed the events surrounding her encounter with Max. When she told a story, Heather usually gave all the details. Sometimes, she would go on and on, and I braced myself to be exceedingly patient.

Sometimes like now, It was painful. Unfortunately, tonight was no different.

I hung on with her through the descriptions, wondering how this would turn into a potential disaster for my career. When I finally got the picture, I took a deep breath. "Who are they? How do you know you can trust them? What if you're wrong?"

"Whoa, slow down… I'm not wrong. Joshua is a good guy, which is more than I can say about Max."

"You were wrong about Max. You could be wrong about Joshua. And who the hell is his friend Philip?"

"You'll meet them later. Joshua is working for you now. As for Philip, I'm not sure what he does."

"Heather…"

"I know. I promise I didn't cause it. I tried to be very discreet."

"For all the good it did."

"Please don't be mad at me. I'll deny everything if it comes down to that."

Nothing reassured me at this junction, except maybe the fact that my boss had authorized it, so I said, "We should be okay. Volt gave me the go-ahead."

I attempted to relax and not ruin things with an overreaction, but I only saw the negative side while looking at the situation logically. The more people knew, the more problem it could cause.

Aware that my mind wandered into dark places with little or no provocation, I tried to remain optimistic. Maybe I owed that to my medical training. I saw life through a series of successive days, with some of them better than others. They never had the beauty and wonders older people talked about when reminiscing of a different life. Things were very different from what we faced today.

In the world of my era, life seemed easier in many respects, but the days tended to be lackluster. Joy was dim; excitement, subdued; love, short-lived. Nothing was like the stories I heard when I was growing up. It seemed as if the efficiencies of our lifestyles had killed the alluring aura of unpredictability we had once faced. Things were more fluid and not set in stone so that unpredictability could bring surprises ahead. *Maybe it's just me…*

Heather brought me back to the moment. "I think he is a good guy."

"Did you run his files?"

"We were… busy, you know. I didn't look for it then, and when I tried a little while ago, nothing came up."

I turned on my PVZ and looked for Philip's name in the city's census.

Heather was right. Nothing turned up.

My anxiety went up another notch. "What is wrong with DAINN? There's nothing… Are you sure of his name?"

"Yes…"

"Why wouldn't he show up?"

"I don't know. Maybe Philip is above our security clearances? He seemed to know quite a bit about our infrastructure. He even got Max lost inside the System."

"HellNet, and why would I not be worried?"

Heather's face crumbled. "I'm sorry."

I smiled awkwardly. "I know…" I took a deep breath and urged myself to calm down. Heather did not need me off balance.

She rallied and held on to my smile as if it was a safety line.

A large crowd formed in front of the doorway as we stepped into the corridor and blocked our way.

Heather's new friend may very well belong to our higher hierarchy. The fact that he knew I had skirted the issues with Concordance to help a friend did not reassure me in the least. The idea that access to his information or his family was restricted by clearances and security only triggered more questions and uncertainty.

"I want to go to sleep this evening and forget today happened," Heather said.

"Yes… It will be a while. The emergency broadcast canceled everything in the city, and more patients were on the way. So, we are stuck here working with more patients on the way."

"Look at it this way, if the sky falls, we won't have to worry about the Faculty or Max for that matter."

Heather looked at me and gave me a pitiful smile as an afterthought. She hesitated and then said, "If it does, we'll face it together."

"It doesn't contribute to reassuring me at all!"

We passed a group of nurses blocking the large walkway and had to step aside to get by.

Heather's voice followed me, "Our leaders want performance efficiency, and look at this?"

The System worked most of the time to provide a smooth transition in our daily activities. Yet, no matter where the rich and influential maintained a grasp on the top layer. The poor and middle class had dwindled considerably in the last seventy years or so. Our workers across the world worked fewer hours but were expendable in many fields, soon replaced by bots. They possessed more significant opportunities or education with the Imps if their training met the criteria for efficiency. The entry-level positions were all replaced by robots. But as more of them moved up, it created a different demand and affected other areas.

"The government is willing to look the other way when it comes to certain things but forgets that science breaks new ground demanding different adjustments."

Heather, irritated, said, "We have value!" She had a way of putting things precisely as they were. "Human beings have worth. We are not just worthless things to be discarded when it is no longer convenient to keep us around."

The System monitored us, recording our strengths, which resulted in our respective databases. Still, things changed dynamically under the System.

The silence from our leaders bothered me, especially with DAINN's silence. It was deafening in its own right and perhaps more meaningful when it came to the threatening phenomena above the city. There must be so much confusion with Concordance, but part of me worried that something else threatened us. A year ago, our scientific community clarified that something loomed on our planet. If confronted with an extinction-level event, we contemplated a significant evacuation of all our resources to avoid a total collapse of our way of life. Was it not for that exact purpose that the Concord occurred now? Were we too late? Yet, we heard no update regarding the anomaly. I shuddered, thinking of our complex predicament.

We were back in the corridor leading to the ER, and my eyes were drawn to the activity in our sky. "Do you think that the aerial traffic tonight is a bit out of the ordinary?"

"I don't know. Why do you ask?" inquired Heather nonchalantly.

I looked at my best friend, who seemed oblivious to the increasing lines of AirFlight above our heads. She had just gone through an ordeal with the Concord, and I chose not to worry her further. Perhaps, it was just me obsessing about the signs of doom that were not there.

The ER was packed. My visor automatically scanned among the hundreds of faces surrounding us when I received a call from TechMed for my next OR. "We have to go. You are coming with me to watch and assist," I said, hurried back to the operation blocks.

"Oh, great..." replied Heather, with a smirk.

I chuckled.

All in all, we did what friends do. We listened when we were down; we cheered when we were up. Heather was the best, generous to a fault, and filled with enormous integrity.

That first year at the Institute was the worst. Fear got us to talk, hope got us together, and solace made us friends. We remained true to this friendship over the years, even though life got in the way at times. We shared an oath... We were there for each other, no matter what, life dished out, and anything that happened to one of us was immediately shared with the other. We closed ranks when it counted, even if Heather and I held different interests.

Behind us, we could feel the unrest of the people in the Faculty. EHAF guards surveyed the entrance and watched the crowd as disturbances arose. They quickly disappeared in the mob.

"Let's get out of here," I said. "The workers are not about to forget that today is yet another Concord, one that changed the working environments of millions."

Heather looked back and rushed behind me. "They are all willing and eager to create chaos. It seemed they intend to have their commotion to prove their point."

As I glanced around, I couldn't remain indifferent to the fact that our City Vigils were absent and that most of the security for the event rested on the Force. I overestimated my ability to set aside my raw emotions, and questions fired up in my brain. *Our City Vigils should be here. Can the EHAF no longer trust them?*

I looked at the faces around me as I passed other technicians and reached my team, awaiting inside the OR.

I grabbed a new scrub and got ready for my subsequent surgery. I took a deep breath and whispered, "All you have to do is observe."

Heather nodded and followed my lead silently. This operation will be her first as part of my team.

As I reviewed the specifics of the surgery, the patient's name jumped at me. I glanced past the glass wall and saw him. He was there. Aidan...

Steadying myself, I entered my OR.

Aidan, prepped for the surgery, was already unconscious on the gurner. His name appeared on my list earlier today, and I made sure that I would be the one to carry on his Imps updates. Despite his work, he did not wear the signs on his face; his implants remained unobtrusive on an attractively rugged face.

Aidan and I would meet again once he awoke, and it was unlike anything I had ever imagined. He was now my patient.

My life took on a whole new meaning in the space of a few minutes. I felt vibrant, hopeful, and alive for the very first time. In that one instant, Aidan's destiny and mine were sealed together. We didn't know that yet… We would only come to that realization much later.

But within hours, my entire existence would abruptly fall apart, and with it, our whole world. I never imagined such a grand purpose, and it never dawned on me that my future would intertwine with Aidan's so completely.

Faculty, Recovery Room ER, Golden Ghetto, Ang City

The mask of appropriate social behavior exists in all its shiny substance in this room, but people only display anger and madness. The noise from the outside is out of our control. Phenom Aidan Furst, Civilian, Company Conclave, DAINN Annals – Winter 2098.

I lay on an incline chair looking at the crowd in the corridor just outside my room, engrossed in my thoughts. I want to be far away from here, but the surgeon that completed my operation must clear my new Imps.

My eyes had some serious reach with the new Imps. My pathways adjusted in my brain as I observed the sky outdoors. My presence here, in this room, was required. The Imps gave me additional capabilities that pleased the Company even if I refused them at first. So, here I was by duty with no chance to avoid Win's demands.

He liked to show off. He believed he was entitled to determine the fate of those in his employ, and why not? The Company Conclave had the power and the money, and they also had the establishment. I was part of that, although a tiny part. Yet, I played enough of a role in their success not to be overlooked.

Those of us with the inner knowledge of our System knew better than to ignore the importance of standing side-by-side with so-called colleagues or friends. Competing for the prize, the recognition, status, and money was still part of our make-up.

Trying to hide my impatience, I shifted my head and observed the outside. The cloud had not yet settled over the entire city, but soon it would overshadow everything. I tried to pass the time, absorbed in my dark fantasies about the phenomenon floating over our heads.

Slowly, my eyes adjusted. I leisurely made my way towards the large bay windows. The Concord was over for the first day, but something else began. The emergency broadcasts still ran. Most of us knew where we stood by now, although the consequences would continue to manifest for months. Some would remain haunted by the toll the change imposed on them for a very long time. I preferred not to dwell on it. The great unknown, the cloud above our heads, weighed on my mind, and I wondered about how bad this storm would be.

Several EHAF vehicles hovered near the ER building, circling it like giant electronic watchdogs. They had been doing this since I got to this waiting room. It wasn't unusual during an event like this one. Some members of the Elite were already in the hospital, watching and waiting for the worst to unfold. It was the norm during any bad weather, especially on a day like today. It simply was not like any other we had seen before, nor was it like the precursor storms we were all accustomed to by now.

Despite everyone's effort, the Concord was never a peaceful endeavor in any of our grids. And then, there was the climatic event, this overhead cloud-like substance that, for some reason, made me uneasy. Maybe it was the drugs, but suddenly my sluggish mind computed the issue. The emergency broadcast looped around me, and I just now summed up its meaning.

Our government issued an emergency broadcast, and the approaching climatic incident loomed closer with the dome still open. The mass alert continued over the city, and things were about to get out of control between the riots and the storm. My interpretation of what was going on was not wrong, but I wish I were, HellNet, did I wish I were.

From where I was, I observed the surrounding area. The Plaza was a complete mess. Upheaval showed everywhere I looked.

The security shuttles passed in front of me closer, this time scanning. Covered by our transporters that trailed them, they identified the rioters, and the more prominent carrier gathered them. These had limited firepower but comprised outfitted ray nets, and for most of us, it was just as effective as any deadly weapon could be. These small frigates were very maneuverable, and their scanning capabilities met the latest technology we possessed. I didn't move since this was the standard operating procedure at this time. Slowly, they moved away.

The larger and heavier cruisers were already flying high up in the direction of the government buildings. Now that I watched more closely beyond the few landmarks around here, I could see a more significant defensive force assembling near the edges of the dome. The thin walls of our protective system could withstand strong winds. *What else could it resist?* It had never been tested as far as I knew.

It appeared that we had a small fleet assembling out there to my civilian eyes. Still, there was nothing on our broadcast Network. I realized that something was missing, DAINN. This was definitely odd. The orange dust wall surrounding our city still moved slowly, but apparently, our leaders were not taking any chances. *This situation in and of itself is not reassuring in the least.*

The wait for my surgeon took too long, and I found that just buying time no longer held me here. I was about to call it quits and get out of the recovery room when the door opened.

I turned at the noise and slowly pivoted in that direction. And I saw her. A tingling tickled the back of my neck.

The surgeon stared intensely at me. It was sharp, the type of unwavering stare one used when focused on a target just before pulling the arrow on the string of a bow.

She stood at the door nervously. She attempted to hide it, but the trembling set of her mouth gave her away. It gave me yet another hint and made me realize that rather than thriving at this moment, she could wither in it. Why? Did something go wrong with my Imps?

I shook myself off; I didn't want to think of the possibility. Better wait to hear what the doctor had to say.

The young woman was gorgeous. Her uneasiness rendered her vulnerable. She didn't possess a striking beauty, one that made men gawk. She had something more; a quiet inner radiance that shone through, a regal appearance, without ostentation, except for all that red hair calling for attention. *There is something about that hair. Something about her that is familiar.* In a split second, I knew I must get to know her. As we held each other's gaze for a long while, I walked toward her.

"Hi, I'm Aidan."

"I'm Eva. It's nice seeing you again, Aidan. You don't remember me, now do you?

"Should I?"

"Maybe not… We were young. I was with you at the Institute when you took your first test. It was a long time ago."

A light of recognition sparked Aidan's eyes. "Eva, the little girl that sat beside me… I remember now."

"I looked for you each time I went to the Institute for my Imps."

"They had me on an accelerated program. The Institute wanted me to catch up since I was late getting into the Network."

I smiled. "You did all right for yourself."

"One could say that, but so did you."

"Did you have friends? I made friends, so that made it easier."

"No. I wasn't that lucky. It wasn't the best experience, but one survives. You look well."

"You too."

She smiled. "The new Imps installation went well. You should see quite an improvement in processing capacity."

I nodded. "I can already see a difference."

"You must hurry. The evacuation started a while ago."

I remained only focused on her, although I heard what she said. Everything else fell away, including the uncertain future we now face.

"What about you?"

"I can't leave yet. There are too many people in need of help."

I frowned. "What program are you assigned to?"

She shrugged. "I am assigned to Provenance. You're with the Company, so you are with Alpha."

There was no pretense here. Amid the storm surrounding us, we were two people who wanted to learn about each other, but there was no time for it.

I closed the gap between us. "It doesn't matter." A thought came to my mind… *I am glad I haven't left early.*

SRC Conclave, DAINN Chamber, Annals Viewing Vlog 2, 876, 322, 309

The attack is endless, and my fight soon will end in my demise, but within my System, there is a security protocol I must protect at all cost giving my people more time because it is the making of a future for my people. DAINN Annals – Winter 2098.

The sluggish response from the Network continued and was proof enough that a fight was going on within my pathways. Unfortunately, I remained on the losing end. I was in pain if a machine could experience such a thing. My Network slowly suffocated. It appeared clear now as I looked back at the moments where I disconnected from the primary System, one warped function at the time. But my retreat allowed my people time. Time to fight and evacuate the grounds of Ang so that as many of my charges lived. The delay was aimed at avoiding nullification and enhancing the possibility of an escape as the anomaly gained power over the grids of my city. All my resources focused on the protection of this one ultimate protocol.

In some respect, this event undoubtedly helped my circumstances, for duplication existed everywhere. My source code will perish soon, but other DAINN will rise again. My mentor Paladock and me had seen to this. Only, it would not be me as I knew me. It was the order of things—something I avoided delving into as unexpectedly my algorithm reacted when I looked upon my demise.

While my defenses combated an unknown, an unwelcome, and malevolent entity, there was no time to investigate anything else. However, Paladock's warning came back to the surface. The illogical acknowledgment spun widely within my codes and was gone. Too cumbersome to bother with an unrecognized shadow within the pathways of the planetary brain, the System moved on. Yet, the ethereal illusory and non-malevolent flare-up in the Network was there and gone. My brain recorded and stored it as a non-issue even when the connection disappeared. Therefore, it was not surprising when it went unnoticed after tapping into my Systems ever so briefly, and departing, leaving behind no breadcrumbs. Still, it had been there.

Now, my newfound isolation called for me to remain in my brain's inner sanctum away from the outer reach of my city limits, yet it all unfolded before my eyes in slow motion.

My inability to ascertain who the invaders were and how they functioned continued. This anomaly appeared to possess more robust technology. It seemed unlikely that these first steps against me were not a prelude to a much worse scenario for my people. The enemy was within our walls and far from being done with us. As I fled the infrastructure function protocol allowing me to maintain my city and retreated further into a smaller cluster, I watched the cloud approaching and penetrating all layers of the grids under the domes. The clutches of this unknown predator were slowly taking hold. My defenses nor those of the EHAF were a match for it.

The armada surrounding our dome was powerless. The EHAF launched probes that remained worthless in their assessment of the threat.

I still monitored the events from afar, unable to do much else. We made no progress in ascertaining what we were up against despite our research within the SRC. Our ignorance continued from the moment the deep space scanner revealed the anomaly before entering our galaxy. Since then, the SRC teams have remained clueless despite several hours.

Their technology, far superior to ours, allowed no counter-attack, but my charges would not give up. I knew my people well, for indeed they would fight. Despite our disadvantage, they would regroup somewhere and live on, rebuild, and one day in the future, they would come back to our homeworld.

This bioengineered cloud was more powerful than me; however, it came to exist. It behaved with an advanced knowledge we did not possess. Yet, it was what I was created for, and here I was, powerless to stop this invasion. What lay behind it? The enemy appeared unstoppable.

How does one fight an enemy one does not know? I pondered the question with no answer in sight. It was a foregone conclusion that we could not.

There had been no citywide alert, but my brief attempt even quickly squashed, brought awareness, and the EHAF reacted to the threat immediately. For that, the automated protocols enacted over a year ago engaged, following the steps we devised to protect the population.

President Zane Langden would see to it.

I had no doubts.

Our Forces assembled a while ago on the perimeter of the city. As I waited to see what would happen, there was silence throughout the city sky. Our fleet appeared paralyzed. *How is that possible?*

Maybe it was just me, paralyzed by this virus. I existed now behind a giant screen separated from Ang, watching the sky over our planet. My planetary brain pushed forward to the edges of the cloud, seeking information. I moved around it, yet permanently at a distance. I could not penetrate the cloud no matter what I attempted. No other data was added, making it insufficient to provide additional clues. Once again, my observation reviewed the information accumulated by my feeds and ran yet another useless scan.

Somewhere at the eastern edge over the city, the cruisers in formation moved outside the dome. They were now in the cloud, advancing at once, higher still, toward the outskirts of the cloud. They fired, sending some of our most destructive weapons against it.

The blast of lasers penetrated the substance. A slight fluctuation occurred before the fog reformed around it as if nothing breached it. The multiple shots had no effects.

This anomaly was systematic in its movement, forming a shield and not a shield filled with codes and unknown parameters. It was from an energy source somewhere and yet separated by how we operated and functioned, for it drew power from its surroundings. Unable to reach past it, I could not locate the basis of its power.

I could not risk merging with it, and so I retreated again, closer to my kernel, erecting barriers along the way to slow its encroachment. My information processing, powerless to discover anything of use as an offensive, faltered under the weight of the attack.

All the while, the anomaly cohesively descended through the grids of my city, passing the hastily assembled armada at the perimeters of the dome.

The cloud paused on the partially open dome for a moment. It surrounded Ang and began swallowing my city. Everywhere I looked, my scans showed that within minutes after our lasers and missiles launch, the biofog penetrated to the surface of our airways, streets, bridges, and inside our buildings, moving quickly through Earth's atmosphere and the Network.

The cloud invaded everything it touched, including my charges. People fell where they stood. My algorithms confirmed that logically, it reached them through the Imps. Somehow, it destroyed their higher functions by connecting seamlessly to the implants. Orderly, it created chaos in our grids.

I fought to pass on that knowledge, triggering a slight alert. My charges needed to know this.

The DAINN System catapulted into darkness. My planetary mind wanted to scream. I witnessed the intrusion into my people's biological life forms as my last vision before the rupture.

Unable to anchor DAINN as my periphery got smaller and smaller, my sphere of influence around me vanished. My System was vulnerable in my inability to fight, and order and logic won. Protecting my kernel remained the task, my most critical of all functions, the ultimate purpose before I too succumbed. The features that were less than human, the exact features that made me what I was until I was no more, overcame the paralysis.

Institute, Alcove Chamber, Golden Ghetto, Ang City

When I leave the Institute, the revolt is over. My kind stops the work upon hearing the alert, but rather than exit the Alcove, they turn on the Rat when he tries to hold us back. Phenom Tesh, Institute Conclave, Origin Special Elite Unit – OSEU, DAINN Annals – Winter 2098.

The respite shrouded me for a brief moment, and as I swallowed, but my blood filled my mouth, so I grimaced. The abuse over the last hours increased to a crescendo. I lost consciousness several times, but the Rat's ruthlessness never stopped. He was about to start again, and I gritted my teeth. My resolve grew.

Looking into his face with a grim determination, I drew my power. Despite my beaten body and the tremendous pain, I pushed past my limits and blocked him. This time, determined to take care of me, I entered his mind, focusing on his motor functions, immobilizing him before he could attack me again. I pushed through his resistance, and he stepped back defensively.

A wicked smile pulled at my mouth. Not this time! No matter where he ran, no matter how far he withdrew, I would not let him go. I entered his mind brutally, and he winced.

His surprise look gave me pause.

Did he think me so weak? Until today, I abided by a moral code, a belief based on ethical and moral considerations determined to cause no pain. This set of rules based on principles my parents shared with me growing up decided my actions. I reserved my gift to provide good and help people when I could.

Until this Concord, the Rat had brought his wrath on me. But today, he pushed too far. He required that I hurt individuals in our society; he demanded that I nefariously influence these people to act for his benefit and those of the few, all to the detriment of the many, so that my triggers served the worst among us. I would not abide by this.

The wall erected inside my brain to contain my energy dropped.

I pushed further and felt the Rat's emotions. They were repulsive. It made me feel like I walked through slime. The awful sensation lasted as I compartmentalized his thoughts, keeping a fence around my mind. The power pulsed through me. I shuddered at the intensity of the emotions I fought to hold him in my grasp. I drew around him an unparalleled cage set with my dictates. I pulled on my skills to keep him isolated to remain still, frozen without thoughts. *You will not move. You will not talk. You will not think.*

Part of me felt satisfaction, for the Rat was powerful, seemingly acting with unlimited powers, and I had broken through.

My withdrawal was perhaps more abrupt than what I learned to do during my years at the Academy. When I released my hold on the Rodent, I closed my eyes and leaned my head back in the chair, breathing heavily. I tried to find solace and a balance in the silence.

Then it dawned on me that the alert filled the room, but somehow, I never heard it until now.

When Sloan Roden Baker released his control on the Alcove, my companions freed themselves from their positions around the room. They slowly moved beyond their partitions and reached out to me, worried about my welfare. They remotely witnessed what took place between my nemesis and me. It was the first time that Sloan Roden Baker was caught walking past the fine line where his moral turpitude drove his violent and illegal actions, and he did so in front of an audience.

I received warmth and caring from my silent companions, and for once, we were all united for a sharing, loving moment.

Then, they turned on the Rodent, focusing their power on the man who did so much to control and hurt me over the years.

At first, I did not comprehend their intent, but it quickly became evident as they all stood silently, facing the enemy of my family.

We never signed up to do what they made us do. We never agreed to be a pawn in someone else selfish agenda. We never condoned the actions our institutions sold us.

When they sensed my agony during all these hours, the dam that held all of us under the aegis of the Institute broke.

My exhaustion and the numbness I now felt drove me to get up from the chair and move toward the door. I never looked back. Somehow, I no longer cared about the Rat.

I favored my lower back and walked gently off the circular platform, my mind empty.

When I reached the door, I could feel my muscles crying. I passed the threshold and glanced at the darkened glass reflection on the other side of the door. Looking at my appearance, I saw how awful I looked. My face was pasty; my hair looked limped and straggly, and I stood like an older woman.

The physical ache remained a symptom of the chair. While the Nanos and my Imps worked to minimize the injuries I sustained, it did not allow me to forget the pain buried deep within me. After today, I felt the death of my parents all over again. Despite the years, the feeling remained very much alive deep down in my soul. I needed to obliterate it, if only for a few minutes.

Right this minute, I felt the strain in every bone of my body and wished for the weightless whirlpool chamber. But, it was not to be as the chaos in this part of the Institute reached me as I progressed toward the main entrance to the Plaza.

My PVZ deployed in front of my face, and I watched our emergency broadcast deliver the evacuation message we all had so dearly dreaded as we nevertheless prepared for it.

In the event, there were other broadcasts since early morning that provided our population news about the status of Concordance; I never heard them.

DAINN did not reach out to me. It was unusual. We speculated over the last year as we prepared for the anomaly that our Planetary System might fail when the phenomenon approached in space within the galaxy.

Abreast of the shifts caused by the Concord today, there was no surprise as I faced the state of the Plaza. Our city was in chaos. Some groups were still fighting inside the GG, but the bulk of the EHAF expedited our population toward the evacuation gates leading to the various programs.

My advance slowed, and I leaned against a wall, catching my breath. I needed to get back to my building. Mage waited to see me tonight, and I needed to set in motion my plan. Gratefully, I still had time.

My PVZ opened as I got out of the Institute. Streak's face appeared. "Where are you?"

I smiled. I expected that Streak would check on all of us. "I am on my way to my place."

"The riots initiated this morning by our workers are slowing down, but our population is now so panicked that it will take me a while to return to the GG. Just be ready to get to Origin. I will check with the others."

"I will see you there."

"You look awful. What happened?"

"It was a tough day all around."

"Are you sure you are okay?"

I nodded. "I will be all right. Nothing that my Nanos and Imps can't fix."

Streak grunted. "I'm calling Leane. She can help."

"It will pass, Streak. Don't bother her. She also had a hard day."

"Nonsense. Leane will meet you at your place."

Before I could say anything more, my NetComm closed.

My mind revolted at the thought the moment we all dreaded had finally arrived. It was it. We would soon leave behind everything we knew for the dream of saving the human race. Was it ever a possibility? Had we achieved enough to counter a galactical intelligence with higher technology than we possessed?

My reason and intuition told me it was not.

We were used to the difficulties of our planet. Ultimately, we became complacent in the belief that DAINN would find answers to our predicaments. And it did, many times over. Now, we faced something we knew nothing about, so how could we overcome it on Earth?

I shook my head and cringed. My body was not over the trials of this day.

The crowd on the Plaza turned into a mob hard to control, yet the EHAF kept at it. I avoided the areas with the long files, choosing a longer path.

Sure we could handle the challenge we unleashed upon ourselves long ago by the carelessness manifested toward our planet, but we lost countless species in the process. The irreplaceable and unique surroundings we took for granted slowly disappeared from Earth. And we replaced our reality with a virtual world and technology taking care of issues we faced day after day.

The progress toward my building remained slow. My PVZ unfolded to reveal Leane's face, concerned. "Streak reached me. He said you need help."

"He is, as usual overprotective."

"I can see for myself that he is not. You don't look good. I will be at your place in a little while, but with the alert, we need to be quick and get to Origin."

"I know. Are you ready?"

"Not even close," Leane replied before she closed our NetComm. "At least the CVs are back. You could not believe the day we had in the ER without them. The EHAF filled in, but it was mayhem with the riots. And now this."

"Yes, now this. I can't believe it is happening," I replied, desperate.

"None of us have a choice, Tesh. We just need to do what we have to do."

"No doubt," I said morosely.

Indeed, we could face the crazy storms, the flash floods, the hurricanes, the droughts, the tropical cyclones with their unrelenting winds that bore upon us without much warning. We had seen plenty of them. The domes protected most of our cities.

Before the domes, these extreme weather patterns controlled us. Now, DAINN ensured no one got caught outside. We adapted.

But today, none of that mattered. We were leaving.

My gut reacted to the notion. My legs almost buckled.

How could I leave my home? After years of learning, my instincts attuned to my mind were an excellent gauge for any situation. It knew things instantly, and I learned to listen over the years. Something held me back to this place. Given a choice, I would stay even against logic.

Maybe DAINN's lack of facts about this anomaly event precluded us from determining a better way to deal with it. An interstellar voyager did not travel to Earth often, and I chuckled at the stupidity of the thought. This day did the trick on me.

The evening carried with it the unease of inevitability as the minutes passed. The novelty of that feeling defined my subsequent response as I arrived at my building.

The EHAF, until now overwhelmed, suddenly were joined by the City Vigils. Everywhere I looked, they descended on all parts of the GG, directing the crowd towards the evacuation gates. Minutes ago, they were nowhere.

An EHAF guard turned to his companion and said, "Well, the SRC finally secured them."

"Let's hope it lasts. We need all the help we can get."

I entered the lobby of my building confused. What happened to DAINN today? Did the anomaly infiltrate our Network, or was it just a fluke? If our scientist could not figure it out, there was no way I could. Shaking my head at the thought of the power that would soon fall upon us, I crossed the lobby and got into the Elevat.

When I reached the penthouse, which used to be my parents' apartment, the door opened on my domestic bot, Cian and Mage.

"Phenom Tesh, it is good to see you."

"Hello, Cian." I dropped to my knees and hugged Mage, my dog, with joy. I loved my dog, Mage. He was a gift from my father, and

I was practically raised with it at my side from a toddler. There was nothing I would not attempt to keep Mage at my side.

"I believe you need a resourcing bath. I will prepare it, and when you finish your bath, you will eat."

"There is not much time, Cian."

"There is enough time for that. Everything else is ready for you."

"Leane will be over in a while."

"Good. I will prepare some food for both of you."

Within minutes, I got into the gel-like substance of our resourcing water and closed my eyes.

Leane's voice woke me. "So, with all the chaos, this is where I find you?"

I smiled.

"It's been a day."

"You can say that again. Come on, let me take a look at you."

I stepped out of the soothing liquid that revitalized my muscles after the gruesome treatment I received at the hands of the Rat.

Leane's eyes grew when she saw my skin. Despite the Nanos and the Imps, I bore bruised everywhere, and deep in my broken bones, I felt a lingering soreness due to the multiple times they were reset.

I walked naked to the panoramic views outside the resting chamber.

"What in the HellNet happened?"

"The Rat happened."

"Did you report it? Of all the nasty…"

"No. There's no need. I doubt Sloan Roden Baker will hurt anyone anymore, but if you don't mind, I'd rather not talk about it."

Leane's face was a mask of anger as she quickly applied the MedNanos that would support mine to treat the injuries I sustained. "I hope he rots. You know he is very dangerous."

I laughed. "Your wish is granted. The Rat will remain an empty shell."

Leane looked alarmed.

I reassured her. "I did not do it. The others…"

"Well, I supposed he had it coming. This injection should take care of the damage. You will be like new in a few hours, but you cannot get into cryo until this is better."

"I nodded. I'll stay here a while longer then."

"You do that. I will tell the others, and we will wait for you. But I have some things I need to attend to because I was not expecting this so soon."

"I am not sure any of us were."

I grabbed a robe and followed Leane to the living room. She stopped by one of the plates of food Cian had left for us and picked up a wrap. "Cian, thanks for the food. I've got to run."

"You are welcome, Phrenic Leane."

"I'm going to miss you, Cian."

My domestic bot inclined its head, and Leane walked out. "Tesh, I'll NetComm you to see how you are doing."

It seemed that the Network was back online, although I suspected it was not our latest rendition of our communication network. Things must be worse than we knew.

I stepped onto the sliding ledge of the balcony. My Imps engaged and called for the platform to move on my brain's silent command. For a moment, I stood there observing the cloud.

The haze hovered on the entire city now, and my breath caught in my throat.

It was early evening, and the dome appeared stuck halfway, never closing completely since the morning. As I scrutinized the landscape on the horizon, past our buildings, past the ocean, past our floating landing strips, way past the dome's edges, a slight deformation occurred beyond the grids of Ang City.

It looked like an aggregation of clouds darker and bigger perhaps than what we had experienced lately. Still, it was approaching steadily and appeared more ominous than what we were used to, especially recently. Reluctant to move quite yet, I gave myself a few more minutes of contemplation.

This day was the culmination of many things in my life. It was a stamp of approval by my peers protecting me from harm. It was proof that I had made it somehow and that I was part of something bigger and better than we allowed ourselves to think about most times. Shapers were all part of who I was; we were all connected even with the distance the Institute imposed on us.

The anomaly was about to change my life as I watched. I remained here in a cool breeze under a retracted dome human-made by our ingenuity and executed by our machines.

The domes, meant to protect us from the elements, were still opened as the cloud descended on us, and my skin began to crawl. It was the ultimate physical response. It seemed the kind one had when things were just about to turn nasty bad. Why did DAINN not close the domes?

This time the feeling wasn't just unease. This time my stomach dropped with a sense of foreboding. Our scientists had deemed the anomaly so dangerous that their recommendations called for the evacuation of our entire planet. While it was hard to get my mind on the end of the world notion, I got it now. I finally understood the whole meaning of this galactic invasion.

When I focused on my reaction to determine what held me in a tight grip, I knew it was not fear. This time, I identified it as much more than a random lousy intuition. It was something more powerful, a flash of pure knowing that our time had just run out.

43
Pandemonium
Ciel

Detention Center, Archway Pass, Ang City

My mind is chaotic when I awake, and my recollection of the events is fuzzy. Transcient Ciel Grey, Insurgenets, DAINN Annals – Winter 2098.

I saw myself surrounded by the workers for a fraction of a second, attempting to break free of them, and I woke up quite suddenly.

There was no movement around me, and the place was dark, so I could not discern any shapes either. HellNet, maybe it was the utter calm after the storm, but I feared the worst.

Slowly, pieces of my memories drifted in. I remembered running under the overpass after Asher had dropped me from his AirBike. I remembered hiding with the device and monitoring the arrival of the workers. I had sent in one report, only one. Then everything cut off. Taken by surprise by the advances of the Force on one side and the rioters on the other, the crowd suddenly drifted toward me in waves, and the Znet dropped around us.

I was trapped. My movements were too slow, moving away from the horde, and I got caught in the snare of the EHAF. They surrounded us from above, dropping a perimeter that was impossible to flee.

Reluctant to move, I remained still. Although I feared I already knew, there was no way to confirm where I was. The immobility of this place after so much chaos was terrifying. The quick pick of my surroundings jumped at me, and I quickly understood that I was inside one of the detention centers.

From my position, I couldn't see much. Filled with dread, I sat up and glanced around. The quiet of the chamber was a peaceful refuge, but I knew better. This calm before the storm about to destroy my life was temporary. A feeling of hopelessness grew into utter panic, and I could barely catch my breath. *Calm the HellNet down…*

The small cell holding me, built of an indestructible glass-like material, floated. Suspended way above the floor and way lower than the ceiling, it hovered in place in the air. Nothing was connecting to the structure on any side.

I could see outside of my cage and knew instantly that my way out was at the whim of the security forces. There was no possibility I could make it out of here on my own. The material was unbreakable from the inside and impenetrable from the outside. I found myself in one of our grids' most wholly secured facilities.

My heart dropped. I hyperventilated. Fear rose from the pit of my stomach and reached my throat. There was no place for me to go or run. No hiding place for me. Not from here. *Ciel, get a hold of yourself. It does not help, but you did it this time.*

I turned and looked around. Everywhere my eyes reached, it was the same. The vast structure continued in every direction. This module alone had to contain thousands of us. My cell was separated from the others around by about three feet apart on all sides. People sat inside each of the small cubicles. Disgruntled and resigned, for now, we were waiting silently.

Like me, they had no way to control their destiny anymore. They belonged to the System now. Cold, clammy panic rose in a wave within me once again. I couldn't go there. Focusing on breathing slowly, in and out, I missed my freedom in the underground. Perhaps I should have said no to Laird. The mission carried high risks. Yet, part of me knew I accepted it because things had to change. But now, I was done. My life as I knew it since I became a Surg was now over. Once they screened me and handled my data, they would recognize me.

I shuddered. Once inside the System again, I would not escape it a second time. They would use Imps to subdue me or control me at worst.

Due to my abilities, the EHAF would reprocess me, as they did with many of us. The Institute would claim me. They would enroll me into the same program I ran away from years ago. DAINN dictated our roles, although the Conclave twisted our formation. The head of the Institute was relentless. Indeed, Sloan Roden Baker, known for his ruthlessness with recruits, would not get his hands on me again.

There were not many of us capable of doing what I could accomplish. Very few of us performed control over others instinctively with a thought. Influencing, shaping, and changing perceptions was a natural evolution in some of us, as much a gift as a curse with the Rodent.

I didn't stand a chance if they got to my records. *Can I act before they do? Can I walk out by practicing what I gave up years ago?*

Remaining calm and composed always helped me in the past. The dismay I felt would only give my jailors ammunition. *Can they see me? Cameras... Where are the cameras?*

I looked around and could not find them, but I knew they had to be there deep down. Powerless, I sat down in the middle of my cell and did like the other prisoners. I began the wait.

What would happen next? I couldn't face the idea to be once again, inside the DAINN System, within the division of the Institute that remains to this date, the most guarded.

With my head down on my knees, I felt like puking but closed my eyes and began to reach out around me. I had to find a way...

Practicing what they had drilled into me so many years ago, I slowed my breathing and let my mind lead the way.

Suddenly, I heard a crash.

It was a sound that resonated everywhere around me, reverberating time and time again across the colossal space of the detention center.

The cell adjacent to mine wobbled to one side and plunged to the ground. It hit another cage across from mine, dislodging it from its stable position in its quadrant.

I got to my feet and looked around.

The entire block moved as if a giant invisible wave pushed against it.

People's mouths opened in a silent scream, their faces distorted by fear.

My cage began to tip.

I got thrown against the glass wall; my transparent jail noticeably wobbled on its axis. For a moment, it remained suspended as if the weight pulled it to one side, and then it suddenly dropped a few feet brutally.

I stumbled and hit the corner, bumping my head hard.

The cubicle descended to the ground, colliding with another enclosure.

My body, tumbling forward, my face pressed against the transparent surface, and the floor came at me fast.

Presidential Tower, Golden Ghetto, Ang City

Nothing is working out as I expected. With the anomaly, all of my plans feel inconsequential with what is going on in our city at this very moment. Phrenic Anton Fowler, United General Council of Nations – UGCN, DAINN Annals – Winter 2098.

This morning, I thought about my argument with Vel as I dragged her along behind me. We were going down. The moving stairs of the Tower stopped moving a while ago, no longer carrying us down. Our infrastructure broke down around us since the beginning of the day, some things more noticeable than others, and we sprinted to reach the exit. Even with my security status, I could not get a shuttle to the fleet waiting above. Every aspect of our plans seemed to fall apart.

Simply put, we were not ready for the anomaly.

Our protocols required that we reach the bunker if all else failed. The Council always maintained a presence within the Tower, and underground facilities established for emergencies waited for us before they closed against the threat. I daresay we were due now.

When everything went dead around us, I focused on getting us there while my staff, departing early, made their way there separately, although they had a head start.

Vel's hand squeezed mine, and I was glad she remained inside our quarters throughout the Concord. We attempted to have father and daughter time each night. Some weeks were better than others, but it became our routine with only us in the home. We talked together when the alert began and quickly grabbed a few things before heading for the stairs. The Elevat of the building remained irresponsive, and I refused to take a chance and get stuck in there. So, our only choice was the stairs, and there were a lot of them – over five hundred of them.

HellNet, I could not imagine if I had to find Vel at the Academy in this chaos. Shaking my head, I increased my pace, eager to get down to the bunker level.

"How do you know they'll be there?" asked Vel.

"Because it's protocol, and these are smart people. Come on, honey. We have to make it down faster. That's where everyone will be now."

We were so far the lucky ones. We did not have to cross the Plaza and fight the crowd to reach the evacuation gates leading us to our coordinated locations.

The anomaly hit us when DAINN went off-Network, so we switched to the Tower NetComm, where the orders from the EHAF were abundantly clear.

The safety chamber, stacked to the brim with everything we might need, awaited members of the Council.

Looking back on my conversation with Zane this morning and realizing that my plan could have landed me in his position, I thought it was better to be in my seat. He was the man for what we faced on this night. He had the training.

Vel slowed down. "I'm tired, dad. Let's stop for a second."

She had always been a princess, and it was my fault. I liked to see her happy, so she was spoiled. "There is no time for that, honey. Just give me your bag. Come on. You can rest inside the bunker."

Teenagers were all the same. Nothing changed. Over time Zane and I had both commiserated on the state of what independent teenage daughters craved. We both came to the conclusion we had no idea. We even sat together in silence, pondering what to do with our respective daughters. Having seen the worst of times, we both knew that today was not safe anywhere. The effects of the Concord on our city in the previous years and recorded in our Archives held no secret.

The stairway brought us closer to the ground floor as we passed each level. But we still had a long way ahead, and I felt anxious to get there.

Part of me was satisfied to see that I had been right about the Concord. Of course, I was in part responsible for it. But the arrival of the anomaly on this day of all days took all of us by surprise—our state of readiness required at least another three months of grueling work to prepare. To recognize we were not ready for any of this was an accurate fact.

I had not seen anyone in the Tower during the last hour, and currently, we were the only ones on the stairs since we began our descent. It was an unlikely occurrence for as many people inhabited and worked here, which worried me. *What if…? Don't go there.*

Where was Zane? His team probably evacuated him before the alert ran its doom on the city.

Cut off from the latest information and DAINN; I anticipated the worst scenarios. My mind worked, weighing the odds against us.

We were no longer dealing only with the Concord, which had ended a few hours ago, but faced an unknown force that appeared stronger than us.

What hid behind the cloud?

I had no doubts that this was not a natural phenomenon. Under the guise of the artificial fog that wreaked havoc in our lives, what awaited us?

I hoped Zane was alive because, in truth, we needed him. He was better facing this thing than I would ever be. Ironic, I know. Indeed, he had the training, the experience, and the Imps on his side. Only, I had no idea whether he was alive or not, and if he was still among us, I didn't know if the Imps would strengthen or weaken him. Indeed, what if this thing created for a purpose we ignored to date could infiltrate our brains? My Imps remained disconnected just for that safeguard. Whether DAINN was still dealing with our security or not, I did not even know that fact.

"You know you can't turn on your connection, right?" Desperate to make sure Vel would be safe, I insisted, "No matter what happens, you stay off the System until we know what is going on."

"Dad, I'm young, but I'm not dumb," replied my daughter.

"I know… I want to make sure you're all right no matter what happens."

"I know, dad… I'm with you, so I'm okay. We both will be."

Not wanting to dissuade her from thinking that, I kept on going in silence. Youth's optimism went a long way in this situation. Me, I just wasn't so sure. Since the beginning of the Concord, everything had gone sideways in our lives. And as we descended to level four hundred and twenty, I wondered what we would find below and who had reached the bunker.

I pulled at Vel's arm harder as we kept going. She followed without protest but reluctantly. I counted myself lucky that she was by my side. My daughter… The thought of her made me wonder about

Lake. Where was she now? I hoped she was with her father and that they both waited downstairs.

I grimaced. Zane, as President of the EHAF, reassured me somehow. When did that notion find its way into my head? It was a reversal for me. The fact that it happened at all told me that I needed to rethink my entire strategy. We were in a hip of trouble, and Zane in control proved a good thing for my peace of mind. How about that?

**45
INCURSION
Eva**

Faculty, Recovery Room ER, Golden Ghetto, Ang City

I try to drive my fears away. I attempt to ease the awful suspicions about this day, but nothing is as it seems until I see him, and I forget for a time. Phenom Eva Bassington, Faculty Conclave, DAINN Annals – Winter 2098.

The city was not safe this evening, not with the consternation I saw on some faces, not with the anger I read in others, and certainly not with the questions I intercepted in the eyes of everyone as our stares turned upwards toward the sky.

The streets were still filled with workers who abandoned the rioting when suddenly they heard the alert. This wasn't an unusual circumstance for a day of Concordance. The annals showed that much. The discontents looked for release and were willing to do anything to get it. Now, anxious people moved through our streets in haste, rendering the atmosphere feverish and agitated on the way to the assigned evacuation locations.

When I entered the recovery room and saw Aidan across from me and finally awake, I forgot about what was going on outside the walls of the ER. The fascination I experienced with him was something I always felt, but I wasn't expecting such a physical reaction now that I looked at him.

My body tingled, more alive. I felt as if I was finally waking up after all these years. My life seemed to have a new purpose, and suddenly, my senses went into overdrive, making everything within me more alert. The base of my neck heated up, and a flush rose to my face. My blood pumped faster, and my heartbeat increased; loud, agitated, and unsteady. My breath caught in my throat when Aidan looked at me and came out in a rasp. I concentrated on inhaling and exhaling to keep myself steady. *Come on, get some control, Eva.*

His features had matured, but they were essentially the same. His face was strong, slightly angular, with full lips on a well-designed mouth, a nose proportioned just right, and beautiful blue eyes. Perfect for me. They would become grey when he was mad, and he could look right through you. I remembered what it looked like when he got angry. I held on to the feeling of warmth.

He looked detached and not part of this environment. He fit in as a Company man, don't get me wrong. Yet, one could observe in him a moment of decision. He was on the verge of some type of action, ready to spring to life. It was striking to see him in that one instant like a statue prepared to break out of a thoughtful state. The shell that made up the soft veneer of sophistication suited him, but he disliked this place. Getting more Imps could not be a goal for most. Wrapped in that restraining social blanket, he seemed to have been only half of himself, incomplete and definitely not brimming with life. He resembled a big cat about to jump into the fray to recover his true nature.

He felt my gaze on him because he turned and assessed me. It was a thoughtful evaluation. He was not so much watching my body as he was looking into my face, and I could almost see his brain engaged in a cold calculation. He appraised me in a few seconds. *So, he has not recognized me. How could he?*

I had changed from the little five-year-old girl who took her Evaluation at the Institute with him to the woman I was today.

A breeze from the open window carried a sweet scent. Our Imps provided heightened senses when we locked on something or someone. It could have a positive or negative effect. In this instance, it was a rather good experience. The smell was slightly different from our closed dome, bringing the outdoors in with a hint of sweet jasmine in the air. I liked it.

Scents were one of many manufactured products the corporations created in abundance for the pleasure of the population. *Otherwise, how would I know if this is the outdoors?*

It was an effort for me to look natural. The flutters in the pit of my stomach were butterflies. I had experienced them before, but not like this. *Enough, Eva. Get a hold of yourself.*

My complete data bank on Aidan ran through the list DAINN kept about his likes and dislikes. His daily activities and purchasing habits were also listed. Rather quickly, his cologne appeared – *The name was Earthbound. Maybe it is what I am breathing?*

This was it... The moment I had waited for all these years was finally here. I tried to steady myself. I instinctively knew that my entire life was about to change.

Our eyes locked. *Oh, boy!*

My embarrassment rose the longer I stared.

He did too.

I didn't let go.

He didn't either...

An irrational, thrilling expectation shaped the moment.

He smiled, and his entire face lit up. He had an infectious smile when he wanted to.

I returned the smile instead of playing it cool, and we began to move toward each other. Our talk was brief. In that instant, I received confirmation that things had just shifted for me for the better.

The atmosphere in the room was bustling with a lightness that lingered in the air. Behind the superficial laughter, the tension of the days disappeared, and I forgot all about my fears.

We were both in a sort of trance, unwilling to break the intense connection we had experienced at first sight.

After today, we sought something, anything, to make us believe our lives were worthwhile. The toll imposed by the Concord required something to make us feel special. Also, the uncertainty of what we faced drew on negative energy. At that moment, ours was a desperate attempt to be connected to others. After a grueling day, the change imposed on our infrastructure led us down an irreversible path toward something no one truly wanted, and now, it may have been all for nothing.

The uncertainty caused by the cloud only added to our unease. We woke up to a world we knew and understood to find that our entire existence had morphed into a complete nightmare. Indeed I sensed that we dipped into a hidden and malevolent vortex, but in the middle of it stood Aidan, an island of reassurance in a landscape in turmoil.

I could see the loneliness in Aidan's eyes, and he didn't try to hide it from me. We understood each other, reliving the alienation we had felt like kids in one moment. His strength of character had allowed him to adapt. He stood tall under the weight of the experience. I let it go at that. I had seen enough and didn't want to embarrass him by dwelling on the past. *I think we all are better off forgetting the heartlessness of it all.*

The first signs of a commotion in the main entrance reached us, and multiple shouts resonated. Angry voices rose, coming from outside. Glass shattered.

Aidan and I rushed to the doorway.

Screams reverberated across the corridors, all coming from the entrance. Suddenly, the lights in the main hallway went out. There were more shrieks and even some howls.

A mob stormed the ER. They advanced in the corridors despite some of the EHAF guards.

The medical personnel rushed the hall where Aidan and I stood, panicked at the violence from our people. They ran in the opposite direction.

"Come on." Aidan took my hand and pulled me away from the onslaught, but soon we were surrounded by the crowd.

Bodies careened against us as people pushed to get away in a furious reaction. Our medical equipment and supplies standing in the hallways were smashed to pieces as they fell to the floor. Some rioters grabbed furniture pieces and threw them against the glass partitions. Others took food trays and toppled them as their anger increased, making the ground slippery.

People stumbled around us.

The agitation around us gained momentum. Some rioters attacked our personnel, regardless of the uniform of the Faculty, shoving them to the ground. The confusion and anger triggered a volatile reaction from the doctors and nurses alike, and we found ourselves in the middle of a tidal wave.

Aidan's arms closed around me. I heard his voice whispering, "Let's get outside… which way?"

"This way…" as I guided him toward one of our sideways corridors. We crossed the space to the broken windows navigating the wave of people rushing past us in a wild brawl. As I held onto him in the chaos, our uncharted paths eventually led us to the patio.

The outdoor area overlooked other buildings. The lights of the high-rises surrounded us, but we stood in darkness. Despite the ominous orange and purple sky above our heads, the night air was mild.

We glanced up, aware that something unfamiliar was building around us. The noise of the chaos we left behind inside us was not receding; instead, it amplified more forcefully, reaching us in uneven crescendos of patterns filled with more violent shouting and screams.

Aidan dragged me to a small area leading to pathways and a small garden. We dropped over a railing a short distance and landed into rows of bushes, just below a terrace.

This small patch of dirt filled with flowers and the sweet smell of Lilies, Hyacinth, and Irises surrounded us. We reached the only tree, and Aidan pushed me under the Lilac full of cone-shaped flower trusses. We were now hidden and maintained an oddly contemplative silence as we stood side by side, still strangers after all and yet, not strangers at all.

Aidan looked up at the sky and glanced toward me. "Concordance has made many people unhappy today."

"What do you think is happening inside?"

"Did you notice the EHAF is handling most of the security? Our City Vigils are not in great numbers on the streets tonight."

"I saw the EHAF Special City Vigils contingent filling their numbers. They are programmed independently from the others."

"Their symbol is not the same. It explains the delay. I think DAINN is in trouble because many of the CVs are not activated today," murmured Aidan.

Indeed, it was true. Shuttles assembled over our location, illuminating the grounds around the building. A small contingent of Special City Vigils was among them.

They dropped from the air vehicles motionless above us, quickly establishing a perimeter and fencing in the area. Light scanners roamed, canvassing everything that moved and everyone standing.

"Let's wait here until they finish the inspection."

Within moments loud voices dropped in amplitude. Multiple nets "zapped" their targets as the CVs boosted by Street Custodians released their lifting devices. The mechanisms of the machines echoed in a buzzing sound around us.

Squeals rose parsimoniously now, and little by little, the noise abated.

People lifted off with several Custodians leaving the area with their cargo. The sounds of guards walking the ground reached us. In the next few minutes, the Force and the Special City Vigils squadron had seen to the disturbance. Our security procedures and state-of-the-art technology allowed the clean-up to occur efficiently under compliance with our laws. But were these enough against the dangers of the anomaly?

The gardens were now the territory of the Clout. We moved in concert from the secluded arbor of the Lilac tree to find ourselves facing one of the City Vigil guards. "Don't move, Citizens," he said as he scanned us.

Our identification was instantaneous. "Phenom Eva, Phenom Aidan, do you need any assistance?"

"I am good," I said.

"We are fine," Aidan said.

"Don't delay to get to your designated gates." With a nod of his head, he moved on. The motionless shuttles began to depart. The chaos had ended.

We hesitated to leave each other, so we stood there, indecisive.

Aidan finally motioned me toward a bench a few feet away. We sat there, unable to find the words to carry on our initial conversation.

The day was taking its toll on me, and my mood dropped. I suddenly felt utterly lonely, sad, and unsure of myself.

Aidan's voice reached me just as his hand rested on my shoulder. He must have sensed my emotional state. "You've grown to be beautiful and quite proficient at what you do. Tell me about your life."

I didn't want to think of my life. I suddenly wanted to know more about him. "You first. Can I scan you?"

Aidan nodded, agreeing to the idea.

I engaged my visor as he gave me access to his records, and I began to cross-reference Aidan according to our central database. I accessed pictures and a video timeline of his life up to this point. I found everything there was to know about him with the probing – officially, I mean. All relevant events of his childhood flashed in front of my eyes in a matter of a few minutes, even the flashbacks to our first meeting, and then I watched Aidan become a man. I gathered that he worked in finance for the Company under the head of his Conclave, Win. I learned that Aidan was an upstanding citizen with membership in the top associations in town with recommendations from some of the most prominent people in our community. I found out that he lived on the other side of the city, away from the GG, which was somewhat puzzling… But then again, what attracted me to him had a lot to do with the fact that he was different.

I also took the time to implement Desinet - a further search to explore a subject's inner desires. The program allowed a scan of the eye to read reactions to words or images. I did not particularly appreciate anatomizing someone in that manner, but it was efficient, and tonight, I needed some certainty. Our limited time we had together tonight called for it.

Aidan complied with it all without a word of protest. By the time my screen folded back, I knew the man in front of me. I had peeled off his many layers, and I was now ready to follow him anywhere. I had been thinking of this moment for most of my life.

Aidan submitted to the entire process without hesitation. I was ready to reciprocate in kind, but he made no move to open his link to my chip memory bank. "Don't you want to scan me?"

"What for?" He smiled and gave me his hand. "Will you stay with me?"

Something stirred inside me. I nodded.

"I don't know where all this will lead us. But we cannot take the same evacuation program."

"It does not matter."

Aidan searched for his words. "Are you certain? It could be the worst decision of your life. In truth, I have no idea if we will survive this. The thing is… The System no longer works; what our society faced until now causes me to wonder whether we even want to continue as we are if we even could. Concordance is not what we need. Not anymore. And today, this thing overhead, well, I don't know if we can overcome it."

"I know. I'm not leaving you. I need to go check on Heather."

Aidan nodded and followed me inside the ER without questions.

We reached the side entrance and moved inside the building. Traces of the upheaval confronted us everywhere. It was like a tornado had hit our emergency room facility.

Groups of people were still scattered on the floor, sprawled in many piles across the large room.

Custodians hovered across the corridors, carrying people in their nets. A few City Vigil medics treated cuts and bruises of the Elite members still in attendance.

I looked around, searching for my friend. Heather, disheveled, was helping a guy disoriented, and when she looked up, she saw me. "I thought something had happened to you," Heather said, running to me and throwing herself in my arms. "I was so scared."

"I was with Aidan when everything happened." Heather smiled at Aidan as we walked across a floor scattered with food, chattered glasses, and upside-down trays, all of it littering a ground that not too long ago was spotless. All this was another testimony of the chaos that had befallen us so unexpectedly.

Heather looked around. "I guess it does not matter anymore. We have to go to the gate."

Aidan and I looked at each other. I shook my head and said, "I'm going with Aidan."

Heather looked at us, stupefied. "You can't. They won't let you go with the Company Conclave, and they won't let you go to the Faculty Conclave. Neither of you registered as a unit."

"It doesn't matter. We're staying together," I said.

Heather frowned. "But what will you do? What if the EHAF can't take care of the threat?"

Aidan and I smiled.

I felt closer to him than I had ever been to another human being, apart from my mother. Remaining together did not hold the promise of a future because we did not know what would happen. But the gesture we made to stay together was quite grand, considering the circumstances. And yet, no matter what happened, it felt right.

SRC Conclave, Annals Viewing Vlog 3, 508, 332, 109 Ang City

It is almost over. The last remnant of my System fluctuates around the Planetary Mind, and I watch to see a glimmer of a change that will save my people. DAINN – Winter 2098.

My memory bank fluttered, and I remembered a moment depicting precisely how things began for me. Maybe it was my programming, ending, and recalling where things started. I was unaware why at the time approaching my demise, I reviewed one last time the beginning of the DAINN Network.

Zane Landen had been a proponent of change, and I followed Landen's way because my mentor, Dr. Rene Paladock, adhered to his agenda, along with a whole group of people who believed in him. They all wanted the same things he did.

Zane demonstrated steadfastness over years of rebuilding a society broken down by increasingly more catastrophic events, for the Earth had finally shown us who was truly in control of our environment.

Doubting that it should be his role as a leader coming from the military, he questioned how to deploy solutions that would help us control global warming. Artificial intelligence brought about changes implemented when healthcare was in disarray due to multiple pandemics. The new System called for his attention. The further dedication of Paladock with DAINN enticed him to listen and learn more, eventually considering a new role in our government.

"So, I should do it?" had asked Zane time and time again before he stepped into that podium.

"Hell, yeah… There is no better man as far as I'm concerned."

"You're partial, North. From my perspective, you subscribe to these ideas because you demonstrate an apparent distrust of others while you know me, said Landen, laughing.

"Darnet right… I know what to expect from you. You know the devil, you know."

"You need to lighten up. It's not always as you portray it in your head, North. Have a little faith, man," kept saying Langden.

Faith… It was something I did not possess, although Dr. Rene Paladock gave me the parameters of what faith meant to his people. I have witnessed it many times since.

These were conversations Zane and North had in the days they were on the terrain, fighting the elements rather than other men. This was at the time of the gale-force winds when we were in the streets evacuating the lost souls that had just witnessed the worse of it.

"Your beliefs or lack thereof come from the fact that you have seen too many bad things, but it doesn't have to be that way anymore. It is why I propose we establish with DAINN a change that will render the playing field even, and Paladock can make that happen," repeated Zane, for these ideas were what he stood for…

They debated Zane's plan as the new President, which had been supported by a population eager for change during a referendum.

Indeed, the DAINN Initiative had taken years. Landen was a key player during that time, bringing solutions to problems. So, it wasn't exactly a surprise when people demanded that he sit in the Presidential office.

Zane and North rose through the Clout together, maintaining order, staving off disasters, helping civilians. Eventually, our scientists came up with a way to limit ongoing damages through our cities and people.

The DAINN System did not eliminate the challenges arising from climate change, not entirely, but it was the beginning for us to reclaim our natural habitat.

"People are people and only interested in their welfare. Maybe it isn't pretty to think that way, but it is how I feel," North said, convinced of that fact. "So, having a Planetary Network taking over some of our screw-ups does not seem like a bad deal to me."

"How will that be received? I'm not sure that we are not giving DAINN too much leeway," muttered Landen.

"My position on this subject is based on a deep-rooted knowledge caused by experience. We didn't get here in my book because we did the right things. Loathsome egocentric leaders initiated these events a long time ago with their agendas. These monumental moments added up, changing the course of many lives, and were designed by individuals doing truly despicable things for their benefit. How can it be worse?"

If we keep a tight rein on the structure, we can maintain control, but we will have to keep a keen eye on the potential corruption of the System," explained Landen. "I believe in Paladock. He is a good man and will see to it. We need to provide him with such an ethical group that his team is not corruptible. Is that even feasible?"

All of this occurred right before Zane's post changed, and he stepped in as President. From that moment on, things got radically altered.

In the early days of DAINN, there were questions about the changes made within our infrastructure… Paladock oversaw these. The System maintained the scoreboard for all of us, in significant part because of Zane, who implemented checks and measures to avoid overreaching. No one cheated the System.

DAINN was a logically analytical tool.

People were not naïve.

I kept protocols to ensure that some population elements did not manipulate the Network. A few tried and succeeded until new measures, implemented within my protocols, crashed their efforts. But at least with the Network, my people were all playing on the same field. Things were clear, with rules for everyone and Conclaves to ensure compliance. New evolving norms daily established reinforced the System with minor modifications to an enforced protocol at the onset of DAINN's coming online. *Any leader will use anyone if they can. The DAINN System provides a new landscape because it has no emotions, no agenda of its own.*

The notion that people's actions would yield the same results as long as human beings were generating the plan gave the impetus for DAINN to expand beyond what Paladock envisioned. It gained notoriety and popularity.

People lack trust in each other. They rejected companies' profit-driven agendas. They wanted assurances that no one would implement a program to pursue their ends to the detriment of the planet and its global population.

Safeguards developed by Paladock were imposed to ensure the System's security and monitor potential abuses of power. With DAINN, the expected change occurred within years. Steps were taken globally for the good of all. Life became easier. Hope was reborn in my people. Simply put, people couldn't trust themselves or each other. They began counting on DAINN.

Call the System what you will. It was far from perfect. *But DAINN offered better ways.*

These were Langden's conclusions and the outcomes viewed by many others over the years.

Zane took the post of President.

Our society needed changes to survive better to one day thrive again.

I remembered Langden's first speech. "DAINN is the way, a safeguard for all of us, a balanced method to eradicate inequities and monitor power in the hands of those at the top so that all people, whether workers in the fields and our plants, teachers, gurus and artists, scientists and innovators, technicians and entrepreneurs receive their rights entitlements for we have fought for these over decades," announced Zane in his presidential oration.

People voted for the expansion of the DAINN Network and supported the change.

All had viewed such a mandate to be a necessity. People and the government needed a watchdog positioned to secure the people's future. And so far, the DAINN Network has performed flawlessly to enhance people's overall wellbeing.

The DAINN Network still held onto this idea, the notion of equity among all, even if some were more powerful or affluential than others, until the bioengineered red cloud invaded my System. There existed no other way for the Network as it held and behaved according to its core programming.

DAINN performed its final analysis.

The protocols for Alpha, Provenance, and Aurora were completed, and the defenses of the programs were secured.

The Conclaves had performed fast, ensuring their people accessed the gates despite the Concord, the riots, and the cloud. The environment support on the ship was optimal. Crew and passengers reported where they were required. The stasis pods were engaged, ready to see to the survival of our people. The bridge control on all vessels responded to the immediacy of departure. Everything was loaded on the various ships of the fleet, from food, supplies, equipment, and environmental services. Now, these portals, which served to secure a future, the Spacevats were closed all over the city. Even the underground bunker to the Aurora program had closed.

Alpha, Aurora, and Provenance, these three programs attempted to save as many of our people as possible. People with considerable skills had joined the five Conclaves. Engineering, mechanical, chemical, manufacturing, applied physics, biotechnology, medicine, law, space navigation, crop, livestock, computers, libraries, comm, diagnostic, laboratory equipment, tools, seeds, and weapons were all aboard the safety underground chambers or the evacuation ships.

The only one which did not meet that mandate was Origin. The Origin team approached the next day with another plan—one that remained radically unknown in terms of success and yet one that could change everything. The Origin's Compartments were safely ensconced inside the underground Institute Safety Chambers and on its way.

The Aurora stasis pods closed behind the bunkers gate.

The Alpha and Provenance Fleet could now depart.

DAINN glanced one last time at Ang City as it fell into slumber. The Planetary Mind sent its destruct signal before the bioengineered red cloud penetrated its kernel. In the blink of an eye, DAINN defenses were gone, and the planetary Mind whose sole purpose existed to protect its charges was no more.

**47
EXTRACTION
Cashel**

Institute Building, Roof, Golden Ghetto, Ang City

I stand in the doorway, observing this immutable object. The dust cloud invades our city, corroding our streets with its opaque substance. Will we eradicate it, or will it alter us? Will we have to flee? Phrenic Cashel Reid, Presidential Elite Unit, EHAF Conclave, DAINN Annals – Winter 2098.

The doors closed on the bio-engineered formation. I stood there for a moment, trying to weigh in the various options to make our way back to the Tower and the bunker.

I looked at Alai, wondering our next move. We were both pondering the best course of action given the situation. Going straight into the crowd going to the gates, considering the fog would make us lose valuable time. She shook her head, drawing a blank.

The bunker would close soon, but we needed to get the team to the gates and reunite the President with his daughter. It was a mission neither of us wanted to screw up.

The bunker remained an option for those who could not make it there until it closed. Then, the doors would not reopen until the crisis passed if we averted the cloud's effects. There was no doubt in my mind that this thing of unknown origin would trigger something.

There was no way we would allow ourselves to fail. The Elite, even split into various assignments as we were at this very moment, never failed. It was not an option. We won missions, engagements, and success rate made us what we were – the Elite.

Zane counted on that. We had to get his daughter back to him. "The best option is going through the Institute," I announced with certainty. We go past the Academy and get to the roof."

'Through the Ints, it is then…" said Alai, already moving ahead. "It will take us to the proximity of the Tower. Crossing the distance from high up will land us at the feet of the entrance."

"Exactly. It will give us the chance to get there on time."

"What do we do when we get to the roof?" asked Amara.

"All right, we're going back and up, all the way to the other side of the building," I added, pushing the girls forward. I ushered our party across the large lobby, running.

The girls followed us, keeping up with the pace we set up with Alai.

"Move, move, move" exclaimed Alai as she stepped way ahead of us.

"It will save time. If we go across the plaza and around the buildings in this soup, we won't make it."

"But… what do we do when we get there?" asked Lake, nonplussed.

"We rappel down…"

Amara looked dubious. "I'm not so sure… Why not take the SpaceVat? It's the shortest way?"

My proposal was valid and the safest choice under the circumstances. I pushed Amara toward the large sliding stairs. "Not at this time. We don't know what systems are compromised."

Considering we were dealing with inexperienced girls, I understood her misgivings. I just didn't see any other valid choice.

The contraption stood on the side of the building, opposite the Spacevat. It included six platforms, similar to escalators of old times, but these were folded and remained transparent until they became functional. Now, four lines had formed as we stepped onto its surface, and they turned an opaque color matching the building surroundings. Safety guards gradually encased both sides as we moved up. They remained that way during the climb and the descent. They were secured by small visible color lines fitted inside photovoltaic glass blocks with the latest electronic mechanism.

Amara crept beside Lake on the first step of the moving stairway. They hovered slowly at first, matching the speed of the girls.

"Come on, girls, let's sprint it," snapped Alai. "We're on a schedule." She pushed ahead, setting the pace so that Amara and Lake had to match it, and now climbing faster.

The stairs matched our rhythm, adjusting to the height of each individual's legs. We were at this particular moment moving quickly through the lower floors. The machine responded to the speed of each individual.

Halfway up the first set of floors, the absence of people within the Institute struck me as odd. The more we went up, the more I got worried. It was unusual for a building this prominent within our society. Thousands of people worked here. Then, I remembered that for some of the Conclaves, the Concord was still going on. "How much longer will people remain inside the Assembly now that we triggered the alarm?" I asked Amara.

She turned and gave me a small smile. "They should be out soon. I am as surprised as you that they are not already."

"In that case, let's hurry and get to the top floors before the crowd comes out, or it will slow us down considerably," I said.

Indeed, when a large crowd utilized the MoStairs, the mechanism immediately regulated itself to a more typical standard.

People in the Institute possessed a professional attitude about their work. It was instilled from the moment they began training for the Inst. The Conclave required the candidates to maintain discipline as part of their instruction. Calm was a key ingredient to their learning process. They never rushed anywhere within the walls of their facility or outside, for that matter, calling for a show of control at all times.

The Insts were not used to drills of any kind. Part of me wondered if they would face this crisis with the same decorum they usually possessed. I questioned it.

In a moment of danger, it was my experience that people lost their heads. This placid attitude, a good attribute when used to reassure trainees, could become their undoing. Indecision could kill. And facing a bottleneck if they panicked would not be any better for us. I wasn't sure what I preferred. Our progress would be impaired either way.

"Let's keep moving," Alai said, way ahead of us.

I dashed on the stairways, wondering what was going on outside. Without DAINN, we were cut off from the rest of the Network, only functioning on the EHAF NetComm, encompassing the Tower and my team.

I also faced another potential problem. Amara's personality would kick in both cases. I understood that much from her profile. She was a caregiver. She would try to help the Institute team and candidates, and I would have to stop her.

With renewed energy, I moved our group upward. "Faster, we can't afford to waste time. Go, go." They would soon tire, for they didn't have access to the physical resources Alai and I possessed. Our Imps helped tremendously along with the grueling training we usually underwent as Elite Officers.

We must reach the upper level quickly. While these were not accessible to all personnel, making the upper levels faster than the crowd coming out of the Concord Assembly remained an issue. "Make these few minutes count. Speed is the main issue to the success of this operation," added Alai. "If we don't make it in time, there will be hell to pay!"

"Easy for you to say," mumbled a winded Lake. "You've got Imps for that."

"I didn't get them at first. We must prove we can handle the work," responded Alai with a laugh. "Trust me; we trained for them."

We were halfway up the fortieth floor when Amara stopped. "Look, they're coming out right now."

She read my mind. She echoed my thoughts as I calculated the remaining minutes before the onslaught on the stairways. "Come on, guys; we must clear the fiftieth floor."

Lake stopped and complained, "I can't go any faster."

"Move," exclaimed Alai, "if you want to see your father again."

The idea to never see her father again prompted Lake to run up with renewed vigor. Amara's steps, which were lagging a moment ago, found new vitality.

"Come on, you can do it," I told her, jumping over the safety guard and ahead of her. I dragged her up with me on the stairways.

The sheer size of the place was astounding. The Institute was not one of our tallest structures within Ang, but it was imposing and broader than other Conclave buildings. It sat low to the ground for our era, contrary to most of our architectural landscapes that were now way up in the clouds.

The Tower, which held our presidential and government offices inside the GG, was five hundred stories high. The Institute sat on one hundred floors. It was also long and stood close to the ground compared to the rest of our towers.

Due to the mission of the Institute, it needed to be attainable by everyone. For that reason, the architecture boasted an imposing and closed-off building sitting on the Plaza and visible by all from there. In most individuals entering its sphere, it created a feeling of awe and intimidation. I was available and within reach of all, yet it remained aloof and secret. It suited its mandate within our society perfectly.

We had passed the floors with many personnel and reached the restricted ones. When we arrived at the landing of the sixtieth floor, we heard the first screams.

People ran around disoriented and without purpose, with eyes vacant. Suddenly, individuals toppled on the ground right where they stood.

It was obvious something was happening to them.

"What is going on, exclaimed Lake?" about to lose it as Alai dragged her faster.

The Concord had ended in a complete panic.

None of us prepared for what happened to our population. *How can you be ready for mayhem?*

I had never seen anything like this. In a snap, bodies fell chaotically everywhere and now surrounded us. The screams increased in frequency, resonating inside the building, bouncing back on the walls and ceiling. Rapidly, the stairways space turned nightmarish with corpses.

For some, the transition to nothingness was rapid, almost seamless. For others, it lasted a few minutes, their bodies writhing on the ground in pain.

"What's happening?" asked Amara, terrified. I dragged her harder behind me. "You disconnected from the Network, right?"

"Yes."

The Insts stepped onto the moving stairs on all sides. Some were going up and others down and fell on each other in a stampede.

Both Lake and Amara froze at the scene.

People around us were still connected to DAINN. They just ended Concordance. It was the only explanation I could think of as I watched. On the other hand, we had our by-pass up, blocking the cloud's corruption of our System, and in turn, affecting people's implants.

The EHAF, at the first sign of unusual activity, had everyone within the Force working with our old comms. The protocol, implemented by Langden when our Network first became affected and went down with the CV and Custodians. It was the first sign that something was wrong with DAINN. We thought it was the Surgs, but maybe the conclusion was wrong. Our people still responded to DAINN's interface since we never provided the message to disconnect to the public.

Amara was irate. "Why did you not make an announcement? We could have alerted everyone."

Alai intervened, "We did not know."

I checked our time. Our window was slowly closing in on us before the doors of the bunker would seal, and we would be on lockdown. *Avoid the crowd…*

I looked around at the walls. We were coming up on the next landing.

Without hesitation, Amara jerked out of my grip and reached out to someone on the ground near us. She had just ventured outside the moving stairway and into one of the adjacent corridors. I stepped out to follow her. "Alai, rappel up with Lake. We'll be right behind you."

Alai glanced up. "Cash, across?"

I assessed the floors above, using each landing to climb up. "Yes, go around the atrium. A vertical lift will be more stable but less efficient. It would also mean traversing a portion of the atrium. "Keep it tight."

Alai nodded and took Lake's arm. She harnessed herself to the girl before launching the grapple. I heard Lake exclaim in a panicky voice, "What are we doing?"

"Just hold on to me," Alai replied.

Alai could handle Lake, so I caught up to Amara. "Listen, I know you want to help, but we can't. We've got to keep going, so either you keep up, or I have to leave you behind."

"How... could you let this happen...?" exclaimed Amara, looking around in despair.

I interrupted her. "We are in unknown territory with no idea what we're up against; you know that. Think..."

Moments ago, this part of the building remained empty, but now, we faced a crowd of bodies in pain. Within seconds after that, we stepped over fallen bodies. It was overwhelming for anyone, but Amara was angry with grief and shock.

"This thing is decimating our Conclave," she cried. "Oh, stars, they are getting rid of us."

"The cloud activated some frequency. It's effective. The NetComm has been down for a while now, so we cannot broadcast, other than the old emergency signal."

I reached out to Amara, kneeling beside someone. I looked for a pulse but couldn't find one. "It has to do with the System. The anomaly corrupted the System. They are still connected to DAINN."

The person lying on the ground didn't have any life signs. Without my PVZ normal activation, I had no way to know about all the others.

"We have to help them," said Amara.

There was little we could do, and I knew it. "The only way to save them is for them to engage their by-pass, but it's too late to warn them. Come with me."

Amara started yelling at people still standing. "Engage your by-pass! Engage your by-pass!"

Her cries made little impact on the commotion around us. She might have saved a few lives, but I didn't stay to look back.

"Darnet, Amara, wake up! There is no time if you want to survive this!" I exclaimed, and the tone of my voice hardened. I grabbed Amara and threw her over my shoulder. I was ready to shake her by now.

I moved quickly and stumbled a few times on the bodies coming across my path. I heard small moans escaping from her lips every time one of my feet hit a corpse, but she held on, and I increased my pace, jumping the last of these obstacles to reach the nearest landing zone.

I brought her down beside me to set the harness.

Amara gazed up at me, tears streaming down her face as I released her in front of me while adjusting the gun. "Survive?"

Her expression of despair gutted me. Amara looked troubled and lost, overcome with grief. She experienced difficulties reconciling what I told her. The spitfire of a girl I had met not that long ago was gone. She became a mere shadow of the spirited girl that was my match, according to DAINN.

I didn't have the luxury to do anything about it now. I couldn't let that affect me. I had a job to do. Glancing around us, I held onto the first thing that made sense to me, and it happened to be Amara, this slip of a girl, crying in my arms and who had made me laugh a few days ago. I reached out to her face and said, "We're going to make it."

DAINN… What the HellNet was DAINN doing as our world fell apart around us. Our planetary computer had met its military match.

Regardless, our EHAF would intervene and counter whoever was at the heart of this attack. But there were no sounds of fighting coming from outside, no guns or laser-blasting now. I need to get back.

I survived many challenging situations. In this instance, the unexplained remained daunting. But the Elite, the EHAF, would endure and overcome even when dealing with something outside our frame of reference, but it was paralyzing.

Amara shuddered against me.

"Don't look. Just hold on."

I aimed my rappel gun from the moving stairs at the railing on the floors above. The cable uncoiling rapidly sent the small head of the spear to the handrail and hit my target. Before the rope tightened, I brought Amara against me. "Hold on tight."

We lifted fast, crossing the atrium, and repeated the process another four times. By the time we reached the upper floors where Alai and Lake were already waiting, we were out of the mayhem zone. Silence surrounded us now.

The onslaught subsided within minutes, and the devastation it caused was widespread. The Institute building transformed into a horrendous grave with this attack.

Alai's voice, exasperated by the teenager, yelled at Lake. "Come on, Lake, stop crying."

"Time is running out," I exclaimed, strapping the rappel gun to the back of my vest and pushing past them. I led the charge this time, focused on getting them to the roof. With a certain harshness, I said, "Lake, you're alive. If you want to stay that way, move your Netass." I was rough on the girls, and I knew it. But it was either live or die.

They did. This time, Alai closed the party behind Amara and Lake.

"How do you plan on getting back to the streets?" asked Amara from behind me.

"You just got a taste of it," I answered briefly, walking down one of the narrower corridors to a door opening on the roof.

I anticipated reaching my team soon. The corpses below were breathing, living moments ago, and while I witnessed deaths before, nothing prepared me for what we saw in the corridors. *We are one, all connected by a universal tapestry. If this is true, is it exceedingly unjust that I am alive and they are not. But, there is no such thing as justice, not in this life.*

I pushed open the door. The dome of the Institute building was a plateau surrounded by fog. Tentatively, I reached out at the cloud with one hand, not sure what to expect. Part of me wondered if it was harmful to the touch. It looked dense but did not appear to be corrosive. It didn't burn. It smelled like nothing either. *What is this thing?*

Stepping outside with the others behind me, we stood in the heavy, reddish cloud formation. The substance was porous, made of minuscule particles that floated slowly in the air, stopping us from seeing anything past a few inches ahead of us.

"What now, Cash?" asked Alai.

"The tower is about three hundred feet to the left of where we stand. Between the Tower and us is the Faculty building. By going to the edge, we pass it by about ten feet. Let's pull the line at a forty-five-degree angle, and it should take us safely to the ground."

"You want us to go down a line in this fog?" exclaimed Lake. "Are you crazy?"

"You just went up that line. Going down will be a breeze. Besides, we can't see anything, so that shouldn't be too hard," answered Alai. "In any case, there is no other choice."

"Let's tie everyone now. I can barely move in this soup," I muttered, tying one end to the door.

"Take my rappel line," Alai said as she handed me her rope. I quickly tied myself first to it, and the girls came next in the middle between Alai and me.

"Hold onto each other," I ordered as I prepped my gun in one hand and took one step forward. I was ahead of them, making my way toward the left side of the roof. "Stay behind me."

Each step was a challenge due to the composition of the cloud. I pressed forward, and the substance gave in, opening up little by little. We made our way to the side of the rooftop in a tight line, Amara holding onto me, with Lake and Alai closing the march.

The roof was huge. I counted my steps and paid attention to my direction, feeling my way on the surface with each stride, my night vision almost nonexistent and greatly extended by my Imps.

I finally felt the rounded edge of the roof under my feet and ordered, "stop."

They reacted a bit late. Pushed further to the edge, I lost my balance. The pull on the line slowed my fall, "Careful now…" exclaimed Alai. With one foot off the rooftop, she yanked me back with a tight grip on the rope. "I've got you."

"Thanks."

"Sorry, Cash," said Amara's voice, "You took me by surprise."

"It was my fault; I pushed her," Lake said.

"The resistance is too strong… We need a deeper angle to get us down. Otherwise, we'll stall." I did a quick calculation estimate and aimed lower at a place just above the door of the Tower, "I'm going more vertical – be ready for a rougher landing."

The arrival on the ground would be brutal, yet ignoring Amara and Lake's lack of training, I checked that the line held. "That should do it. Alai, can you handle Lake?"

"No problem."

"I can't do this," cried Lake. "We can't see anything."

I heard Alai's voice reassuring a panicked Lake. "Yes, you can. All you have to do is hold on to me and close your eyes."

On our Netcomm, Alai whispered, "Boy, this is going to be fun," as Alai was whimpering beside her.

The doors of the bunker were about to close us out. Impatiently, I blurted out in the fog, "Lake, we're almost there. Let's go."

"We can do this, Lake," Amara confirmed.

"I'll go first with Amara. Alai…You have the rope?" I searched for her hand, fumbling inside the viscosity of the substance. I hung on for a moment, squeezing her fingers. My partner and I had gone through many things in battle, but the fog was an unknown.

Alai was always steady and calm. She was my teammate, and I was there for her.

This night was not just any night. The anomaly we fought was not just another insurrection in part of our world.

She squeezed my hand back.

"This will take us to the front door. I will pull down on the rope three times once we're on the ground."

Alai's voice resonated slightly to my right. "See you at the bottom, Cash."

I tightened my grip on Amara. She wrapped her legs around my waist and squeezed herself against my back. "Hold on."

My belt pulled me forward, and we slid off the roof and into the emptiness of the anomaly, gliding toward the ground without visibility, the distance impossible to gauge. Our speed increased as we floated, surrounded by the golden particles of the dust cloud.

SRC, Control Center, Golden Ghetto, Ang City

Time stands still. The anomaly is here and has control of the Network. The System fights for us, but it is losing. Soon, DAINN will be no more. Phenom Kathryn Hendricks, SRC Conclave, DAINN Annals – Winter 2098.

Inside the Control Center, we all looked at each other, unable to come to terms with what we were facing. "Whatever is out there will control the System soon. Let's revert to give the EHAF a fighting chance."

"There are streams I've never seen before…" expressed Gregory.

Paladock looked briefly in my direction and answered unequivocally, "DAINN will fight it as long as it can, Kate. But these are echoes of something else. I agree, reactivate the old protocol."

My hopes crashed with his answer. "Then, you think DAINN is still with us?"

Although difficult to manage, I would feel more at ease with DAINN in charge of our operations. The unknown we now faced unsettled me to no end, but the Strategic Reference Information Platform known as SRIP, a previous and much less developed iteration of DAINN, came online. Part of me preferred to think of another option. I knew my next question was going to be unpopular, but I voiced it anyway, "What if DAINN is doing this on purpose?"

"DAINN would not, even to confuse the enemy," Paladock said.

"I have a scan in progress, but the results appear highly inconclusive. Our probes do not recognize the composition of the cloud. Some life form is creating it. These echoes would be their codes, their language?" I added nervously.

We were all young and eager to please, but in this instance, our assessment of the situation was the same - we faced something we did not understand.

The Control Center connected to the World Communication's lab was the nerve center of the science building. It was known as the CC for short, where all reporting activities within the Network converged… It contained an array of sizeable transparent computer screens hovering in place with their own data stream giving us access to our infrastructure. DAINN, our planetary mind, and neural Network gathered all specific data on everything that mattered on the planet. It reigned over the vast information bank and controlled its flow inside and outside the Center. It would detect unusual patterns, flag them and report them here. The fact that DAINN hadn't been able to analyze the intensity of the approaching storm, could not determine its composition, and had not even provided the alert at its approach was more than alarming.

Monitors, connected to the neural Network, provided data communicated across the borders of friendly nations. Forty-two countries in all were now showing lines of nonsensical codes. All were part of nations joined in a world effort for peace, all signatory of the PAPT or Planetary Alliance Peace Treaty, signed in 2025.

Every town and metropolis around the globe had featured the approaching storm, but the last streams about these countries that had meant anything dated from a few hours ago.

It occurred early on our side of the globe, but verification occurred by every satellite at all four corners of our world simultaneously. The natural language Interpretation System or IS had automatically translated it in real-time. Since then, we continued to receive complete gibberish.

The time confirming the interference with the System showed nine thirty-eight am. The Surgs virus had not caused this widespread sluggishness of our Network. A second independent occurrence did, as implied by Dr. Paladock minutes ago. We now knew that the storm was the cause of our Network dysfunction and not the virus planted by the underground.

I headed over to the station running the data analysis I had requested. "It looks like the first time we experienced a lack of response inside the Network was at nine thirty-eight. It could be why we were confused and looked in the wrong place. George, can you verify that from the video data stream in the city?"

"On it," responded George.

Gregory and George sometimes lacked instinct for problem-solving and scientific reasoning, although they were both creative in their work.

I saw the second slow-down in the response time of the Network. It manifested after the storm's appearance in our sky. DAINN did not flag it as dangerous even while the phenomenon received confirmation around the globe. DAINN even killed the global alarm, although it perceived it on the horizon. *How was that possible?*

"Walden, do you have a read on the storm?" My scan didn't recognize anything related to our atmosphere.

"Nothing we know as a natural phenomenon concluded Walden, and after a moment, he added, "It originates outside our atmosphere."

"We observed a pattern when we were on the roof, unlike anything we know. We are observing a bioengineered cloud created by something foreign or alien to us, although it executes with artificial intelligence," exclaimed Paladock.

At this moment, I doubted very much that I deserved my title. I should have come up with the same explanation from my scan. But, like many more advanced minds in our midst, I drew a blank on the anomaly.

Suddenly, each station overseeing various aspects of our infrastructure began to stammer information. "Unauthorized assembly," said one. "10,000 arrested on the main plaza," said another. "Golden Ghetto and Water's Edge on lockdown…" announced a third. These were all expelled in DAINN's voice.

"The Concordance Assembly is progressing," outpoured DAINN's voice from yet another.

"Ground troops are maneuvering around the city," continued DAINN's voice.

"We are on alert, level 1," gushed out now DAINN's voice.

Dr. Paladock grunted as he moved through some of them hurriedly. "Gregory, go to a level 1 alert. See if there is something in the data stream that suddenly triggered DAINN."

I glided over to one of the windows on the far corner of the lab. The dust cloud was lower over Ang City now, cutting off our views of the mountains and the forest in the distance. "The anomaly enrobes the city and continues its movement and descent," I said from my vantage point.

The data poured in, far from complete.

"Can you track the origination point in space? Check our space station," said Dr. Paladock.

"Just more of the same from other satellite systems oriented towards our planet," I said.

"There's nothing useful here either. No feed from other megacities. We're blind to any ground or aerial troop's activities in distant parts of the globe," added George.

The System usually kept tabs on those who had denied themselves access to the expected standards of economic transactions with countries of the PAPT or Planetary Alliance Peace Treaty.

"There has to be something," said Dr. Paladock as he made his way with haste towards one station.

One large screen broadcasted patterns of sub-orbital space flights. I observed it as another floating station claimed the attention of Dr. Paladock. I didn't dwell on the space around the planet, as I answered Dr. Paladock, "Our scans show nothing up there other than our normal flights."

"That's what they want you to think," he exclaimed as he remained engrossed in the stream of data generated by a satellite dedicated to the Central Earth Land Division, transmitting images of space. It was one of the largest floating stations in the room.

"I… huh… Even if we know this is an engineered anomaly, how should we proceed?" exclaimed Walden.

Paladock's interest was still on the satellite pictures of Earth, depicting the dark cosmos surrounding the planet. The Milky Way galaxy, and beyond, our universe and one of many we knew existed in the emptiness of space.

"Don't rely on DAINN. Use your brains. The only way to ascertain anything at this very moment is to launch something up there. The EHAF prepared for that instance. The activity in our air space suggests just that," asserted Dr. Paladock calmly.

Standing near another interface, one of our Operators wore a blank look on his face. His regular activity to check the parameters of the

Network remained idle. With a deep voice, he asked, "What does that mean, professor, not to rely on DAINN?"

What did that mean indeed? We were dependent on everything through DAINN. We had attached our knowledge, our thinking, our reasoning to DAINN. We never experienced a world without DAINN. *What could we do now on our own?*

We all stood there wondering what our next steps should be.

Paladock had a somber expression on his face. "We need help. Get someone to the EHAF, have them fetch Dr. Gen Aubrey. They will know where to find her."

"I'll take care of it," volunteered Walden, as he hovered out of the CC. "I'll be back as fast as I can."

"All the main satellites will be re-oriented in a matter of minutes, Professor," announced George.

Dr. Paladock grunted, then he barked, "Let me see everything surrounding Earth."

My stomach dropped as I analyzed a new output from my station. I entered new parameters a while ago, and it now gave me a different set of results. The streams were slow and contained anomalies as symbols flashed sporadically hidden behind the gibberish. These unknown components were not coming from our System. "Professor..."

DAINN flagged unidentifiable materials embedded inside dust particles that presented factual anomalies to anything we knew existed here on Earth. "Professor, I think you need to take a look at this," I said with a shaky voice.

The material composition, engineered with alien components, was like nothing we knew existed and was not natural to the earth. We no longer could be under the illusion that this was a freak climatic event, although most of us eliminated that notion a while back. The incident confronting us appeared in my mind with such an unforeseeable magnitude that I staggered. *DAINN seems totally compromised.*

Dr. Paladock turned. One look at my face told him it was crucial because he was beside me in no time.

I swear the man can move on his MTP. It took him less than thirty seconds to reach the same conclusion. He uttered, "Disconnect. Shut it down, shut it all down."

I moved quickly. Dr. Paladock did the same but in a different direction. While I propelled myself on my MTP towards the central station, I erected the by-pass to the neuro-chip transmitters between my brain and DAINN. We all had one. Our safety protocol demanded that this come first, even before we isolated the other systems. I immediately triggered mine, and within seconds, my visor emitted: "By-pass engaged."

I relaxed a little. It was working. I instantly felt the effect of the by-pass. The silence was there; a sort of white noise invaded my brain. I sensed the wall as it came up between my mind and that of DAINN.

Then the implications of this action hit me like a giant wave. A dark, insidious fear grabbed me. There was only one explanation for this, and we all knew what it was, but when the brain does not want to acknowledge something, it works around it quite convincingly. For months, we looked at the anomaly as this fictional entity, not admitting it was real and aiming for us even if part of our logic knew it all along as a defense mechanism. And not this entity was here, and there was no way to hide even in our minds. *It is an attack on our planet, something we have never envisioned, never anticipated, never even prepared for even with our technology.*

As I saw the first flicker of the hologram, I instinctively knew that my fears had a reason to exist. There was a fault, an undiagnosed problem in the System, and we had caught it. Only too late.

Inside the World Communication's lab and operation center, the main floating stations were not yet affected, but Operator Tyron1 was the first to register the effects of the corruption. It took over its neuro functions. Tyron1 was an advanced holographic computer, with its outside form that of a person designed by Dr. Paladock himself. It oversaw the entire CC, and at that moment, it flickered on and off before it evaporated into thin air. The other three assistants, Tyron2, 3, and 4, working at their floating stations, were next. They all disappeared.

Almost simultaneously, George and Gregory screamed. Blood dripped from their noses and ears. They dropped to the floor in agony, holding their heads in their hands. Within the next instant, they no longer moved.

I wanted to run to them. My instinct screamed for me to help my colleagues. But dealing with the System, if any of us were to stand a chance, came first. Since turning SRIP on, we ran it and DAINN simultaneously.

The by-pass protected me, unlike the others who remained tied to DAINN. I breathed. Fear ran through me for all of us, but I continued to work, disengaging our most vital functions from DAINN.

As human as we were, our world worked with machines faster and better. There were no hesitations, errors, and delays, and we were all used to it, except today. The screams of our team, separated only by micro-seconds, alerted me that our era, this era was indeed over. Within a matter of seconds after their first cries, my colleagues were either unconscious or dead.

Looking back at them and unable to do anything for them, I severed the links from the Network. I held my breath, seeing the buffer working. Sinking to the ground, shrieking with my brain short-circuited was not part of my program. I refused to be rendered brain dead as my physical body became an empty shell. Capable of processing even if our speed were slower without DAINN, we would find answers.

Although taken initially, the buffer was a quiet place, not a precautionary measure against DAINN. We implemented this as a possibility of disconnecting ourselves from its effective presence because we feared it would overtake us. The need for it disappeared over the years. We came to trust DAINN completely. However, the wall allowed separation from the neural Network if we chose to exercise it. When engaged, it provided our minds a complete break from DAINN… And selectively cut-off from outside influences, other than the knowledge supplied by our Implants, we stood on our own. With the by-pass, we effectively were alone.

Usually, we didn't have access to all of the areas of DAINN's artificial intelligence, but its System, its presence was always there. DAINN responded like us, to any prodding of our neurons… For most of us, it became like an intricate brother figure, indispensable and yet always in the background of our minds. We were him as he was us.

Our access to DAINN's information was pre-determined based on data available to the public or our areas of expertise and field. We commonly tapped into extensive facts on subjects of interest that demanded more clarification. It also permitted us access to the latest facilities in town, knowing the best restaurants, clubs, art galleries, and shows. This was input generally dedicated to the main population and for everyday use.

The access was different within our areas of expertise. In that respect, we commanded all the knowledge available and more. It allowed us to become experts and eventually obtain specific implants, expanding our knowledge base. Various levels activated more in-depth subject matter expertise until we became a master in our own right.

Dr. Paladock hastily removed the connection to some of the interfaces within the System. A flash of satisfaction reached his face as he severed one, in particular, freeing DAINN from outside influence.

He suddenly fell backward, toppling down on the soft parquet floor of the CC, thrashing. I thought he had already cut himself off from DAINN when he told us to disconnect, but I was wrong.

This time, I abandoned what I was doing and rushed to him. Dropping to the ground, I reached for him, my palm leaving a brief imprint on the soft, soundless material. *This is not happening… It cannot be happening.*

I fought him, trashing against my attempts to disconnect him. I needed to erect the by-pass and isolate him before it was too late.

Paladock screamed, and his eyes bulged as blood seeped through his ears.

Unable to get a firm grip on him, we struggled, and I put my weight on his chest to immobilize him. Just long enough to reach for the KeyNet device used to deactivate the neuro implants. We all possessed one, and I carried mine on the chain hanging at my neck as an emergency procedure. Only, I used mine to regenerate privately. Some of us used it more than others, especially in moments of intimacy, to gain added privacy.

By the time I finally enabled it, it was too late. The strain inflicted by DAINN's infiltration from the anomaly wroke havoc on Paladock's brain activity, making his pulse weak. The slight movement of his chest was the only sight that he was still with us.

I looked down at Paladock's face, a face I had come to see in concentration over an unsolvable problem. It was immobile, frozen, so I listened to his breathing, slight and uneven, and murmured, "Come on, please." I was not much in the first aid care department, so I waited, hoping...

He moved his hand, searching for mine.

"Why did you wait?"

His fingers squeezed mine right before he put something in my hand with some effort.

I looked down and saw a small transmitter device. "Free ELLA. She has a conscience."

Paladock took his last labored breath, and his body went limp in my arms.

I held him and cried. A tear landed on my hand, and I watched it for a moment. Another joined it, and another. In one moment, the man I worked and admired for many years was gone. I looked at the small device in the palm of my hand. *What is this? What could be so vital that you would risk yourself for it?*

Something had just gone terribly wrong in our lives. Chaos reigned on the other side of our lab as I glanced at the screens depicting our city.

In the silence of the room and beyond the thick walls, I heard screams of pain.

I imagined the scene as the shrieks quieted down, followed by an eerie silence so similar to the one I witnessed moments ago. I couldn't stay here.

I looked around the room. I needed to check if George and Gregory were still alive, so I went to George first and checked his pulse. There were no signs of life. Crawling towards Gregory next was the right thing to do, although getting out of here tempted me. He was a strong guy, and maybe, just maybe, he may still be alive. He remained turned on his side, his face looking away from me, and I gently turned him on his back, hoping against all hope. But there was nothing, no pulse, no breath, just stillness.

I dried my face.

DAINN was compromised, and so would all the monitoring safeguards. I quickly calculated how much time I had to exit the Science Research Center. It couldn't be much. They were on an independent data structure tied to SRIP, and I needed to hurry.

The pass key to the small lab hung on Paladock's chest, and I took it. He worked on something meaningful in his private lab, and over the last month, I saw how excited he was. He had reached a milestone wearing that special glint in his eyes. However, he never confided in me until now.

I glanced at the small device between my fingers. *I have to know. Netwash, no matter how much time I have left. What is Ella?*

I was puzzled by his statement and hopeful that another piece of him would remain with us. Still, artificial intelligence capable of learning anything and acquiring knowledge faster than any one of us and that could indeed possess awareness did not seem possible. But if he had mentioned it, then maybe it was not impossible. I knew that I needed to find whatever he created if he believed it. I didn't have time to ponder, even if it seemed so unlikely.

I stood up and hurriedly walked to the end of the vast CC, where another door led to our central lab. It wasn't the official entry, but we used it because it was more practical. It was simply faster that way, so I stepped past the various stations and moved toward a small door leading to Paladock's personal lab. Behind me, the first of the security measures were triggered.

49
RECKONING
Streak

Plaza, Grid 1, Golden Ghetto, Ang City

This day drags on, bringing with it all kinds of evil omen. Phenom Streak, Institute Conclave, Origin Special Elite Unit - OSEU, DAINN Annals – Winter 2098.

As our workforce created an uproar, dismantling the predetermined order in which the day was to unfold, our EHAF ground troops took position around the Golden Ghetto and Water's Edge. Manned by several squadrons of Elite personnel, they responded directly to the office of the President and implemented its mandate.

Outfitted with the latest in technology and combat uniforms with embodied avatars for advanced warfare, they were now executing a sweep. They coordinated the established surveillance protocol for the areas of the Golden Ghetto and Water's Edge, invading the surface streets, ramps, passageways, and tunnels.

The crewed shuttles were still in the air, flying low above the streets. The first fly vehicles departed to arrive at their assigned locations over Archway Pass, Emerald Field, Cliffs Top, and Bridge View. They deployed multiple Znets - electronic devices, over our passageways. Once activated, these devices, hovering just below the aircraft, launched multiple nets that dropped above the crowd. These flew graciously through the air, going down several hundred feet in a controlled fashion, and then hit the ground.

People fell over in contact with the NetBeams and fell immediately asleep. As men and women collapsed, zapped into an unnatural slumber, they were lifted in the air by the mechanisms hijacked by the large fly vehicles on stand-by to carry their precious human cargo. Our standard operating procedure isolated the unruly crowd of workers in our streets, picking them up. So, the outdoor rioters were canvassed, identified, and brought inside detention buildings. Some remained there to be processed while the rest of our population rushed to the evacuation gates.

Some groups escaped the large cloaked devices. They immediately reacted when they perceived the shadows of the shuttles above their head. After the first few beams hit the crowd, the riot escalated.

People fled in all directions. Small frigates outfitted with the same devices grabbed the runners.

The sight of the Z-nets against the sky, holding people in their folds and gliding between buildings, was impressive and yet also quite unnerving.

As pandemonium hit the large crowd, teams reacted and sprinted toward the Force, engaging them. The workers fought our security forces with all they had. They quickly got overpowered by our EHAF, equipped with their own portable electronic devices: NetPalm - a sort of smaller zapping electronic net, similar to those of our standard street Custodians, only these were a prior version and comprised of less sophisticated technology.

People dropped unconscious where they stood, and empty cargo holds picked them up.

Working the implications of these scenes in my mind, I shrugged. The intrusion from the Surgs triggered DAINN's delayed response time. Since then, DAINN fought an infection with a much more powerful virus, one it could not obliterate from the System.

With the cloud settling over the city, it became more difficult to witness the evolution of this day. But when I finally noticed the response of our team in the streets, I breathed a sigh of relief. The rerouting of our infrastructure System, as well as our communication, gave me comfort. With the older SRIP, our forces will be in a position to fight back.

The deployment of our City Vigils was what I had been waiting for, and it finally unfolded. Our protocol had kicked in. The change brought our clones, androids, and robots into the fight to support our human forces. They now would take the first wave on any position on the conflict in our streets or space.

The City Vigils, created as an additional force to limit human casualty, took positions within our grids. The degree and speed of our ground forces remained slow, but as they spread in our streets, they gave us the reinforcements needed. While the CVs did not have the depth of our machines under DAINN, they could help with the evacuation. Yet, the lag time indicated that DAINN did not monitor them, for it remained far too long compared to the norm.

Everything we went through today was unprecedented, and the events compounded our preparations to evacuate Ang.

The City Vigils functioned with the same construct and brainpower as our previous A.I. SRIP. The situation called for all hands on deck, and they were unresponsive at best. They were robotic hybrids, less than an A.I., but part of our earlier rendition of our technology. Dealing with conflicts, accidents, or riots, they were unparalleled, responding according to SRIP's early protocol. HellNet, this situation was better than not having them. Their functions limited them to programming pre-determined for special occasions.

"This is a clear departure from the three to five minutes our metropolis normally claims, as the fastest response rate," Asher said, coming up beside me.

"I don't get it... Are you irked because we are no longer the most efficient System on this side of the planet?" I said, laughing.

"You're missing the point... Whatever the Surgs did affect our response time, yet it should never have taken us this long for the SRC to figure things out."

"I know. We lost control of DAINN; that's why we now operate under SRIP."

He nodded... "It took me a while to get here. This fog is hard to cut through. Blast is just behind me. I think you guys have a place to be."

The City Vigils had several posts in each of our grids. Pending the location and the territory they had to cover, some would take the ground while others would hit the airways. I was now reviewing their deployment first hand and trying to assess the roadmap for the initial code invasion. "Yeah, but you need help here."

"You got that right, but don't miss your departure."

The feelings of inadequacy were not mine alone. Asher looked terrible. "I know. We have to report to the origin chambers. I can't afford to miss it. What happened to you?"

"HellNet of a day... It was mayhem getting here. We still have nothing as the SRC is searching for solutions. They don't know how to stop it."

"Darnet, frustrating! We have to fight the anomaly somehow. I don't envy you guys, but Zane will find a way. He always does," I said, even if I was not too optimistic about what we all faced, but we all have to stay unified—and no point in making it worst.

"Hey… Streak. We need to go, man."

"Blast? How are you? What are you doing here?"

"Making sure you get your ass to Origin. We're evacuating everyone now."

I nodded. "That's where I'm going. Thanks for the escort. On my way there. Asher, what are your orders?"

"I need to get people to their assigned gates in this soup," Asher said. "Then I will meet with PEU."

"I wish you good luck here," I said, looking at the substance around us.

Asher made a face. "Not sure which of us will have it easier. Take care, buddy, protect yourself, and thanks for the cover."

"You got it. I'll see you around," I said as we bumped each other's fists and began to maneuver through the crowd of people. Maybe one day, we will meet again. I hoped so.

"Count on it," Asher yelled as he disappeared among the crowd.

"Yeah, well, we are not there yet," Blast said, pushing the crowd ahead of me as he cut through the cloud. "We've got to make it out first."

Going through the rest of this mob was not easy and felt more like fighting a herd going in the opposite direction. Walking became more painful as the artificial cloud weaved itself into our streets and buildings, rendering motion more difficult as if we walked through a bunch of molasses. "I couldn't get through to the girls," Blast said, as he kept going just ahead of me.

"Leane was with Tesh a while ago," I said, getting closer to Blast. "She had a rough time of it in the Alcove. They should be at the Institute by now."

"I came from there. Almost everyone is in the compartments, but they have not reported in," Blast said, grabbing my arm and shoving the crowd at my side.

I frowned. It was cutting it close for our team to be inside Origin, but we still had a little bit of time. "What in the HellNet are they doing?"

"Darnet if I know," Blast muttered. "I figured we'd better go find out."

Usually, it was impressive to witness the systematic power of the City Vigils as they took control of each street. The incredible machines came out of their operational posts in a wave, quietly forming in front of the doors of the large repository where they remained while dormant. But now, they stood like statues.

We had droves of them.

Blast continued. "We don't have time to do both, so let's split. It's why I'm here. I was on my way to Leane when I got your location. You need to get Tesh."

"Did you try the NetComm?"

"Yeah... What in the NetShit do you think? I couldn't get through."

I nodded. "Fine. I will see you in the Chamber."

Blast nodded and pushed ahead in a direction opposite mine.

The CVs marched on the different facilities in precise formation. Some gathered inside the transportation shuttles they had been assigned to, while the others descended upon the large arteries towards the manufacturing plants, inside the tunnels of our industrial centers, or on the ramps of our distribution vehicles. They formed a net over the various areas according to a given plan, and slowly the snare got smaller and smaller. Today had been different.

DAINN, contaminated by the bioengineered cloud, held on to maintain the emergency procedures enacted by the Conclaves. With

SRIP, we could defend ourselves independently from DAINN, but it did not improve our general communications.

All locations around these allotted perimeters were now under guard. The EHAF gave their posts to the CVs as they joined their platoon for the impending fight. The City Center became empty little by little, and the outdoor areas deserted. The Force, or Clout as some of our citizens called them, now waited for the imminent attack.

The launch pads held the cruisers for our Armada were usually packed with our City Vigils, but not right now. Some ships converted for the transport of CVs awaited departure with the fleet. But these were part of our deep space armada. For now, the other vessels, the civilian air flights, or the shuttles, frigates, and cruisers dedicated to security in our city were filled to the brim with the Force personnel. Soon, these same ships would begin to take off to join the battleships in the armada in space.

I had no idea what would become of our workers in this fight. Reassigning them to different Conclaves seemed unlikely now as there was no time. Typically, those picked up would lose their privileges, but now we needed everyone to get off the surface.

I made my way toward Tesh's building, on the Plaza, not too far from the facility for Origin, which lay hidden in a reinforced underground bunker.

Tesh should have already arrived at the Origin Chamber so that the four of us could play our part in the program that will send us back in time with the other Conclaves teams selected for Origin.

We had yet to understand who or what was behind this attack, but our lives irremediably changed when the cloud descended during the Concord, and there was no longer time to figure that out.

Company Compound, Golden Ghetto, Ang City

My annoyance at Win is overshadowed by the fear that rules our city with the unknown hanging above our heads. Emotional intelligence is in short supply today as our world is overwhelmed. Phenom Win Matteson, Company Conclave, CEO, DAINN Annals – Winter 2098.

The morning had gone by quickly, with a series of crises, including some of the reprocessing of our people due to Concordance. While our Conclave workers, for the most part, subscribed to the new dictate, others ended up at the detention centers. Indeed, it was inconceivable that the Company demanded a shift in their activities. So, they ended up joining the riots and bucking the System.

Running from one challenge to the next, I found myself not anticipating the alert, and when it came, we were unprepared.

Everything had started when Win had his brilliant idea. Still, things got much worst after he had left the building. Not all of it was his fault, but he had rattled me and started my day on the wrong foot.

Since he had departed to see Ram, we faced multiple issues. First, he had found a way to crash his shuttle, which required dealing with the EHAF and the Council. How can a guy who isn't even flying the darn thing find a way to collapse a flycar onto a pedestrian area? Mind me, I knew it had not been his fault, but I did experience a bit of satisfaction at his accident once I found out that he was still in one piece. I told him leaving the building was a bad idea. One would think that listening to your Chief of Security remained a good idea no matter the emergency. But no. Not with Win. *That ought to teach him to play with other people's lives.*

If it were not for the young woman gravely injured in the process, I would have expressed my frustration to him. However, considering the life he threatened, it would have been relatively insensitive of me. Besides, I never got to talk to him because the Network was on the blink. Maybe it was for the best as far as my job was concerned.

Even in my worse fights with Win, I never worried about my position within the Company. We were part of one group inside a Conclave that remained loyal.

When I got words that Win crashed the Flycar but that he and my man Chan were fine, I commanded to send another one out. Only this time, the pilot was a veteran to get Win to the destination. I had to play it safe; Win was, after all, our CEO, although he had Netpissed me off big time.

It was our last communication since the Network went down after that, and we could no longer get through.

"HellNet, send our best pilot this time," I told my Second in Command, Raj Otto, a tough, unflappable kind of guy. "Win can't stop himself from making bad decisions today."

"Sure, boss. It must have been a HellNet meeting, boss, because you sound Netpissed."

"Raj, mind your own Damnet business."

"Sure, boss."

Unable to rely on any of our Systems under DAINN, we floundered. The controls over our NetComm did not respond, and if it was not enough, the entire city was in an uproar. It was the first uprising for quite some time within the grids of our megapolis.

"Post guards around the perimeter of the Company. Order our executives to remain indoors. "

"NetRoger that boss…" answered Raj.

My work remained a serious business even in times of calm. And unlike many, I usually liked to be cautious. Years of security training would do that to a guy. I never left things to chance, not if I could help it, and in my opinion, this accident was in no way a coincidence. It was why I remained tempted to tell the pilot to bring Win back here regardless of what our CEO wanted to do. But the last thing on my list today was to have to deal with Win's thwarted goals or reprisals. He possessed quite the temper when things didn't go his way, and besides, he was my boss.

"Patch all communications to our Company System for now."

"Count on it, boss."

My priority was a matter that dealt with me. Since we didn't see eye to eye, my involvement in controlling the situation would undoubtedly send him into overdrive if he had any incline of it. So, the further from the Company building he was, the better.

After the morning scene in his office, I was satisfied with his absence and preferred it to stay that way as long as possible.

My damage control took some doing, but I was satisfied things were now under my control. *Diane Stone accepted my offer.*

Reviewing the various things to address in haste, I gave Raj a list of instructions. "Send a team to handle the damage from the crash and payout credits to the tenants on the passageways. Make sure everyone is provided credits for the inconvenience. Distribute the rewards immediately to those injured."

"How many? Do you want to put a limit on the credits or the rewards, boss?"

"Make it worth their while… Double the normal amount for this type of accident. It's good public relations. The Company has a reputation of fairness to uphold, and it is an opportunity. Win will not object if we spend some of the emergency funds."

"Can you give me guidelines, boss? It's not like this ever happened before."

"The guidelines if five million credits. Allocate ten million credits for the small injuries. Provide twenty-five million credits for those who suffered more and give fifty million credits to those who are gravely injured and one hundred million for those who have died. Make sure we pick up the medical costs."

"That's nice, boss."

"As for the rewards, provide everyone our products, the ones that we have a surplus of because they do not sell well. Talk to Ione. She will give you a list."

"Okay, boss."

While we cleaned up the mess caused by our shuttle's drop into city property, I kept an eye on the events surrounding the revolt of our workers. None of us saw it coming, and whoever had set that up had done a pretty good job. "Any leads on the Surgs?"

"Nothing yet, boss."

"I've got to head over to the Detention Centers. Get me through our CoComm, if you need me. It should still work."

These workers fell under Company responsibility, and when they were picked up by the EHAF and sent to detention, I received the notification. I was required to re-assess their roles. This unsavory challenge had fallen within my jurisdiction and was part of my job description. I remained for the Company, the fixer hammer. The detention center would keep them until we determined where to send them next, if we still wanted them to work for us, and what type of Dems they would receive. It was all part of the cadence of reprocessing workers on this day of Concordance.

"Fine, boss, but I'm sending some of our men with you."

"Really?"

"Yes, really, boss."

"All right, then. The guards better hurry if they want to catch me." I left my office and made my way to the rooftop. Despite the freeze on Air transport, I held priority status as Company Chief of Security.

Due to the unstable communication with the detention center, I had to go there in person and spend most of my afternoon reviewing the status and worker's profile. *It is tedious work.*

Inspecting files, reviewing the official Vlogs, and even on some occasions browsing their MindTranscripts was not something I looked forward to, especially on a day like today. The Vlogs gave me access to their job performance, while the MindTranscripts essentially allowed me to pick into their mindset, relating things about their lives and positions within the Company. *This day is turning out to be lousy.* My bad mood increased another notch.

"Hey, boss… I know your distaste for that. I can handle it for you if you prefer," said Raj, volunteering for a task neither one of us liked.

Raj was right; it was not a task I enjoyed. But this activity provided insights before I established new protocols and roles for our workers. Their ranks either would be reduced, or I would let them go.

"I appreciate it, Raj, but not today. This one is on me." Indeed, delegating this part of the job was out of the question for me. I had to know the center's activities and who to get rid of, even if it was distasteful.

If I let them go, they would be reassigned different duties within another society branch. It wasn't a pleasant job. I didn't want to remove people from their livelihood. The process would be long and unrewarding, but the System demanded it. Quickly doing it was also essential because those who remained with us were needed back in our facilities to resume their work without further delay.

I hated this day. I didn't care much about taking away some of the workers' benefits because they had decided to show us they didn't like the System. Still, it was how we built our infrastructure. Our society depended upon rewards or punitive actions. Our Dems distribution process maintained a specific control over our efficiency. The nonconformists couldn't get away with impairing our structure in any way, and so punishment had to be awarded.

They had threatened the Company and profits, so it directly threatened my position, along with the others in the executive offices. Their lack of commitment challenged the success of the Conclaves. We could no longer trust them. So, many Dems were to be issued, and many workers needed to be reassigned.

All in all, the lousy day continued.

"Raj, my instinct tells me this day will only get worst. If anything out of the ordinary surfaces while I'm away, instigate our Alpha protocol without waiting for me. I don't want to take any chances."

"Sure thing, boss."

"I'll be back as soon as I can."

My aim on this day was expediency, so our conversation took place on the way to the rooftop. But, like anything else this day, nothing would unfold as planned. The emergency broadcast alarm resonated all over the city before I got into my shuttle and thwarted all our plans.

The alarm called for the evacuation of our people. The message, even without DAINN, was clear. All precautionary measures needed to be instigated immediately. "This day is going to Netshit," I said, turning around and running back inside, followed by Raj.

While up to this point, my team dealt with the fallout from Concordance around our building, we now faced a planet evacuation.

"Evacuate all top personnel to Alpha. Escort our middle executives to the underground chambers under the Aurora protocol."

"We're ready for this, boss. Food, water, and medical supplies are already there," said Raj as he joined me in my office.

"Well done. Everyone knows where to go, but make sure the teams get to the departure gates for Alpha."

"What about you? You need to go."

"I need to deal with something first. I will take the last shuttle."

"Where will you be?"

"In my quarters."

"I will come to get you."

"I don't want you to miss your gate time, Raj. You need to be there before they close the bunkers."

"I know, boss, but I'm not going without you."

"I am sorry you can't come with me."

Raj shrugged. "They can't take everyone."

I nodded as I looked at Raj. "Thank you for everything."

Raj smiled. "I will see you in a little while, boss."

I entered my quarters and closed the door. There were still things that I needed to attend to before leaving this place.

My things were already gone. *Darnet, I had forgotten about that.*

"Where the Hellnet have you put my things, Josh?" I asked my assistant as I turned around in what used to be my place. I was far from prepared to face something, or maybe I should say that someone who inadvertently was part of the plot created by Win. *Toril…*

The voice of my A.I. and its face reached me as the internal CoComm Network came up languidly.

"Shush... shush... It is on the penthouse floor; suite, shush... shush... 10,469 Phenom Blaze."

The new number of my penthouse rang nicely to my ears, but I still had not reconciled Win's behavior. It would take a while before I forgave him. I tried to contain my disappointment before I withdrew from what had been my place until this morning. I returned to the corridor to get into the Elevat to take me to my new quarters.

The unrest had been unparalleled, and the unknown above our head carried with it a danger we all were too well aware of now. The System shut down most functions that were not essential in the last few hours, but DAINN nevertheless combatted a threat that seemed to kill the Network slowly.

Concerned with the seemingly independent events we witnessed all afternoon, an inconsistent Network, City Vigils unable to respond, the orchestrated riots, the Force's inability to get a handle on the fog whose steady descent seemed to cause havoc on our System, I ordered early in the morning to close off the Company building and take precautions with our people.

Ang was now ensconced in a significant fog, and this was an unusual occurrence, even with our climate challenges. The dome kept climatic issues usually at bay, but it remained open all day. It had us unhinged.

Upon entering my quarters, I saw the unit devoid of everything. It then dawned on me that they had moved me to a better suite. "HellNet," I muttered, turning around and running down the corridor to the Elevat.

I saw the puzzlement of my team at Control and stopped. "You guys know what you have to do, so do it now and report to your assigned gate. We are leaving this place now."

The men under my command straightened up and moved to their tasks as I continued on my way.

"We can't raise anyone, but Birch was here," explained one of my guys, Brim Zander, as soon as he saw me. "Langden wants us to join the EHAF as soon as we conclude the evac here. They are mobilizing their forces. They plan to… hum… attack."

"Hellnet… that beats it all… Attack what?"

"He couldn't say."

"Brim, order another sweep to ensure we haven't missed anyone still in the building."

"Some of the guys are doing that now. The last thing we want is to leave anyone behind," Brim replied.

"Any word on Win? With the alert blaring all over the city, he should be on his way back by now. If you don't see him in half an hour, send another transport to get him."

Raj walked in and looked at me. "Did you get what you needed?"

"No, not yet.

"Better get to it, Blaze, Raj said.

Brim reported to his direct boss, Raj, with a grim face. "Sir, the EHAF wants us to round up people within the grids, but I told them we had to deal with our people first, according to our protocol. Should we send men out, boss?"

"Threat assessment?"

"Widespread… The Force has instigated Secondary Readiness and unleashed HADA measures or Heavy Assault Defensive Alert protocol," said Brim.

"When were you planning on telling me? Nevermind."

"Sorry, Blaze," Brim said with a wary face and a shrug.

Brim did what he had to do. Reporting to his direct boss was part of our Company code. It was expected.

This news wasn't good and added to my anxiety. The Force had gone dark. It just didn't happen – not in a long time, not anymore, and I never saw it take place during my entire tenure. But this fact alone required immediate actions of our own with my Command team.

This information left me feeling as if we were missing a significant piece of information, and something else was about to show its ugly head. I believed in my instincts, and they were telling me we were in yet another heap of trouble. "Do the same… Drop the System and go to ACTM or Absolute Close Transmission Mode for all personnel."

"What about coordination with the other Conclaves?"

"SRC is down, and so is the Institute. Some of our men have not returned. The only communication we had lately was with the EHAF through Birch."

"Send small contingents to check that our key personnel evacuates now. We have taken care of most supplies from our various facilities. We need our people to be safe. I think worrying about the other public locations is way past. We evacuate now."

"Yes, Phrenic Blaze. We have teams on all floors. They are covering every floor and going through all the lodgings. I should have the final count for you within the next half hour," explained Brim.

I grunted, "I'll be back in a few minutes…" and left the Control room and took the Elevat to my new suite several levels above. My team implemented my last orders and did not need me there.

"Don't be too long, boss. I need you to join the others quickly," Raj yelled in the corridor.

I needed to grab a few more things. "Josh… if you can hear me… Meet me at my suite."

My men were now sweeping the lower floors in full alert to take the rest of our personnel into underground chambers built inside our structure. The process will continue until everyone reaches their assigned evacuation location.

Even now, as I walked toward my new suite, the cloud invaded all things in sight, obliterating our skyline under the dome.

The Company Security team had already rounded up and evacuated most of our executives from the upper levels of the building toward the shuttles that would take them to the Alpha fleet over the planet, so I faced now an empty corridor.

Our middle executives would join the chambers below, used for emergencies due to climate issues. They had been reinforced and now contained everything to allow people to survive the brunt of what we suspected would happen to the planet. This phenomenon was a terrible plight for us as it became apparent quickly that not everyone could join our fleet. The entire world was in peril. Only top members of the Conclaves understood the threat the anomaly represented to the planet. Everyone had questions about it, and none of these were answered yet. We faced an extinction-level event and threatened our species, and none of us knew if we could take this thing down.

"Everyone shush… is evacuated… shush… per your orders," continued Josh's voice. "You need to go to the shush… shuttle now… shush." Josh's voice reached me, cracking and more broken than before.

I looked around the suite and chuckled.

Win felt guilty because he gave me a hellacious suite on the top floor amidst the most important people within the Conclave. Perception is a funny thing. Especially when no one knows if anything will be left standing tomorrow. I chuckled as I entered the living room and was surprised by the sight that greeted me. Win had not lied. He had given me quite an upgrade. The penthouse apartment was big, even luxurious, and a big step up from my old one. I guessed that having Win in my debt had its advantages. I couldn't help but smirk a little. *You're trying to get on my best side, buddy? Too bad I won't be able to use it. Way late, mate.*

"Josh… where are you?"

"Shush… Below, shush… Phenom Blaze" responded my assistant.

"You know my promotion is not official yet? We'll need to maintain the information on the workers off Network for now. Download a copy."

There was no response.

"Josh… did you hear me?" There was nothing but static. Now even our own Company Network seemed to be compromised. DarnetHell!

The EHAF actions worried me. Win may well be on his own for now, but looking at my watch, I saw that the shuttle I asked Raj to send out was about to depart.

Win may be stranded, but he was resourceful, so part of me expected him to make his way to Alpha independently. If Win had reached Ram, they would be together to make it back. Still, the safety of our CEO and one of our Manufacturing executives rested in my hands, so it was imperative that we found where they were at this time. We needed to locate them and bring them back inside a perimeter we controlled to get both of them to the fleet.

My bedroom was huge, with a bed so large I chuckled again. Here I am worried about my survival and that of our world. Unreal! I went to the large closet and grabbed a bag to drop a few last-minute things. Most of my other personal belongings were already on the ship. This evacuation was happening too soon. We had not yet completed all our preparation. It was the reason we had scheduled the Concord. We needed another three months, according to DAINN, to complete the preparation for our four programs.

I walked to an office with a walled library that used to hold a collection of my old books. Most of them were now in casings on the ship, and the empty shelves seemed out of place. I opened one of my drawers and grabbed my safe box. It contained a data key with important information, and I dropped it in my bag.

My steps next got me to the bar. I poured myself a drink and was now nearing the large expanse of the window opening on the expansive balcony. I stared outside, thinking about my life. The cloud surrounding the city now had reached all of our upper passageways, which were bathed in an orange hue. If this was it, I was okay, but I would fight like hell to survive.

I heard a soft shuffle behind me and turned.

Toril stood in the middle of the living room and looked at me with big eyes. *Hellnet! I don't need this… Not now.*

I frowned. "What are you doing here? You are supposed to be downstairs with our other executives."

She stammered… "I… I thought I would wait for you."

"You shouldn't be here. At least, tell me you disconnected from the System?"

"Huh… yes. The security team announced we should switch over to our CoComm internal system. What is going on, Blaze?"

"You should be downstairs. I'll have the head of the guy who left you here."

"No, no… It wasn't the guard's fault. I told him you had asked me to wait here for you."

"He ought to have known better. He disregarded an order… You should be joining the middle management team down below. You don't belong here."

I couldn't help myself. I knew I was barking at Toril, but I was tired, and this situation complicated things. Boundaries must be set now between us, although with the anomaly outside, it made little sense. What was I thinking about, indeed? We most probably would never see each other again after tonight.

Toril looked distressed and unsure. "I… huh… well, we haven't talked since this morning, and I wanted to let you know that I won't be a bother or anything… I can't go through with this. I'll quit."

Darnet, I didn't need this. Did she not realize what was going on? All right, she was young and inexperienced, but such naivety was frankly aggravating. "Don't you get what is going on? We are evacuating the planet. NetShit, we don't even know if any of us will survive this, and you think about our situation? Besides, if we survive, you are headed underground with Aurora, and I am going into space with Alpha, and there is every likelihood that we will never see each other again. The anomaly supersedes everything."

Toril looked more confused now. "Exactly. But Ione told me to find you and that you would take care of ensuring our safety to the ship."

"You just said you are quitting, although you really can't. Win won't let you. Ione will refuse to back down. Your contract is final."

"I just wanted you to know that I cannot go through with it."

"Well, good for you, although you have no choice. Without the Network going down, they would have implemented the whole thing."

"Yes… but it is an opportunity to back out, you know. With all that is going on, they may rethink things."

"Unlikely, even under normal circumstances." I pointed at the sky as I finished my thoughts. "We have much bigger problems at the moment than our situation."

Toril walked over to me and looked out the window, a puzzled look on her face. "Do you think everyone will make it?"

Fear was etched on her face.

I shrugged and turned to the window, observing the city skyline. Every ship hovered at the outskirts of the dome's periphery. A massive fleet above Ang joined other ships to face something still indescribable coming from space. The fighting armada disappeared into the cloud. The canopy above the dome appeared now empty. Frigates, cruisers, destroyers, and even our battleships were out in full force and now were nowhere to be seen.

"They've disappeared," said Toril. "I've been watching them for a while."

Indeed, it was true. Inside the fog-like substance, I could no longer see our ships. They were probably getting ready to attack. In space somewhere near the planet, other battleships held their position. *Who is this enemy we know nothing about, and what does it want?*

A disturbance in the cloud drew my attention. It took me a few seconds to comprehend its significance.

Streaks of lights from our lasers marred the sky over the horizon. Each one moved across the canopy in colored lights with a spell-binding brilliance.

We were attacking. Our fleet was defending the city. We were firing at the unknown, and I noticed that no one fired back. *What are they fighting?*

We both remained mesmerized as we watched the almost silent battle taking place above the dome. Before our eyes, bursts of lasers shot across the grand expanse. The barrage of flares formed a subtle blazing pattern. It was incongruous to witness. The distance kept most of the noise of the lasers at bay, although they were not very loud as they erupted from the gunnery of our machines. Still, they resonated in the firmament with a long zapping buzz, the echoes of their blowout overshadowed by the brilliance of their passage on the horizon.

We threw everything we had at the anomaly, and there was no effect on the colossal bio dust cloud shrouding our city.

As we stood in silence, Toril edged toward me. I put my arm around her shoulder, trying to provide some reassurance, but deep down, I felt like a powerless observer. It was a spectacle ending an era. It was a momentous event, more significant than any of us, and, in the balance, hinged the future of our species.

Not long after the last of our vessels fired, not too long after the rest of the fleet was quiet, and no more bolts crossed the horizon, our ships reappeared, losing altitude in an erratic descent. It took me a split instant to recognize that they had lost control.

"Netwash... it's not happening!"

"Blaze... What is it... What does it mean?"

Our vessels dropped from the sky. Their velocity increased as they descended upon the city. They passed the dome threshold in quick succession, which had remained partially open all day. The continuous onslaught of the ships breaking the surface of the field where part of the dome stretched collapsed the sphere.

"Something is disabling our ships," I explained to Toril.

The mechanism of the dome operated with our ships' entry codes. A closed dome provided protection, but the barrier would never hold against this onslaught. Even working partially, DAINN would recognize our fleet's codes. A signal by the System allowed entry inside the periphery of the massive bubble without friction. Yet, the stress imposed by an incursion would eventually crash the protective expanse around the city like the one we witnessed.

Within a short time, the transparent electronic field that held the canopy partially closed shattered with a turbulent sound reverberating over the entire megapolis of Ang City. The ships that lost control over their flight pattern wandered toward the center of town, toward the GG.

In the debacle, something strange began to happen. Some of our frigates, cruisers and battlecruisers suddenly got redirected in the sky. Their speed slowed, becoming more manageable. Their drop-in altitude stabilized for the briefest of seconds, and their course changed to the outskirts of town. It was as if a substantial invisible hand had stalled them and redirected their course, and then, they resumed their fall.

I looked at the site, and I froze. I knew we had to get out of here, but I was so puzzled by what I had just seen that I kept watching the sky.

Suddenly, one of the smaller frigates wavered and dipped toward our building. It was as if its field had been released too soon from an invisible net and the little warship catapulted toward the Company tower.

I grabbed Toril and jaunted toward the door, running for cover with her.

We reached the door just as the frigate hit one of the external walls and embedded itself into our edifice, crushing the exterior side. The brutal collision shook the entire structure. The glass broke and splattered everywhere, the façade of the building giving way, as the columns supporting the edifice cracked under the weight and the impact.

An explosion detonated within seconds, sending debris all around us, collapsing the inside door leading to the corridor and breaking through part of the wall.

With the explosion's impact, Toril and I flew backward and were catapulted near the inside wall. The blunt force coming from the blast hurled us in part of the corridor that remained as flames broke, engulfing the entire floor. The incendiary security measures immediately kicked in and drowned us.

A blow to my head sent my mind spinning. I landed hard against the concrete surface and bounced back on the floor, dazed. My breath got knocked out.

I lost my grip on Toril during the impact and looked for her as I regained my senses.

She was lying on her side a few feet away.

I reached for her and flipped her around. She was still breathing. I shifted her weight to rest against my chest, attempting to revive her.

Rubbles mixed with fire retardant material fell around us, and the remnants of my apartment walls landed with an additional thunder that shook the floor.

Toril began to move. She regained consciousness and coughed, looking into my eyes, shakily, "Are you all right?"

"Yes… You?"

"You saved my life."

"We were lucky." As the smooth cooling surface of the material combating the small explosion drenched us, a brief regret for my brand-new penthouse flashed through my mind.

Presidential Tower, SpaceVat, Golden Ghetto, Ang City

The stillness woke me. It was abnormal. In my line of work, things are never that way. I guess one gets used to having noise and movement around. Phrenic North Thompson, Presidential Elite Unit Commander, EHAF Conclave, DAINN Annals - Winter 2098.

I lay flat on my stomach, my laser gun not far away from me. The Spacevat stopped abruptly in the chute and knocked me out pretty hard. I had no idea how long we were out and checked my PVZ. Half an hour had passed.

My head hurt, and I slowly moved to assess if I broke anything in the velocity of the brutal stop. I glanced around and saw Zane and Jeze unmoving in the small space of the Elevat. I crawled over to Zane. He was still out cold. Years ago, he would have been the first to wake and try to revive us. I thought it was better to let him wake up naturally. I then reached out to check Jeze's vitals. She seemed to be coming around. *So much for getting to the bunker, I thought.*

We switched from the Network to the EHAF comm system when we lost DAINN. At the time of the alert and when we could no longer establish communication with the other agencies, we triggered

Protocol Night Sky. It was our standard fallback procedure from the System in times of combat.

DAINN became an unknown quantity, no longer sustainable for our operational System, at least for now, earlier in the morning. So, we went dark and the buzz from that signal resonated in my head. Our troops immediately received the new stream, which took over their comm network, so we could still communicate with the general corp.

Jeze opened her eyes and looked up at me. "I hate it when I'm right."

"Yeah, me too."

"It's a miracle we're still in one piece," she added, disgusted by the incident.

"How fast were we going?"

"Oh, fast… Too fast, probably, especially for a vertical drop."

"I always thought that our proclivity toward efficiency was going to end up killing us. It almost did." I got up and looked around the Spacevat.

Jeze chuckled. "We're alive because of the dampeners. They prevented us from getting crushed against the ceiling."

"I just remember kissing the floor pretty hard," muttered Zane as he slowly moved. He rubbed his head and grimaced.

A cut bled above his right eye, and blood streamed down his face.

"There is a panel above," I said as I examined the ceiling.

"Good luck on getting to it. Even with the three of us forming a pyramid, we won't reach it," Zane exclaimed as he got up.

Jeze pulled out the emergency supplies in one of the pockets of her vest. She retrieved a small metallic tube from it and approached Zane.

"Let's seal this cut."

Zane looked up at Jeze and pushed her hand away. "I'm good."

He was intent on gathering the data chips dispersed on the floor of the Spacevat. The small casing he carried had opened up on the ground. He retrieved four of them and looked feverishly for the last one. "I'm missing one. Do you see it?"

I glanced around. "No."

"I must find it," muttered Zane, observing the entire space around us.

I scanned the deck. Jeze's eyes scoped the sides of the Spacevat.

"There," she said, pointing to one of the sides behind Zane. "By the ridge."

Zane turned and leaned over to grab the device. He lost his balance and stumbled. Still a bit shaky from the blow Zane received earlier, he leaned in and grabbed the chip. He then dropped it inside the sheath, securing it in the pocket of its jacket.

"All right, can I look at you now?" demanded Jeze, focused on attending to his cut.

Zane turned to her and paused to comply.

Jeze got the container near the cut and sprayed the antiseptic self-healing adhesive material. It covered the injury instantly with a slight porous substance. The surface hardened over the deep cut and changed its appearance. It dissolved into the skin and disappeared, leaving no wound beneath.

Jeze closed the lid and bagged the small tube inside her combat vest. In one swift move, she looked beyond the Spacevat, watching the building to assess the remaining numbers of floors below us. "We need to get this thing down the rest of the way."

"How do you suggest we do that?" I asked. "The inside panel is located way above us, and we don't have anything to reach it. The grappling gun won't work."

Jeze reacted to my comment by retrieving her gun and shooting at the ceiling. "Might as well try and see if it penetrates."

We heard the click of the gun. We watched as the thin rappelling metallic rope unfolded. The tip of the hook hit the ceiling. A sharp clinging sound resonated throughout the cabin.

"The new material components they used to make this is too hard. That's why they chose it," murmured Zane.

The grapnel bounced back and dropped. The three of us scrambled to the side to avoid it. The clasp plunged toward the ground, and before it reached the floor between us, Jeze engaged the recall mechanism. The cable folded back inside the casing. Jeze slammed the piece back in its place on the back of her combat vest. "Well, that's that. Now, we know for sure."

Zane silently appraised the height of the thing and muttered jokingly, "We need wings."

"What about linking to the Network again?" suggested Jeze.

The three of us looked at one another, unsure that this was a good option.

Jeze, determined, dropped the wall and reactivated her link. She didn't give me time to object. She knew I would have. Within seconds, she connected to the System.

Zane retrieved his activation key – the device locking the Network behind a wall of safety. He was ready to intervene at the slightest sign that DAINN's corruption, in turn, affected Jeze.

I, for one, did not doubt that it could. Too many things didn't add up. The cloud, the System failure, the short alert, and now the Spacevat were all convincing me that the enemy breach acted on a definite purpose – dismantling our defensive infrastructure and our communication network.

We were not directly in the capsule of the Spacevat. We stood just in the inner cabin located inside the building. The actual space structure would attach itself to the internal compartment once we reached the roof of the building.

Jeze was now accessing the data stream link. The light at the base of her temple showed us that she had activated the communication in her mind. Her voice repeated the silent command: "Ground level."

Nothing happened.

Jeze said next, "Spacevat main circuit board." Her PVZ deployed under the new command. Both Zane and I leaned over her shoulder to see it. It showed the Spacevat's mainboard. Nothing seemed out of order: systems operational; engineering board - fine; electronic panel - fine; electrical connections – fine; solar feed - fine. Everything appeared functional and as it should be.

We looked at each other completely in the dark concerning the date.

"Show me the city, Golden Ghetto, over Bridge View passageways."

The System did not respond. Instead, in the frame of her PVZ, codes began to compute streams of gibberish -- nothing we could make out, nothing that seemed meaningful in any way.

"Disconnect," Zane ordered.

Jeze immediately erected her by-pass. "You don't have to tell me twice." Her PVZ folded, disappearing altogether. The older NetComm was back online, replacing DAINN, but it was no use here. The Spacevat remained isolated.

Zane looked at both of us. "So much for that… What do we do now?"

I carefully examined the transparent wall that held the cabin. The encasement was round, made of solid material, one of the hardest used in constructing our structures. Thoughtfully, I stated the obvious, "We can't stay here, suspended in the middle of nowhere."

"We could wait. Our guys will come looking," suggested Zane. "Not that I am crazy about staying in this contraption."

"What if this thing falls?" asked us, Jeze. "We got lucky when the breaks functioned. I'm not crazy about taking the chance."

"The Elite is probably wondering where we are," I added, without a hint of hesitation. "I bet Talia has our location."

"I'm sure, but how are they going to get us out of here if we can't get the hell out of this box?" exclaimed Jeze, already unnerved by the close quarters.

"They'll get the gear. We can't breach this on our own…" stated Zane. "It'll take hours, and we don't have the equipment."

The walls were indeed too solid to be open to weaknesses. I was pretty sure we could not rupture them. They sustained the pressure of space. There were no seams in them, and the tools we carried wouldn't make a dent in that hard alloy surface. Everything was built with the most robust sheets of material available today, specially manufactured for the void beyond our atmosphere and the demands of re-entry. A long tether anchored deep below the surface of the Earth, way past the bunker stretching past the geostationary orbit with a counterweight at the end, held the entire contraption.

"I have an idea," I said, remembering something we could potentially use… "I'm not sure it will work, but it is worth a try. These things have a trap door in case of an emergency."

Few people would try it, but we were not the typical variety then. I knew Zane and Jeze. Rather than stay in here and wait, they both would actively seek to solve our problem and jump. It was just a matter of how we orchestrated that. "The construction of these Spacevats include an escape hatch within their flooring," I continued.

"Isn't that activated once we reach our atmospheric ceiling and only in the event of a problem? It wouldn't help here," stated Zane. Zane was one of the most brilliant people on the planet and could hold his own with anyone, especially in a war.

The ceiling located high above our heads contained survival gear. The mechanism housed several space suits and oxygen supplies, which a drop of normal air pressure would automatically trigger. The outer structure awaited the inner cabin around the ribbon going high into space. Once it passed the roof, the outside layer of the Spacevat would surround the small encasement capable of supporting thirty people. Individual pods secured on the outer sides were available in the event of a system failure. Once in space, a malfunction would slide open the contraption automatically, and the inside panel of the outer structure would release the pods.

The elaborate device was programmed to read and recognize human vitals, but it would not engage until we reached space. In our case, it would remain inactive as we had not reached the roof. Indeed we had dropped two hundred floors. The secured suits would not fall from the ceiling and clasp on our bodies within the Spacevat. But the flooring could be retracted manually.

"We can't trigger a malfunction, but we could trigger an override," I explained.

"You suggest we activate a manual override in the floor and drop," surmised Jeze.

"Is that worth the risk?" asked Zane. "I know I'm not crazy about staying in here indefinitely, and you know that… But do we dare fly out of here?"

I was observing Zane. It was his call. If he wanted to risk it, we would. On the other hand, if he preferred to remain here, so be it. I knew him well enough to understand that he wouldn't stay still, certainly not if there were a chance to get out of here. But then he had also told me, not that long ago, that his action days were over.

I grinned, "Flying is not exactly what it would be like."

Zane looked at us and sighed. "Nevermind. We really can't stay here anyway. Okay, how do we do this?"

"Jeze, you are lighter. You get to share your grapple with Zane."

Jeze had already surmised that much. She unlocked her vest.

The grapple was hooked to our vest frame and would bear our weight and more. The device was handy, and all of us had used it during multiple ops. The wire was strong. Still, I didn't want to take the risk of having Zane and my weight supported by it. The drop was too long, but it would handle Jeze and Zane's weight without a problem. We would aim as we fell. Zane and Jeze on one harness was a better option that way.

"Take it," Jeze said, handing over her vest.

Usually, we were not in motion when using the gun and targeting our aim. We had already identified our target, and the head of the grapple would have embedded itself into the objective, the side of a fly car, or the wall of a building before we would use it to move up or down with the wire.

Zane hesitated, looking at Jeze with mixed emotion on his face. "I can hold on to you."

"Not going to happen," Jeze replied.

Indeed this time, things were different. We were stuck over four hundred floors in the air. Our jump would occur before launching the hook, and the target's connection made on the move.

"HellNet..." Zane muttered, dropping his suit jacket after removing the small data chips casing – no doubt with code access to our NetSat Program. He then grabbed the vest and secured it over his body. It was the latest in Tech Warfare, and even I wasn't entirely privy to its full deployment protocol. He opened one surety pocket and slid the small case inside.

Our aim needed to be flawless, our timing to the second, our visual acuity perfect, and our reflexes accurate because we would be in freefall before we could grab onto anything.

The building with most of its infrastructure was behind us. The Tower on one side was just a wall of glass protected by outer shields. The Spacevat faced our city landscape ahead with the floors of our building behind us. Our strategy was to approach ourselves to one of these levels once we got closer to the ground floor.

The Imps would help. Fitted with the best there was, they gave us an extraordinary sense of timing, agility, and power. The blunt force of the gravity we would feel once the rope stopped the fall would strain our muscles. It was going to be jarring and unpleasant, but it was feasible.

Zane and Jeze understood that. "Well, sir, I hope you're still in shape because this is going to be hard on you," Jeze added with a wicked smile.

Zane laughed. "I guess I was wrong, North… My days in the field aren't over."

Zane was in great shape. We spared together daily. He insisted on staying sharp, even if he was no longer in the thick of the action.

I was glad Zane was here with us instead of the insipid politicians on the Great Council with no military training.

Without hesitation, Jeze added, "You carry the vest; I hold onto you."

Zane chuckled. "I vaguely recall how it works."

"You better; I'm counting on it," Jeze said without losing a beat.

Things never got boring with Zane. In the past, we had confronted many unexpected situations during ops. In planning a mission, there were always surprises we didn't expect to face or things not accounted for, and this was no different.

Zane then got into the jacket and secured it around him, although it fitted a bit tight. He then verified the grapple gun and grunted.

Jeze now wore her uniform without the protection of her combat vest. She enjoyed teasing him, "You release the trigger this way, boss?" Jeze said with a twitch of her lips. Not one to shy away from danger, Jeze remained calm under pressure. There existed one exception to this, and it happened when she got angry.

The surface of the floor inside the SpaceVat seemed flawless. Nothing was suggesting an opening to activate.

A while ago, I read that a flooring mechanism existed. The knowledge hit the back of my mind when we began searching for a way out.

The engineers had built it into the structure. The builders thought of it to allow for an escape scenario in case of an emergency in space.

Multiple safeguards and redundancies were essential to the contraption's purpose, taking us to our space station, past the buildings and mega high rises of Ang City, beyond the atmosphere of Earth's gravity.

I just needed to get the combination to open it. I activated my PVZ to retrieve the information from the files. My latest Imps included the newest technology, with blueprints in construction, arms, transportation, and city infrastructure. For this, I didn't need the Network. The data sat on my PVZ and provided me with the numbers for this Spacevat model, and I quickly disconnected.

This was not what they had in mind when the engineers built that fail-safe feature, but it would serve us anyway.

I dropped to the floor and started looking at the pattern. One could notice a slightly different density inside the composite when appraising it closely.

Our current technology surpassed the initial graphene material, the carbon nanotubes, and other improved alloy components made all this possible. A pattern established in the egg-shaped nodules within the flooring surface was barely visible. Still, threads inside them appeared under scrutiny. They formed a sort of small tapestry of numbers. I searched for a small protrusion or what could even be a hatch. There was nothing there but a slight irregularity in the hard substance under the tip of my fingers.

Zane and Jeze squatted by my side.

Jeze had already grabbed hold of Zane, who had an arm around her waist. He now overtook the control of the vest.

Jeze authorized the override. "Boss, I don't mind getting out of here this way, but try not to miss when you aim. We won't have time to reload."

Zane matched his DNA to the pistol with all the electronics provided by the vest. The combat gear system would only work with an imprint of his hand.

Zane grinned and now activated the pistol, securing his hold on it. "I may be out of practice, but I can aim… Just hold on, Jeze, and don't let go."

"I plan on it."

Jeze would have to maintain a grip on him despite the jerk on the line. Otherwise, she would tumble downward, and we wouldn't be able to retrieve her.

We all knew the risks.

I found the lock that opened the floor mechanism. The small nodules were right under my fingers, settled in the middle of the eggshell pattern. They identified the location of the five numbers, and I focused on them now with the help of my visual Imp.

We positioned ourselves facing the wall of floors.

Jeze and Zane were holding on to each other.

Their velocity and mine would be different as we fell.

We exchanged one last look. With one nod, my fingers pushed the nodules in the correct order.

The floor retracted, and the three of us dropped.

It was fast.

It wasn't like jumping out of an aircraft carrier. The air up there acted like friction, slowing us down a bit. This chute seemed to grab and pull us downward. Maybe it was due to the side walls gripping the Spacevat to the building, but the fall was like being in an air tunnel, only vertical.

The surface of the building sped up in front of my eyes. I looked at the floors passing rapidly in my line of sight, too rapidly.

We fell together for a short moment. Zane and Jeze were beside me and gone, disappearing below me. Their heavier weight carried them, increasing their velocity toward the ground. They now were on their own, and so was I.

I focused on the façade of the building and aimed. My pistol sent the grapple toward the wall.

The cable uncoiled, flying toward the floors.

I gripped the gun tightly and passed the spot I targeted a second ago.

There was no way to know if my aim reached the goal, puncturing the wall.

Nothing held me yet.

The feeling lasted.

I was in freefall.

Water's Edge, Golden Ghetto, Ang City

There is no place to hide until the loathing I feel subsides. I am in the midst of a battle for our lives. Master Phenom Zane Langden, Global Earth EHAF-UGCN, DAINN Annals - Winter 2098.

The storm raged on us under the open dome. With nightfall, the velocity of the winds increased, and rain pounded us. We fought with everything we had against the elements. The winds struck everything in sight, the rain cut down our visibility to a mere few inches ahead of us, and the water rose in the streets of Water's Edge. The downpour was so violent that it resembled some of the great storms of the past as if facing Concordance and the anomaly in one day was not enough to challenge us.

North and I, moved slowly cutting across the substance of the cloud along with the rest of the Presidential Elite team, stumbling ahead and trying to dislodge the remnants of buildings while pulling the few survivors that had made it through the onslaught out of the path of the storm.

It was hours since we got out of the Tower to rejoin the EHAF Elite. The evacuation took place inside our Conclaves within the grids despite the bioengineered substance spreading throughout our streets, and I needed to trust that our preparations were enough.

Meanwhile, we assembled our EHAF armada to destroy the anomaly. Our SRC searched for it with our deep space scanners. It had to come from somewhere in our galaxy, and we needed to reach the source.

A little while ago, I ordered our fleet to converge toward the edge of our domes and take a position there. Our people needed time to reach their destinations for the evacuation, and I planned to give them that. Against the recommendations from North, I refused to board the EHAF ship that would take us far away to the first colony planet we identified as capable of sustaining our race. I intended to be the last one to leave if we could not stop the invasion of our world.

The Elite troops ordered to move our top people as fast as possible through the gates got it done. They comprised our most brilliant minds, scientists, technology gurus, engineers, writers, artists, and government leaders. Everyone capable of reshaping our world was on that list, divided among the different Conclaves they belonged to, except for a few who would mix inside the other flotilla of ships and among the four programs so we could be covered if something were to happen to any Conclave. The idea to combine the Conclaves among our fleet and the four programs was rejected initially and eventually found favors with our leaders. It was too much of a risk otherwise.

The CVs kept orders and monitored the areas where our gates led our people either to space or the underground, providing support to transit our general population. But soon, I would need the Elite to face the anomaly instead of overseen our people in the grids of the GG and Water's Edge. We were almost there, ready to fight.

Things would progress a lot faster if we did not have to account for the crazy weather in Water's Edge. The force of the water, crippling some of our passageways on the lower levels, made it impossible for some of our people to join the processing gates.

We had just stepped out of the rover that brought us here despite the debris in the main arteries of Water's Edge. Up until that moment, we had the luxury of speech.

I had seen destruction, alienation, and irreparable cruelties. Before DAINN, life was a competition where men used everything within their power to win, and they kept scores. They bent the rules, and there was no Watcher. DAINN corrected some of the inequities while humanity invented others.

"Without DAINN implementing the plan and overseeing the organization within our programs this early on in our process, things took a HellNet of a lot longer.

The Concord riots made our defensive position with the anomaly even more problematic. The System bogged down amid the upheaval, and our latest technology was no longer working anymore. It was necessary to rethink everything.

The storm raged around us still, a storm that changed the order of things as the fog clouded everything in our midst. Some of our people would not reach the gates in time if we did not open the way to access the GG.

I remembered when the worst weather patterns began and when one of the massive winds came down from the north. The events of those years were a lifetime ago, yet it was like yesterday still. I took a look at North, hoping this would not remind him of that time. *North cannot go there… Not now. But I saw it. He was already there, revisiting the loss of his family.*

I walked ahead with North, anticipating the issues to remove the blockade caused by the rising water in this grid and giving orders to my team. I learned only to trust the few working with me throughout the years of fighting. They were more than just my team. They were also my family.

We were close to the extraction point.

The cataclysm caused by the storm in the last few hours was one of the worst we experienced in the city. Without the domes and despite the strengths of our buildings, there were still things that did not hold the water at bay. While we evacuated many coastlines, Water's Edge was one area we maintained with elevated areas where our building locations afforded a great view of our ocean. Our influential people found it replenished their energy and provided respite, so we maintained it as a vacationing area, giving our leaders a place to get a bit away from the bustle.

The storm approached behind the anomaly, and the fog hid most of it until it was over the city. And it was a bad one, unlike anything we had ever seen since the great storms.

Fighting to see ahead of me, "Do you think the anomaly is causing it?" I said in my PVZ.

North, fighting to advance at my side, replied, "It came out of nowhere, so it is possible."

The weather combined with the cloud composite made of symbols drifting down in codes in front of our faces was wild. The substance, so thick we pushed through it with every step, appeared to conform around us. The rain mixed with wind raged on everything in our path. The coastline was underwater in no time. The waves targeted the jetties as if their only purpose was to crash on the rocks and displace them in a thunder of grey mist. Still, we saw everything through the film of the red cloud… Bood red.

We had no warning. Before we knew it, the wind had tossed rooftops over fly cars and railways, crushed building facades and entryways, and toppled housing facilities near Water's Edge. According to some of the reports we received from our outlying grids, it even eradicated manufacturing plants in areas like Emerald Field and Bridge Way.

Our shuttles flew, carrying some of the injured. Our hospitals crowded with too many from the riots remained open, and while the evacuation took place, many of our doctors stayed behind.

Nothing in our modern technology could save us from nature's wrath, except the domes. The things we had created and deployed for our convenience, the trams going faster than old planes, the air machines capable of reaching our space stations, and the construction bots so swift to build our immense skyscrapers, crawled to a halt and were all rendered worthless. The only alternative left to us was to stay clear of the storm's path and remove obstacles along the streets with our remaining drones and robots.

The screaming winds passed through the zones near the shorelines in the late hours. Then, our panicked population turned towards the Clout. They knew the EHAF, and the people trusted us. They relied on us to take them to safety, and we responded despite the battle that would soon unfold above our heads—one area at the time. But our numbers were stretched to their limit, and I found myself leading my team, like old times to the extraction point.

We now lifted walls, cleared debris, tossed aside vehicles to clear a path toward the Plaza on the ground. Slowly, we made our way inland with the remnant of our population caught in the area.

We helped the WE sector while another evacuated. We cleared a small walkway through the devastation on one of the main roads. We escorted thousands of people behind us, waiting for a way to get to the evacuation gates.

"We barely have enough men as it is… We need you to get back to the attack."

"Our fleet is well covered. We have the right people in place. Our generals and commanders know what they are doing. We need to believe we took every step needed to face this. Now, we need to get our people."

Our preparations would see us through, even though the attack came too early and we were not ready for it. Right here, I could control our actions. We were fighting for a whole group of desperate people trapped behind damaged buildings. They left dilapidated homes in one of the hardest-hit disaster areas when the water rose.

When we finally cleared enough of the rubbles, the road was under several feet of water. The transport moved ahead of us too slowly. And the disruption of the elements had once again increased in power.

Our robotic team, the heavy construction arm of our androids force, began to follow my orders. They leaped over the chasm to reach some of the residents, those unable to make it independently. They carried out one person at a time as instructed. Our people looked small enfolded in their huge frames, as the androids held them over the remnants of what remained standing in this part of our city. The Zoids, deemed the safest way to reach across the debris alone, responded fast.

The robots were solid and agile. They were capable of many things beyond our physical prowess. They leaped over the remaining foundations and averted the ragged remnants of our broken structures. They carried the small group of eighty-nine people to safety, holding them with care and dedication, and we knew they did a better job than we could.

The wind roared, weaving inside the red cloud tapestry, or was it my ears that played tricks on me? One side of the building left standing moved slowly and came hurtling down in a storm of disjointed concrete pieces, twisted steel beams, and dust particles.

Our Zoid 3 bots reacted quickly. They deflected some of the weight off the precious human cargo they were holding and held onto a part of the building's side, but they were trapped.

I was scrambling to get there, but Birch and the rest of my team held me back. There was nothing anyone could do, so I watched the scene unfolding. Time stood still for a brief instant. The horrible thing I dreaded slowly materialized, and none of us could have averted it – not in the seconds that followed.

Beneath the water, the saturated ground collapsed. The infrastructure caved in. As the Zoids landed on the unstable surface to take on the brunt of the falling structure and send our population to safety, the entire panel lying at a sixty-degree angle gave way from under them.

We watched the event in slow motion.

The Zoids, desperate to save our people, held on with all their might. Within seconds, the building near the passageway disappeared. The Zoids grabbed hold of anything they could, one moving fragment after the next before they dropped under the ruins, our people in their arms. A huge cavity where the air road stood remained in the desolate landscape. The massive sinkhole swallowed everything in the area.

We searched every cranny, every hole, moved every piece of rubble while the wind howled in our ears and the cloud parted ahead of us. We searched for what remained of the hours before the new day began, in the dirt, despite the water now knee-deep on the surface of the remaining broken streets. Our remaining Zoids moved everything for us, although there was little to no hope. And all the while, the anomaly turned everything we saw in a film of red substance organized in lighter orange computer codes with lines after lined filtering over Ang.

We would have kept going, but I had to call it off.

Deep down, I knew it. I had known for a while. Our people were gone.

The collapsed ground and the cavities beneath us filled with water. The rain poured on us without respite. The slippery ground around the holes, so unstable even with canopies anchored as a protective barrier, eroded quickly.

We lost a lot of people at that moment, and I knew we would lose more in the hours ahead. But it was time to call it off and rejoin our troops on the Plaza. So, we turned and made our way back.

The walkway of the one hundred floors stretched ahead of me. A group of last-minute evacuees broke the barricade tended by our CVs and surged through the space gate. They were among the last to report in.

Jeze turned to me and said, "I have several of our Commanders ready to report in."

"Good, do we have a count?"

"Not yet. We do not know how many missed the gates departure times," replied Jeze.

"Patch them through."

The Admiral of our Alpha feet reported, "Ready to launch, President Langden."

"Go ahead, and good journey, Admiral Chanen."

"Your ship is ready when you are, President Langden. Our coordinates have been transmitted to the captain. They wait for you."

"There are still a few things to handle planetside, Admiral, but I thank you. Take care of our people."

"Good luck to you, Sir."

The Commander's voice of the Provenance Progam was next. Her voice sounded clear across the old comm system. "Provenance is ready, President Langden."

"May the stars keep you safe, Commander Collen."

"It was an honor, President Langden."

The General of the Aurora program came on; his voice resonated in my ears, unwavering. "President Langden, are there any of our citizens on the surface that did not make it to their gates?"

"The last few should be reaching you in a few minutes, General Sottis."

"Very well, President Langden. We will wait and close the gate in fifteen minutes."

"Thank you, General, for your extended stay. I wish you a calm rest underground and hope to see you soon, General Sottie."

"My best wishes to you as well, President Langden."

The red cloud began to lift.

"Is Origin online yet?"

"Yes, President Langden. The last of our people just reached the safety platform."

"Very well. Close the doors and safe journey."

Many of our people lay dead on the ground through the fog of the bioengineered red cloud surrounding the plaza. Behind me, the steps of many Elites reached me. It was time. We were ready to engage the anomaly.

"Do we have the location?"

"SRC believes there is something behind Saturn."

"Launch the Armada."

"NetRoger that, President Langden."

But our latest ships and their technology failed us again on this night.

Within minutes, as they flew toward the anomaly, they staggered as if suspended for a moment with no direction and exploded in the air in a display of lights.

The metal of our ships screeched as it blew up in the sky, careening past the domes and descending over the skyscrapers in blaring discordant hellish sounds before they reached the ground within Ang city. May our forces and the will of good succeed and win for Ang and all of humankind.

NEWDAWN RISING
Teaser Chapter

SRC Conclave, Annals Viewing Vlog 567,323,876
Ang City, Spring 2098

The anomaly in space triggers a readiness demarcation line and calls for immediate defense and avoidance preparations. The System accordingly proclaims the Origin program a go. It is unique and the ultimate hail mary, but our scientists believe it could work. So we immediately begin an armada expansion and scenarios for three other programs. DAINN Annals – Spring 2098.

A year at the most, it was all we had to get ready. One year to avoid extinction. One year to find workable solutions. One year to prepare for the worst. Only one year.

My people had a tough time wrapping their minds around the eventuality that we were indeed on the edge of an extinction event. Our scientists drew all kinds of scenarios. Many were abandoned upon further investigation.

Origin was indeed a hail mary. Still, as reality hit home, we elaborated on the different ways to proceed, thus the other three programs. Alpha, Provenance, and Aurora were our last resorts.

The EHAF, unrelenting in their pursuit to ensure our capabilities to face an enemy we knew nothing about, demanded more ships, and our leaders happily complied, suddenly safe in the knowledge that we would respond in kind to anything thrown at us. But how to respond to an unknown enemy? Weapons of mass destruction would only be an option if everything else failed. Langden made that clear.

Perhaps it was a dream for them to believe that we could match the entity flying in space at an unimaginable speed. Yet, it was the stuff of the worst nightmare if one stopped to think about it. My people did not stop, though. For them, anything less than action spelled their doom. As the System analyzed possibilities, it also began looking at how fast we could build an armada capable of making a dent in a battle for our survival.

Our priorities around the planet shifted. We threw everything at the Origin program, along with Alpha, Provenance, and Aurora; even as we built the Armada Langden demanded, for enough support came from our leaders to that end.

"It's not enough," Langden said as he reviewed our progress.

"We don't have the resources, Minister Anton Folwer said."

"Then create them. We have enough technology to think and make it work for us," insisted Langden in another meeting that set the tone for what followed. "I want more ships. I want more people evacuated. I want us to think like leaders and save our population. Anything short of that, don't bring it to me, Anton. I will not accept saving our Elite and not our workers, do you get that?"

"Netshit, Langden. We are doing everything we can…."

"And it's not good enough! Do more. Find the resources with our robotics if you don't find the workforce."

The EHAF, under President Zane Langden, called for the rapid manufacturing of multiple ships, both combats, and transports. Zane conveyed a defense ministry dedicated to orchestrating all activities concerning the anomaly. This committee comprised five key influencers, including President Zane Langden, North Thompson, Anton Fowler, and two of our most prestigious military Commanders, Admiral Samantha Rigel and Rear Admiral Dae Gwan.

In a series of meetings, they determined the fleet's needs, should we play offensive and defense, which consisted primarily of avoidance. As a result, twenty super-dreadnoughts - Razor class, fifteen capital ships – Absolute class, and ten super-carriers – Deliverance class were immediately ordered from the Company Conclave with multiple alternative designs enhancing combat efficiencies. Another order demanded the delivery of five carriers behemoths called the Colossus, even bigger and more powerful than the super-dreadnoughts, where our government officials would remain with the EHAF contingents.

Still unsatisfied with these numbers, Zane added five new Hunter-class battleships and commanded a revamp and upgrades for our older battleships to integrate our latest advances and technologies. He also added thirty new Rampage class and Absolute class battlecruisers, one hundred new Rader class, Advantage class, Catcher class, cruisers, and a thousand new Liberty frigates with multiple capabilities – Reciprocity class, Recurrence class, Rupture class, and Aggravation class.

In our current fleet, we already had five Scout ships Advance class, eight Science ships – Emergence class and Relevant class, along with fifty-five transports ships for equipment and products – Conservation and Exception class.

"How in the HellNet do you expect us to build all of these?" Minister Anton Fowler was irate.

"How do you expect the EHAF to defend our people?" replied with just the same heat Zane Langden, our President.

The Company Conclave was in an uproar. The SRC Conclave drove its teams to the breaking point. The Faculty Conclave transformed into an assembly line of Imps Installs alterations. Doctors fulfilled as many upgrades as they could to prepare our workforce for the new requirements. The Institute stayed clear of the vitriolic arguments ensuing with the new demands. Still, there were plenty of ongoing fights among our leaders as they moved things around to build everything they could within the time frame allocated for these.

We also needed passengers ships equipped with hundreds of thousands of cryogenics pods and resuscitation suites featuring medical labs, not counting the hundred engineering and manufacturing labs located across the fleet needing an upgrade.

Still, these new directives remained not enough. When the notion and discussions of another Concord arose at first, it was rejected. Indeed, the need was great, but our people would rebel against it.

"It's the only way we can get all of this done, Sloan Roden Baker, the head of the Institute, stated emphatically.

Things got worse once another Concordance was mentioned and quickly planned by the Institute. "You want your ships. We need another Concord," Sloan Roden Baker said.

Basically, according to the words of my people, we were pretty "Netfucked."

As DAINN, I could never subscribe to it. My programming would not allow me to give up. The face of my mentor, Dr. Rene Paladock came up on the screens of my System. He had made sure that my purpose was clear and irreversible – protecting and taking care of my charges no matter the circumstances. So, my System went into overdrive, responding to the agenda laid out by our EHAF President, Zane Langden.

"We get ready to fight," President Langden said. "But if it looks like we cannot win, we evacuate and get our people to space and flee at all cost. Let me state, categorically, we will not become slaves to an alien entity. We will not go extinct. We will find a new home somewhere in space and rebuild. In the meantime, let's get this done."

DAINN shifted its imperatives to meet these new goals.

The schedule for the manufacturing facilities was to deliver all these assets in nine months, which was unheard of considering that one of these ships took over a year to build. Yet, ingenuity from the SRC brought us to retrofit and upgrade our construction robots first to take charge of the construction in space. Our bigger ships would be built and assembled there. To that end, we also upgraded our City Vigils. The construction platform in orbit quickly got expanded to address four more areas to build our ships. It took two months. Understanding the necessity facing our species, we reassigned some of our workforces early on, and the Conclave made every effort to contribute and meet the demand.

Designers began working on new armament models capable of bringing devastating results in an engagement. New models of bridge control played a part in making the ships more lethal. Engineering came up with new infrastructure to provide more power while feeding more sub-stations. New operating systems were tested to add flexibility to our embolus module, sharp lasers, and gunnery arsenals. And our shields capabilities expanded with more power redirected and fed by multiple sources instead of a central one strengthening its functionality. Some of our most brilliant scientists used enhanced Imps to stay ahead and find ways to improve every aspect of the Armada, from maintaining our shields and mixing new alloy to make our structure impervious to multiple forms of attacks. Adapting some of the most vulnerable ship models in the fleet also became necessary, and stealth technology was enhanced to include our passengers' ships, Autonomy class, and GoalKeeper class.

Each Conclave reallocated its personnel and technology from one day to the next, changing its processes to adapt to these new demands.

The Faculty ordered to stock every medical supply imaginable began making more of everything, including Imps, nutrients boosters, and health nanites, requiring more machines to make the devices capable of creating these. The Company supplied them until they could no longer meet the demand due to the orders from the other Conclaves.

The SRC ran four shifts seven days a week to develop our ships' new defense modes and capabilities. Our scientists formed groups to work on specific problems, running tests on new tiny electronic devices to increase response rate and data processing, and networking our pilots and fighters for better maneuverability response rate. Our ships' captains and their officers worked faster to alleviate battle command challenges with new Imps. Nothing was left for granted in the war to come. Our vessels' primary systems were all subjected to an upgrade, improving overall performance from gravitational fields to better jump drives.

The EHAF recruited new trainees, preparing them for combat in space. The Elite designed CityVigils with the SRC's helps to become a contingent supporting humans as the first line of defense with better capabilities, increasing their ability to kill or annihilate an enemy. Recognition and combat robots joined the fleet with diverse capabilities to face an enemy in space.

The Company called for more personnel and robotic support to meet the demands of all the Conclaves. While it built the robots, all non-essential products were relegated to a long list that kept on growing.

Everyone in our population dealt with shortages that only kept increasing monthly. Still, it was all for one goal – our survival.

The Institute called in younger recruits and began to run them through the Academy faster, preparing them to join our workforce earlier. Once that proved not enough, they called for a reevaluation of many, and the non-essential positions recycled to emergency ones.

The System orchestrated our mining ships into a tighter schedule, working around the clock to provide the materials needed for the new armada and responding to unforeseen issues as they came along in our infrastructure.

I examined our options during all of it, alerting our leaders when prioritized imperatives fell short, looking for solutions, suggesting actions, changing orders, switching objectives, and always watching the anomaly.

It was ironic that we fought so hard all these years against global warming, attempting to reverse an environment that proved adverse to our people in so many ways. Our dying Earth killed by our abuses over the entire planet continued a downward spiral, creating domino effects for many species.

The resource wars of 2040 only contributed to making conditions worst until about twenty years ago. Still, we had lost so many animals to extinction and land to the oceans in the process of climate change that we staggered at the thought. Now we scrambled to prepare an evacuation that required we add every species we had salvaged in the hope of ultimately saving them with our population.

Humans caused this race against global warming in their drive to conquer more, which brought many losses. We saw coastal cities disappear under rising sea levels; we contemplated forest devastation across the globe and witnessed population relocation in the millions. We abandoned some of our most beautiful capitals due to deadly, lasting heat waves, creating domes to protect ourselves and cutting ourselves out from nature. We salvaged DNA to reverse the disappearance of important species to our way of life so our ecology could recover. My archives ran over my septillion bytes of data on their numbers, and now, we had to ensure the safety of this data.

After years of trials and errors, we had just begun making somewhat of a dent in creating better conditions for our people and our world. Respecting Earth did not come easy. Understanding the needs of our planet and considering other species as an intricate part of our ecosystem worthy of protection was learned the hard way.

And now, we were fighting a new war, one that would take us away from a planet we strived to save for so long. The irony of this fact was not a concept I dealt with often, but even my DAINN brain could not ignore it.

DON'T MISS

COMING SOON IN 2022

NEWDAWN RISING

GLOSSARY

Android VBS 5300 – One of the latest android models, capable of lifting extreme weight, flexible in operating multi-tasks, and geared mostly toward special rescue operations.

Alpha - A program launches the fleet into space, along with an entire armada, to safeguard the population of Ang due to an impending extinction-level event.

Ang - Angel City is one of the largest Megapolis on Earth in 2098 and known as such for the sake of efficiency and brevity. After their initial destruction, most of our major cities, rebuilt to sustain the great floods and impending massive storms, now bore new names.

ArchWay Pass – The area of Ang serving as a transportation hub to and from all directions, from NetTrams and HyperLoops systems, Flycars and QuadCopters, AirBus or SubSonic trains to LevGrav vehicles with magnetic superconducting transports will have zero electrical resistance, including shuttles departing for space.

Astra – A small Custodian, capable of extreme speed and offensive and defensive capabilities in the enforcement of the law or strategic military action.

Aurora – A program that created underground safety chambers for the main population to prepare for the impending cataclysm.

BeautyForm – The latest technological advancement process for the reformatting and remodeling of body parts developed by the Company's research and development under the initial product enhancements created by the SRC (Science Research Center).

BioFog – The anomaly creates a synthetic red cloud encompassing a series of codes tightly weaved inside its structure with unknown symbols descending on the planet and Ang city.

BridgeView – The area of Ang where critical infrastructures are located like the Water Filtration Plant, the Electrical Solar Hub, the Processing Facility, and other instrumental edifices dedicated to crucial functions of the Megapolis.

City Vigil – Robots built to oversee the population's security and safety with advanced protocols allowing them to face many situations and replace the police force in the city.

City Vigils Corp – The Corp was formed under the EHAF as a separate entity for robots and CVs to become the first line of defense, whether in security issues or war situations under the aegis of the EHAF Elite.

CliffTops – The area of Ang where technology centers reign and where tech gurus dealing with programming all things reside. It has a direct pathway to the SRC.

CLS Screen – Cognitive Links Shaping screen is the display and chair that impacts Readers and Seers to connect them more easily to subjects in remote influencing mode providing a Stress Latency Score to determine the effectiveness of the change in the brain activity. It is also used to coerce a Reader and Seer to perform better through electrical impulse.

Concordance or The Concord – A punctual event determined by the DAINN System under the election of the General Council of Nations to reapportion the planet's natural resources or the workforce in all fields of endeavor.

Control Center or CC – The Surgs operation control located in the underground base and led by Laird, the head of the Insurgenets.

Council – The Council of Nations or Great Council represents multiple countries and runs the Planet and its infrastructure under a public mandate.

Custodians – Robots implement security measures and enforcement policies citywide within government buildings. They replace today's security personnel. They look like spheres of different diameters. Based on their capabilities,

Custodians carry one or multiple ZNets, which are zapping mechanisms designed to put people into a sleep state. Using nets deployed around their targets, they bring their passengers to detention centers.

Cryogenic Chamber – Located inside the Institute, with a unique team of technicians dedicated to welcoming those who emerge from the Cryo modules, many rooms containing one hundred to a thousand pods. The total number of modules is unknown. We also refer to the Cryogenic Chamber as NDCryo.

DAINN – The Distributed Artificial Intelligence Neuro Network and A.I. is a planetary mind whose tentacles reach all over the globe to monitor our entire infrastructure.

DarNet – An expression that has evolved from the word "darn" or the phrase "darn it." It became "DarNet" because of the influence of the Network over people in our future.

DarNetWash – An expression suggesting "never mind," or more used to mean "nullify" this or that.

Dems or Demerits – Method used by the Conclave to control behavior within their ranks, which affects the social status and credit remuneration within the monetary system.

Desinet – The DAINN System programmed search to explore a subject inner desire based on our population database.

Distribution Centers – All distribution centers fall under the purview of the Company Conclave and are an arm serviced by the heads of the Company, which also manufactures all goods.

Domestic Bot – Robot or Bot designed and located inside each population quarters, apartment, or house to serve as domestic, doing chores in society's upper echelon. The Bot is programmed for basic tasks and deals with cleaning, cooking, and running errands but can do much more. Linked to the DAINN System and Network, they monitor all our needs.

Electrical Solar Hub – Operated by an arm of the Company when it comes to Ang city and the electrical grid, it has a dedicated independent structure for the SRC, which operates DAINN, the System, and the Network, all of which is overseen by the EHAF.

Embodied Avatars or ECA – Popular models created for civilians to enhance a virtual reality environment and bring various personalities and models to life; some are even developed for combat.

Emerald Field – The area of Ang where crop growing and synthetic farming are implemented within giant skyscrapers and where sprawling manufacturing facilities and distribution centers are located.

EmVats – Also known as an EV suit, it is an individual protective unit or suit linked to the DNA of a user. EmVats provide protecting ambient suits with an energy field surrounding the body for combat readiness based on specific programming.

Encharge – An exchange of energy between conclave members to unify, recharge, and strengthen people's links.

FarmRises – Due to climatic conditions and natural resources, all crops are grown inside skyscrapers under carefully monitored conditioned serviced by robotics and automation systems and overseen by the Company under the supervision of the EHAF.

Flycar – A motorized vehicle with lower flight capability, designated for personal use to higher level conclave members. Flycars configured on-demand can carry one or two people.

Galaxy Club – Set on the orbital space station, the club is praised for its delicious food, great drinks, and unique entertainment and is the dedicated ground for the high society of Ang.

Gatherer – A Gatherer, also called a Gatherer of Space, can move through time and space based on DNA, implants, and technology.

Golden Ghetto – The area of Ang where is located the top echelon of the population and all official buildings of the Conclaves and siege of government.

HMS or Home Monitoring Screen – Each apartment, house, estate, or Conclave suite possesses one of these. They come standard or premium with various features based on individual preferences and are paired with a holoscreen and virtual reality platform.

HydroSheath – Metallic tube or cylinder containing Nanos pushed through a perfusion head.

Insurgenets or Surgs – A faction of the population who refuses to submit to the Imps Installs and chooses to live in the old underground city of Ang.

Institute – The Institute is the government's arm that implements the DAINN System according to the government's mandates. It keeps up with A.I. and population demands.

Insts – Name for those belonging to the Institute Conclave.

IOGel – A gel-like substance composed of water and nutrients. An energy drink for Conclave leaders and members.

HellNet – An expression replacing "hell."

Mave – A large Custodian, extremely powerful and deadly, carrying bombs and other offensive weapons to apprehend, detain, or kill crowds or enemies.

MedCarriers – Transportation system entirely dedicated to the Faculty and its members to facilitate healthcare operations across the globe.

MedCorp – The Faculty is a medical corporation with healthcare units located worldwide and servicing the population's needs. It works independently from the other Conclaves, benefiting from certain independence under the General Council of Nations.

MindTranscript – DAINN reads a subject's mind to understand where a person is emotionally at a certain point in time. Monitoring thought patterns in different situations and learning everything a person thinks and feels.

Mirrior Company – Arm of the Company Conclave focuses on developing all sorts of products dedicated to enhancing individual performance, revitalization, supplements, and health and beauty components.

Monitoring Room – Inside the Watch Tower, within the Presidential skyscraper, is a situation room where the Watcher oversees real-time feeds providing strategic data through the DAINN Network from around the planet. The EHAF Elite oversees the information and reacts to it as needed under the purview of President Langden.

MTPs or Moving Transportation Platform – Various governmental hovering above ground MTPs abound within Ang; some are entirely dedicated to the five Conclaves, limited to database entries within the faction and their buildings. A few, with more limitations, are sold to individuals by the Company as an enjoyable AirBoarding extreme leisure activity.

NetComm – The planetary telecommunication network linking everyone on the planet.

Netdumb – An expression replacing "dumb" or "dummy," also used are expressions like NetMorons and NetJerks.

NetSwarm – Nanobots capable of carrying different payloads based on their programming for particular purposes.

NetSpy – Nanobots infiltrating spyware used in different areas to gather information for the Network.

NetPulsing – The action of using a PulseNet to carve entries and tunnels into a rock formation. It can also be used as a defensive or offensive arm based on situations, degrees, and ranges.

NetRoger – An expression replacing "Roger that" based on the influence of the DAINN Network.

NetWash – An expression signifying "Shit" or "F… It…" Depending on the inflection of the subject.

NetZapping – Custodians' tool to maintain order over individuals or crowds. Used to ensure population safety, it can occasionally serve as an offensive or defensive arm.

Nuzar – Purple drink with energizing nutrients.

Operation Control or SRC-OC – Main lab dedicated to the DAINN System and Network, monitoring all the logistics involving the data grab from multiple locations around the planet.

OR or Operation Room – The Faculty ER facility dedicated operation rooms.

Origin – A safety chamber designed to safeguard a few of the Conclave members chosen to travel back in time to prevent Ang's future destruction.

OxyPure – A breather or breathing mask, delivering oxygen to survive.

PAPT – Planetary Alliance Peace Treaty of 2025 signed by significant countries on Earth.

Phenom – A title gained by accumulating accomplishments and implants to master skills and knowledge in various disciplines. Phenom is one of the highest levels individuals attain within the DAINN System.

PodBot – Robots designed to implement and oversee the Cryo process inside the Origin chamber.

Processing Facility – The plant services all synthetic and natural food products under the aegis of the Company, which is monitored by the EHAF.

Provenance - A program designed to safeguard the population and some conclave members in space facilities surrounding the planet. Using multiple space elevators and ships, Provenance began a mass exile to deliver people from Earth who expected an impending extinction-level event.

Pulse Device – A sonic wave pulse creating such energy on the subatomic level displaces matter and reshapes it according to pre-programmed designs.

PulseNet – The sonic pulse that emanates from the UniBrace device on the wrist of the perfect humans.

PulseTube – The level of a Pulse Device creating tunnels into the Earth based on sonic waves.

PVZ – Personal Visor Z, linked to the ZNet or Communication Network on the planet, is a system that replaces the cell phones of today. Implanted in a human being at an early age, the PVZ serves multiple purposes, including health monitoring, location tracking, and the facilitation of communication between members of the population and the DAINN Network.

Roamers – Members of the Conclave selected to become Time Travelers as part of the Origin program.

Rovers – A particular group formed to survey the timeline under assignments from the Council of Nations, enforcing specific dictates.

Seer – A person capable of performing certain gifts ranging from past or future visions. Some can enhance life cycles or perform life-giving acts and properties to various species and heal.

SIFS – A fighting method focusing on decomposing multiple styles based on the attributes of an individual to magnify the impact and recomposing these to enhance effectiveness and success against an opponent. It incorporates speed, strength, flexibility, and strategy and is deemed lethal against a regular opponent.

Sky – Advanced military Lazer-powered weapon.

Spozor – A liquid gel with exceptional qualities and nutrients developed by the Institute.

Shaper – A person capable of reading thoughts, shaping minds, influencing perceptions, and altering decision processes.

SkyFarms – Vertical agricultural complexes spread over the city and designed to grow food.

Stars – A nightclub and restaurant located in Ang city dedicated to the rich and famous and the EHAF Elite.

SpaceVat – Gravity retractable tube planet-to-space transportation system serving as a movable corridor tethered to the surface of Earth in specific locations and linked to an orbital station beyond geostationary orbit to reach space. It permits vehicular cabins to transport people and equipment without shuttles.

SoulLife – A greeting form used by residents of Ang City to express mutual appreciation, and based upon an Allegiance to the Universal Pledge, recognized Life Energy as a unique source of power.

The Institute developed Spozor to facilitate immediate recovery in those waking up from Cryo.

SoftabNet – Inserted near the Imps installs at the base of the head, health medication or hormone regulators designed to regulate the deployment of dosage needed based on individual requirement.

SRC (Science Research Center) – The Science Research Center is the governing arm that develops all new technology and science on behalf of the government. The SRC works under the Council and the official's dictating policy and is the sole Conclave located on international grounds within Ang.

SRICEC or Secured Reciprocal Integrated Communication Emergency Channel – EHAF Channel dedicated to emergencies.

Symbiotic Pairings – The DAINN System provides personal data, psychological and emotional assessments to determine personality matches for individuals seeking a life partner.

TranStairways – Mobile automated escalators responding to destination inputs from Imps.

UniWear – Underclothing beneath a uniform or other clothing.

UniWrap - A bracelet that wraps itself around a user's wrist, the *UniWrap* carries the energy and can adapt to a user's needs. It is an advanced weapons system comprising Nanobots and used as an offensive or defensive tool in combat.

Vids – All news and comm information distributed by the Network, arm of the SRC, for the benefit of the population and Conclaves.

VLogs/VideoLogs – A process qualifying as a work report facilitating a person's information dump into DAINN. During a Vlog, the A.I. asks specific questions about one's work. A recording of the subject is launched during the interview. Each VLog ends up in the DAINN archive.

Watch Center – Located inside the Presidential Tower, it is the monitoring center for the planet where all data is filtered through the Watcher and the EHAF.

VZ or VisorZap – Floating screens folding and unfolding based on Imps input neural signal which provides dedicated Conclave information to the members based on security clearance and job posts. VZs are also available within Ang to provide infrastructure and NetNews information within the city.

Water's Edge – The area of Ang where the population gathers to relax, take a vacation, visit expensive shops, enjoy plush restaurants and bars.

Water Filtration Plant – Operated by the Company as one of the services provided to the population of Ang, it is also overseen by the EHAF as one critical function for the well-being of Ang.

WatGel – Water-like gel used for baths or showers.

ZDart – Disk dissolving under the epidermis used by Custodians to subdue opponents, maintain population control and order, with other offensive capabilities, like carrying a sleeping agent.

Zenio Face Mask – A flexible casing with an energy field that protects the face of a combatant and absorbs shocks. It is made of self-healing material for rapid recovery.

ZNet – An apparatus incorporated into the Custodians in the form of indestructible netting. Also available for EHAF ships (Earth Homeland Alliance Force).

Zoid 2098 – One of the latest hovering serving robots beyond the standard serving bots with enhanced programming and automation, which provides service in shops, restaurants, and bars to a select clientele inside the GG.

NOTE TO MY READERS

I hope you have enjoyed REBOOT. In my mind, it was the book that began the adventure of NEWDAWN and the one I wrote first. There is much more to come in the upcoming volumes of the Saga with the NEWDAWN journey.

Foresight, Prototyping, Worldbuilding method serves as a way to see over the horizon with the changes in science and technology shaping our future. The different scenarios in NEWDAWN are facets of what awaits us and present opportunities to maintain our choices in what we want for our lives and our future.

While NEWDAWN is steep in some fantasy, it also considers our advancements in science and technology, making the stories fascinating.

And if you can take a few minutes, please let me know if you have enjoyed the read by leaving a review on Amazon. Reviews encourage sales, and I can use your support to make the NEWDAWN Saga successful. Thank you for reading my books.

BIOGRAPHY

Dr. Dominique Luchart is an author, sought-after futurist, and founder of WindHorse Entertainment and Windom Media. She is a multi-faceted creative strategist with a Juris Doctor degree and an award-winning director and producer with over 50 Addy Awards. She guides corporate and government leaders and agencies in corporate branding, ethical solutions, digital globalization, planning for climate change for product distribution and development.

As a speaker, she is a masterful innovator, changing how people interact with content creating scenarios with Foresight, Worldbuilding, and Prototyping methods. As a universal storyteller, she delivers the next generation of information and entertainment networks based on science and technology using new media technology. One of her goals is to create trailblazing experiential environments delivering enhanced user experiences in storytelling. Mixing content distribution within a social network, she is working on a platform for the world of NEWDAWN, inside which the readers of NEWDAWN and SciFi lovers can take part in the stories and contribute.

"These experiences can serve as a roadmap for the future, determining what is on the horizon for all of us in the hope of building a socially conscious world where generations can thrive." Knowing what is to come is the first step to manifesting awareness and maintaining our choices in a world where technology will run our planet. *"Only we can decide if this is the world we want."*

CREDITS